GIVEN

TIME

Given Time

R.L. Roush

Red Engine Press
Fort Smith, AR

Cover art by Jennifer Rodriguez

Library of Congress Control Number: 2024946157

ISBN: 979-8-9895620-5-3

For Eden Jeanne

ONE

EDEN WALKER RAN DOWN THE STEPS and out the front door, allowing the screen door to bang shut behind her. Upstairs her mother had heard, and shouted after her, "Don't be slamming that door, young lady!"

In a huff, Eden flung herself onto the porch swing next to her twin brother, Aiden, causing it to swing forcefully back and forth. Rolling her eyes, Eden said, "Great! Mom and Dad aren't even listening to reason! I just tried explaining to them that expecting us to go to a brand- new high school in the middle of nowhere for our senior year was beyond cruel. We'll be emotionally scarred for life!"

"Hmm," Aiden continued reading his tablet.

"So, I told them what Jenny Harris's parents suggested. You know, about us staying with them for our senior year, and then joining them at the dig after graduation. We would only have to be there for the summer before we started college."

Aiden, smirked. "And what did they have to say about that idea?"

"Oh, you can imagine! They launched into their go to speech about how we're a family, and how we are going to continue to stay one by remaining together no matter what!"

"Well, what did you expect them to say?"

"I expected them to say... Oh, oh, crap! I don't know, Aiden! That they understood and we could stay with the Harris'?"

"Really?"

"I know! I should've known better than to think they'd change their minds. But really Aiden... why now? And right before our senior year? Sending us to live with Pap and Grammy Walker in

Florida would've been kinder than making us move to Western Pennsylvania to... what's that tiny town we're moving to called?"

He grinned, "Ohioville?"

"Oh, yeah, Ohioville." Sighing in defeat, she glanced at Aiden. "How come you're staying so calm about all this? I thought you'd be really upset about having to leave Jenny."

"Seriously, Eden! You know Jenny and I haven't been a couple since the eighth grade.

We're only good friends now." Aiden placed his tablet on the stand between the porch swing and chair.

Pleased to get a rise out of him, she giggled, "Yeah, I know. Still, she's the only friend you've got outside the Chess and Baseball teams." Sharing the joke, the two of them burst into laughter.

Aiden, who had started the chess team in the eighth grade, only had four members counting him until he joined the middle school baseball team that spring. After hitting the winning runs in the first three games, membership in the chess team exploded, with everyone claiming to be his best friend.

As their laughter died down, Aiden said, "I know you're upset. I am too. Living in Western Pennsylvania will be different than it is here in Carlisle. And since I don't see any way of changing Mom's and Dad's mind, we need to warm up to that idea fast, especially since this type of Paleo Native American dig is exactly what they live for. Them getting asked to be a part of an archeological study with the potential this one has is next to zero during a Professor of Archeology's career."

"Yeah, I know. I was just hoping when they took the teaching job at Dickinson it would be our last move until we got into college," Eden said. "I guess we've been lucky though. I mean, after all, this is the longest we've ever stayed in one place."

"Yeah, I was hoping for that too, Eden.

Come to think about it, we have lived in a lot of odd places. Haven't we? Remember that tiny, old, beat-up town in New

Mexico we lived in for six months during a dig back when they were just starting as professors?"

"Oh wow! How could I forget that place?" She grinned. "Isn't that the old mining town we named Spook'sville? We had to be about... six. Remember how we were so afraid to go outside to ride our bikes because we thought we'd run into a ghost!"

"Yeah, that was back when we were scared of our shadows. But this time it's different.

We're not six years old anymore. Besides, they're only taking a sabbatical so they can consult on this dig. And they're going to be renting out our house for a year. When the actual digging is completed, they'll come back and finish up the study here at Dickinson."

"Geez, Aiden, I know we're not six! But stop and think about the timing. By the time the actual digging is done, you and I will be in college, or possibly grad school. This could end up being a one season dig or a lot longer depending on what's found. I guess what's really bothering me is that our last year of high school will be shared with a bunch of people from Ohioville that we don't even know."

"Really? That's what's bothering you? The way you are, you'll end up knowing the whole school before the end of the year," Aiden laughed, wrapping his arm around her head, and messing up her hair.

"*Stop... it... you... brat!*" Eden accentuated each word with a playful punch.

"Well, it looks like you're in a much better mood, Eden," their dad said, while elbowing the screen door open as he struggled with two heavily packed cardboard boxes. "Now, if you two are done picking on each other, your mother has more of these boxes ready to go into the moving containers."

Aiden reluctantly let go of Eden. As he got up from the porch swing to help, he managed to avoid another one of her punches. Then he took one of the boxes from their dad, all the while smirking at her.

"These go into the storage container on the right," Frank told Aiden as they walked down the porch steps together.

While they were loading the boxes in the pod, Eden went to the screen door and stood there trying to redo her ponytail. Unsuccessful, she gave up and took it out. Having messed up hair might be a good look for Aiden, but not for her.

Standing there watching her dad, Eden had to admit he did look happier lately. He seemed to have a new bounce in his step. Except for the slight touch of gray running through his dark wavy hair, she could see how people were always thinking he was someone much younger than he was. She was glad her parents had careers they enjoyed instead of the dreary jobs most of her friend's parents had. "Happy parents, happy family," Eden thought. "You know, given time this move might turn out to be a good thing."

As her dad and Aiden came up the porch steps, Eden opened the screen door for them, smiled and said, "Don't worry, Dad. We've got this."

TWO

THE WALKERS WERE ON THE PENNSYLVANIA Turnpike for nearly two hours before pulling off into a rest stop. Slightly carsick, Eden stumbled from their SUV, moaning, "Oh... good grief! How much farther is this place anyway?"

"You forgot to take your motion sickness pill before we left, didn't you?" Eden's mom, Barb, asked.

"Yeah... I guess so."

"Well, then, you have no right to complain, Sweetie. But you might want to take a pill while we're stopped here. We have about two hours left to go before we reach Ohioville."

"Two hours! Mom! Dad! You guys are killing me! Anyway, where exactly is this place?

Are you sure the moving van's going to be able to find it?"

"Well, now, I'm not so sure! Let me see, I believe it's smack in the middle of the boondocks, right next to nowhere," laughed her dad. "Take it easy, Squirt! They have our address, and they have GPS," he said, putting his arm reassuringly around her shoulders as the four of them walked into the building together.

No sooner had they entered the food court than they received a phone call from the director of the site, Dr. Maxwell. "Sorry kids. Mom and I must take this call," their dad said handing his credit card to Aiden. While holding his hand over the receiver, he whispered for them to go purchase some food and drinks while he and their mom looked for a quiet spot to talk.

In possession of the card, Eden and Aiden went into the main area of the building while their parents headed back outside to talk to Dr. Maxwell.

Once inside the food court, Eden and Aiden checked out the different venders. They settled on grilled chicken sandwiches with side salads. They also grabbed some bottles of flavored vitamin water along with two strong coffees for their parents from the coffee vendor, before looking for a table. Finding one near the front window, they sat and began eating while waiting for them to finish their phone call and join them.

Eden opened one of the bottles of water and took her motion sickness pill after having a few bites of her sandwich. As she swallowed the pill, she prayed it would not take long to work. "Being car sick stinks! You don't know how lucky you are, Aiden." Car sickness was one of the few things that differed between the twins. Aiden never got motion sickness of any kind.

"Yeah, I can tell." Aiden responded, glad that was one trait they did not share.

Fortunately, they did not have too long to wait for their parents to return. As soon as the conversation with Dr. Maxwell ended, their mom and dad found them eating at a table near the coffee vendor and joined them.

While they were munching on their salads, their mom told them, "Sorry, kids. We weren't expecting to have any phone calls from Dr. Maxwell until later tomorrow. But it seems something exciting has come up. He couldn't wait 'til then to tell us about it," Barb told them.

"Yes, apparently some very interesting data has come back about the initial artifact that was sent to the University's lab for testing. Even though the artifact is a significant find by itself, it's showing some other unusual results. So, Dr. Maxwell wants us to come to a meeting at the site tomorrow morning for an hour or two so he can run the data by the whole team at the same time. He's a strong believer of everyone being on the same page," Frank told them.

"So, it looks like we'll need to leave you both alone for a while tomorrow. Think you two can handle things while we're gone?" asked Barb.

"Sure!" Eden and Aiden answered in unison, wincing as soon as they said it. Though they were fraternal twins, occasionally they would slip and answer as one, or finish each other's sentences, always dreading whenever it happened.

Their mom, paying no attention, asked, "So, I was thinking, while we're at the meeting, would you two unpack the boxes in the other rooms after you've finished with yours? You won't need to worry about unpacking our bedroom or the room we'll be using as our office. We'll take care of that after we get back."

"Yeah, Mom, you know Eden and I'll be glad to help out any way we can."

"That's such a relief! You two don't realize how much pressure that takes off your father and me. We were supposed to have until Thursday before we reported to the dig. Now, because of this report, we won't have the time to settle in as we'd planned on. So, you two unpacking more than your rooms will be a big help.

Now, the house is largely furnished. So, there'll only be the few pieces of furniture that wasn't put into storage for the movers to bring in. Mostly it will be boxes. I'll show them where I want the furniture. The boxes are all marked, so the movers will be putting them in the rooms where they belong.

After they leave, we'll need to unpack enough to make our beds, get some personal items, and organize the kitchen somewhat for breakfast. Tomorrow you two can pick a room to work on. Whatever rooms you decide on will be fine with us.

Oh, and that reminds me, Frank, before we get to the house, we'll need to grab a few things from the local market for breakfast, and something for lunch for the kids. We can do the heavy shopping for everything else after Dr. Maxwell's meeting tomorrow."

Popping the remaining bite of his sandwich into his mouth, Frank automatically nodded his head in agreement as his wife continued talking. He wisely let her handle the moving details, letting her put her fortes into play, while supporting her decisions, and being the heavy lifter. Her organizational skills were one of her many assets that had first caught his attention years ago; not to mention she was the only grad student he had ever seen who could still manage to look gorgeous with dirt on

7

her face. His only concern right now was whether the grocery store would be well stocked since he did much of the cooking.

Eden, finally feeling some relief from the car sickness, said, "Yeah, Mom, what Aiden said. You know you can count on us. We'll hold down the Homefront tomorrow, while you and Dad go meet with Dr. Maxwell."

As they were finishing up their meal, Barb made a short grocery list for that evening while adding more to the one she had already started for tomorrow. When they were done, they gathered their trash and tossed it on their way out. Always about recycling, Eden spotted a bin and threw their plastic water bottles into it before heading back to the car. But, not before Frank had grabbed two more coffees, water, and some cookies for the road.

Within a few minutes they were back on the turnpike, heading for the unknown wilds of Ohioville.

THREE

BY THE TIME THEY WERE APPROACHING the last interchange on the Pennsylvania Turnpike, Eden found herself liking the scenery. But one troubling thing she did noticed was there were a lot of farms and woods, and not much else. Sighing, she thought, "I'm doomed! I'm going to turn into a country bumpkin!"

Aiden heard Eden sigh, glanced over at her, and grinned. In this case, telepathy was not needed. Just looking at the expression on her face gave him a pretty good idea as to what she was thinking.

Before leaving Carlisle, Aiden had thoroughly researched the area of Western Pennsylvania they were moving to after their parents had told them about the move. He had not shared that fact with Eden. As he delved into it, he learned there was a mall not too far from their new home, an Outlet mall north of them, and that the city of Pittsburgh was less than forty miles away.

Seeing her dismay, he debated on telling her now that her idea of culture was only a short drive from where they would be staying or letting her wallow in self-pity a bit longer. The decision to let her wallow won out.

After exiting the turnpike, they turned south onto Interstate 376 until they reached the Brighton Township exit. Taking Tuscarawas Road, they headed west towards Ohio. About five minutes later they saw a small shopping plaza with a Shop' N Save grocery store. There were a few other shops in the same plaza, one of them being a pizza place which Aiden noticed right away.

As they pulled in, Aiden's stomach growled. Hearing it Eden laughed, "We just ate two hours ago and you're hungry again? Your stomach's a bottomless pit, Aiden!"

"I can't help that I'm a growing boy, I mean man."

"Ha, you had it right the first time!"

Aiden tossed his crumpled cookie wrapper at her, and asked their parents, "How about we get some pizza for supper?"

"You know, that's not a bad idea. Why don't you and Eden go get the pizza, while your dad and I get the groceries? That way we just need to make a salad when we get to the house."

"Better get two large pizzas, one for us and one for him, Mom. You know what his appetite is like!"

Their mom laughed. "I think you're right, Eden! Here's my card. Get two large pizzas. Whatever kind you get will be fine with us."

Pulling into a parking place near the front of Shop'n Save, their father parked and turned off the car. While their parents went to the grocery store, Eden and Aiden headed to the restaurant.

The minute they walked through the door Aiden liked the place. He had spotted several vintage pinball games, a newer pool table, and several flat screen televisions set in various places around the restaurant. On the walls hung recent and vintage pictures of local landmarks, and events, giving the atmosphere a relaxed feeling.

He counted a dozen booths and almost as many tables, some sitting in front of a small, raised stage. There were a handful of people scattered about at the tables and in the booths talking and eating. They barely noticed Eden and Aiden as they went to the counter to order.

"Hey, this looks like a great place to hang out."

Eden rolled her eyes at her brother, and said, "Yeah, it's probably the only place around for miles and miles."

Grabbing a menu off the counter, she scanned it for a few seconds then pointed out a couple of the selections. Aiden nodded his head in agreement. Just as they had decided on what they wanted, a young woman with a friendly smile, came out of the kitchen and took their order.

"It will take about twenty-five minutes," she said, as she rung everything up.

"Cool! That will give me some time to play a few of those sweet pinball games," Aiden said, walking away. Eden shook her head and sat down at the table nearest to the counter ready to sulk while Aiden played his games.

"We have free Wi-Fi," the young woman told Eden, pointing to the sign near the cash register before turning to go back into the kitchen.

"Hey, thanks!" Eden called after her.

"At least there's one redeeming thing about this place," she mumbled to herself while she pulled her phone from her pocket. Connecting to their Wi-Fi did not take long, and soon she was checking her text messages.

It seemed like no time before the young woman brought out their order. Eden paid and called for Aiden. Picking up the boxes, they headed to their car to find their parents already loading the groceries. Holding up the boxes, Aiden exclaimed, "These pizzas smell fantastic!

And the place isn't too bad inside either. Pizza and vintage pinball! What more could a guy want?"

"A life!" mumbled, Eden.

"Well, I didn't see you complaining once you found out they had Wi-Fi." Aiden countered, as he placed the pizzas in the back of the SUV along with the groceries, various boxes, and suitcases.

Eden stuck her tongue out at him as she slipped inside the vehicle.

Once again, they were back on the road taking the last leg to their new home. Within a few minutes, they had finally reached Ohioville. As they entered the borough, Eden could not help noticing the fire and police stations, and little else. A few minutes later she saw the municipal building and then a small country church. When they passed the church, she nervously thought, "This is it? It's quaint, but there's nothing here. I can see me dying from boredom now!"

A few driveways past the church, her father slowed and made a right onto a private gravel road. As soon as he had turned off onto it, Eden and Aiden perked up.

At first all they could see were the thick woods on either side of the road, but after a few hundred yards they abruptly gave way to huge fields of growing wheat, soybeans, and corn. Then suddenly as the corn disappeared, there directly in front of them was a large, stone farmhouse, not unlike those seen in Eastern Pennsylvania.

As they got closer, they could tell that some sections of the house looked newer. These additions, however, closely matched the farmhouse's original style without being obvious.

Slightly to the left of the it sat a quaint homey looking stone cottage. Beyond it and the house, they could see part of an impressive wooden barn. Off to the right they could see the tops of a large group of trees that appeared to be surrounded by more wheat. Eden fell in love with the house immediately, while Aiden drooled over the possibilities of what could be in the large barn.

"Well, here we are!" their dad announced, enjoying the look on Eden's and Aiden's faces as they viewed the house for the first time. The unexpected silence coming from them caused him to chuckle, as they were hardly ever at a loss for words.

"So, what do you think?" their mom asked, as their dad drove the SUV around the cul-de-sac and parked in front of the main entrance.

"Wow, it's absolutely great! Nothing like I was expecting," Eden answered as she opened her door.

"I'd say you and Dad hit the mark with this place! If the inside is as amazing as the outside, this is by far the best one you've ever picked. Hey! By the way, just how did Mom and you ever find this gem?" Aiden asked, shutting his door.

"We can't take any credit for finding it. The house belongs to Dr. Maxwell's brother, Sam, a retired architect. At his request, his brother loaned it to us as long as it's needed while we're involved on the dig," their dad explained.

"We were told it's one of a dozen different homes Sam owns around the world. This one's from the pre-colonial period. It's been here since the early 1700s. Dr. Maxwell told us it caught fire back in the late 80s and remained empty until the 90s when his brother bought and restored it. Up until they retired five years ago, he and his wife lived here. Now they are living in Sardinia, Italy.

Since this house is coincidently just over the hill from the dig site, Sam graciously loaned it to us as long as we are part of the team. Better keep that in mind before you two decide to get rambunctious!"

As they gathered the groceries and pizzas, Frank pointed to the small homey-looking cottage setting off to the left of the main house. "See that guest cottage over there? That's where Dr. Maxwell, leader of the team, is staying. That means it's off limits to you two unless he invites you."

"Geez, give us some credit, Dad. We're not going to be knocking on his door like a couple of little kids!" Eden protested.

Frank chuckled. Still, if he knew his twins, they would make it a point to meet Dr. Maxwell before the week was over. Both Dr. Maxwell and his cottage were a mystery, and he knew how they both loved a good mystery.

As they walked to the front door, Eden and Aiden eyed the quaint little cottage sitting under several tall trees, wondering why he had taken the smaller place allowing them to have the larger house. The cottage was small, but they had managed to live in much smaller places while their parents were working on site.

The cottage looked homey and inviting. There was a field-stone chimney, which meant it had a fireplace, and what looked like a private, fenced-in garden behind it. It was surrounded by flowers, some of which had wound up and around parts of the fence. There was also a mossy, flagstone walk leading from it to the driveway that went behind the main house towards the barn.

As they were taking the time to look over the cottage while waiting to get in, their mom took a key ring from her bag holding old-looking keys. Finding the largest of five ancient looking keys, she placed it in the keyhole and turned it to the right. The unusual click it made as it struck the tumblers drew Aiden's attention right away.

"Whoa! What kind of key makes a sound like that?"

Holding up the key ring so they could see, she said, "Well, they are mostly colonial era. This one here is the main key to the original section of the house. This newer one is to the back door; this chunky one is for the barn; this one here is for the cottage, and this odd-looking one is for... now what did Dr. Maxwell call it? Oh, yes, the *Mystery Key!*"

"The *Mystery Key?* Ooh, I wonder why they call it that?" Filled with curiosity, Eden reached for the key ring.

Handing it to Eden, her mom said, "He didn't say why. He did mention though, that when his brother, Sam, bought the property from the last owners they told him they had no idea what the key was for, but not to lose it because of the legend."

Shifting the grocery bag and her purse to the same arm, she then lifted the latch with her free hand and opened the door.

"Legend?" asked Eden and Aiden together without cringing this time.

"Yup, that's exactly what your mom just said, 'legend'. Now, let's not all stand here on the front porch talking about it right at this moment. These bags are getting heavy. Besides the groceries, we must get our suitcases and boxes out of the SUV and move it before the van gets here in a few hours," their dad informed them.

"We can talk about it while we're eating supper," their mom suggested as she walked into the house.

Eden, having set her two grocery bags down when she was handed the key ring, was carefully studying each of them, paying particular attention to the one her mom called the *Mystery Key.* The other keys looked like other types of antique keys she had seen before, but this key was different.

Even though all the keys were antique, the *Mystery Key* looked ancient. Where they were made of brass or pewter and mostly plain in design, this one appeared to be made of an unusual type of metal. It was banded with a beautiful pattern embossed around the stem, and bow, stopping short at the collar. The bit even had a cut out that seemed familiar, but she could not recall where she had seen it before.

While examining it, she was absent mindedly running her fingers over the design becoming mesmerized with its pattern. It felt rhythmical to her. She began to imagine she heard music playing. Not just any music, like an Irish jig, the type that causes you to tap your foot and feel like dancing to it.

Slightly perplexed over what she was experiencing, Eden raised her head to say something to the others, when she was caught off guard by a sudden flash of light. Looking in the direction of where she thought the flash had come, Eden found she was facing the lonely group of tall trees, and the possibility of another intriguing mystery.

FOUR

THE FLASH OF LIGHT COMING FROM the group of trees not only happened once, but several times. When it occurred the second time, Eden was looking directly at it. It seemed as if someone was intentionally trying to get her attention. Standing there staring at the trees, she was at a loss wondering what or possibly who could be causing it.

She quickly came back to her senses when her mom called out, "Honey, bring those groceries in here. Don't worry about the stuff in the SUV for now. We'll get the boxes and suitcases unpacked after we eat." After pocketing the keys, Eden picked up the bags, but before she stepped across the threshold, she paused to glance back at the trees. Seeing nothing out of the ordinary, she sighed, stepped inside, and gave the door a push with her hip, shutting it behind her.

Once inside, Eden glanced around before heading to the kitchen area. She noticed how the open floor plan made everything look spacious but kept a homey feeling. The large fieldstone fireplace and the wide plank pine floors reminded her of their home at the University. She also spotted a swimming pool through the French doors at the end of the well-designed kitchen. However, she put all that information into the back of her head, as her mind was still on the weird flashing lights she saw coming from the lonely cluster of trees.

As she entered the kitchen area, Eden heard her mom telling Aiden, "We don't have the time to show you two the house right now. We'll have to wait until after supper. And, since it's getting dark, sometime tomorrow after the meeting we'll take you around the grounds."

Eden placed her bags on the kitchen counter nearest the large stainless-steel refrigerator and began taking out the groceries. She placed some of them in it and the rest where her mom showed her in the pantry. After emptying her bags and storing them with the others, she turned toward her family, and asked, "Did any of you see those flashing lights out in that bunch of trees when we came into the house?"

"Nope!" mumbled, Aiden, while munching on an apple. "But what I did see was that sweet swimming pool, and some cool ATV's sitting outside that awesome barn."

As they were talking, their mom had set the pizzas on the table while their dad, making a salad, paused to answer Eden. "No, I didn't see any flashing lights, Squirt. But I'm sure it's nothing to worry about. It's probably just the sun bouncing off some old farm scrap or a junk pile hidden out in the trees. But, about that barn, Aiden, it's being used to prep, store and catalog the specimens we find. And those 'cool' ATVs belong to the site team."

Seeing the disappointed look on Aiden's face caused Frank to laugh. "Hey, no frowning, mister! There's been one assigned to you and Eden. You'll have to talk to… Charles, I believe. He's the grad student in charge of site transportation, and Dr. Maxwell's right-hand man. He'll assign you one. Once he does, it'll be both of your responsibilities to take care of it, not his. Also, you'll need to wear helmets while riding."

Putting his hand up to stop Aiden's expected protest, Frank informed him, "That wasn't my idea. The insurance the University is carrying on the dig requires everyone to wear helmets. Still, personally I don't think it's a bad idea. Oh, and before I forget, the bunk house on the far side of the barn is off-limits at all times. The grad students and support staff are staying there and…"

Eden, growing frustrated that her question had not been taken serious interrupted, "No! Really guys! I did see flashes, and not just one, but several!"

"Geez, Eden! Don't get all worked up over some imaginary flashing lights you thought you saw. Like Dad said, it could be anything," Aiden snickered.

"Now, Aiden!" their mom scolded, as she gave him a look.

R.L. Roush

"Well, Eden, if it's bothering you that much, go do some exploring this week and check it out. But, if you do, remember to stay on the tractor paths, and don't go cutting through the fields ruining the crops." At that moment her dad set his delicious looking strawberry, blueberry, and spinach salad, topped with feta cheese on the table.

"You two have the whole farm to explore this summer, so make good use of your time," said their mom.

Aiden, standing at the other end of the kitchen, was looking out the French doors leading to the outdoor living area and pool. Turning around, he said, "Talking about exploring, I think I'll be exploring that awesome looking pool sometime tomorrow!"

Disappointed, Eden crossed her arms across her chest, walked over to the table, and sat down in a huff, saying, "Well, everybody! Don't say I didn't warn you if some brain eating zombies break in during the night and suck our brains out our ears while we're sound asleep!"

FIVE

ONCE THE KITCHEN WAS CLEANED up from supper, the Walkers quickly unloaded the SUV. When they were finished, Frank moved the vehicle around to the garage attached at the back left of the house so to give the moving van room to unload.

As Barb picked up one of the boxes, she said, "Now that Dad's back, let's go see the rest of the house, and while we're at it get some of these things where they belong, and out of the way. Before we know it, the rest of our stuff will be here." She waited while they each picked up a suitcase or carton before turning and leading the way towards the stairs.

As they were going up the steps, she explained, "When Dr. Maxwell gave us a tour of the house a few months ago, your dad and I decided we would wait to tell you what the second floor holds. There are four bedrooms. Two are large and have their own bathrooms. The other two are smaller and share a Jack and Jill style bathroom.

You have the choice of any bedroom you want. Just please don't want the same one," she begged.

Eden and Aiden snickered. Their mom knew them all too well. They often wanted the same things at the same time, but most times it was not because they were trying to be difficult, it just happened. After seventeen years they had gotten used to it occurring and blamed it on being twins.

Upon reaching the second-floor landing, it dawned on Eden and Aiden just how big the house was. They could see that the upstairs landing was rectangular shaped with the rooms on its outside. The steps led to the middle of the back length of that rectangle, facing the rear of the house. There was a small lounging area there, as well as two windows on either side that overlooked the pool and outside entertainment area.

The smaller bedrooms were positioned in each of the front corners of the house with the bathroom between them. They both had queen-sized beds, and generous walk-in closets with shelves and cubby holes for storage. These bedrooms, although smaller than the other two, where larger than the bedrooms Eden and Aiden had back home. The enormous bathroom between them boasted both a shower and a tub, with double vanities.

The other two bedrooms were located at the back corners of the house and were much larger due to being opened to the attic, allowing for two floors. Each had a sleeping loft, along with its own dormer and a window seat. Despite the sloping roof, the lofts were very roomy. The windowed dormer let in fresh air and brought in a lot of natural light.

Below, the lounging and study area was overlooked by the sleeping loft, while the bathroom and closet were tucked under it. The living area contained a loveseat, recliner, and study desk set in the window surrounded by a bookcase with some cubby holes containing storage baskets beneath it.

The bathrooms under the lofts had soaking tubs, as well as ample showers. A large, well-lit mirror overlooked a decent sized vanity, and there was plenty of personal storage. At the back of each bathroom was a walk-in closet like the smaller bedrooms, but with more shelves and storage. There was also another window in each closet that let in the natural light.

As soon as Eden and Aiden saw the larger bedrooms, they could not believe their luck.

This was something they would never have dreamed of. All that the bedrooms were lacking to be apartments was a kitchen.

"Well, this is a no brainer," Aiden said, "there's no way we wouldn't want these bedrooms!"

All Eden could think as she looked around was, "Wow!"

Standing inside the left bedroom doorway, Aiden set down his box, and said, "I'll take this bedroom with its picturesque view of the barn, unless Eden really wants to see it every morning."

"No, that's quite all right. You go ahead and take it. I can see how you've fallen in love with it."

Questioning their good fortune, Eden asked, "Mom, Dad, I'm confused. After years of living in campers, shacks, and smelly tents, how did we happen to luck out here?"

"Yeah, it's amazing, isn't it? Almost dreamlike when you compare it to some of the other places we've stayed. But you can thank Dr. Maxwell and especially his brother, Sam, for our good fortune for our accommodations during the site excavation."

"Yes. Your Mom and I are extremely fortunate to be part of this project, especially since Dr. Maxwell personally requested us to assist him. If we hadn't have met him back when we were grad students, we wouldn't be here now."

"Then I'll be sure and thank him, *when* I get a chance to meet him," Eden said, looking at Aiden.

"Yeah, same here!" Aiden said, as he had his back to his parents. Winking at Eden, he knew exactly what she was inferring. However, neither parent had picked up on their intent.

"Hey, by the way, where are you two sleeping?" Eden asked when she realized they had not seen a master suite on the same floor as their bedrooms.

"Well, downstairs of course! Don't you remember seeing the doorway off to the right of the living area, past the fireplace? Their mom explained, "It has its own sitting and study area, and a private bathroom with a steam shower. The French doors in the bedroom open onto the pool area. It's like a little slice of heaven!"

"Oh... I bet Eden didn't see it when she came in, Mom! Remember? She was too worried about zombies attacking us and eating our brains."

"Oh, shut up, Aiden!" Eden warned. "Just remember, you owe me. I'm letting you have the bedroom with the barn view." Even though they were all laughing, she still could not shake that odd feeling after seeing the lights earlier.

"Oh, come on you two, quit teasing each other! There's more boxes and suitcases to bring up," said their dad.

Eden set her boxes in the opposite bedroom from Aiden's. As she put them down on the loveseat, she thought about how their move had turned from a negative into a positive for them. Maybe she just needed to relax and give this place a chance. "I wish I could see what the future holds," she sighed as she left her room.

Rushing back down the stairs, she grabbed more of her boxes and took them back to her room. Working together they quickly had everything that was brought in from the SUV put in their new rooms, and even started settling in. Not too long after making the last bed, the moving van holding the rest of their belongings pulled up to the front door.

Eden breathed a sigh of relief when she heard the truck pull up. The movers had found this place after all! Even though she would never admit it, she was worried they would get lost.

In no time the men had the boxes off the truck, and into the house. As they began moving in the office furniture, she could tell her mom was in her glory directing them where to place stuff.

Eden thought it was strange that the only furniture her parent's chose to bring with them had originally been in their study. Not exactly what she would have chosen, but her parents were weird that way. Oddly though, it all fit perfectly in the master study as if it were meant to be there. And it was the only room in the whole house that was not furnished.

When the movers had finished, their dad thanked, and generously tipped them. Pleased with their gratuity, they loaded up their covers and straps and headed back east. As they left, Eden was surprised that she was not as sad as she thought she would be when earlier she had thought about joining them.

Later, when she was in her new bedroom, she began opening her boxes, putting away her clothes, and setting out some of her mementoes. Tomorrow, when she had everything set up the way she wanted, she planned to take some pictures of her new bedroom, the house, and grounds. and send them to her friends back home to show them just how bad she had it here.

"I definitely don't want to turn into a country bumpkin, but who knows, given time this place may grow on me," Eden smiled.

SIX

THE MORNING SUN CAME POURING into Eden's bedroom waking her early. Not that she had slept all that well anyway. Between dreams of flashing lights, and zombies chasing her wanting to eat her brains, she got very little sleep that night.

She tried lying still hoping that she would eventually nod off. When that did not work, she tried covering her head, blocking out the sun. That only made her hot and sticky. Hearing the birds' chirping louder and louder outside her windows was all she could take. Raising her head to get a look at the clock on her nightstand, she saw it displaying 6:00 AM. It was then she made the decision to get up.

Throwing off her covers, she swung her feet over the side of the bed and sat up. Rubbing her eyes, she moaned, "Ugh! This is no way to start the day."

Standing up, she yawned and stretched before turning and grabbing ahold of the covers. Quickly she made her bed and when she was done, stood back, and took a look at it. Not perfect, but it would do, she thought while taking a few pictures to post to her friends.

As she was climbing down the loft's ladder, she stopped and took a few more pictures. Without thinking she glanced out the window facing the group of trees where she had seen the lights the evening before, when she noticed something.

There sitting under the window was a box marked 'EDEN BATHROOM' in black capital letters that she must have missed the evening before. Walking quickly to the window, Eden placed her phone in her t-shirt pocket and picked the box up. But before taking it into the bathroom, she lingered a little, watching the breeze stirring the trees. After not seeing anything unusual, she shrugged her shoulders and said, "Maybe they're right. It's nothing, but my imagination."

Taking the box into the bathroom, she sat it in the middle of the floor and opened it. Pulling out her shampoo, conditioner, and body wash, and placed them in the shower. The remainder of the items she quickly put into the drawers of the vanity. Finished, she snapped a few more pictures.

Eden tore the tape off the empty box and flattened it. Then she took it into the walk-in closet, placing it along with the others she had emptied from the night before. She figured she would check with her mom later to see what to do with them.

Going to the shelves along the closet wall, she selected her clothes for the day, grabbing a pair of sneakers from one of the shoe cubbies in case there was a chance to take a walk to check out the group of trees later. Before leaving, she set the clothing down on top of one of the cubbies, and stripped off the t-shirt she had slept in, tossing it into the hamper next to the closet door.

Grabbing everything, she walked into the bathroom, and stood there trying to decide whether to take a quick shower or a long bath. Afraid she would doze off while soaking in the awesome looking tub, the shower won out.

Setting her clothes down on the vanity, Eden went to the shower and turned the water on to get it warm before stepping into the stall. When the temperature was exactly right, she slipped into the spray.

As the water poured over her, she reached for her shampoo. The scent of mint filled the air as she lathered it into her hair. Shampoo, rinse, shampoo, rinse, condition, rinse, the routine was almost robotic since she was tired. Standing in the shower longer than necessary, Eden said aloud, "Come on, Eden, snap out of it! Get a move on!"

Shutting off the water, she squeezed as much of it out of her long hair as she could.

Reaching for one of two towels she had hung up the night before, she wrapped it tightly around her hair drawing out more of the water. The second towel she wrapped around her after patting herself dry. Stepping out of the stall, she was beginning to feel more like herself.

While she dressed and went through her morning routine, her thoughts were on making breakfast for her family. With her parents having a meeting with Dr. Maxwell and the staff later this morning, it would be one less thing on their minds before heading out. Besides, Eden always enjoyed making a big breakfast for them at least once a week and today seemed to be as good as any other day.

"You can't send your parents out to face the past on an empty stomach," Eden giggled, looking into the mirror. The decision was made while she ran her comb through her damp hair. It would be 'Big Breakfast' morning.

Grabbing an elastic hair tie, Eden gathered her slightly damp hair into a loose bun.

Standing back from the mirror, she gave her reflection a quick check. Not completely satisfied with the result, she gave up and shrugged her shoulders.

Before leaving to make breakfast, she tidied up the bathroom. On her way out she took one more glance in the mirror, pausing a few seconds to cross her eyes and stick her tongue out at her reflection.

Laughing at herself, Eden picked up her sneakers and walked into the lounging area of her room. But, before reaching the door, she felt an urge to go to the window and take one more look at the trees before heading downstairs.

Standing in front of the window, Eden watched as the breeze intermittently danced through the leaves and smaller branches lifting them gently then setting them back down again. Just when she was about to leave, Eden saw a sudden flickering of light stirring in the trees. The light seemed to move quickly through the lower branches until it shone directly into her window, bouncing off the far wall. Then just as suddenly, it was gone!

Eden was shocked. Dropping her sneakers, she rubbed her eyes. Did she just see what she thought she saw, or was it just her imagination playing games with her mind because of a lack of sleep?

She went to the window and pulled up the screen. Putting her hands on the windowsill, she leaned out slightly to get a better look. After looking around for a bit, she saw nothing out of the ordinary. Letting out a sigh of disappointment, she pulled her head back inside hitting it against the bottom of the sash as she did.

"Man! That hurts!" she complained out loud, rubbing the spot.

"Boy, I'm losing it! I think Aiden might be right about my imagination. Maybe I am seeing things," she said.

Once her head felt a little better after some rubbing, she pulled the screen back down.

Grabbing her sneakers, she went to leave. But, as she put her hand on the doorknob, she thought, "There's no way I'm telling anyone about this! Besides, if Aiden knew, he would tease me all summer, and there's no way I'd willingly make myself a target for his sense of humor."

Quietly pulling the door shut so not to wake Aiden, she headed to the kitchen. Walking down the steps, she tried to keep them from creaking too much. When she reached the last one, she noticed that the door to her parent's bedroom suite was still shut. "Good!" she thought.

Setting her sneakers by the French doors, Eden stopped to listen to hear if anyone was stirring. After not hearing anything, she went ahead and started a pot of coffee. "This ought to wake them up," she thought.

While the coffee began slowly dripping into the pot, she took some bacon from the refrigerator and put it into a skillet and set it to low. Grabbing some of the fruit at the same time, she cut it into pieces and made four fruit cups to go along with the bacon, toast, and omelets she was planning to make. Just as she had begun whisking the eggs and milk, the door near the fireplace opened, and her dad walked out rubbing his eyes.

Eden could not help but laugh seeing her dad unsteadily walking towards her wearing his flannel sleeping pants and the tie-dyed t-shirt she had made him for Father's Day when she was twelve.

"That coffee and bacon's smell'n good! What else you make'n there, Squirt?" he asked as he kissed her on the top of her head.

"Just some veggie and cheese omelets with toast. Fruit cups are chilling in the fridge."

"You make'n the bacon crispy?"

"Yup, just like you like it."

"Great! I'm swiping a couple cups of that wonderful smelling coffee for your mom and me, and then I'm going to chase your Mom out of that steam shower. Give us about twenty minutes before starting those omelets."

"Sure, no problem. It'll give me a chance to make myself a cup of tea. Oh, and Dad?"

"Yeah?" he asked, while walking away with the coffee.

"Cowlick!" Eden answered, while motioning at the back of her head with her hand. "Oh, right! Thanks!"

As he disappeared through the door with a mug of coffee in each hand, Eden laughed. After all the driving and the moving yesterday, her dad must have really slept hard. "Well, I'm glad at least someone here had a good night's sleep," she mumbled, as she went back to preparing breakfast.

While her tea was steeping, she busied herself by cutting up a few mushrooms and vegetables, then grating the cheese for the omelets. Seeing the bacon was cooked, she took it off the stove and placed it on some paper towels to drain off the grease. Now she was ready for any special omelet requests from her family when they were ready.

When her tea was done, Eden took her mug and went to the French doors. After opening them completely, she stepped out onto the stone patio barefoot. Looking around briefly, she chose the table and the chairs closest to a landscaped waterfall and made for them.

R.L. Roush

As she sat there listening to the water, she began to unwind and appreciate the beautiful morning and her peaceful setting. The pleasing scent of the flowers planted round the pool hung in the air. They, along with the shrubs, trees, and the waterfall, created the ideal retreat.

After snapping some pictures of the pool, she sent them to her friends back in Carlisle. While sitting there contentedly sipping her tea, and listening to the water, she noticed she could just see the tops of the trees where she saw the mysterious flashing lights yesterday and again this morning. Studying them, she made the decision to go explore them, either with or without Aiden, as soon as they finished unpacking the remaining boxes for their mom.

Just as she decided to check out the trees, she was completely caught off guard by a booming, male voice coming from behind her, saying, "Good morning young lady! Enjoying this beautiful, sunny morning, are we? Well, you couldn't have picked a better spot for it!

You must be Frank's and Barb's daughter. Eden, isn't it? Your parents were right about the fiery red hair. I also hear from your parents that you have a twin brother, Aiden, who happens to be a rather good baseball player."

Caught totally off guard, Eden almost choked on her sip of tea.

While coughing, the old man, who had now reached her, apologized, "Oh, sorry about that! I didn't mean to frighten you."

As she stood, Eden sputtered, "No... no, that's okay!"

"I guess I should have quietly announced myself before barging in like this and catching you by surprise."

With a twinkle in his eyes, the old man reached out his hand and said, "Now for a proper introduction. I'm Dr. Maxwell. Pleased to make your acquaintance!"

SEVEN

AFTER EDEN HAD STOPPED COUGHING, she found herself facing an elderly man extending his hand for her to shake. He had kind brown eyes and appeared to be in his late sixties, early seventies. He was medium height and had a solid physique. His gleaming white hair, platted into two braids, fell nearly to his waist.

As she shook his hand, she could not help noticing he had a good firm grip. His demeanor was pleasant, and rather endearing, putting her at ease. Strange though, the minute she had touched his hand she was overcome with a feeling that somehow this was not the first time they had met. But, for the life of her, she could not recall when or where.

"Pleased to finally meet you too, Dr. Maxwell.

I don't know if you know it, sir, but you've become quite a celebrity in our home. Mom and Dad have talked so much about you since they accepted your offer that it's almost like you've become a part of our family."

"Well, if that's the case, then maybe I should come for Sunday supper," he grinned, setting two sets of keys on the table.

"Now, the reason I'm here so early is to drop off these keys for your parents. They belong to the ATV's that my aide, Charles, has assigned to them. Just let your parents know they are over with the rest of the vehicles by the barn in the lean-to, in parking spaces one and two.

Tell them when they are ready to come to the dig site, they can follow the path directly behind the barn. It leads down to Little Beaver Creek where they'll find several canoes and kayaks they can use to paddle to where we're set up.

I'll get Charles to give you yours and Aiden's keys in a few days and have him go over the rules for operation and care. I know you'll both want to do some exploring this summer before you start school. The farm's a good place to start. It's over two hundred acres and has many interesting places to discover."

"Like that cluster of trees, I keep seeing those lights in," mumbled Eden.

"Exactly!" Dr. Maxwell answered.

Shocked he had heard what she had barely muttered to herself, Eden glanced at him to see if she had heard him correctly.

Dr. Maxwell gave her a slight wink, and continued without a misstep, saying, "I know you and Aiden will wear your helmets, and ride carefully. Just remember to stay on the tractor paths, no matter what. The farmers who rent this land, work hard farming it, and would not appreciate having their crops destroyed."

But, before Eden could ask him what he knew about the lights she had been seeing in the trees, he quickly went on to say, "Now, I've got to be going. Charles is waiting for me."

Dr. Maxwell started towards the far side of the garage, but after taking a few steps, he turned back and took Eden's hand in his. Patting it, he told her, "This weekend, when it's raining, you and Aiden come to the cottage. I'll make us some popcorn, and we'll have a nice, long chat. Oh, and whatever you do, Eden, don't lose the *Key*. I suggest you wear it."

Right away Eden was puzzled. Rain? She heard it was supposed to be sunny until next Monday. And whatever did he mean by *key*? There were two sets of keys lying on the table, not one. How could she lose them when she was going to give them to her parents in a few minutes? Why wear it, or them? And, most importantly, how did he know about the lights in the trees?

At this point, Eden did not know what to think. Maybe he was confused since she had mumbled, or maybe he was a mind reader. It did not matter to her either way. She wanted… No, she *needed* answers to her questions.

He let go of her hand and proceeded to leave. He was almost at the corner of the garage by the time she regained her senses, and called out, "Dr. Maxwell! Dr. Maxwell, wait!"

Continuing to walk, he smiled and waved goodbye while calling out to her, "Can't. I've got to get going! Charles is waiting. See you this weekend!" Then he quickly disappeared around the corner.

Eden ran to the edge of the garage and around the corner hoping to catch Dr. Maxwell, but no one was there. "Boy, for an old man, he sure can move fast!"

Left with a bunch of questions and no real answers, she felt like a deflated balloon.

However, she did have one question finally answered. Now she knew what Dr. Maxwell looked like.

Walking back to the table, Eden grinned, "Just wait! When Aiden finds out I got to meet Dr. Maxwell while he was sound asleep. He is going to have a fit!" Pleased with the morning's outcome, Eden picked up the keys and her cup and went back inside.

She set the keys on the breakfast bar, and busied herself with setting three places for breakfast, one for her and the other two for her parents. Eden knew Aiden would continue sleeping until noon if no one bothered him. That was another way they differed. She managed to get along fine with just six or seven hours of sleep, whereas Aiden needed more than eight.

Taking the eggs she had whisked out of the refrigerator, as if on cue, the door near the fireplace opened and her parents walked in. Dressed in old jeans and t-shirts, they reminded Eden of past archeological digs they had been on.

"Hey, looking good guys!" Eden teased.

"Well, you know how we're so fashion conscious," laughed her mom as she set her Boonie hat and sunglasses down on the table.

Noticing the keys setting next to their plates, her dad asked, "Hey, Squirt, where did the keys come from?"

"Dr. Maxwell dropped them off about fifteen minutes ago. He said they're for your ATV's parked in the lean-to by the barn. They're in spaces, one and two."

"Oh, so he was here. You should've come in and gotten us, Honey," said her mom.

"Well, I would have, but he said he was in a bit of a rush, and that a Charles somebody had been waiting long enough. And, then he took off like a flash. You know, I've never seen a man his age *move* so fast," Eden said while adding the cheese to the omelets.

"Yeah, it's hard to believe he'll be eighty next year," said her dad.

"What! You've got to be kidding. Eighty? I thought he was in his late sixties or early seventies," Eden said, almost dropping her spatula.

"Yes, he was sixty-two when we met him as grad students. It still puzzles me as to why he took us under his wing, convincing us to change our focus to the Paleo Native American period," her mom said.

"Hmm… I still think the reason he took an interest in us was because he found out you were pregnant," Eden's dad teased her mom, but she just rolled her eyes at him.

"You have to admit though, he called it when he said you would have twins, a boy for you, and a girl for me." He winked at Eden while reaching for the coffee pot. He then poured two mugs and handed one to his wife.

"Lucky guess," she laughed, taking the mug from him.

"Hey! How come I'm just finding this out?" Eden asked as she set out the fruit cups.

"Well, could it be because you weren't born yet?"

Handing her dad the plate of bacon, and her mom the toast, she said, "Very funny! Ha! Ha!"

Checking the omelets, Eden said, "Looks like their done."

"Umm…they smell delicious, Honey!" said her mom. "Yes, they do! Let's eat!"

Eden handed them their omelets and joined her parents. Conversation soon gave way to the sounds of eating and did not let up until their stomachs were full.

"Well, that hit the spot, Squirt! Now I'm ready to get to work."

"Yes, it was particularly good, Honey. Thanks for cooking this morning."

"Well, I didn't want you two eating your first breakfast here at the site's canteen. Besides, Dad gets grumpy when he's not fed." Eden laughed when her dad growled and tossed a dishtowel at her.

"Here, let's help you clean up before we go," said her mom, reaching for a dish cloth.

"No, that's okay. Just put them in the sink. I'll run the dishwasher after Aiden eats breakfast. Well… if, he gets up before noon."

Grabbing her sunglasses and hat off the table while Frank placed their dishes in the sink, Barb said, "Well, don't let him sleep that long. He's not leaving you to unpack the remaining boxes while he gets to sleep in."

As her parents headed to the French doors, Eden said, "Oh, I almost forgot! Dr. Maxwell said for you to follow the path behind the barn to get to the creek. When you reach it, there'll be some canoes and kayaks you can take to get to the dig downstream."

"That sounds like fun! See you around supper, Squirt." said her dad, as they walked out the door.

Smiling, Eden went about tidying up some while waiting for Aiden. A few minutes later, behind the garage, near the barn, she heard the noisy motors of the ATV's revving up.

"Ah, and off they go!" Eden smiled to herself, as she put the milk back in the refrigerator.

After shutting the door, Eden was startled to find standing behind it a bed-headed Aiden, yawning, still in his sleeping briefs.

While scratching his head, Aiden asked, "Thought I'd heard some ATV's. What'd I miss?"

EIGHT

EDEN ROLLED HER EYES at Aiden, punching him in the shoulder as she walked by him on her way to the stove. "Ow! What was that for?" he bellyached.

"For scaring me!"

He frowned at her, while rubbing his shoulder.

"Aw, come on! I didn't even hit you that hard. So, sit! While I'm making you breakfast, I'll catch you up on everything that's happened while you were dead to the world," Eden commanded.

Aiden obediently pulled out a chair at the breakfast bar and sat.

While Eden got the ingredients together for his omelet, Aiden quickly devoured the cup of fruit she had handed to him along with his glass of milk. As she was cooking his omelet, she told him all about Dr. Maxwell's unexpected visit, and what they had talked about, especially, the part about him asking them to come to the cottage this weekend.

"Man! Who'd of guessed he'd show up this morning!" Aiden grumbled.

"It was no big deal, Aiden. He just wanted to give Mom and Dad the ATV keys before they went to the dig site."

"So, what'd you think about him? Do you think he's an okay dude, or someone we'll have to steer clear of while we're here this summer?"

Handing Aiden his omelet and jam covered toast, she said, "I'm not really sure. I only talked to him for all of ten minutes. He seemed okay."

"But?"

"But, what?"

"Eden! You're killing me here!" Aiden said, dramatically smacking his forehead, and in the process getting jam all over it.

Eden wet a paper towel and threw it at him, saying, "Wipe."

"Thanks, I think."

As he wiped, Eden told him, "I can't get rid of this weird feeling that I've met him before, but for the life of me I can't remember where. Mom and Dad said the first time they met him was when she was pregnant with us. But I didn't know that until they told me this morning."

"True. Still, you could have met him at the University, or at least seen him passing by," he mumbled as he stuffed the remaining omelet into his mouth.

"I guess it's possible, but it feels like... well, more than that. It was more like the feeling you have when you've known someone for a while. I just don't get how that could be possible though. It's really unsettling since I'm usually right about the feelings I have about people."

"Yeah, you are kind of weird that way."

Eden rolled her eyes at him, saying, "Gee, like you don't have your own odd quirks!"

Aiden laughed at Eden as he scraped off his dishes before putting them in the dishwasher.

In the meantime, Eden wiped off the counters and put away the food items. As she was shutting the refrigerator, she asked, "Well, are you going to go take a shower now, or just get dressed and get started on the boxes?"

As he set his glass in the dishwasher, Aiden answered, "I'll take one after everything's done. It shouldn't take us more than a couple of hours. Besides, I still must finish unpacking my room. I'll wait until then."

"Gross! It figures! Stinky brothers!" Eden pinched her nose.

Aiden laughed at her as he opened the first box. Time flew by, and soon they had all but one box unpacked, and most of the items put away where they thought their mom would want them. She could move them later if needed.

As Eden opened the final box, she removed a picture of their family. "I think this would look nice on the left end of the mantle."

"Yeah, whatever," said a tired, grumpy, and sweaty Aiden.

Waiting until Eden had finished adjusting the picture, while her back was to him, he picked up a throw pillow and tossed it at her, hitting her in the back of her head.

Eden turned and glared at him. It was at that very moment the doorbell rang. "I'll get it!" they called out together.

As they made a mad dash to the door, Aiden leapt over the couch beating Eden. Opening the door triumphantly, he found himself looking into the scowling face of the local sheriff.

NINE

AIDEN FLUNG THE FRONT DOOR OPEN to find a large, intimidating, uniformed man wearing a badge, standing there scowling. As the man eyed Aiden up and down, his eyes stopped at Aiden's snug briefs. The man's frown deepened even more.

Right then he remembered he was still in the briefs he had slept in. Wishing he could disappear, Aiden cursed himself for beating Eden to the door.

After what felt like several minutes to Aiden, but was really only a few seconds, the man spoke, "I'm Sheriff Ward. Are your parents at home?"

Aiden was having trouble finding his voice and was just about to speak when a cushion came flying out of nowhere, hitting him in the side of his head. Again, the man looked at Aiden, and the pillow lying at Aiden's feet, before saying, "I'm taking that as a no."

Right at that moment Eden slid into Aiden and nudged him with her elbow. "How'd you like that throw, Stinky? You're not the only one in this family with a good arm."

Then without missing a beat, Eden extended her hand to Sheriff Ward, saying, "Hi. I'm Eden, and this smelly guy here is my twin brother, Aiden."

As she was shaking Sheriff Ward's hand, she answered his previous statement, and said, "Yes, you're right. Our parents aren't here. They went down to the dig with Dr. Maxwell. Are they okay?"

He nodded, "Yes, as far as I know."

After she let go of Sheriff Ward's hand, Eden noticed the right corner of his mouth twitch slightly, almost as if he were trying to hold back a smile. It appeared to her that he had to have a sense of humor. Right then she decided that she liked this big moose of a man.

"Well, Dad, are you going to introduce me now, so I can give them Mom's casserole, or are you going to let me stand here all day holding it?" an impatient voice coming from behind the sheriff, asked.

"Well of course I'm going to introduce you, Savanah! Just as soon as this young man here covers up," answered her father eyeing up Aiden's briefs again.

As soon as Aiden heard Savanah snicker, he realized a girl was standing behind the sheriff. Quickly he grabbed the pillow from the floor and held it in front of him before turning a bright shade of red. Thankfully the pillow was large enough to hide everything. If he had not been so determined to beat Eden to the door, he would not be in the predicament he was in now.

The girl the Sheriff had called, Savanah, poked her head out from behind her father, and said, "Hi there, I'm Savanah, but you can just call me, Savage. Everyone around here does."

Sheriff Ward moved out of the way as Savanah handed the casserole to Eden, since Aiden was securely clutching the pillow in front of him. "This is a tuna casserole Mom made you for supper tonight. She said to tell you to bake it at three hundred and fifty degrees for half an hour. She also wanted Dad to invite your family to come over for supper this Sunday at six."

"I'll speak to your parents about supper when I stop by the excavation." Turning, Sheriff Ward looked directly at Aiden, and added, "And, when you come to my house pants are not optional young man."

"Yes! Yes sir," stammered Aiden.

Tipping his hat, Sheriff Ward took his leave, but once his back was to Eden and Aiden, he smiled. When he reached the bottom step, he called, "Let's go Savanah. I still have several stops to make today, and it's almost noon."

"Okay, Daddy! Just give me a minute," Savage begged.

Turning to Eden, she said, "My brother, Colton, is off tomorrow. He and I, along with our cousin, Wade, were planning on doing some kayaking and fishing on Little Beaver Creek. Do you and Aiden think you'd like to join us?"

"That sounds like fun. We'd love too!"

"Great! We'll pick you up at seven sharp tomorrow morning. Don't worry if you don't have kayaks, we have extras. Oh, wear old clothes and shoes, and don't forget to bring sunscreen and some water. We'll bring lunch."

"Come on, Savanah! Get a move on!" Sheriff Ward shouted impatiently from inside his cruiser.

"Ugh! He's always in a hurry. We'll see you both tomorrow then, at seven." But, before going down the steps, Savage took a few seconds to check out Aiden. As their eyes met, she flashed him a huge smile.

"Please, tell your mom thanks for the casserole," Eden said, as Savage descended the last step.

"Sure will! See you tomorrow, Eden, and you too, *Pillow Boy*," Savage said, as she opened the door to the cruiser.

Eden and Aiden watched from the front door as they drove away. "Kayaking sounds like it's going to be a whole lot of fun tomorrow. And, from the look Savanah was giving you, you might have your very own personal tour guide, *Pillow Boy*."

TEN

EARLY THAT EVENING, AFTER CALLING it a day, Dr. Maxwell decided on walking back to his cottage alone. As he ambled along the creek, his thoughts were of the first time he had laid eyes on the twins. They were younger now than when he had first met them. Then again, that was the problem with *Time*. It was never the same if you were going against the flow. He should know. It was a lesson he learned several lifetimes ago.

It had turned out to be a beautiful day. The mud from the rains had dried up. The sun was shining. The birds were singing, and flowers were blooming. Summer would soon be upon them. He was not aware of any of it as he was walking along Little Beaver Creek. His mind was lost in time, thinking about the future past, and how he was going to tell the twins what he needed to tell them this weekend, without scaring them senseless. He had no choice, it was necessary, before time caught up to them all again.

He needed time to think, to clear his head, to prepare for this weekend when the twins would come, along with the rain. And if the timeline was correct on this loop, they, their friends, and he would have their talk, forever changing their lives.

Besides, he needed a break from Charles, who had been hovering over him. Despite what he knew would transpire over the next few weeks, he did not need Charles's fussing at him now.

As Dr. Maxwell took the worn path leading to the cottage, he had to cross over Little Beaver Creek using the large stones as a walkway. Once he reached the other side, he had only taken a few steps up the hill when behind him he heard a twig snap.

Thinking it was Charles, Dr. Maxwell turned to tell him that he was okay and to go back to the dig. He could get to the cottage just fine on his own. But, before he could utter a word, a blur of leaves, straw, and flash of blue came hurdling towards him, catching him off guard, pulling him off balance and knocking him backwards into the water.

Surfacing quickly, he immediately began coughing up the creek water he had swallowed. As the swift current began pulling him downstream, looking towards the shore he briefly caught sight of a figure and a flash of blue eyes, camouflaged in leaves and twigs, disappearing into the undergrowth.

Struggling to keep his head above the swift, cold water, the elderly Dr. Maxwell began to realize the dire predicament he was in. Even though he was a decent swimmer, he was not a spry sixty-year-old anymore. It was right at that moment he heard a splash, and his name being shouted. It was Charles!

"Hold on Dr. Maxwell! I got you! I got you!" Once Charles reached him, he began pulling him to the shore.

"It was her, Charles! Did you see her?" coughed Dr. Maxwell, as Charles helped him onto the bank.

"I saw something, Sir. But I'm not exactly sure what it was. It kind'a looked like a bush."

"That's it! That bush was her! Darn it, she's found us again! But how did she do it, Charles? We've had our Time locators removed, and we've taken all the necessary precautions covering our tracks." Dr. Maxwell said, wiping water from his face.

"That's true. But you did wander off outside the plasma damping fields by yourself, leaving yourself open for an attack."

"Yes, yes! I know, but I had to do some thinking by myself. We're so close. A few more days, maybe a week and we might be able to resolve this broken *Time Displacement*. We just can't let her get the best of us. Not now, not when we're so close!"

"What do you need me to do, Sir?"

"Nothing right now, Charles, just make sure none of our precautions have been tampered with. Help me get back to the cottage so I can get into dry clothes before I catch something."

Charles smiled, took the old man's arm helping him to his feet.

ELEVEN

EARLY THE NEXT MORNING, EDEN AND AIDEN were up by dawn getting their gear ready for their kayaking trip with Savage, and her brother, Colton, and cousin Wade. Once their parents had left for the dig site, they gave everything a final check. After putting their water in their daypacks, they felt they were finally ready.

They did not have long to wait. At seven sharp a beat-up pickup truck pulled up to their front door, followed by a newer SUV. In the bed of the truck sat five kayaks.

Eden and Aiden quickly grabbed their gear and were heading to the front door when Eden remembered to check for her zinc oxide. Not waiting for her, Aiden went on ahead. When he opened the door, he was surprised to find himself standing face to face with Savage readying to knock. Upon seeing her he was caught off guard and an unexpected surge of emotions welled up in him. Catching his breath, he could only manage to stutter, "Hi."

When Savage saw that it was Aiden who had opened the door, she was surprised by how happy she was to see him. Giving him a huge smile, she said, "Good morning, Aiden! Or should I call you by your alias, *Pillow Boy*?"

Immediately Aiden turned red. Even though he tried as hard as he could to keep it from happening, he could feel the blood flowing up the back of his neck, and the tips of his ears beginning to get warm. "Ah... Aiden's fine," he answered.

Savage was amused that she could get Aiden to blush easily but was left wondering why she liked having that kind of effect on him. Besides the fact that she thought he was cute, there was something endearing about his awkwardness. And, after their first meeting yesterday, she found that she could not stop thinking about him.

Taking the opportunity to playfully tease him some more, she said, "Glad to see you've decided to leave your pillow behind today, and wear something more fitting for kayaking. Daddy would approve."

Coming up behind her, Colton, said, "Cut the chit chat, Savage. We're wasting time here. Those fish aren't going to be waiting around all day just for us to catch them!"

Extending his hand to Aiden, Colton said, "Hi, I'm this pest's older brother, Colton. Glad to have you along this morning."

As he was shaking Colton's hand, Aiden found his voice and answered, "Thanks for inviting us. Glad to have the chance to be meeting someone else other than grad students and professors. With our parents' line of work, they tend to forget we also need to meet people our own age."

Colton commiserated, saying, "You think that's bad, try being the son of the local sheriff.

That's a whole other set of problems on its own." "I can only imagine," Aiden said.

Absentmindedly going through her daypack as she walked to the door, Eden thought, "I hope I didn't forget anything."

Bumping into Aiden, Eden smiled when she raised her head and saw Savage standing there. But the minute she saw the tall, dark-haired guy slightly behind Savage, Eden jabbed Aiden hard in the ribs, saying, "Introductions... please!"

"Ouch! Eden! Was that necessary! If you'd given me a chance, I'd a..." Aiden groused, before being interrupted by Colton.

"That's easy enough to fix! I'm Colton, Savage's brother. And the guy in the truck bed checking the kayaks is our cousin, Wade." Upon hearing his name, Wade looked up and gave everyone a thumbs up sign.

Colton then offered his hand to Eden as he had for Aiden. However, just as their hands grasped, a slight electrical spark discharged, surprising them both.

"Ouch!" they responded, quickly letting go of each other's hands. Both began shaking them from the stinging sensation.

Confused and to diffuse an awkward situation, Colton joked, "I'd like to say that shock was due to our electric personalities, but I think it was just plain static electricity."

"Yeah, most likely," Eden hesitantly replied, while rubbing the stinging palm of her hand. Normally, she would have gone with that explanation, and not given it another thought. Normally... except for the fact the *key* that was attached to the chain hanging around her neck was now slightly vibrating against her skin. And this was not just any key, this was the very same one that her mom called the *Mystery Key*. It was the only key she could figure that Dr. Maxwell wanted her to wear.

In response to its vibration, Eden had absentmindedly placed her hand over where she had it securely tucked under her top. It was then she caught Colton's eyes following her movements and saw the half smile on his lips.

Now, just what was it he was finding so interesting, she wondered?

TWELVE

EDEN PULLED THE FRONT DOOR SHUT, locked it, then quickly caught up to the rest waiting for her. As they reached the truck, Savage said, "Eden, you'll be riding with me in the SUV. The guys will all be riding in the truck."

Eden glanced at Savage as soon as she had picked up on the under tone of disappointment in her voice. It gave her the feeling that Savage was not happy about Aiden going with the guys. At that moment it dawned on Eden that Savage might be developing a crush on her brother.

Once they got inside the SUV, Savage said, "We plan to leave this vehicle at the Ohioville Boat Ramp and take the truck to our launch point at Beaver Creek State Park. One of Colton's and Wade's coworkers will meet us there to bring the truck back to the boat ramp. That way we won't have to make two trips when we're done kayaking.

Actually, Mia jumped at the chance to help out when she heard Wade was coming with us. Don't tell Wade I told you, but she's had a crush on him since graduation, when they all started working together at the plant. Wade won't admit he likes the idea that she likes him, but then he's never been the type of guy who goes looking for a girl's attention. I think your brother's kind'a like that. Too bad her niece's first birthday party is this week in Canton. Mia's a lot of fun. The three of us would have had a blast!"

As Eden was listening to Savage, Colton signaled they were leaving and jumped into the driver's seat of the pickup. Starting the SUV, Savage then followed them down the driveway. As soon as they had pulled onto the main road, she casually asked Eden "I guess it had to be hard for you and Aiden to leave all your friends behind and move here?"

But, before Eden could answer her, Savage added, "Well, that was a dumb question! Of course, it had to be hard. I mean, especially, if you had to leave someone behind you were really close to, like a boyfriend or girlfriend." Eden smiled to herself. She instantly saw through Savage's line of questioning. She was fishing, trying to find out if Aiden had a girlfriend back in Carlisle.

Not letting on she knew where Savage was leading with her questions, Eden said, "Yeah, it was really hard leaving our friends. Living in Carlisle was the longest we'd ever been in one place because of our parent's jobs. We left some good friends, but no one close like a boyfriend or girlfriend." Eden noted Savage seemed relieved to hear that.

As they traveled the back country roads, Savage continued asking Eden questions, but these questions were not intrusive. She would have been asking the same ones, trying to get to know the other person better herself. In turn, she asked Savage quite a few questions... questions about their school, the activities, the teachers. And she questioned her about where to go shopping and what they did for fun. Eden also asked Savage some personal questions, and even threw in a few questions about Colton and Wade. So, by the time they arrived at the boat launch, Eden knew what the type of person Savage was, and decided she liked her.

Still, there was one question Eden had not asked Savage that she was dying to know the answer to before leaving the SUV. So, as Savage pulled into the parking lot and began parking under the shade of a tree, Eden asked, "Savage, I have one more question I wanted to ask you before we join the guys."

"Yeah, what?"

"Would you mind telling me how you got your nickname?"

Turning off the vehicle, Savage grinned, "It's one of those goofy family things. You see, when Colton was four, and I was two, I adored him. I was his little shadow, and whatever he did, I mimicked.

According to our parents, our family was watching a nature show about animal families. You know, the PG type, where they showed domesticated and wild animals feeding their babies. The narrator was talking about the wild, savage beasts being gentle parents when feeding their young, so Colton decided to try and feed me some of the cheese curls he was eating.

When he tried to give me one, I guess I made a squawking sound when I bit down on the cheese curl, accidentally biting his fingers. I was only two and didn't understand that I'd hurt him.

Of course, he cried because I didn't just bite his fingers, I'd bruised his feelings. It took a bit for Mom and Dad to calm him down and that's when he called me 'a little savage'. Later he shortened it to just, "Savage". I guess it's stuck since then."

"You have to be kidding me! That's adorable!"

Over their laughs, they heard the truck horn, and Colton yelling, "Come on Savage, Eden, get a move on!"

Grabbing their daypacks, Eden and Savage were still laughing as they exited the SUV and headed to the truck. They were about to climb into the back seat, when Savage remotely locked the SUV, and pointed to another vehicle parked in the lot. "That's Mia's Jeep. You'll be meeting her when we get to the park."

Acknowledging Savage's comment with a nod, she held the door open allowing Savage to slide in next to Aiden. Eden figured this was a chance to play Cupid, and she was going to take it. Aiden could just thank her later. Besides, she thought, Savage's cheerful, fun personality was exactly what Aiden needed to keep him from becoming too serious.

Sensing something was up, Aiden leaned forward in his seat and looked over at Eden.

She could not resist smiling and raising her eyebrows up and down at him a few times. He knew that smile and that look. He also knew she was scheming something. He decided that later when he had a chance, he was going to get it out of her.

Eden had barely shut the door and settled into the back seat when Colton pulled out of the parking lot and headed towards Beaver Creek State Park. It would take about fifteen minutes for them to get there, and he did not want to waste any more time than they already had. Since he was working full time, it was not often on a beautiful day like today that he was able to go fishing and kayaking. "Those fish aren't going to wait around all day," he thought as he turned on the right turn signal.

Before pulling onto the road, Colton had caught the look that Eden had given her brother in his rearview mirror. He knew that look all too well. It was the same one Savage gave him when she was up to something, and it usually meant trouble. Still, he found the way Eden's face lit up when she smiled, rather attractive.

Earlier, after being introduced to Eden and Aiden, he had not given her much thought. At that time, he was more interested in finding out what sports Aiden liked, and if he fished or hunted or both. That was why he had Aiden riding along with him. Colton wanted time to scope him out without Savage's interference, especially after Aiden was all Savage could talk about since she met him the day before. He knew Savage had taken a liking to Aiden. And now here he was, checking out Aiden's sister.

"Wow, what am I doing? I'm as pathetic as Savage!" he thought. Bringing his focus back to the winding road in front of him, Colton figured he would have plenty of time today to find out more about Eden. Even so, he could not resist taking another quick look in the rear-view mirror. As he did, he noticed she was smiling back at him.

Caught off guard, Colton nearly ran off the road. "Gee, Colton, watch where you're going!" Wade complained.

"Sorry! Pothole."

"I didn't see any dang pothole." Wade said checking his passenger side mirror.

"Don't worry about it, Wade! Anyway, this road's always a mess after winter."

"Yeah, you're right about that."

"Thank God, we've finally reached Echo Dell Road!" Colton thought. While breathing a sigh of relief, he turned right onto the road. "Only a minute or two and we'll be there."

A little further down the road they came to Beaver Creek State Park. Taking the first right past Vodrey Chapel into the parking lot, they pulled into the area next to the creek to find Mia with her bicycle, excitedly waving at them.

THIRTEEN

MIA HAD ENJOYED HER RIDE FROM the boat launch to the small park. It had taken her around an hour, but it was an hour well spent. The scenery was beautiful. The bright blue sky with fluffy white clouds, and the many shades of green, white, and pink from the budding and blooming trees was like being in one of the travel shorts people post on the Internet. And to top it off, she got to see a doe and her fawns grazing in the grass as she entered the park.

She was sitting on a picnic table eating her breakfast and listening to her favorite group when the truck she was waiting for pulled into the parking lot. Popping the last of her granola bar into her mouth, she stood up and brushed off any of the lingering crumbs and began excitedly waving at them. She smiled when she noticed Wade in the front seat.

Mia placed her helmet on her bike seat and put her earbuds in her bike pouch while Colton backed the truck close to the creek to unload. She was still smiling as she began walking towards the truck. She was happy she was getting a chance to see Wade today, even though it would only be for a few minutes.

Before the truck came to a complete stop, Wade began to get out to see Mia. Colton turned off the engine, and while rolling his eyes at Wade. He said, "Let's get those kayaks in the water. Rate we're going, it's going to be noon before we get down creek to that sweet fishing hole."

Eden and Aiden opened their doors as Savage teased Colton, "All you talk about are those fish! You sound like you're in love, Colton!"

In one fluid motion, Colton reached back, tugging Savage's Boonie hat down over her face. "Geeze, Colton! Really? Look at this! You messed up my hair!" she yelled, checking it in the rear-view mirror.

"Cry me a river, Savage! It's already messy. What are you worried about anyhow? We're going fishing. Those fish aren't gonn'a care what you look like," he said, before sliding out of the truck.

"It's called a 'messy' bun, you jerk!" Savage yelled after him as she tried fixing her hair.

Eden laughed. She had seen and heard the whole thing before shutting her door. It appeared to her that Colton and Savage were a lot like her and Aiden when it came to teasing one another.

Colton walked to the front of the truck where Wade was talking to Mia. He gave him a slight push as he passed him, calling him, "Loser!" Wade laughed and pushed Colton back.

As Colton turned to walk towards the back of the truck, he told Mia, "Thanks for offering to do this, Mia. We would've had to have Dad and Mom take the truck back to the boat launch. And, since he's starting the midnight shift tonight, that would have cost him some sleep. You know how grouchy he gets when he can't get a full eight hours."

Mia smiled, glanced coyly at Wade, and said, "No problem, Colton. Glad I could help out. Besides, it gave me a chance to ride my bike. By the way, how long will Deputy Mike be on vacation?" she asked.

"He'll be back on Sunday. At least Dad's only working two nights instead of the whole week. The other officers jumped at the chance to get the overtime leaving him the weekend night shift. If Wade would hurry up and finish his Criminal Justice classes and enroll in the Police Academy like Dad wants, he could take that empty position when he graduated. Then his uncle wouldn't have to fill in for the rest of the officers when they're out on vacation." He winked at Wade, as he began to unstrap the kayaks.

"Yeah, you try working full time and taking evening classes, Colton. It's a good thing CCBC is on semester break and I'm off work today, or I wouldn't be here."

Wade walked to the back of the truck and began helping Colton. Mia had followed. She stood there watching them for a few minutes when Aiden climbed into the truck bed. He was handing Eden the paddles when Mia asked, "Aren't either of you guys going to introduce me?"

Colton and Wade stopped what they were doing, each wearing a confused look on their faces. "Boys!" Savage complained, as she came from around the other side of the truck after fixing her hair.

"Mia, this is Eden and her brother, Aiden. They've just moved here from Carlisle," Savage said, as she took the vests Aiden was holding out to her.

"Eden, Aiden, this is Mia Cooper, Colton's and Wade's coworker," Savage said as she set the vests next to the paddles.

"Hi, nice to meet you," Eden said, as she shook Mia's hand.

"Nice to meet you both. Wade, you didn't tell me they were twins."

"Is it that obvious?" asked Eden.

"Well, you two do look a lot alike." Nervously Mia placed a strand of her curly, black hair behind her ear. She could not believe she had said that out loud after just meeting them.

Colton and Wade snickered, and Wade said, "That's our Mia. Always truthful."

"I'm sorry! I didn't mean to be rude. Sometimes stuff just slips out."

"Don't worry. You weren't even close to being rude," Eden smiled. Yeah, you should hear all the stuff people have told us or asked since we were little. That wasn't rude at all. But remember, although we may look alike, I am the better-looking twin." Eden rolled her eyes at Aiden.

Unlatching the last kayak, Colton said, "Okay, let's get these into the creek." Picking up a kayak, he asked Eden, Savage, and Mia, "Would you guys grab that stuff and bring it closer?" As they grabbed the equipment, the guys carried the five kayaks into the creek. Anxious to get going, Colton had the equipment organized and distributed in no time.

In the meantime, Wade had gotten Mia's bike and put it in the truck bed for her. Handing her the keys, he walked her around to the driver's side. Out of sight, they stood there talking for a few minutes when Colton called out, "Wade! Get a move on!"

Strapping down a small cooler onto the front seat of his two-person kayak, Colton looked up and thought he saw Wade kissing Mia. But, from how he was kneeling, he might have been mistaken, too many shadows from the trees and the clouds. "Better be sure I saw what I thought I saw before I start teasing him about it," he thought.

But there was someone else who was one hundred percent certain Wade had kissed Mia, and more than once, but that wasn't all they had seen. They had seen everything from the time the girl had arrived on her bike, to the moment the five young people had paddled away from the shore. They had seen everything because this was not the first time all of them had been here.

FOURTEEN

1138 A.D. in County Meath, Ireland

CIARA WALKED ALONE UP THE STEEP HILL to the well as she did every morning since being chosen to make the Greeting of the Day offering to their god protector, Dian Cecht. Carrying the small golden bowl containing finely ground barley, wheat, oats, and rye, she stumbled momentarily in the darkness, as the bottom of her ceremonial gowns, now heavy and wet with dew, wrapped around her bare legs. Fortunately, for her, none of the offering spilled.

Dawn was drawing nigh. As Ciara reached the summit of the hill, she could make out the shadow of the sacred well. Moving with purpose, she took her place by the wellspring facing the east to await the rising sun. Setting the small bowl on the stones of the well, she removed the veil from her head, and arranged her beautiful, raven-black hair over her shoulders preparing to present her offering of grain.

As soon as the sun broke the horizon, she lifted the bowl above her head and sang the incantation she had been taught by Elise the Elder, her Druid master. Ciara's strong, enchanting voice carried down the hill and into the valley below reminding the villagers of Slane how fortunate they were to be living near the sacred well of healing, the well that Dian Cecht had blessed for the battle injured Tuatha Dé Danann, the tribe of gods.

When the sun was fully above the horizon and the song ended, Ciara poured the offering into the water below, and bowed. After the grain had mingled with the water in the well, she drew up the bucket and filled that same bowl with the water, careful not to spill a precious drop. Once that was accomplished, she pulled her veil over her head, as well as the water she carried, so to preserve her and the water's purity until she delivered it safely into Elise's waiting hands to be used in that day's healing rituals.

As Ciara reached the level section of the pathway, she allowed her mind to wander without fear of stumbling and spilling the sacred water. She remembered that the first time she had walked this path five summers ago when she was twelve. She was old enough then to be given in marriage, old enough to take her place with the other village women, to have a husband, care for a household, and hopefully to bear children. But that was not to be.

Elise the Elder, while passing near the creek one wash day, had heard Ciara singing as she pounded out her family's clothing against the rocks. She was singing because she was happy as she had just been pledged in marriage to one of the Chieftain's sons, Rory O'Connor, with the marriage to take place in only a few weeks on the summer's solstice. Her singing rang clear as she was also pleased, because all her time spent planning and plotting had worked.

Ciara was not like the other girls of her village. She had ambitions beyond just marrying well and having children. The man she would marry would need to be someone who would be important, have power and wealth, a man who gave orders and not take them like her father. And once she was married, she would find a way to unseat any other wives, and then when the time was right, co-rule with her husband, or perhaps even by herself.

When she had overheard some of the women gossiping that Rory was looking to take a second wife after the stillborn death of his first-born son that winter, she put her plan in motion. Every chance she got to be seen by him she took. Helping her father deliver supplies where Rory was to be, learning Rory's schedule from the household servants so she would be seen in the street shopping, and allowing him to see her washing her beautiful hair in the stream were all steppingstones to help her gain her goal. And, she had. It was in her grasp. That is, until Elise heard her singing.

As soon as Elise showed up on their doorstep and announced her intentions to take on Ciara as her apprentice, Ciara thought her world had come to an end. But, looking back on it now, she could see it was a blessing in disguise.

Disappointedly, Rory was not even upset when Ciara's father told him she had been chosen by Elise. Instead, he went and married her older fourteen-year-old sister Rose on the summer's solstice, the very day on which they were to have been wed. The following spring Rose bore him twin sons, and in the years since, another son and a daughter.

Instead, Ciara applied herself over those five years to learning all that Elise was teaching her. At first, she was upset that her plans were ruined, but she soon saw that as a Druid, Elise welded more power than Rory would ever have, even if he, by some small chance, would become the High King of Ireland. At least as a Druid, she did not have to take a husband to obtain power and wealth; she only needed to learn all that Elise knew.

As Ciara approached the door of the cottage, one of the servant girls was waiting to open the door for her, allowing her to enter without taking her hands from the sacred bowl. Once she was inside, Ciara immediately walked over to the elderly woman seated near the fire and knelt in front of her holding up the bowl. Elise removed Ciara's veil and took the water from her, handing it to another servant who placed it on Elise's altar.

Patting Ciara's cheek lovingly, Elise smiled, and told her, "Well done, child. Go now and put on some dry robes. Lessons are about to begin."

With that no sooner said, there was a knock at the door. The day's lessons had begun.

FIFTEEN

ONCE THEY WERE IN THE WATER, THE GUYS had only one thing on their minds, fishing.

Paddling as fast as they could, they were determined to get to Colton's secret fishing hole before the sun got much higher, and the day hotter. Before long they were a good quarter of a mile ahead of Eden and Savage.

The girls were not in a hurry. They were taking their time enjoying the scenery, talking, laughing, and occasionally splashing one another. As they paddled along, Savage pointed to a few of the historical sites along the creek. She also told Eden how Little Beaver Creek became protected back in the 1970s because scientists found that the creek bed had seen five ice ages. That made it prehistoric. And because of the unique variety of its plants and animals, it was the only place like it in the whole world.

Savage explained how it was this variety of life that made Little Beaver Creek very appealing to the many Native American tribes, who lived, fished, and hunted along its banks and tributaries eons ago. What was left behind by one or more of those tribes in one of the caves along the creek was why Eden and Aiden's parents were now downstream working at Dr. Maxwell's archaeological site.

Leisurely paddling along enjoying the morning, several minutes had passed before they were aware that they could no longer see or hear any of the guys. Realizing they were left behind, Savage complained, "That darn brother of mine, and his so-called secret fishing hole! He just can't wait to get there and start reeling them in." Both girls understood how single-minded their brothers could get about something like fishing.

However, not seeing the guys would not have been an issue normally, except for this time they were unknowingly being stalked. Oblivious of this fact, the girls continued to leisurely paddle on.

"We're coming up on Rough Run. It's a small creek that merges on the left. Little Beaver splits a few places after it and forms some islands. I think we should stay to the left, where the water is deeper. We've got a few small rapids among them as well, so we don't want to hit any large, unseen rocks or they could easily flip the kayaks.

If the water's too low on the right, we'd end up dragging or grounding out on the bottom. Then we'd have to get out and pull the kayaks, and that's no fun. But, after we pass Rough Run, we have to move to the right because the channel flows that way, then we'll be okay."

While Savage was talking about the plan to follow the channel, up ahead on their right near the edge of the trees by the rocks, they noticed something odd. "Hey, what's that over in those rocks?" Eden pointed at what looked to her like a figure in the shadows along the shoreline of one of the islands.

Looking where Eden was pointing, she answered, "Not sure... sort of looks like a person, maybe a woman?" At that moment, the figure stood up and began waving their arms above their head.

"Over here, over here!" the figure shouted frantically, while waving their arms.

As the girls drew closer, they could tell that the person was a woman. She appeared to be in her early thirties, with black hair braided into a single braid draped over her shoulder. There was a pair of binoculars hanging from her neck. They noticed she was soaking wet and favoring her right leg as she stood there waiting. It looked as if her kayak had flipped and become filled with water.

Concerned, Eden and Savage decided to check to see if they could help. Paddling up to a nearby sandbar, they got out and pulled their kayaks out of the water onto it. After making sure they were secure, they went to the woman's aid.

R.L. Roush

As she watched the young women changing direction and paddle toward her, the woman had to quell her excitement. She was close, so, so close! After so many centuries, finally the chance to rid herself of Airmed, the daughter of Dian Cecht, and her friend, the blonde warrior-poet, Brigid, was finally here.

While waiting for the girls, the woman rested against a large rock. Although, it was not just any rock. She had chosen one with large inclusions of quartz running through it. The woman was aware of quartz's electrical properties. It was enough to help power the Time Bender she had stolen centuries ago and kept hidden on her. She also knew if things went the way she planned, in the next few minutes she would be able to return to her time period, no longer having the need for it.

Fortunately for her, the old man from the future was not here to ruin her plan this time.

He was such a busy body, always showing up at the most inopportune moments wrecking everything. She had tried to drown him yesterday when she had pushed him into the creek, and would have succeeded, except that his servant had jumped in and pulled him out. But now here she was, alone with just Airmed and Brigid. This time there would be no one to save them.

After getting rid of the young women, Airmed's brother, Miach and his friends, Brigid's brothers, Cermait and Aengus, would be next. As soon as she had put an end to them, there would be no one left to stop her from returning to her century. There, with all the knowledge she had gained traveling through time and space, she would change her fate and the fate of Ireland as well.

She had lofty plans, plans that would make her the most powerful Druid Ireland would ever know. Then once that was achieved, she would become the first High Queen of Ireland. She knew she had the fortitude to see her plans through no matter what might happen. She only needed patience, because she already had plenty of time.

These two girls paddling towards her did not matter. They were in her way. She felt the cost of their lives, or of any others she would decide she needed to take in her pursuit, would be a small price to pay for the chance to rule not just the Ireland of her time period, but the larger world in which it was but a small part.

While the woman was lost in her delusions, Eden and Savage, began making their way around and over rocks and debris to where she sat waiting. As they got closer, the *key* hidden around Eden's neck began tingling uncomfortably. It also felt as if it were growing heavier.

Thinking it was her imagination, she tried to ignore it. But the closer they got; the more Eden was sure it was not.

Absent-mindedly, she placed her hand on her shirt where the *key* lay and rubbed it. This caught Savage's attention, and more importantly, the woman's.

Watching Eden vigorously rubbing her shirt, Savage whispered, "Eden?"

Eden whispered back, "I'll tell you later."

When the girls reached her, the woman, who had an Irish accent, said, "Bless ye' girls! I can't tell ye' how happy I am someone finally passed by! I've been stranded here for hours!" She smiled, pushing her long braid off her shoulder.

Eden thought it strange the women had said that, because there was no way she would not have seen the guys paddling by earlier. That lie, along with the woman actions, made Eden cautious. There was something about her Eden did not trust. At least that was what her gut was telling her, and her dad had always told her to go with her gut.

Seeing Eden, hesitant for a few seconds, also gave Savage a moment of pause. Unbeknownst to Eden, she was not sure about this woman herself, she also had no reason why. She also was finding it strange that the woman did not see the guys passing by but was unable to let Eden know about her concerns.

"Aye', I'm Ciara. I'm so pleased to meet ye' both. I'm from Maynooth College in Dublin. I'm working in the U.S. on an ornithology project. I guess I was paying too much attention to the birds, and not enough on my kayaking."

"Yeah, you definitely got into some trouble. Let's see if we can help get you out of it and get you on your way," Eden suggested. Keeping their distance from the woman, they walked to Ciara's water filled kayak and began checking it out.

Trying to decide on a course of action, they let their guard down. They turned their backs to the woman so they could flip the kayak over to dump out the water. As they watched the water draining from the kayak, the woman stealthily reached for one of the large broken limbs laying near her feet, while thinking, "Aye', ye' can help get me on my way. Ye' can help me by dying."

Just as the woman rose with the limb in her hand to attack the girls, someone began shouting from the water, "Savage! Eden! Where the heck have you two been?"

Looking downstream, the girls saw Colton angerly paddling towards them.

SIXTEEN

COLTON COULD FINALLY KICK BACK and relax! It had been weeks since he had been able to get to his secret fishing hole. Since he was working full time to save for college by trying to pick up any extra shifts he could, he had no free time. As he saw it, those fish had gone too long without a reckoning from him.

After pulling their kayaks onto the bank, it did not take long for the guys to retrieve their fishing poles and bait them. Watching Aiden, the guys had to grin. They could tell by his enthusiasm that he had an appreciation for a sweet finishing spot. As the three of them sat on the rocks along the bank casting their lines into the creek, they decided it could not get any better.

A good hour later they had managed to catch a five-pound Largemouth and two three-pound Smallmouth Bass, a Rainbow Trout and five good sized Crappie. It was when they were admiring their fish, Colton realized the girls had not caught up to them and he began to worry.

"Those two should have been here by now. I don't know what could be holding them up."

"What did you say, Colton?"

"I said Savanah and Eden should have caught up to us by now." "Well, if I know my sister…" Aiden trailed off.

"Yeah, and I know mine. Savage is always in some sort of a predicament. Trouble just seems to find her."

Laying his fishing pole in Wade's kayak, Colton said, "I guess I better go check on them."

"Wait, I'll come with you."

"Yeah, you two go right ahead. I'll stay here and keep fishing while you check on them," Wade, grinned.

R.L. Roush

"Nah, not necessary, Aiden, I can manage finding them on my own. No sense in all of us losing fishing time."

"You might need some help with Eden though. Most of the time she's okay, but she can be stubborn. Are you sure you don't want some help?"

"Oh! I just got another hit!" Wade exclaimed, setting the hook.

"Great! Reel it in, Wade. Hopefully, while I'm gone, you two will have caught enough for the fish fry on Sunday."

Colton did not think Eden would give him any trouble since he was not her brother, although he did get the impression, she was not the type to turn down a chance at an adventure. Now, Savage, on the other hand, could be difficult. If past experiences had taught him anything, she would give him a hard time just because he was her brother.

"Don't be long, or there might not be any fish by the time you get back," Aiden laughed, setting his hook into a fish.

"Believe me, I'm not planning on it." Colton said, as he began paddling upstream away from them.

Colton sighed. Babysitting his little sister was not what he wanted to do on the only day he had off this month. Did she not understand those fish were calling his name? It was just like her to take her good old time, and not think about other people's plans. On the other hand, when he thought about Eden, the idea of spending time with her did not seem like it would be such a terrible sacrifice.

Paddling upstream, Colton's strokes were powered by his frustration. His kayak cut easily through the water, as his strong shoulders along with his annoyance aided him maneuvering against the strong current. He was thankful that it had not rained a lot this past week or he would have been struggling despite his strength.

Colton put his focus on finding the girls. Normally he would be enjoying the beautiful scenery around him, and the wildlife, but all he was aware of at that moment was that Savanah was going to get a chewing out from him once he found her.

62

Coming to the islands, Colton stayed to the deepest part of the channel to make his way around them. The largest island he would have to check on both sides. But the smaller islands were easy enough to check since the underbrush was not fully grown allowing him to see to their other side.

Coming around the last and largest of the islands, Colton could see Eden and his sister standing on some rocks piled along the east side of the creek looking at an old, beat-up, kayak. He also saw a woman standing behind them holding onto a large branch.

Once he got a bit closer, he could see the expression on the woman's face better. It was then the hair on the back of his neck started to rise! He had never seen a face twisted with so much hatred and loathing. He did not know who this woman was, but it was plain to see she meant to do harm to Eden and Savage.

When Colton realized her intent was to hurt the girls, he tried to get their attention by shouting, "Savage! Eden! Where in the hell have you two been?"

Neither Eden, and Savage, nor the woman, had seen Colton approaching from downstream. So, when he started to shout, they were all startled.

"Oh, crap! We're in for it now!" Savage told Eden.

Angrily running his kayak onto the sand bank, Colton quickly got out and furiously walked towards the girls shouting, "What were you two thinking? You had all of us worried something had happened!" After he said that, he turned and glared at the woman.

Ciara, who was standing behind the girls, and grasping onto the limb she had chosen to use to take the lives of Airmed and Brigid, could barely hide her anger. With Cermait standing in front of her yelling at his sister, Brigid, she saw her chance slipping away. It could be a hundred or more Time Bends before a chance like this came again. She could not let that happen.

Eden and Savage were facing Colton, while their backs were to Ciara as he was yelling, so they had no clue what he had seen when he paddled around the island. They only felt confused believing he was overreacting just because they had been lagging.

"Chill, Colton! We were just trying to help Ciara. She flipped her kayak in the rapids and couldn't get the water out of it because she hurt herself," Savage told him, acting like there was more she wanted to say.

Colton knew his sister, and immediately picked up on her tone. He glanced at Eden and the look on her face confirmed what he thought Savage was trying to convey to him. Plus, Eden was oddly rubbing her shirt again adding to the importance of Savage's rolling eyes. Colton noted that it was the same area she had placed her hand on when they had been shocked after shaking hands earlier that morning.

Right at the instant Savage had finished talking, from out of the corner of his left eye, Colton saw some sort of movement. Not wasting any time, he quickly turned to his right, towards Eden, pulling her out of the way. As it was, he barely had enough time to grab her as the limb came crashing down grazing Eden's left arm, knocking her to the ground.

Ciara, then calling Savage, Brigid, and swung the limb hitting her across her midsection, knocking the air out of her, and pushing her backwards onto the rocks. However, Ciara's main goal was not to kill the girls immediately; it was only to disable them long enough to attack Cermait. She knew he would come to their aid. So, while he was distracted, she planned to strike his head with the limb when he stepped forward to assist them, knocking him out. After that, it would be no problem killing them all and removing the *Key to Immorality* she knew Airmed was wearing around her neck.

But Ciara had misjudged Colton's reaction. Instead of him stepping forward and bending over to check the girls as she had thought, he instead stepped forward grabbing onto the limb as she brought it down again. He knew the girl's injuries were not life threatening. And, having had self-defense classes at his father's insistence a few years ago, he was prepared for Ciara's tactics.

Grabbing ahold of the branch, they struggled back and forth for a few minutes before Colton was finally able to wrestle the limb from her. Surprisingly, he found that Ciara was much stronger than he had anticipated while trying to take the branch from her.

Losing the limb to Colton, Ciara wasted no time in deploying her backup plan. With surprising agility, and despite her claim of having hurt her leg when her kayak flipped, she scrambled over some debris to the large rock she was sitting on earlier.

Colton immediately clambered after her; however, she had a few seconds lead on him and used it to her advantage. No sooner had she reached the rock, than she stood on it. Reaching out her hand, she employed the visibility control on the Time Bender, then placed her finger on the main control and deployed it.

Colton hesitated when he saw Ciara reaching out her hand thinking she may have a weapon on her. When he saw that she had on a strange-looking, metallic bracelet, he charged ahead. A few feet away, he reached out to grab her. But before he could grab her, she sneered menacingly at him, calling him Cermait, and disappeared.

SEVENTEEN

EDEN, SAVAGE, AND COLTON COULD NOT believe their eyes! It was though Ciara had vaporized into a slight cloud of smoke. They were left dumbfounded.

While shaking his head in disbelief over what he had just witnessed, Colton hurried to check on Eden and Savage. Reaching Savage first, he took the hand his sister offered him and pulled her to her feet. As he fussed over her, she reassured him she was fine now that she had gotten her breath back.

Although she was sore across her midsection where Ciara had hit her with the branch, she was more concerned that her bottom was going to be bruised from the hard landing she had taken on the creek rocks. Despite feeling several nasty bruises beginning to form, she chose not to say anything to Colton and Eden for fear of risking embarrassment, deciding instead to just deal with it.

Once Colton realized Savage was all right, he turned his attention to Eden. She had managed to get to her feet on her own and was examining her bleeding arm when he reached her.

The limb Ciara had struck her with had only skimmed her arm after he had pushed her out of the way. Even though Colton had saved Eden from certain death, the glancing blow had scraped her arm causing it to bleed.

Colton went and got the first aid kit he always kept in his kayak. He cleaned it, then applied an antibiotic cream to the abrasions on Eden's arm, after which he expertly wrapped a gauze bandage over them. As he worked on Eden's injuries, he was relieved to find that when he touched her now, they did not get shocked like they had earlier that morning. He was also experiencing relief he had been able to push her out of the way in time, or the outcome would have been unthinkable.

As soon as Colton knew his sister and Eden were fine, he went to inspect the rock Ciara had been standing on. As he examined it, he immediately noticed the quartz inclusions that ran throughout it were extremely melted and brittle to the touch. Frowning in confusion, he shook his head. He had never seen anything like this before.

Reaching for his first aid kit, he knelt and proceeded to take out the adhesive tape he had just used on Eden. He cut a small strip from the roll and rubbed it against the crumbling quartz pulling off some of it along with crumbled bits of the surrounding stone. He then took the empty pill bottle he kept in the kit that he normally stored extra matches in and put the sample in it. Capping the bottle, he placed it back into the kit for safe keeping.

Eden had been standing beside Colton scrutinizing everything he was doing, watching the whole procedure from beginning to end. She was all too familiar with her parent's investigative practices and was comparing Colton's with theirs. When he shut the first aid kit, she said, "That was smart. You hoping to get that analyzed?"

Colton picking up his kit, stood and said, "Yeah, I'd like to. Maybe it could give us a clue as to what happened to that deranged woman. But, having it examined might prove to be harder to do than figuring out what happened to her."

"Why do you say that?"

"Well, to get it looked at, I'd have to explain why I wanted it tested. Can you imagine what my dad would think? Plus, as soon as the guys at the station heard about it, I'd be laughed at."

"I'm not sure that's true, Colton. The three of us all saw the same thing. Don't you think your dad would consider that fact?" asked Eden.

"I don't know. Since I graduated and disappointed him by not going off to college for criminal justice immediately, it's been hard to tell what he'd think."

"Well, I think he'd listen if Savage and I backed you up. You should tell him. Give him a chance. By the way, that woman's name was Ciara."

"Huh?" asked Colton distracted again, his mind hashing over what had just taken place.

"The woman, she said her name was Ciara. She also said she was from Ireland," Eden told him.

Colton absentmindedly nodded his head, even though his thoughts were elsewhere, he had heard what Eden had said. He was concerned for their safety. If she could do that and she survived, what else could she do?

Walking to his kayak, Colton knelt and secured the first aid kit back in its place. Looking up at Eden and Savage after latching the compartment, he told them, "Well, there aren't any remains, so there's no evidence. Other than the beat-up old kayak, which I don't really think was hers, we can't prove she was even here. After what's happened here, I think we should get the hell out of here in case there's a possibility she wasn't disintegrated and could come back."

"Leave? Colton, you must be kidding! After what she just tried to do to us, we need to get all of Dad's guys from the station down here right now!" Savage shouted.

"I think your brother's right, Savage," Eden said calmly. "What would we tell them? We have no proof that anything happened. There's not a body left to show anyone. No witnesses other than us. And our injuries look like we took a bad spill in some rapids. People could just say we were making the whole story up. Besides, Colton's right. We need to go. There could be a possibility she could come back, since we don't know what exactly happened to her," Eden urged, as she nervously rubbed her hand over the *key* concealed under her shirt. Both Savage and Colton again noticed Eden's uneasy gesture.

That made Savage ask, "Eden, what's wrong? You were rubbing your chest earlier when we first met Ciara. Remember? I thought you were having a heart attack, but when I asked if you were okay, you said you'd tell me later. So…?"

Eden sighed as she pulled the *key* hidden under her shirt from around her neck to show them. She said, "Well, I guess I should tell you two about it, but only if you promise not to laugh."

Colton shrugged, and said, "Sure," while Savage crossed her heart and smiled.

Eden smiled back. Holding the *key*, she explained, "This *key* was on the key ring Dr. Maxwell gave my mom and dad when we moved here. Mom said Dr. Maxwell called it the *Mystery Key*, because no one could remember what it was used for, and it didn't fit any of the doors at the farm. The previous owners warned him not to lose it.

It's odd, but the first time I held it, it felt familiar, like it belonged to me. I know this sounds weird, but it was as if I had held it in another time and place a long time ago. As I rubbed my fingers over the design, I even thought I heard a faint melody that sounded like an old song.

No, no… that's not right!" Eden hesitated, trying to remember.

After a few seconds she tried to explain again, "No, it was… it was more like a melody from another time. That's it!" she said, as she snapped her fingers.

She smiled, and then said wistfully, "It made me want to dance, but I didn't have a partner."

Colton, after listening to Eden's explanation and seeing her wistful smile, caught himself wishing he could be her partner.

"You mean like a waltz?" Savage asked.

"No, nothing so formal, Savage. It was more like an Irish jig, but from an older time. It was a lively tune. I could hear fiddles," Eden told them.

Colton took the *key* from Eden's hand. He noted it was heavier than it looked. The longer he held and studied it, the more he felt compelled to run his thumb along the design the same way Eden had the first time she had held it. As he rubbed it, he noted how it had a rhythm to it, one that seemed familiar. In no time he too had become mesmerized just as Eden had two days ago.

As he continued rubbing the *key* with his thumb and index finger, he began to hear music too. The same type of music Eden had described. It was a spirited tune, making him want to tap his foot. But, no, it was more than that. It made him want to join in, to dance along with the others.

Colton took a deep breath and exhaled. The *key* was pulsating now. Glancing down at his feet, he saw he was no longer wearing the old athletic shoes he used when kayaking, but a pair of fine, polished, black leather boots. Startled, he quickly looked up at Eden to find her smiling back at him.

But only she was different. Her hair was pulled up, a few loose curls touching her bare shoulders. She was wearing a shear, silky veil, held in place by a thin, golden band placed around her head like a crown. The tartan shawl that was draped across her shoulders was pinned with a golden, leaf shaped brooch at her breasts. The gown she was wearing was a rich shade of green, embroidered along the neckline, while the under dress was a matching shade of light green; the long sleeves were sewn with gold cord to the bodice. Around her waist was a belt woven from the same golden cord.

Not knowing why, Colton was filled with unexplainable happiness. He took Eden's right hand in his and placed his other arm around her waist pulling her close. As they were preparing to dance to the music with the others, he leaned into Eden and lowered his head, passionately kissing her.

Shocked at Colton's odd behavior, Savage could not believe what she was seeing. Her brother never acted like that. Besides, he had only just met Eden. Upset she yelled, "Colton! What on earth do you think you're doing?"

When he heard his sister's voice, Colton came back to reality. But, when he opened his eyes, he was still kissing Eden. Realizing what he was doing, he let go of her and stepped back, only to have to grab her again, as his kiss had caught her off guard and left her unsteady on her feet.

"What the heck was that all about, Colton Ward?"

As soon as Eden had had regained her senses, she laughed, "Don't be mad at him, Savage. It wasn't his fault. It was the *key*."

"What...?"

"The *key*. It has this hypnotic power that lures you into it. You can't help yourself. It's like watching a movie playing out in your mind," explained Eden.

"A movie?"

"Like a movie. Colton just got caught up in its spell. But you better believe I have a lot of questions for Dr. Maxwell about this *Mystery Key*. He's the one that said I wear it and keep it close. Still, I do have to say it did kind of warn me about Ciara by getting heavy and tingling as I got closer to her. That's why I grabbed it."

"Gee, thank goodness it gave you a bit of a heads up about her. But, if that *key* does that hypnotic sort of thing to people, do you think you should be wearing it? Do you think it's safe?"

"Yes, it might be strange saying that, but I do. I think we must be careful when we hold it, and not allow it to pull us in."

"Humph!" Savage said, not quite in agreement. "You know, I think I'd like to be in on that conversation you have with Dr. Maxwell. Anyway, with Colton getting hypnotized, mesmerized or whatever the heck you called it, I agree now. We need to go," Savage said, then stomped off to her kayak.

Before Eden had a chance to follow Savage, Colton grabbed her arm and returned the *key*. He apologized, saying, "I am so sorry, Eden! That was so unlike me! I guess… I guess I got caught up in that music." He was too embarrassed to tell her anymore.

Eden smiled, but before going back to her kayak, she stood on her tiptoes, and whispered into his ear, "You're forgiven! But, if you ever want to kiss me again, you need to ask."

Surprised by Eden's calm reaction, Colton burst out laughing as she walked away.

Once they reached their kayaks, they quickly prepared to leave. As Eden slid into hers, she slipped the *Mystery Key* back around her neck and out of sight under her shirt, unaware that all this time, she, Savage, and Colton were being watched.

Looking through her binoculars from her hiding spot several hundred yards away, Ciara saw Eden slip the *key* back under her shirt, and gasped, "Aye, just as I thought, Airmed does have the *Key of Immortality!*"

EIGHTEEN

AIDEN AND WADE HAD REACHED their limit on the Bass but were still working on the one for the Crappie. Up to now, they had caught fifteen fish between them. By the time they saw Eden, Savage and Colton paddling their way, Wade was reeling in a Trout, making it number sixteen.

As Eden, Savage and Colton pulled up to the bank, Wade, grinning from ear-to-ear taunted Colton by holding up their string of fish, yelling, "Well, it's about time you guys showed up! We've just about fished your secret fishing spot dry, Colton." But, when he noticed the serious look on Colton's face, and saw the bandage wrapped around Eden's arm, he suddenly stopped his teasing.

While Wade was trying to annoy Colton, Aiden had reeled in his line and set his pole down to help them pull up their kayaks. It was when he went to give Eden, Savage, and Colton a hand, he noticed Eden's bandage. But, before he could help, Eden waved him off since Colton was at that moment helping her out.

Savage, on the other hand, was having some difficulty getting out of her kayak all by herself. While they had been paddling there, the bruising on her backside started causing her difficultly sitting, and her back was beginning to stiffen up. Happily seeing Aiden standing there, she reached out her hand and asked, "Hey there, *Pillow Boy*! Can you give a girl with a sore butt a hand here?"

Aiden instantly turned red at Savage's mentioning of yesterday's incident with the pillow but took ahold of her hand anyway. But, when he grasped it, they suddenly felt a sting.

Fortunately, Aiden had a tight grip on her hand because Savage instantly let go of his the second they were shocked. If he had not held on, she would have ended up falling back into the kayak or into the water.

"Ouch! What in the world was that?" shouted Savage.

Puzzled, Aiden suggested, "I'm not sure. Static electricity, maybe?"

Wade, after adding his newest catch to the stringer, set it carefully back into the water, and walked over to Aiden and Savage. Laughingly, he said, "What's the matter, Aiden? Don't you know a man shouldn't hold a girl's hand quite that tight?" After which, Wade playfully slapped Aiden's shoulder.

Immediately, he received a shock.

"Geeze! That stung!" yelled Wade, shaking his stinging hand. Eden and Colton exchanged knowing looks.

"It's the *key*," said Eden.

"Yeah, she's right. It's that blasted *key*," Colton added.

"What?" Wade asked, still rubbing his hand.

"A key?" Aiden asked, frowning.

"Yeah, Aiden, the one your sister's been wearing around her neck," Colton answered.

"Oh... so that's what you were doing with that *key* this morning, making a necklace out of it," Aiden said, finally understanding.

"You didn't happen to touch it, did you?" Eden asked him.

"Well, yeah, I picked it up, and looked at it," Aiden said as he finished helping Savage up the bank, "so what?"

"Did you notice anything strange or unusual about it?"

"Nah, not really," said Aiden. Eden, Savage, and Colton looked at each other confused. "Unless you count that fiddling music I heard as strange."

"Did you see anything odd?" Colton asked, hoping he hadn't.

"See anything? No, I just heard music. I put the *Key* down when Mom and Dad said good morning to me. I thought the music I heard was coming from the radio they were playing when they were getting ready. But I'm guessing from the way you three are acting, it wasn't," Aiden said.

"Wow, not just good looking, but smart too!" Savage said, smiling.

"Really, Savage!" Colton scolded.

It was then Aiden became aware he was still holding onto Savage's hand. Quickly letting go, he muttered, "Sorry!"

"Mm, but I'm not..." Savage said, as she gave him a huge smile to let him know she meant it.

"Wait! What's all this stuff about a key, and hearing music?" Wade asked.

"I guess I should start at the beginning," Eden said. "You see, it all began with Dr. Maxwell's visit yesterday morning. He suggested I wear this *key*. In a way, I'm kind of glad he did, or I wouldn't have had any warning about Ciara."

"Ciara.... Who's Ciara?" asked Aiden.

Savage began, "She's this perfectly awful person, beautiful on the outside, poison on the inside! Try helping her out of a bad situation, and she hits you and your friend with a log!" She excitedly recounted, upset at what had happened to them.

"Wait! Someone hit you two with a log! Is that why you're walking all stiff, Savage? And why your arm is bandaged, Sis?" Aiden asked.

"Savage, you've interrupted again! Hold onto your comments until Eden's finished, and don't butt in again!" Colton scolded.

Ignoring Colton's suggestion, Savage happily said, "Oh! How sweet, Aiden! You noticed I was hurt."

"Of course, I did. I'd have to be blind not to notice you," Aiden replied. This time it was Savage's turn to blush.

"Oh, for heaven's sake guys, you can flirt with one another later!" Colton complained. "Let Eden finish telling the story."

"Fine!" Savage said, angrily crossing her arms.

Eden continued, "Savage and I were paddling along relaxed, talking about the history of the creek and other stuff, when we came to the islands. That's when we saw someone waving us down. As we got closer, the person looked like they were in distress. So, when we paddled up to a sandbar to see if we could help, that's when this *key* I'm wearing started getting heavy. At first, I thought it was my imagination, but as we got closer to the person, it started tingling as well. The woman who waved us down told us her name was Ciara, and when she started giving us this story about what happened to her, the *key's* tingling started to hurt. That's when I grabbed my chest. Remember, Savage?"

"Yeah, that's why I said I thought you were having a heart attack."

"For a second, it felt like it. Still, if the *key* hadn't acted like that, I wouldn't have figured out it was a warning. I think she would have succeeded in killing us both and Colton would have found us dead."

"By the way, how'd you figure it out so fast?"

"Well, every time I got close to her, the *key* would begin to vibrate and get heavier. If I moved away, it lessened and got lighter. When I grabbed my chest and you asked me about it, I couldn't say anything just then. We were too close, and I didn't want her to overhear us. But, come to think of it, I do believe I saw Ciara's eyes widen when I grabbed my chest."

"That's right! I remember seeing that, too. Now that I think of it, I think she suspected you had the *key*."

"Savage! Let Eden finish," Colton moaned.

"Anyway," Eden continued, "before we checked out her kayak, she gave us this story about being here from some university in Ireland to study the local birds. She said because she was watching the birds, she overturned in the rapids and had been stranded for hours.

We had just started inspecting her kayak when Colton showed up. Once he beached his kayak and came storming on shore, all hell broke loose."

"I acted like that because you two didn't see the look of pure evil she had on her face. When I saw her picking up that branch, I knew I had to act fast," Colton told them.

"We're glad you did! If you hadn't pushed me out of the way when she swung down with that branch, I'm sure I wouldn't be here. I'm fairly sure Ciara tried to hit Savage in the head as well, but I think the momentum it had when it glanced off me caught Savage across her stomach."

"Woah! You two got attacked and almost killed by some crazy woman! Man, that's insane!" Wade exclaimed. "But, hey, when we paddled through there earlier, we didn't see anyone stranded, did we guys? If you think about it, it looks like she was waiting for you two."

"You might be right about that, Wade."

"Oh, now that's enough to send a cold chill up my spine," Savage said, wrapping her arms around herself, and visibly shaking. In empathy, Aiden put his arm around her shoulders.

"There's still more," Eden told them. "Wait 'til you hear what happened to us next. You see, after Ciara tried to hit us with that branch, Colton grabbed onto it and wrestled it away from her. Then he fought her hand to hand until..." Eden stopped and said something she had wanted to say earlier to Colton.

"By the way Colton, you have some rather good fighting moves. I think you should show us a few of them later. You know, just in case we ever run into her again."

Embarrassed, Colton mumbled, "Sure. Yeah. Later."

"And? Then what happened next, Eden?" asked Aiden.

"They continued fighting until Ciara suddenly broke away, running towards this large rock with Colton in hot pursuit. As soon as she reached it, she climbed on top of it and held out this smooth, metal bracket looking thing on her hand. But, before Colton could reach her, she pointed it at us, then pushed something on the top of it, disappearing into a puff of smoke."

"No way!" shouted Wade.

"Are you all sure you really saw her disappear?" asked Aiden. "It could have been an illusion. She could have used a common magician's trick. Now, if she blew herself up, there'd be a lot of evidence."

"No... we told you, Aiden, she didn't 'blow up'! She just disappeared into thin air. In fact, Colton examined the area thoroughly and took some samples of the rock she was standing on. You'd have been impressed. His investigative skills are quite good! He's better than most of the grad students Mom and Dad have taught over the years."

"Well, if Colton has samples, then we can have them analyzed. Maybe that would tell us what happened to that psychopath."

"No kidding! Don't you think we already thought about having them examined?" asked Eden.

"Yeah, we thought we'd have my dad submit them for analysis, but that would require an explanation. Can you imagine what he'd say when we try to tell him why we wanted the samples tested?" explained Colton.

"Oh, yeah! I can just hear what Uncle Norm would say!"

"Dad can be quite skeptical. With our history, he'd probably think we were trying to prank him again," Savage said.

Eden, shocked at Savage's admission, asked, "You pranked a Sheriff?"

"Yeah, well, he's not just the Sheriff, he is our dad after all. Remember three Halloweens ago, Colton, Wade, all the fake blood and the dummy?"

"Humph! All I remember is being grounded for a month!" mumbled Colton. Wade snorted, and Colton threw him a look.

While the rest of them were talking, Aiden was extremely quiet. He was trying to figure out a way they could get the samples analyzed, when the answer hit him... *Dr. Maxwell!*

NINETEEN

KEEPING TO THE SPARSE UNDERBRUSH WHILE time jumping in fifteen-minute intervals, Ciara was able to keep herself hidden while still following Airmed, Brigid and Cermait. As she had anticipated, they had unknowingly led her to Miach and Aengus. Now that she had the five of them together, she hoped they would soon lead her to Dian Cecht and Lugh.

Unable to hear what they were saying, she did not want to chance getting any closer and risk losing the concealment of the undergrowth. So, instead she patiently watched them from a distance. After observing twenty minutes or so of conversation between Airmed and her friends, followed by a quick lunch, Ciara could see they were preparing to leave. She desperately needed to follow them, just as she had the day they came through the Portal of Time, the day that everything changed for her.

While she watched them packing their belongings, Ciara's thoughts drifted back to that fateful day. She had just made the Greeting of the Day Offering and was carefully bringing the sacred water back down the hill when there was a sudden flash of a bright light behind her. She was curious, and had to find out what the light was, but she also had to make sure not to spill the water.

Cautiously removing her veil, she draped it into a lose circle with one hand on top of one of the many large rocks along the edge of the path to the well. After positioning the veil into the shape she desired, she securely set the bowl inside it, covering it with the loose end.

Once she knew the sacred water was safe and would stay pure, she quickly went back along the path towards the well, driven to find the source of the light. As she approached the crest of the hill, she thought she could hear voices. Cautiously she dropped to her stomach, wondering if the light was coming from a friend or foe. Unable to see from where she lay, she crawled on her hands and knees, not caring if she stained the ceremonial robe she wore, to hide amongst the bushes that grew near the ruins closest to the well.

Secure in her hiding spot, Ciara was amazed at the sight forming before her. In front of the well, there was a swirling ball of light around ten feet in diameter, yet no thicker than a strand of her hair! The same voices she had heard earlier, she could have sworn were now coming from inside it even though she knew it was impossible.

As she sat there pondering what kind of magic had conjured this light, she quickly concluded it had to have been created by one of the Tribe of Gods, the Tuatha Dé Danann. Especially, since this was the well Dian Cecht had created to heal their battle wounds. No sooner had she come to that conclusion, six figures emerged from the swirling light: two young women, three young men and a boy.

They looked to be around her age, except for the boy, who appeared to be around ten. All of them were dressed oddly in clothing made of skins sporting long fringes and decorated with colorful beads and feathers. The young women had their hair pulled into braids and wore what Ciara thought were jewel encrusted crowns with a silver medallion at the center, and feathers hanging from the back. Their legs were covered with decorated leggings reaching above their knees and fastened to their leather shoes.

She also noticed the young men of the group were wearing same type of leggings as the girls, except theirs went to their thighs. The fringed breach cloths to which the leggings were attached were the same style as the girl's tunics and leggings. They also carried some cloth folded over one shoulder, like the men in her village, but she was unable to see what clan's tartan they claimed. The headpieces they wore were not as ornate as the girls, but they did have the same silver medallion at the front, and the same kinds of feathers.

The young boy, Ciara noted, was dressed like the young men except for his hair. Where his head was shaved at the sides with a

R.L. Roush

strip of black hair left along the top, the young men had theirs tied back at the nape of their necks. The boy did not wear a headpiece but did have a feather attached to his hair.

The redheaded young woman who emerged first, had caught Ciara's attention not only because of her royal bearing, but because she was grasping an odd-looking key hung about her neck. Those two things gave Ciara the impression that this girl was someone of importance and was a higher status than the rest, including the athletic, redheaded young man, who appeared to be her brother.

The one other significant thing Ciara noticed was the fact that they were all carrying weapons. The young men carried several distinct types such as spears and daggers, but also clubs, bows and arrows. Each of the young women had spears in their hands and sheathed daggers at their waists. Even the young boy had his own bow and full quiver. To Ciara, this meant the Tuatha Dé Danann had just been to battle and had come to the well for healing or respite.

As she watched them, she figured that the redheaded young woman and young man had to be Airmed and her brother, Miach, the children of Dian Cecht. The other young woman had to be her friend, Brigid, the warrior-poet. In turn that would make the commanding, dark haired, young man, Cermait, Brigid's older brother, and the slim, athletic male with lighter, curly hair and bronze skin, her younger brother, Aengus. But she could not place the boy; perhaps he was only a servant or a page, but he could be one of Dian Cecht's grandsons.

As they stepped out of the light, they were arguing with one another and continued to do so, even after Cermait pointed a device at the light causing it to disappear. Since they were quarrelling loudly Ciara could clearly hear them talking in her language, but their strange accent made their conversation hard to follow. What she had grasped of it was that they had to return quickly, because of what one of them called a *time displacement*, but first they needed to get their bearings.

As she intently watched them, the young man she called Miach went to the well and lowered the bucket. When it was full, he took a strange device identical to the one Cermait had used on the light from his hand and set it on the rim of the well to better grab ahold of the pail's wet rope. When he pulled it up out of the water. the young woman who Ciara thought was Brigid walked over to him. After speaking to him, she took a drink from the pail as he held it for her.

The others followed suit and drank as well.

Once everyone had their fill, Miach grabbed ahold of the pail with both hands, and took a long drink for himself. After finishing, he poured the remaining water over his head. This made Brigid laugh.

Being shorter than him she had to get on her toes to lean in close to brush away some of the wet hair from his eyes. Teasingly, she slowly ran the back of her hand along the side of his face. Miach grabbed ahold of it, kissing her palm. They were not paying attention to the device on the ledge and knocked it into the well.

The others watching what was happening, suddenly began shouting at Miach and Brigid.

Cermait rushed to the well, plunged his arm into the water, and began searching for the apparatus. Miach quickly tied the bucket out of the way and began doing the same. Aengus also joined it. But, despite all their efforts, they could not find it.

Realizing it was lost, Brigid put her hands over her face and began weeping. Airmed, comforting Brigid, placed her hand on her shoulder and spoke soothingly. The young boy had even wrapped his arm around her waist to comfort her. Eventually, Brigid stopped crying and stood there miserably, until Miach came over and hugged her.

Ciara remembered how shocked she was to see Brigid crying. She was led to believe that warriors never cried. She was taught this from an early age and told that it was a sign of weakness. It was also confusing for her when she saw Brigid accepting comfort from Miach and the others, as friendship was a concept she did not understand.

Because of their duress, it dawned on Ciara that the device they had knocked into the well had to be of great value, if not only for the gold and jewels it was made of, more importantly for the magic it could create. It seemed that if it could stop the swirling light, one must be able to use it to create it. It created the doorway they emerged from, so maybe it could create another to go into or even possibly on to other places.

Ciara also recalled how at that time she had thought that the Tuatha Dé Danann had to be great and powerful Gods to create such magic. But to date, she had learned they were like everyone else. "Ha! Powerful gods, indeed! I was such a child," she snorted. She knew now that she was just like them. The only difference between them then was they had knowledge that she did not.

If she had not rushed to the well as soon as they had disappeared back into the light and found the device lying on the small shelf of stone a few feet under water that only she knew of, and then used it to follow them, she would have gone to her grave still believing that they were gods. But, because she had found the device and chose to use it, circumstances had changed.

Now she hid, watching as the five of them paddled downstream. Reaching into her pocket, Ciara pulled out the Time Bender, placing it over her hand. Narrowing her eyes, she said before pressing the accelerator, "Circumstances have changed, indeed!"

TWENTY

AFTER A QUICK LUNCH EATEN IN TOTAL silence, Eden and the others hurriedly packed up their fishing equipment and belongings. Once they had loaded up their kayaks, they prepared to begin their final leg downstream.

While everyone else was busy packing, Wade was carefully putting their stringer of fish into a holding compartment in his kayak. He figured with all the excitement of that morning, he did not want to lose any of their precious catch, crazy woman, or no crazy woman.

Once the others had gotten into their kayaks, Eden and Colton hesitated for a few seconds before getting into theirs. Colton nodded at Eden after she had given him a frown. They had a feeling they were being watched, so before they began paddling away, they warily glanced around. Giving into her jittery feelings, Eden reached for the *key* to calm her nerves and felt a slight tingling vibration coming from it. She knew then Ciara was close even though they were unable to see her.

Colton saw her fiddling with the *key*, and asked, "Well?"

"Nearby, but not close."

After they joined the others, he said, "Wade, you lead the way. Eden and I will be last. Just don't get too far ahead. Everyone, stay in each other's sight. Eden, you're with me. I want to know the minute that *key* starts acting up."

Under other circumstances, Eden would have argued with Colton for telling her what to do just as she did when Aiden tried bossing her. Instead, she just quietly nodded her head and got into place. After this morning's events, she figured being next to someone who had already proven he could handle himself in a fight was not a bad place to be.

Eden waited and watched as the others began paddling downstream. She was not too worried about the others. Aiden could handle himself if Ciara decided to make a sudden appearance, but with Savage and Wade alongside him, she was less concerned than if he would be by himself.

Colton aligned his kayak with hers, and said, "Keep your eyes open, Eden. She could be anywhere. Let me know if that key of yours starts tingling and getting heavy. I don't know how I know, but I'm positive she could pop up anywhere, and at any time. I'd just like a little warning before she does."

"I agree with you, Colton, I think she'll try it, too. But you don't have to worry. If this *key* begins vibrating anything like it did when Savage and I first saw her, you'll be the first to know."

"Got ya'! Hey, I see the others have a bigger lead than I'd like, so we'd better catch up. How about you stay slightly ahead of me, but close enough that we can talk? Also, I was thinking, after we get to your parent's dig, we should stop and go ashore for a while before heading to the boat ramp. Maybe that might help throw Ciara off our trail."

"You're positive she's going to try something again. Aren't you?"

"Yeah, I am. It doesn't take much to figure out that whatever her reasons are she really wants us dead. Plus, she has this ability to appear and disappear at will and now it seems she's following us. I mean, if I had the imaginary issues she has, and could disappear and possibly reappear on a whim, I'd take another chance and try it."

"I was afraid of that, but I was thinking the very same thing. So, what'd you think we should do?"

"I think our best bet is getting to the dig, so we can talk to Dr. Maxwell about testing those samples and ask him about that key of yours. I'm hoping he'll be able to give us some information we can use or at least tell us something to point us in the right direction. After that, I guess we'll go from there."

"Yeah, there's about a million questions I have for him about this *key* and Ciara."

Hesitantly, Eden asked Colton, "Have you ever met someone that you were sure you had met before, but you can't remember when or where?"

Colton shrugged his shoulders, which Eden took to mean maybe. So, she continued, "See... when Dr. Maxwell stopped in yesterday morning, I got a feeling like that. The other odd thing was how strange he was acting. Almost like he had something he wanted to say, but then thought better of it. When he went to leave, out of the blue he suddenly turned around, then invited Aiden and me to come to his house this weekend for popcorn."

"There's nothing strange about inviting someone over for popcorn, Eden"

"Yeah, I know, but that wasn't the weird part. It was when he told me to come. He said to come when it rains."

"It's not supposed to rain until next Monday."

"That's exactly what I told him, but he just smiled, and took off before I could ask him about it."

"That's a little unusual, but he might have had something on his mind."

"True."

Soon they reached three large rapids running through a narrower section of the creek. As they studied them, they noticed some larger rocks scattered throughout them and knew this would make it a little tricky to navigate. They knew keeping alert as they paddled around them was important to keep from spilling.

"Oh! Yeah!" Wade shouted excitedly as he positioned his kayak. "Keep your eyes on me and follow my lead. I'll get you through without spilling." Then he dug his paddle deep into the water and pulled.

Wade shot through the first rapid with ease. Savage and Aiden paddled right behind him with less finesse. Then Eden and Colton followed without any incident.

After successfully navigating the second rapid, which was closer to the first than the third, they recouped before attempting the last and hardest of the three. Wade pointed in the direction he was going to take. But, as they began lining up, Eden's *key* began vibrating and increasing in weight. Immediately she alerted Colton, who signaled to Wade to keep his eyes open.

After scanning the rapid ahead of them, along with the shores on either side, Colton could not see anything odd or unusual, so he signaled Wade to go ahead. Pulling on their paddles as hard as they could in the water, Wade, Savage, and Aiden made it through the rapids and past the last of the large rocks without any incidents.

Now that Wade, Savage, and Aiden had made it without any mishaps, it was their turn. Once they moved into position to follow were Wade had went, they began paddling hard.

Colton, who was following a foot or two behind Eden, suddenly saw a swirling light materializing over the largest of the rocks sitting along the channel they were taking. Shouting to Eden, he pointed at the rock trying to get her to change course. But it was too late. Ciara was coming at her from the center of the spinning light.

Catching movement coming from her upper right, Eden reacting on instinct, swung her paddle up as Ciara came at her. But before the paddle could smashed into her, Ciara froze in midair. Suddenly she was yanked back into the light. In those few seconds, all Eden could see was a pair of surprised, blue eyes and a black braid jerking away from her. Then just as quickly as the light had appeared, it vanished, along with Ciara.

As soon as Ciara was gone, Eden crashed hard into the rock. The force of the impact caused her kayak to suddenly turn onto its side spilling her out into the water.

Fortunately, she kept her wits about her. After coming to the surface, she immediately brought her knees to her chest allowing the fast-flowing water to carry her through the rapids without bashing her against the rocks. The force of the flowing water floated her to where Aiden, Savage and Wade were waiting. Grabbing onto Aiden's kayak, she held on as he paddled her to shore.

"You okay, Sis?" Eden gave him a thumb's up.

"What in the hell was that!" shouted Wade.

"Did I just see what I thought I saw?" exclaimed Savage.

"Yeah, that was Ciara all right!" sputtered Eden, as she made her way onto the bank.

"So that's the idiot who attacked you, Savage, and Colton?"

"Yeah, Wade, that was her," answered Colton, towing Eden's kayak behind him.

"Did you all see how she just snapped back into that light?"

"Yeah, we were all there, Savage! Eden, you, okay?" Colton asked.

"I'll live."

"Wade, can you give me a hand with Eden's kayak?" Colton asked. Between the two of them, they dragged the kayak onto the bank and set about turning it over to empty out any water.

Savage pulled up on shore to check on Eden. She shook out Eden's helmet as Eden tried to wring out her hair.

Aiden was watching from his kayak, trying to figure out what they had just seen. When he finally figured out what happened, he started to say, "Hey guys, I think I know what happened to..." But, before finishing his sentence, he looked up and saw a man standing on the opposite shore, smiling, and waving at them!

TWENTY-ONE

AIDEN SWALLOWED THE REST OF HIS SENTENCE the moment he saw the stranger standing atop the steep bank on the far shore. When he had gotten quiet, everyone immediately stopped and followed his gaze. They all were astonished to find a grandfatherly looking man, around five feet, eight inches, on the opposite shore chuckling at them.

As soon as Eden saw him, she suddenly gasped and called out happily, "Dr. Maxwell!" "That's Dr. Maxwell?"

"Yup! That's him, Aiden."

"You didn't tell me he was Native American."

"You didn't ask."

At that moment, Dr. Maxwell put his hands to his mouth, and shouted to them, "Come on over! I'll wait for you here."

Quickly they got into their kayaks, and after a few strokes arrived at the creek bank where Dr. Maxwell was waiting.

When they were close enough to the steep, rocky bank Dr. Maxwell was standing on, he said, "Well, hello there, Eden! Good to see you again!"

When he went to acknowledge the others, he clapped his hands, and said, "Ah, I see we have your brother Aiden, along with Savage, her brother Colton, and cousin, Wade. Good, good, you're all together! That's what I'd hoped for. Wonderful!"

Noticing that Eden was sopping wet when the others were only slightly, and that she had a bandage around her arm, he added, "Oh, but I can see from the bandage, it seems you all ran into a little trouble. Or should I say, you've all ran into Ciara."

"Ciara! But, how in the world could you know about Ciara?" Eden asked.

Just at that moment, his assistant, Charles, came out of the woods on one of the paths that ran along Little Beaver Creek, and whispered something into Dr. Maxwell's ear. When Charles was finished, Dr. Maxwell nodded his head, and Charles turned and disappeared back into the woods.

Then Dr. Maxwell said, "Why don't you all paddle down to the site? It's not far. Charles and I will meet you there shortly. I can't wait to show you the site and what we've just found." And, before they could say anything else or have a chance to ask him any questions, he turned and disappeared into the woods.

Wade asked, "What just happened?"

"I'm not sure. But it sure sounded to me like he knows about Ciara," said Aiden.

"But, how in the world could he possibly know about her?" Savage asked.

"None of us know, Savage. I guess we'll find out when we get to the dig site. Just keep it together until we get there, Sis."

Eden reached for the *key* for reassurance and was surprised to find it no longer pulsing.

Colton noticing, asked, "Ciara?"

"No tingling, no pulsating, nothing. She must not be anywhere close."

"Well, I got the impression she didn't know what was going on from the look on her face before she disappeared or at least if she did, she sure wasn't happy about it."

"Yeah, you're right about that, Colton. She was completely caught off guard from what I could see. Maybe, whatever grabbed her flung her far from here."

"Humph! We can only hope!" Savage said.

Aiden said, "Hey, we're not going to get any answers sitting here in our kayaks talking amongst ourselves. So, why don't we paddle down to the site and meet up with Dr. Maxwell like he asked? Maybe we'll get some answers from him since he seems to already know about Ciara."

"Yeah, Aiden's right. Better than sitting here, and taking a chance she'll find us again," said Colton, as he dipped his paddle into the water, pushing away from the shore.

Staring at Colton's back as he paddled away, Savage thought, "Yeah, let's go talk to this Dr. Maxwell and find out what he knows. But one thing for sure, he better not tell us we imagined everything, because my sore butt is telling me otherwise!"

TWENTY-TWO

ONCE THEY ROUNDED THE BEND RIGHT ABOVE the dig site, they could see Dr. Maxwell and his assistant, Charles, standing on the bank waiting for them. They hurriedly put to shore and beached their kayaks, as Dr. Maxwell had instructed them, all in anticipation of getting answers to their questions.

Dr. Maxwell happily shook each one of their hands, told them how glad he was to see them, and then introduced his assistant, Charles. As soon as the introductions were finished, they all at once began telling him about what had happened, especially with Ciara, and asking questions.

"Hold on there! I promise I'll answer some of your questions while I'm showing you all around, but I'll also tell you that there are some questions that I won't be answering now."

At his assertion they all grew silent, looking at one another in disbelief.

Thinking they were being put off, Eden grew frustrated, and asked, "But if you know, why not? We've got to have answers to what's going on, Dr. Maxwell! We were attacked!"

"Yes, you were, and violently. And I promise you'll have your answers, Eden. You all will. But it must be at the proper time. There are reasons why I can't tell you about everything here. Let's just say it isn't completely, ah, safe. That's why I want you all to come to my house when it's raining this weekend to hear the whole story. I'll make us popcorn, hot chocolate, and we can relax and talk in privacy," he answered her.

"But it's not supposed to rain until Monday," Eden and Colton both answered shocking each other.

Aiden snickered. It was strangely satisfying hearing someone else saying the same thing as Eden instead of him. But Eden did not care for the smug look on her brother's face and elbowed him knowing later he'd gripe to her about it.

Colton was surprised when he said the same thing as Eden. It felt as if his and her thoughts over the last few hours were becoming the same. There were moments earlier when he felt he knew what she was thinking. But that was impossible.

While he was thinking about Eden, he slowly came to realize he had developed feelings for her. This self-realization then triggered a physical reaction that he tried his best to stop but failed. Feeling the heat slowly creeping up the back of his neck, he wondered if anyone else saw him blushing. Not knowing if they had, caused him to fidget, whereas normally he was calm.

It only took a few seconds for Savage to notice her brother blushing and shuffling. After rolling her eyes, she shook her head and sighed. She had a good idea as to what had caused it.

Even though Colton was older than her, she felt he was less capable of handling feelings for the opposite sex than she was.

Wade was confused over how Colton was acting. He was trying to understand why Colton got weird because Eden and him happened to say the same thing at the same time. That sort of thing happened to people at times. Nothing to get bent out of shape over, he thought. Still, he wondered if he had missed something.

However, Dr. Maxwell had not missed anything. He had seen their reactions many times before and knew exactly what was happening.

Colton wanting to change the subject since the situation had become uncomfortable, said, "I think I have something you might want to see, Dr. Maxwell." Going to his kayak, he retrieved the samples of the melted rock he had taken earlier.

When he rejoined the group, he handed Dr. Maxwell the medicine bottle containing the wrapped bits of quartz and stone from the boulder Ciara was standing on when she disappeared. Colton said, "After Ciara attacked Eden, Savage, and me this morning, I took these two samples from the large rock she jumped on when she vanished. If you look closely, you can see the difference between samples. One type I got from the quartz veins and the other is from the rock around those veins. We believe these samples could give us a clue as to what happened to her. And, um… we were also hoping you could have them tested for us."

"That was a smart move getting both types of samples, Colton. I'll be more than glad to have them tested for you," Dr. Maxwell said, turning the container as he looked at the samples.

Handing Charles the samples, Dr. Maxwell told him, "Run this through the standard artifact testing, plus have it looked at under the electron microscope. We'll see what we have and after that, go from there."

"Yes, Dr. Maxwell. I'll add it to today's specimens," Charles told him, as he placed the bottle in one of the pockets of his cargo pants.

Colton was relieved hearing that the pieces of quartz and rock he had collected were going to be tested. And he was especially relieved Dr. Maxwell had not laughed at him when he asked, as he knew the officers at the station would have.

"See, told you it would be okay," Aiden said as he nudged Colton.

"Thanks, Dr. Maxwell."

"No problem, Colton.

By the way… before we get to the site, there is something I need to talk about with all of you. It's about what happened earlier today, the attacks by Ciara. For the time being, it would not be wise to talk about it to anyone outside of this group. It's not safe for anyone else to find out about her, especially considering what I need to tell you all when you come to my cottage. I know I'm asking a lot of everyone. But, for the safety of the others here, will you keep quiet about her until I say it's safe?"

Eden and Aiden did not like keeping things from their parents and were questioning if they should fully trust Dr. Maxwell even though they knew their parents were fond of him. But at the same time, they were concerned about putting anyone else in Ciara's cross hair. The same with the other three as well. They knew without some sort of evidence; their dad and uncle would be highly skeptical of their story. So, in the end, they all agreed to keep it quiet for the time being.

Once it was agreed, Dr. Maxwell smiled then excitedly rubbed his hands together, saying, "Now, everyone, let's go see my latest excavation!"

Following Dr. Maxwell and Charles up a well-trodden path winding through some rhododendrons, and other flora, they were surprised when they reached the crest of the creek bank to find spread out before them an active dig taking place in and around a large cave. And there, in the middle of it all, were Eden's and Aiden's parents, along with fifteen or so other people performing various tasks about the site.

"Welcome to my world!" Dr. Maxwell said, as he happily watched the astonished expressions forming on their faces. "Now, come meet my team and see some of the amazing things we've found."

They all followed Dr. Maxwell, while Charles took Colton's samples over to a table where two interns were busy cataloging that day's specimens that were to be taken back to the barn for further analysis. Once Charles saw that Colton's samples were safely logged in, he went to a computer nearby and proceeded to check on something. When he had finished, he rejoined the group but seemed to be preoccupied. He did not give them any clue as to what was bothering him though. He only whispered into Dr. Maxwell's ear.

For Eden and Aiden, being at a dig site was old news. And, even though Savage, Colton and Wade had all been to the Meadowcroft Rockshelter for school field trips, this was the very first active site they had ever seen. It was uncovered unlike the Meadowcroft Rockshelter, except for the few canopies where the canteen was set up and the specimens were being bagged and cataloged. The largest one was set outside the entrance to the cave to shield the test pits they were digging there.

Wade and Colton observed the two interns Charles had passed Colton's samples to were sitting at a table receiving the tagged and bagged items from students working at various locations in the dig. Once they cataloged them, they secured them for transportation to the barn by safely placing them into the cargo hold of an ATV.

The idea of sitting there cataloging the findings into a computer did not seem overly exciting to Colton and Wade, but what did get their attention were the students carrying dirt buckets to be sieved, looking for artifacts. Getting down and dirty was more their style.

Before Dr. Maxwell took them into the cave, he first led them to the test pit where the Walkers were working so he could introduce Savage, Colton, and Wade.

"Frank! Barb! Look who I found kayaking by our dig. Eden, Aiden and their friends, Savage and Colton, Sheriff Wade's children and his nephew, Wade."

"So glad you and your friends stopped by," Barb said, while the group stood looking down into their pit.

Hunkering down at the edge of the nearly five-foot-deep pit her parents were working in, Eden said, "Looks like you two are having lots of fun."

"Yeah, Squirt, we've been finding some unique artifacts. From what we're seeing, it's looking like this site was a major gathering place for many Paleo-American groups for quite some time. Who knows, once we start studying the artifacts more in depth some of these finds might be up there with the Meadowcroft Rockshelter's clovis point," her dad told her, handing her a piece of broken pottery.

Eden took the piece from her dad and studied it a bit before saying, "I'd say this looks like it's from the early Monongahela Era, Dad. The design is a touch different, though. More decorative." She then passed it to Aiden to look at before handing it back to her dad.

"That's my girl! You're right on both accounts. Of course, we'll need to look at what else is being found at this level and... well, you know the drill," her dad told her, aware he was starting to ramble on.

"Dad, Mom, Savage and Colton have some artifacts they've found along Little Beaver Creek that I bet you both would like to look at. And, since we've been invited to their house for supper on Sunday, maybe you both could check them out. Who knows, they might lead you to another site," Eden suggested, as she stood up.

"Sure, we'd be glad to! It's always good to check out other people's finds. You never know what they may lead to," said her mom.

It was then she noticed Eden's bandage. "What in the world happened to your arm Eden?"

Setting her tools down, Barb was reaching for the ladder when Eden said, "No, Mom! My arm's okay. I just got scraped by a tree branch. No big deal! Colton took care of it. He cleaned it, slapped on some cream, and wrapped it. All's good! Actually, he's rather good with first aid." Eden began blushing slightly when she realized she had given Colton a compliment in front of everyone.

"Are you sure you're, okay?" asked her mom, noticing Eden's flushed face. "Yeah, it's fine," Eden said trying not to make a big deal of it.

Aiden, being Aiden, could not resist, and laughed, "Don't worry, Mom. If it scars, it'll match her face."

TWENTY-THREE

BEFORE ENTERING THE CAVE, EVERYONE SAID their goodbyes to the Walkers, leaving them to get back to their work. Before the last goodbye had barely left their lips, Dr. Maxwell was hurrying them to the front of the cave.

Stopping under the small rock shelf at the entrance, he reached into a box handing each of them a headlamp and flashlight, explaining, "You'll need to use these since we haven't had a chance to run any lighting to the area of the cave we will be visiting. Without any lights, it is so dark you won't be able to see your hand in front of your face. These headlamps and flashlights will provide us with the light we'll need. Just yesterday we discovered something quite amazing in the section I'll be taking you to. And even though the lighting isn't set up, I really want you to see what we came across. Let me say that I think you'll find it remarkable! Now that you know why you need the lights, I'll tell you all a story about it. How the discovery was made is quite amusing in and of itself. When we were exploring the passageway yesterday, an intern sat on a large rock to take a break. It wasn't stable and rolled away. They ended up falling flat on their butt exposing a fissure. That happy mishap led to the finding of a previously unknown chamber!"

Everyone but Savage, found it humorous as they followed Dr. Maxwell through the opening of the cave. Instead, she quietly mumbled to herself, "Humph! Bet their bottom's nowhere near as sore as mine."

Continuing to follow Dr. Maxwell, Eden and Aiden were busy checking it out. They were surprised to find how large it was. They figured it could hold up to a couple dozen people comfortably. Drawing on what they had learned from their parents, they could easily imagine Native Americans making use of this cave year-round eons ago. So, they were sure it contained artifacts.

Watching as Dr. Maxwell skillfully moved along the uneven floor of the cave, they noticed they were approaching a large fissure, when he and his light suddenly disappeared into it. All of them, except Charles, stopped short wondering where he had gone, until he poked his head out and said, "Well, come along! You're not going to get to see what we found by standing there!" To their relief, when they reached the inky dark gap and looked inside, they saw his lights bobbing ahead of them.

Trailing behind Dr. Maxwell's bouncing headlamp and flashlight, they hiked deeper into the cave. They walked single file for about fifteen minutes until the passageway began to widen enough that two or three people could walk side by side comfortably. It was here that Dr. Maxwell stopped. After turning off his flashlight, he reached down and picked up a larger flashlight that was sitting in the passageway. He pointed it at a large pile of stones that had at some time in the distant past slid down the wall of the corridor, piled there for who knows how long.

Charles came from the back of the group, as if the turning on of Dr. Maxwell's flashlight was a signal for him. Without saying a word, he began moving a few stones away from the wall. Once he had repositioned the larger ones, he then checked them making sure none of them would roll. Satisfied they were safe, he then rolled away the last of the stones exposing a sizeable opening in the wall of the passageway. Getting on his hand and knees, he crawled into the void and disappeared.

"Charles is going into the chamber first to check for any snakes, bats or humans that may have wandered in there since yesterday. And to check on one of our many dampening fields that's keeping your bioelectrical signatures from being seen by Ciara. So, while we wait on him, I have a few instructions for you all. You're not children, so you know it goes without saying to be incredibly careful once you're inside the chamber. We've only had a chance to do a cursory examination of this cavity. But... well, you'll understand when I show you. And one more thing, once we're in there, please let me know if any of you have any questions! There's no such thing as a dumb question."

Right away Eden asked, "Dr. Maxwell, what's so special about this discovery that you specifically had to show it to all of us right now?"

"Ah, that's the most important question of all, Eden. And, as soon as we're all inside, you'll see your answer."

Eden thought, "Well, that's kind of cryptic. See my answer? What does he mean by see?"

At that moment, Charles called out to them, "Looks good, Dr. Maxwell! No critters of any type to be found and the field's running great unlike earlier. So far, no incursions, but not from a lack of her trying."

"All right! Let's head in," Dr. Maxwell said, as he dropped to his hands and knees to lead the way.

In turn, each of them got down and followed behind Dr. Maxwell into the inky dark crack. As they came out of the short passageway into the chamber on the other side, Aiden felt something creeping across his face. Jumping up as he exited, he ran his hands over his face and yelled, "Spiders! There're spiders in here! I feel one crawling in my hair!"

Savage who had been in front of him, turned around to face him, and with a hint of amusement in her voice, calmly said, "Here, Aiden, drop your head and let me check."

Aiden stopped his fidgeting long enough to allow Savage to examine him. Gently she checked out his face, down his neck and raked her fingers through his hair. She must have been enjoying that part and had taken a little longer than her brother Colton thought she should, because he cleared his throat.

After throwing him a look, Savage removed her hands from Aiden's hair and handed him a dusty old cobweb saying, "Here's what you felt, Aiden. No spiders."

Aiden, embarrassed about panicking, and the fact he had obviously enjoyed Savage mussing his hair, mumbled, "Geez, thanks, Savage. You don't understand how much I hate spiders."

Eden watched Aiden's panic attack with feigned interest. Personally, spiders never bothered her, but Aiden had always hated them. So, feeling slightly annoyed at his outburst, she shrugged her shoulders and sighed. Then without thinking, she looked in Dr. Maxwell's direction. That action caused her headlamp to light up the wall of the chamber behind him. After a few seconds she realized what she was seeing, and gasped, "Oh my, goodness!"

When the others heard Eden catch her breath, they all looked her way to see what had happened. Noticing she was focusing on the wall of the cave behind Dr. Maxwell, they drew closer to see what had captured her attention.

As their additional head lamps and flashlights began lighting up more of the wall, they were in awe of what was revealed. The figures and bright colors decorating the wall appeared as if it had only been painted yesterday. After being enclosed for centuries in this small chamber, they were beautifully preserved.

As they carefully examined the walls of the cave, they realized there were six figures, two females and four males. Although, from what they could tell, one of the male figures was depicted was smaller than the others leading them to surmise that it might represent a child. The figures were placed about in various panoramas. Some were typical hunting and fishing scenes, while others were of daily life, not unlike other pictographs found in caves throughout the world.

However, there were two unusual views that stood out from all the rest that Eden noticed right away. These views both showed an elongated swirling disk, mirror images of each other.

Nudging Aiden, Eden pointed to those views without saying anything to him. She had seen this figure before at other sites and in her parent's reference books. If she was recalling what she had read correctly, some of these disks had something to do with the passage of time, portals, acoustics, or even in some cases, star positions. Still, these disks were not the same as those in the books because of their elongated shape.

The disk that tilted to the left depicted all the figures moving away from it, except for one male figure, with red lines projecting from his head representing hair or feathers. That figure appeared to be stepping out of it. Oddly, this was also the only scene without the male child.

The swirling disk tilting to the right showed the figures walking towards and into it. The last of these figures were the two females, each holding onto the smaller male figure's hands as if leading him.

While they were all examining the paintings, Savage had taken ahold of Aiden's arm, so when Eden nudged him and pointed to the disks, Savage looked also. When she stepped closer to study them, she let go of Aiden's arm. It was then she noticed, besides the two figures with red hair or feathers and the child, there was a female figure with what appeared to have blonde hair or feathers. She tentatively pointed it out to Eden.

As Eden and Savage began talking among themselves about what the figures on the cave walls could mean, Aiden's attention was drawn away by Colton's and Wade's conversation. He wandered over to the other side of the cave where they were talking excitely about other paintings that contained various hunting scenes, leaving Eden and Savage absorbed in their discussion about the figures and the disks.

Something in one of the views had caught Colton's eye, and he said, "Hey! Look! This guy with the red hair brought down a huge twelve-point buck with just a spear!"

It was Colton's excited remark that suddenly sparked Eden's and Savage's realization that the figures in the panoramas were meant to represent them. And, as that fact sunk in, both Eden and Savage turned, and faced Dr. Maxwell, who was standing there smiling at them.

When Eden and Savage had abruptly stopped talking, the guys noticed it had gotten quiet. They stopped their discussion to see what was happening with the girls.

Noticing they were staring at Dr. Maxwell, Aiden asked, "What's up, Sis? Savage?" Eden began to raise her index finger to signal Aiden to wait, as she was about to ask Dr. Maxwell some tough questions. But, before she could speak a word, Dr. Maxwell told his assistant, "Let's see what they think about this, Charles."

Turning his back on them, he walked over to the crevasse they had crawled through to enter the chamber. At first, they thought he was leaving, until he reached up into a small niche above the opening and removed a small, dusty, carved, stone box.

The very second Dr. Maxwell picked up the box, the key Eden was wearing under her shirt began vibrating again, but it was a different type of pulsing this time. It did not hurt like it had around Ciara, nor did it grow heavy. Eden was able to ignore it for the most part, as her attention was focused on the beautiful box Dr. Maxwell held in his hand.

As he brushed the dust off it, Eden had placed her left hand over the *key*. Even though she was unaware she had done so, Colton and Savage noticed it. They had seen her use the same mannerism earlier that day when they had met Ciara. Because of this, they knew the *key* was vibrating.

Savage whispered, "Is it Ciara?"

Eden, not taking her eyes off Dr. Maxwell and the box, shook her head and answered, "No, it's different. No, pain or weight."

Going to Eden he handed her the box, and excitedly said as she took it, "Why don't you look and see what it holds, Eden? You see, I believe this box, and its contents, belong to you."

Eden was confused, thinking, "Wait! What on Earth can Dr. Maxwell mean by the box being mine?"

She frowned after she had ahold of the box. As she examined it, she could not help noticing its striking design was familiar. Its weight seemed oddly comfortable in her hand, almost as if it was accustomed to it. So did the Celtic carvings on the lid as she ran her fingers across them down to the very tiny chip on the lip of the lid where she remembered having dropped it. Next, she gave it a gentle shake and heard something inside.

"Hmm... I recognized this box. But how...?" She mumbled to herself.

While Eden was examining the box, Colton had moved to her side. Placing his hand on her shoulder, he stood watching her. He, too, was beginning to feel like he had seen it before. He even recognized the beautiful, intertwined Celtic knots carved on it.

When Eden hesitated to open it, Colton reached for the lid without thinking, removing it before Eden could stop him.

When he saw what was inside, he said, "No, it can't be! It's the golden brooch I gave you for our engagement when we were stuck in Ireland centuries ago!"

All of them, except for Dr. Maxwell and Charles, were stunned to hear what Colton said about the stone box and the brooch it held. As they were each trying to wrap their minds around it, Dr. Maxwell startled them all by clearing his throat, then mumbling, "Interesting."

Colton, himself, was as surprised as they were with what he had said. Still standing close to Eden with his hand on her shoulder, Eden looked up at him in disbelief. He knew she was wondering how he could have known about the beautiful piece of jewelry she was holding.

Filled with confusion, Eden said faintly, "How... how did you know this is mine? This is the very same brooch I saw in a vision I had earlier today. I never told you or Savage about that, so there's absolutely no way you could have known about it. And even though I know beyond a shadow of a doubt that this brooch is mine, and that you did give it to me as a pledge of marriage in Ireland, how could that even be possible? We only just met this morning!"

"What Eden's saying is right, Dr. Maxwell. The first time we've ever met was this morning. Gee! I don't get why I said what I said about that broach. I know it sounds like I'm totally wacked, but my heart and my mind are both telling me it's true that I did give it to Eden as a promise of marriage. In some ways it feels like it's Deja vu, like... I'm watching a movie of things that I have done, but I don't remember doing them. Still, deep down I know it's true. But how in the world can that even be possible?"

After Colton was done talking, something that morning after Ciara's disappearance became clear to Savage. She said, "Ohhh...! So now that kiss you gave Eden makes sense! Well, sort of."

"Kiss? What kiss?" asked Aiden and Wade, wondering if they had missed something. "The kiss Colton gave Eden after our encounter with Ciara."

"Really, Savage! You had to go and mention that now?"

Figuring that Aiden and Wade were going to ask questions that he did not have answers for, he said, "Stop right now. You know just as much as I do."

Through all of Eden's and Colton's conversations, Dr. Maxwell had remained silent, watching, and listening. He only stood there with an odd smile on his face, as if it was familiar.

His silence bothered Eden, and at that point she began to be concerned. Going to the different panoramas, she said, "Besides this broach, what about all these cave paintings? I can tell they're ancient, but they're about us! See, here's Aiden spearing a deer, while Colton, Savage, Wade, and I are hunting with him. Over here there's scenes of us cooking, building lodges, planting, and canoeing along with a young boy and other natives. And, then there're these two views with swirling disks that looks like we're coming out of one and going into the other one and taking the young boy along with us."

Right at that moment she paused, and wondered, "Although, why a child with us is kind'a puzzling."

As soon as the child was mentioned, Dr. Maxwell told her, "You're right Eden. These paintings are about all of you and the boy. And it looks like I must tell you all everything sooner than originally planned considering Ciara's attacks today. So, because your lives are in danger, I needed you to see them first to help me explain what is happening. Even so, it's not safe to talk about everything here at the dig. I'll explain a few things now, but most of what I have to say will need to wait until you all come to my cottage this weekend when it's raining."

The second he stopped they began asking him questions, but Dr. Maxwell stopped them. When they had quieted down, he continued, "Let me enlighten you first about the rain. You see, the atmospheric energy a storm creates keeps Ciara from finding us so she can spy on or attack us. The bigger the storm the safer we are. Here at the excavation, we use several small plasma dampening fields to create a larger one to protect us, but it requires a lot of power to maintain it for a short time. Whereas a storm is raw, natural energy, and we can use that energy to create a larger, stronger, and longer lasting field to block her from spying or attacking. Even though these smaller fields in and around the camp are keeping everyone safe for now, Ciara is trying to punch through them to find us. Eventually she will succeed. Regrettably, some of you know firsthand how dangerous she can be. Now, about the paintings and the swirling disks, how can I explain in terms you'll all understand?" he pondered, as he rubbed his chin.

Suddenly he had an idea, and said, "Ah, let's try this... the swirling disks painted on the wall are what you could call a hole in spacetime. It's an artificially created portal that allows a connection to be made from one time to another. It allows a person, or persons, to move through time periods forwards or backwards. It's what you have been taught is a *wormhole*, but on a much smaller, friendlier scale."

"No way! You're talking about time travel, aren't you?" Aiden asked excitedly.

"Yes, exactly!"

"Whoa, no way!" Wade said.

"But that's not even possible with today's technology, is it? We won't have that kind of technology in place for a while," Savage said. "Besides, Einstein and Hawking both said you would need..."

Noticing everyone had gone quiet and were staring at her, Savage stopped talking. Then she snapped, "What? You all know what I said is true." Angrily tossing her blonde hair behind her shoulders, she crossed her arms and stood there looking at them defiantly.

Even though she was first in her class, excelling in math and science, Savage never liked sounding like a know-it-all. Usually, she chose not to say anything, opting to let others answer instead, but occasionally when she did speak up, they took notice.

"Wow! Smart and beautiful," Aiden said. Savage began to blush.

Dr. Maxwell, patted her shoulder, saying, "Yes, you are right, Savage. We don't have the capability to travel through time presently. But, using a Time Loop, we most likely will be able in your lifetime."

"Wait! How could you know that? You make it sound like it's a done deal," she asked.

Dr. Maxwell laughed when Savage said, "No, let me guess. You can't tell us now, but you'll tell us all about it when we come to your cottage when it's raining this weekend."

"I'm sorry. I know, it sounds like I'm putting you off, but really, I'm not. It's just not safe to talk about certain issues now because…" he was trying to explain when the alarm went off.

"It looks like she's trying to punch through unit three's plasma damping shield, Dr. Maxwell. That's on the other side of the compound. Give me a second to reinforce it," Charles informed him. But, no sooner had Charles reinforced that field, another alarm went off.

"Seems like she's fishing, sir. What do you suggest?" asked Charles.

"Reinforce it all around but run pulsating plasma widths. That will keep her guessing for a while," he told Charles.

"Well, it looks like Ciara's back at it, so I better make this quick so we can get you all safely out of here, and on your way home before she finds out exactly where you are. We especially wouldn't want her finding you here in this cave with all these paintings. She's not aware of this place in this Time Loop. Before we go, there is something of importance I want to tell you all now. Questions we'll discuss later."

"The *key* that you are wearing, Eden, is for all intents and purposes called a *Memory Keeper*. It has other names as well. Ciara calls it the *Key to Immortality* because she mistakenly thinks it will allow her to live forever. What it does do is allow the one wearing it to see the correct path they need to take, but only if they have been on that path in time before. Another thing it does is react to danger. As you found out earlier, when you first saw Ciara. Always wear it, Eden. Trust it. It won't fail you!"

"Now, the visions you and Colton had today were shown to you by the *Memory Keeper* and are about previous memories from other Time Loops." When he noticed she was about to interrupt, he continued without any hesitation, "Yes, he had the same vision as you about the time when you were stuck in Ireland, but that was a very small part of why he kissed you."

When Eden and Savage heard that Colton had the same vision as Eden, and had not said anything to them about it, they expected an explanation. Instead, he ignored them by pretending to be paying attention to Dr. Maxwell.

"You'll need to let Savage, Aiden, and Wade touch the *Memory Key* before you leave so their memories will be fully activated for this loop. You and Colton already have touched it, but they haven't, only people who had touched it..."

"Ah, excuse me, Dr. Maxwell," interrupted Aiden. "But I did touch the *key* this morning before Eden made a necklace out of it."

"Well then, good, good! That just leaves Savage and Wade. Eden, would you take out your *key*?"

Eden was still holding the box containing the pin, so she handed it to Colton. He replaced the lid and slipped it carefully into a pocket in his cargo shorts. Once her hands were free, she lifted the *key* from under her top, and removed it from around her neck, protectively cradling it in her hand.

As Savage and Wade drew closer to get a better look, Dr. Maxwell told them, "Each of you need to hold the *key* and run your fingers down the shank and around the bow to activate it."

Seeing their hesitation, his eyes twinkled as he smiled. "Don't worry. It won't bite or sting much," he cautioned. Both Savage and Wade gave Dr. Maxwell a side eye.

Wade was the first to reach out and take it. As he ran his fingers up and down the stem and about the bow, a half-cocked smile appeared on his wistful face. Before handing the *key* to Savage, he nudged Aiden saying, "Yeah, definitely old-style fiddle music. Still, it isn't half bad to listen to."

Dropping the *key* into Savage's hand, Wade jokingly told her. "You're up, Cuz!"

At first, Savage was holding the *key* in her hand like it was some kind of big scary bug, but as she studied it, she noticed how beautiful the designs were on the shank and bow and grew less fearful of it. Before long, she could not help herself, and began rubbing it, feeling the minute pattern, and becoming mesmerized with its rhythm.

After a few moments had passed, Savage looked up from the *key* and asked, "Hey guys! Is there a radio playing or someone's ringtone going off? Cause, I'm hearing fiddles."

TWENTY-FOUR

A FEW DAYS AFTER MEETING DR. MAXWELL and the attack by Ciara, the weather conditions began to change. Early the week was beautiful, especially the day they went kayaking on Little Beaver Creek. Now all that was ending. Rain was coming.

When they were getting ready to leave the dig, Dr. Maxwell had again implored them all to promise to keep quiet about Ciara. He reminded them that innocent people might be hurt if she was aware that they knew about her. They understood Dr. Maxwell's logic in not wanting them to say anything to anyone about Ciara. They also knew if they reported her attack to Sheriff Ward and the officers at the station, it would be dismissed as a prank or a misunderstanding of events. So, they agreed it would be best to keep quiet, until they had some hard evidence they could share.

Right before leaving, Dr. Maxwell had Charles hand out wristbands to Colton, Savage, and Wade, instructing them to always wear them. He called them bio-electrical field disruptors. He explained that the bands would hide their biological and electrical signatures from Ciara, so she would not be able to target them once they left the protection of the plasma damping fields covering the dig.

He did not give Eden or Aidan any wristbands, so they were a little confused until Dr. Maxwell explained that they would not need any as there was a larger plasma damping field on the farm. As long as they were there, Ciara would not be able to find their electrical and biological signals. And, if they were with the others, they would be protected by their wristbands if they stayed within six feet of them. Hearing this put their minds at ease as much as it was possible under such circumstances.

After leaving the dig, they all decided that until the rain came, they would stick close to each other's homes as much as possible. Eden and Aiden would remain at the farm. Savage would stay home.

Colton and Wade would only go to work, head straight back home, then they would all meet up at the farmhouse. Fortunately for Wade, Sheriff Ward and his wife would not be wondering why their nephew was at their house. Since both his parents were pilots in the Air Force, he was there all the time during the summer anyway.

They also planned to keep in constant communication with one another when they were apart. Most of their time was spent on their phones and tablets talking. Of course, Colton and Wade still had to work, but they managed to contact everyone before they left in the morning and during their breaks. If for any reason they were unable to meet, the three of them would be on their tablets with Eden and Aiden until bedtime. With Sheriff Ward working the night shift, Colton's and Savage's mother was glad that they and Wade were spending so much time at the farm allowing him to sleep undisturbed.

The first time they were together at the farmhouse, Eden retrieved her mom's reference books from the study and showed everyone the pictures of the disks like the ones they had seen in the cave. They spent a few hours poring over them but did not find any photos that looked exactly like the ones in the cave. The disks in the cave were unique.

Later, Aiden and Savage researched various time travel theories that they discussed during the next few days. When their minds became stuffed with information they were trying to understand, they would take a dip in the pool. Later, they would order from the pizza shop or make snacks. So, by the time the rain began, they had gotten to know each other quite well.

In the middle of all their bonding, Eden was aware that Aiden and Savage had become close, maybe a little too close in such a short time. More than once, she had found them with Aiden's arm innocently draped around Savage's shoulders and their heads nearly touching, while poring over Time Travel articles.

Though things seemed to be happening faster than normal in their relationship, Eden was happy Aiden had found someone he liked, and even more amazing, someone who liked him. She worried that back in Carlisle he was cutting himself off socially, but now she could put those concerns to rest. But one of the benefits for her if they became a couple, was that she and Savage had become good friends.

When Eden woke up Friday morning, the blue sky contained only a handful of clouds and looked like it was going to be another beautiful day. But when she went out the front door to get the mail later, she was met by a heavy wall of humidity. Looking towards the southwest, she could see a line of darkening gray clouds that appeared to be coming their way. As she walked down the driveway to the mailbox, it looked like Dr. Maxwell was going to get the huge storm he had told them about after all.

Upon reaching the mailbox, she gave the area a quick glance around looking for anything suspicious. Not seeing anything, she reached into the mailbox and pulled out the mail.

As she was walking back, Eden quickly scanned through the mail she was holding. She did not see anything for her or Aiden, just some envelopes for her parents. Taking her time, she let her mind ponder what Dr. Maxwell was going to tell them. Personally, she was having a tough time believing he was going to be forthcoming about everything, since he had deflected all their questions they had asked him, using the excuse it was not safe to disclose information because of Ciara. Tonight would tell.

Reaching the porch, she bounded up the steps but thought she had heard something.

Turning around, she looked out at the fields and down the lane she had just walked up and saw nothing. Shrugging her shoulders, she turned back around to open the door. Right at that moment she caught a flash of light reflecting on the door.

Spinning around to face the trees, she saw another quick flash in the leaves and then nothing. She stood there for five minutes or so hoping it would happen again, but it did not. Also, while she was watching, she was listening but did not hear anything except buzzing bees and chirping birds.

Sighing, she opened the door and went inside. As she shut it, she said, "Probably zombies."

TWENTY-FIVE

STANDING PENSIVELY AT HER WINDOW, CIARA was not focusing on anything. Even though she gave the appearance of being calm on the outside, inside she was boiling with rage.

Abruptly, she crossed the floor and checked the data on her screens and instruments for the hundredth time in the past hour. Again, nothing! She was at a loss trying to understand why her plans failed and how she had lost Airmed's, Brigid's, Cermait's, Miach's, and Aengus' electrical and biological signals.

Everything, in her mind, had been executed perfectly. She had successfully lured Airmed and Brigid to the shore by pretending to be injured in a kayaking accident. And she would have succeeded in killing them, except Cermait had ruined everything by showing up just at the moment she was going to strike. As it was, she barely escaped from him after their fight with hardly any time to spare to create the portal to escape.

And once she was safe, she continued tracking their signals until they reached the three rapids. It was at the last rapid, the perfect place for an attack, where she decided to create the second portal so she could focus on solely ambushing Airmed. She was surprised as she was coming through her portal to see another one unexpectedly form inside hers. The gravity from this portal pulled her in and flung her out of range. Again, she was denied success! This failure increased her anger even more. She was so close she could see the surprise in Airmed's eyes. But by the time she was able to create a third portal, she could no longer find their electrical and biological signals.

"It has to be that old man from the future, Dian Cecht, and his grandson, Lugh! They have to be the ones who created that portal pulling me away from Airmed!" Ciara screamed, as she slammed her hand on the desk, rattling her equipment.

"They think they have eluded me. But watch! I'll find them," she said. Sitting, she began franticly searching the immediate area after the rapids, looking once again for their electrical and biological signals, sending her probes where she felt there was a possibility they could be.

Once she calmed down, she realized that not only could she not find any of their signals in the area after the rapids, but she could also not find any other human signals as well, even though there were people in that area hiking, fishing, and boating. Looking closer at her data, she found that her readings were showing small fluctuations and realized that someone had set up a plasma dampening field over the lower third of Little Beaver Creek.

"Well, well, well! What do we have here, a protection field? I should have known Dian Cecht and Lugh would go to such extremes to keep me from finding them and the others. They should realize by now that their pathetic precautions are not going to stop me!"

In no time she was studying the ebb and flow of the plasma field, probing it for any weaknesses. "Humph! Let's see how they'll manage this!" She sneered.

Making some minor adjustments to her instruments and increasing their power intake, Ciara tried to punch holes into the dampening field to allow her to insert a probe to see what they were hiding underneath. She knew the only way she could accomplish this was if she could match the frequency and the strength of their field but given her lack of resources, this was going to take time.

Besides setting off several alarms on Dr. Maxwell's and Charles' instruments, her first attempt failed miserably. This had not discouraged her but caused her to become more focused to find the correct frequency she needed to break through the fluctuating plasma field. She became obsessed with finding inconsistencies so to insert her probes. But little did she know that Dr. Maxwell and Charles were on to her, working on countering any of her attempts.

After her second try, the field was weakened slightly but not enough for her to create an opening. This attempt did not give Dr. Maxwell any cause for worry. He knew Ciara did not have the power she needed to accomplish inserting a probe. In fact, he thought her efforts were rather humorous. Instead, he toyed with her, allowing her to believe she was making headway. Still, he did know that eventually she would find some other way unless he distracted, or as he liked to say, "redirected" her.

For now, he was only concerned about keeping her out as long as Eden, Aiden, Colton, Savage, and Wade were under the field. Once they were gone, he would have Charles collapse part of the field making it look as if it were gone. This would show the electrical and biological signals of any human not attached to the dig, along with any animals, so she would believe she had succeeded.

Of course by then, they would be long gone, protected by the wrist bands which were, as he told them, bio-electro field disruptors. His main concern was to keep them all safe until the rainstorm came and, more importantly, the morning after.

He needed to give them vital information he had to help them understand what had happened to them recently, and the knowledge they would need to know before undertaking an extremely dangerous quest that he would ask them to go on. He longed to tell them everything, but he knew that it would not work, because he had done so in previous failed Time Loops.

"Only tell them enough, and don't overwhelm them," he mumbled. Most importantly they had to learn to trust themselves and each other. Eden especially, needed to learn to trust herself and the *Key* or it would fail again miserably.

When the alarms went off for the third time, Dr. Maxwell looked at Charles. "Don't worry, Dr. Maxwell. I got this!" Charles reassured him, while turning his attention back to his instruments.

"Dear Charles. What would I do without you?" Dr. Maxwell asked himself, as he watched while Charles worked to prevent Ciara from poking through the plasma field.

Dr. Maxwell was thankful Charles had been assigned to him, even though at the time he wasn't thrilled about it because they were good friends. But after the last three Time Loops, Charles had been a God Send. Especially during the Loop where Ciara had stranded him in time over a thousand years ago. If Charles had not found him when he did, he would have died there alone. As it was, he had physically aged sixty years. That was the problem with Time. It was all relative.

One thing Dr. Maxwell was relieved about was, if they could not repair the time displacement during this Loop, Charles would be around to see it repaired on the next one. He knew very well his time was running out and that this would be the last time he would be able to aid them. His body would not survive another Loop. Although the Sentinels repaired much of the damage caused to him after he was stranded, he doubted that they would be able to do so again.

Then, added to everything were the Sentinels, who regulated Time Loops. He knew after this loop they would not allow him to continue. After all, there had been a total of eleven failed loops already, hopefully this would not be the twelfth. If it were not for the two young women, the very two that had given the first real love and security to a frightened ten-year-old, he would have retired by now and let the Sentinels manage the Time Loops. Although the first mistake was made by the five of them, the second and bigger mistake was made by the Sentinels.

Then again, who knew that the beautiful, blue eyed, dark haired seventeen-year-old, with the golden voice, who found the lost Time Bender and followed them through the portal, would turn out to be both a genius and a sociopath?

TWENTY-SIX

THE BLUE SKY AND THE HEAVY WALL of moisture that Eden met with that Friday morning had given way by late afternoon to darkening gray clouds approaching from the southwest. During supper, the rain began falling hard, accompanied by thunder and lightning.

After meeting Dr. Maxwell a few days ago, they had planned to all be together for supper that evening. Fortunately, Colton, Savage and Wade had arrived at the farmhouse before the storm hit. They showed up bearing shredded chicken, shrimp, and beef tacos from a local taco shop in Beaver that they insisted the Walkers had to try.

While everyone was enjoying the food, there was a lot of friendly banter going on between them. It reminded Eden of meals they shared as a family back in Carlisle when their friends from school or her parent's graduate students from Dickinson joined them for supper. The memory of it made her smile. Maybe, given time, living here would not be as bad as she had thought.

Barb was laughing at a comment her husband had made when she noticed Eden smiling cheerfully at the friendly teasing going on around the table. She and Frank had talked about meeting the Sheriff's son, daughter, and nephew at the dig site. They were pleased that the five of them had quickly become friends. Watching how they were interacting with one another eased their concern about their decision to pull Eden and Aiden out of their school for their senior year and have them attend Western Beaver. Now, they could put that worry aside.

Since meeting Colton, Savage, and Wade at the dig, they had been running into the three of them off and on at the farmhouse. Being college professors, they did not mind having young people around. Years of experience dealing with them made them good judges of character and from what they could tell from their brief interactions with them, they seemed to be pleasant and capable young adults. Besides being polite and respectful, they pitched in cleaning up their messes before leaving, which was a plus in her eyes. The three of them also showed a genuine interest in how the site excavation was coming, asking questions about their findings.

Still, she and Frank could sense some uneasiness amongst them. It was not anything they could put their finger on nor was it, thankfully, anything they could see directed to or from any individual in the group. In fact, they all seemed to get along. But the tension was there, lurking in the background. Especially, when she and Frank asked a few open-ended questions about their kayaking trip, it seemed they all gave short evasive answers.

They also noticed how Aiden was paying a lot of attention to Savage, and it appeared she did not seem to mind. In her mother's heart, she was glad for Aiden. It seemed to her that they liked a lot of the same things, and she was able to get him to relax and open up in a group. As his mother, she knew he tended to be an introvert, but it appeared Savage was able to get him to join in.

She was also aware Colton was watching Eden, sneaking glances when he thought no one else knew. She was not too worried about Colton's interest in Eden at this point, because she knew Eden would say something if his attention was not wanted. He had already proved he had his head on straight when he had dressed Eden's arm better than she could have after Eden's accident kayaking. And the scratch was healing beautifully. Still, Barb decided that at an opportune time, a few carefully chosen words with Eden about him would be best since he was a few years older than her.

Barb could not help but chuckle to herself as her eyes fell on Wade. It was obvious that he and Colton were closer than brothers, and that one of their favorite pastimes was getting on Savage's nerves. Although, she did have to say, Savage gave as good as she got.

Wade did seem to be a little down tonight, but she knew it was due to not being able to see Mia, as she had left for a family get together this weekend. He and Colton had just discovered at work that they would be furloughed until Tuesday as new machinery was arriving earlier than expected and the company needed to install it immediately. Only the manufacturing engineers and machinists would be working, so this meant he would not be able to see her for another day than originally planned.

"Ah, to be young and in love!" Barb mumbled, thinking back to when she and Frank had met.

However, she didn't have long to reminisce. Eden interrupted her thoughts by saying, "Mom, Dad, this is the night Dr. Maxwell wants us to come over. So don't worry about the kitchen. We have a little time yet, so we'll clean it up, then head over when he texts us. You two can just relax. You'll have the whole house to yourselves for at least a few hours." Then she laughed.

Frank was busy eating. Swallowing the last bite of his taco, he said, "My! Those tacos were delicious! I can't say I've ever had better. Thank you, guys, for getting them. But, Squirt, you needn't be worried about bothering us tonight. Mom and I were planning on going up to the barn and working with some of the artifacts that were found this week before we ship them out to the lab at the end of the month."

At that very moment, lightning flashed then the thunder cracked, causing the lights to flicker. Momentarily, everyone stopped talking.

"Wow! That one was close! Hopefully, we won't lose our electricity. If that happens, we might have to power up the generators. Maybe we should head to the barn now, Frank. At least if it does go out, we'll be right there to get it back on since the generators are in the lean-to outside the barn."

"I think you might be right. We better grab our raincoats, and get going," he said, before downing the last of his drink.

Heading to the mudroom, Barb told them, "Thanks, you three, for bringing the tacos. They were delicious. Just be careful when you go over to Dr. Maxwell's in this storm. There's extra raingear in the mudroom if you need it," Barb added, as she pulled out hers and Frank's raincoats. Quickly they put them on, said goodbye, leaving by the garage side door closest to the barn.

As soon as they were gone, the five of them quickly cleaned up the kitchen. It did not take them long, especially since there were no leftovers to put in the refrigerator. Eden whispered to

Savage, "Out of all those tacos you guys brought, there are zero left. I thought it was just Aiden, but all guys must have bottomless pits for stomachs." Savage laughed. She was well aware of how much food Colton and Wade could consume.

As they finished cleaning, another bolt of lightning hit close by, followed by its thunder.

"Boy, listen to all that wind and rain! According to Dr. Maxwell, all that energy from this storm should keep Ciara from snooping or from trying another attack when we're together tonight. I sure hope he's got that right."

"So do I, Aiden," Colton agreed. "That first attack was brutal. The second was devious. It shows how very capable she is of just about anything."

"True. But what I don't get, Colton, is why was she even trying to kill us? We've all been racking our brains the last few days trying to think if any of us have ever seen her or had any interaction with her, but none of us have come up with anything. The only one who seems to know anything about her is Dr. Maxwell. And you better believe he's going to tell us all about her tonight. No matter what!" Savage said.

"Yeah, I'm more than ready to hear that explanation," said Eden.

Suddenly Eden had a thought. "Hey, Colton. Something just popped into my mind. I just remembered that Ciara called you something right before she vanished. It was a name… of sorts, I think. Ah… Cer… Cermait? That's it!" Eden said, snapping her fingers.

"You mean like the frog?" snickered Wade, elbowing Aiden.

Colton threw his wet dish towel at Wade. But Wade, anticipating Colton's move, saw it coming and moved away in time for it to hit Aiden in the face.

"I owe you one, Wade!" Colton laughed, pointing his finger at him. "Sorry about that, Aiden."

"No harm done," Aiden said, picking the dish towel up off the floor and tossing it into the washer in the mudroom.

"Okay, Colton. Was that what Ciara called you or not? I was too far away to hear anything."

"Yeah, Savage. That was what she called me. I was focused on trying to catch her and really wasn't paying attention to what she was saying. But wow, Eden! I didn't remember that until you just mentioned it."

"Cermait? I wonder why she'd call you that?" asked Aiden. "Hmm, let me check something." Walking into the living room, he picked up his tablet from the coffee table, plopped down on the couch, and began searching for it. Curious, the rest of them grabbed a seat, and waited for him to finish.

"Okay, let's try this. You said Ciara had an Irish accent, so let me cross reference that with the Irish spelling of Cermait and see what it shows."

"Ooh, look here!" Savage said, as she took the tablet from Aiden. Once she realized what she had done, she told Aiden repentantly, "Sorry!"

"Go ahead. It's okay, Savage. You read it," Aiden said.

"Well, it says this Cermait guy was a member of the Tuatha Dé Danann and had a brother named Aengus. Apparently, this Cermait was a smooth talker. He was the god of poetry and eloquence," Savage read to them.

"What's a Tuatha Dé Danann?" asked Wade.

"It literally means, the folks of the goddess Danu, or the shorter version says, tribe of gods. They are also referred to as, 'The Shining Ones'."

"Gods, huh? 'The Shining Ones', you don't say."

"Oh, for heaven's sake! Don't let it go to your head, Colton," Savage scolded. Everyone laughed.

They searched the site on Tuatha Dé Danann and found there where several gods associated with the group called The Shining Ones. They also found that Cermait had two brothers called Aengus and Aed. He was killed by someone called Lugh.

"This is all interesting, but it doesn't say why Ciara called Colton, Cermait," Eden said, when she was alerted by a text message.

"Hey guys! Dr. Maxwell just texted me. He's ready for us. Well, looks like it's Interrogation Time!"

Grabbing some raincoats, they pulled them on and headed out into the storm. Once they had, they immediately wished they were back inside. The cold rain was coming down so hard it stung when it hit them, making it hard to see where they were going. The wind was just as bad, pushing them around causing them to walk like drunkards. It took them a few minutes to reach Dr. Maxwell's cottage, and they were soaked through by that time.

Charles greeted them as they came up onto the front porch, and quickly ushered them inside where he took their soaked coats. He then took the coats to a room down the hall. They heard a few soft banging sounds, and then the humming of a dryer before he came back with some towels for them to dry off with.

Grateful, they took the towels and began drying off before he disappeared again. Eden, Savage, and Colton walked over to the fireplace and stood in front of the fire. Wade sat on the hearth rubbing his head with a towel when he caught a whiff of something delicious.

"Is that popcorn I smell?"

"Yeah, I think I smell it too," said Aiden.

"You're always thinking you're smelling food, Aiden."

Just then, Dr. Maxwell came into the room with a large bowl of popcorn and several, empty smaller bowls. He was followed by Charles, carrying a tray with mugs of steaming hot chocolate. The delicious smell of the hot chocolate and freshly popped corn made their mouths water.

Dr. Maxwell and Charles set the popcorn and the drinks on a sideboard in the Livingroom. Once things were arranged to his liking, Dr. Maxwell turned and spoke, saying, "Welcome Airmed, Brigid, Miach, Cermait, and Aengus to my humble little cottage! Let me introduce both of us, I am Dian Cecht and this is Lugh."

TWENTY-SEVEN

THE FIVE OF THEM STOOD THERE WITH their mouths open. Did they hear Dr. Maxwell correctly? That he and Charles were Dian Cecht and Lugh, members of 'The Shining Ones'?

Eden's knees buckled a bit as his words sunk in.

The *key* she had been wearing since the morning they were attacked by Ciara began pulsing as Dr. Maxwell made the announcement, but not in the same way it had when they had encountered her. Out of habit, Eden reached for it.

Colton noticed her reaction and grabbed her arm. He whispered, "Are you alright? The *key's* pulsating again, isn't it? Here, let's sit down." Before she even had a chance to answer him, they were sitting on the nearby sofa.

"I'm fine, Colton. It's not vibrating in warning."

"I don't know how, Dr. Maxwell, but it's like the *key* is confirming that what you just told us is correct. But how can that be true? All that stuff is ancient Irish folklore that may or may not have happened centuries ago."

"Yes, Eden. You are right about the *key* confirming what I said was correct. You are beginning to learn what the types of vibrations mean. Also, you need to be sure to follow any of the *key's* visual promptings as well because the *Memory Keeper* remembers all the Time Loops; what failed as well as what succeeded. It will tell you if what you are hearing or seeing is the right truth, relative to that time period. Remember, the *key* will never fail you.

The *key* is working to synchronize your senses. And because of that, you're now beginning to feel the differences in the pulsations it sends you. In essence, it is adapting to you. It has also shown you and Colton in-depth visions of some of the Time

Loops. The others either saw glimpses or heard snippets because they have held it too. But it is up to you to learn to read what the *key* is giving you. This is so you can guide the others, the members of your team.

As far as the Irish folklore part, I am Dr. Maxwell, as is Charles is Charles, but in Ciara's mind, we are Dian Cecht and Lugh. Just as you are to her Airmed, and Savage is Brigid. Your brother, Aiden, is Miach, Airmed's brother. Your brother, Colton, Savage, is Brigid's brother, Cermait, and your cousin, Wade, is your brother, Aengus. At least this is all how Ciara sees things from her viewpoint."

"Okay, I understand all that. Sort of. But what I can't understand is why me? Why was I chosen to be the leader of our group?"

"That's a simple enough question for me to answer, Eden. It's because the *key* chose you. It recognized you as having the right qualities to do the job."

"That's true, Eden, you were always organizing, directing events and getting people to work together back in Carlisle. Remember the clothing drive for the local homeless shelter you headed, and that awesome Bookfest you were able to pull together at the last minute?"

Eden glared at him, but Aiden only smiled. Then suddenly a thought came to him, and he asked Dr. Maxwell, "Whoa! Wait a minute! You're saying that Ciara thinks that we're all gods? That she actually believes I'm a mythological person called Miach?"

"In Ciara's mind, yes. You are all some of the gods of the Tuatha Dé Danann, or Tuatha Dé, The Shinning Ones."

"You know, I recall seeing some info on the Tuatha Dé Danann when I was searching on my tablet for Cermait. There were a lot of names. It mentioned they were also called the Tribe of Gods. If Eden hadn't said she'd heard Ciara calling Colton Cermait right before disappearing, we wouldn't know what the Tuatha Dé Danann was."

Dr. Maxwell was listening to Aiden's explanation on his search, and was surprised when Aiden exclaimed, "Man, we're only normal teenagers! We're not any mythological characters with superpowers. So, she must have a really good reason to call us by these god's names. Why would she do this, Dr. Maxwell?"

"Well, yes, it's all tied into the first time we wrongly showed up in Ireland."

Dr. Maxwell's remark caught Colton's attention and he asked, "What exactly is that supposed to mean? The first time?"

"Yeah! I think I might have missed something here too because I'm totally confused. How many times were we in Ireland?" asked Wade.

"You're not the only one that's confused," Savage said.

"Excuse me, Dr. Maxwell, you might want to start the explanation at the beginning. But, maybe after everyone has a chance to get some popcorn and hot chocolate first?"

"Oh, my, goodness! Where are my manners? Please, all of you help yourselves to the hot chocolate and popcorn while it's still warm. Get settled and I'll explain more."

When everyone hesitated, he urged them, "No, go ahead! Get some food and get seated. I'll wait for you all to settle before explaining more." Then he went and sat in the old brown leather chair nearest to the fire.

Looking around the cottage as everyone was getting their popcorn and hot chocolate, Eden liked the ambiance and the charm of the place. It was homey and gave off a warm, comfortable feeling. Even though the living area was much smaller compared to the main farmhouse, it still had the same architectural style. Dr. Maxwell's brother had made sure the cottage had the same amenities even though it was smaller.

Once everyone had their hot chocolate and popcorn, they found a place to sit. Wade took a seat on the sofa with Colton and Eden. Aiden and Savage made their way to the hearth next to the fire. Aiden placed a pillow on the stone for her to sit on. And Charles, after handing Dr. Maxwell a steaming mug of coffee, sat in the chair opposite him.

Eden's thoughts about the cottage were interrupted when Dr. Maxwell said, "Everyone set?" After they nodded, he rubbed his hands together, and said, "Great! Let's get to it then. By the way Charles, good idea suggesting that I start at the beginning. You know how I get distracted and can ramble on at times."

But before he began, he pondered to himself, "Although, when dealing with Time, the idea of a beginning is relative." Then he sat his coffee down.

"Now, let me start off with saying that the beginning of all the deviant Time Loops concerning Ciara began with you, Eden," he said kindly. When everyone heard this, they were taken aback and immediately began asking questions.

Even though he had surprised her with his claim, she knew he was right. The *key's* vibrations were identical as to what they had been when he told them he and Charles were Dian Cecht and Lugh. However, Eden had to ask, "Me? But how can that even be possible?"

"Well… it all began with the creation of your very first Time Loop. For now, let's just say after you obtained your mission objective, there was an event that took place and in turn that event created a serious situation. In response to it, Eden, you reacted from a place of fear and created a Time Loop to an incorrect period in time, which brought you all to Ciara.

While you all were in that time period, she was somehow able to obtain what she calls a Time Bender, which is actually a Spacetime Generator, STG for short. Believing you to be The Shinning Ones, she attempted to create a Time Loop to follow you after she saw you create one to leave. However, the Time Loop was unstable, causing it to repeat itself again, and again with different variations each time. This is now the twelfth time that it has been repeated.

I'm not blaming you for panicking when you were faced with danger from that event, Eden. But you are the leader, whether in the past or in the future, you cannot afford the luxury to panic. I can only stress from here on out to learn to trust the Memory Keeper, your training, and most of all, yourself."

"Training? What training, Dr. Maxwell? I've had driver's training, various kinds of sport's training, and if you want to count them, piano lessons. But I've never had any training with anything called an STG and a Time Loop."

"True, but you soon will. In fact, you all will. But you will be the only one in charge of the Memory Keeper, Eden. As I said before, learn to trust it. Learn to follow its prompting, and more importantly, learn to trust yourself or Time will be doomed to repeat itself yet again for a thirteenth time," answered Dr. Maxwell.

Here he paused and thought to himself, "And I might not be here to help guide you during the next Time Loop."

"Dr. Maxwell, if I heard you right, you just said we all need training with the STGs and Time Loops. Everyone here knows time travel doesn't exist nowadays. I'm not saying I don't believe you, but how can we have training with something that doesn't exist?"

"Time is relative, Colton. It all depends on the point at which you are observing it. An oversimplified way to explain it is to look at our country's time zones. What might be 8:00 P.M. for us on the East Coast, is 5:00 P.M. on the West Coast. If you travel West, you gain time, when you travel East you lose time. Time is relative to where you are in this case. Just because something doesn't exist now, doesn't mean it didn't exist in the past or exist in the future.

I wish I could explain it better to you but here I don't have the proper equipment or aids. Don't worry, though, when you meet the Sentinels they will help you understand Spacetime and Time Loops. They have equipment to show you how Time Loops work. And they will be able to give you the training you need to make any necessary changes in this Time Loop."

"Sentinels?" Eden and Aiden both asked.

"Well, to give you a brief explanation, they are a benign organization of principled individuals that was established many, many millennia ago. Their main responsibility is to prevent unnatural disruptions in the fabric of Spacetime throughout the universe. Each populated galaxy has its own designated team. For the most part, humanoids are the largest group represented in the Sentinels in the Milky Way, but there are many other lifeforms.

On occasion, they will train a select group of individuals to aid them, short term, in resetting an unstable Time Loop or they will recruit subjects who possess a certain temperament for, let's say, a permanent assignment. Many of these subjects are orphans. The Sentinels take them in, care for them, train them and become their family, but only with their permission. No one is forced."

"Okay, so we have this elite group of beings taxed with keeping the Timeline straight, and who take in an occasional orphan. That's great! But what I'm most interested in knowing is what was the reason we were there before Eden made the mistake that took us to Ciara's time period?"

Dr. Maxwell said, "Ah, yes, Colton! The purpose that you were all there. It's a twofold reason. First, it was because the five of you were chosen. Chosen by the Sentinels to rescue a scared, unloved, nine-year-old orphan and safely deliver him to them. And secondly, because the five of you have a unique skill set that is perfect for this situation."

Perplexed, Aiden asked, "Okay, Dr. Maxwell. I got the rescue of the orphan part, and I agree we all are awesome. Well, some of us more than others. But I don't get why you and Charles could possibly know about all this?"

"Right! Why would you and Charles know about all this?" echoed Eden.

Dr. Maxwell grinned at all of them, before saying, "That's because Charles and I are members of the Sentinels."

TWENTY-EIGHT

NEARBY A STREAK OF LIGHTENING FLASHED across the sky, quickly followed by the loud crack of thunder. However, apparently no one in the cottage was aware of what was happening outside, as their minds were focused on the news Dr. Maxwell had just delivered.

Abruptly, the silence was broken by Wade's laughter. Standing, he asked, "Wow! Guys, don't you get it? We all should be jumping around the room in excitement!"

"Get what?" scowled Savage. While she sat there looking at him as if he had lost his mind. She had no clue as to what he was referring to and neither did the others, except Dr. Maxwell and Charles.

Wade could see that they were drawing blank. So, he tried to explain, "Okay now, just think about it! If Dr. Maxwell and Charles aren't insane, and if they're not messing with us, and given the fact we are assuming we can trust them, then that implies they have to be telling us the truth."

Normally Wade was uncomfortable having the focus on him, but at this moment his excitement overcame his discomfort. "Listen! Here's the awesome part about all of this, the five of us are going to become *Time Travelers*!"

He remained standing, happily looking around at everyone over the prospect, only to be disappointed at not seeing the same excitement on any of their faces.

"I think you're insane!"

"Stop and think about it, Colten. Dr. Maxwell said we were selected by these Sentinels to find a nine-year-old orphan, who apparently is not in our local time period, and then deliver him safely back to them. So, how else are we going to be able to do this unless we do some Time Traveling?"

Charles hid his smile, as Dr. Maxwell said, "Excellent, Wade! Your assumptions are correct! You deduced everything quite nicely. You know, I really think you should give more consideration in pursuing that career in criminal justice that you're interested in. I believe you would make a topnotch detective or even an exceptional FBI agent."

"Ah... thanks, Dr. Maxwell," Wade said, puzzled how Dr. Maxwell knew that he wanted a degree in criminal justice.

While Wade was talking, Eden and Aiden were each considering everything they had been told along with Wade's assumptions and excitement over Time Traveling. Now that he had finished, Eden looked at Aiden and raised her eyebrows. Aiden, realized what she meant, nodded his head for her to go ahead with what she was planning.

Eden then said, "So, help me see if I'm understanding it correctly. You're saying that there is this group of *time watchers* called the Sentinels, who you both belong to that look for unnatural disruptions of Spacetime. And, that they want us to fix this disruption I caused, while at the same time retrieving and delivering to them an orphan from the past?" As she was speaking, she had reached for the *key* hanging around her neck. Holding it, she could feel it pulsating and released it only when she was reassured the vibrations were calm.

"Yes, that's correct, Eden," Dr. Maxwell took note of her reaching for the *key*. He did not bring it to anyone else's attention, but he was pleased to see she was learning this Time Loop to use the *key* and rely on it much more quickly.

"How about Charles and I make it easier to understand, and at the same time prove to you all that we are being honest with you and are indeed telling you the truth?" Considering his proposal, they agreed.

"Wonderful! Charles, a quick demonstration, please." Charles, got to his feet.

Dr. Maxwell explained, "Charles is now going to create a portal and move into the future by twenty seconds. He will then reappear in this room somewhere else of his own choosing other than in front of the chair he has been sitting in."

At that point, Charles took a metal device that looked like a bracelet from the pocket of the hoodie he was wearing. He then placed it onto his left wrist, sliding a section of it over the back of his hand. Once it was in place, the object seemed to react to the shape of his hand, forming itself to fit it.

As Charles took the device from his pocket and placed it on his hand, Colton recognized it. "Guys, that's the same type of device I saw Ciara put on her hand before she disappeared!"

Charles held out his hand pulling up the sleeve of his hoodie so they could get a better look. He said, "Yes, this is what Ciara calls a 'Time Bender'. It's basically a STG with added force field and translator options. It generates a warp field around an object, in most cases a person, allowing them to move forwards or backwards through time.

The force field is used for protection since you never know what you might be walking into when you come through a portal. There's also an automatic stealth mode setting that will keep you hidden until you want to be revealed. That option's extremely helpful once you're moving around in the time period and there's a chance you could end up in the middle of a battle or worse.

The translator is straight forward. It's especially helpful when you need to understand local dialects. It allows your brain to process their language so you can speak theirs. However, you'll still be hearing in your language as you speak and hear theirs. It's only used for short-term teams now, like yours.

Protocol was changed after a few colleagues damaged their STGs and became stuck in a time period unable to understand the language. The Sentinels had to come up with another option, which they did. Now they can easily enhance the brain so that function in the STGs is not necessary.

"Super! Brain enhancement," Aiden said.

Savage thought about the bands they were currently wearing and asked, "Those bands that you gave us when we left the dig, are they STGs?"

"No. Those I gave you, Colton and Wade are different. They only have the force field capability to mask your bioelectrical signals, and they don't use much energy."

Admiring the object on Charles hand, Aiden commented "Even though that mechanism you're wearing looks small, I bet that STG must pull a boat load of energy."

"Right, it does! It's made with some elements that have not been discovered yet in this time period and with others that have but have not had their full potential realized to date. When these elements are combined and processed under certain applications, they can produce a warp field."

Savage interrupted, "Oh, now I understand! Because of the STG's energy surge, the energy coming from the storm outside will mask it from Ciara. You and Dr. Maxwell have been trying to protect us from what she might do if she knew where we were. That's why you didn't want to tell us about all this before and couldn't show us until the storm happened tonight.

Without the energy the storm produces, it would be like putting a bull's eye on us. Since the storm's activity hides the energy signature the STG produces, I'm assuming it also draws energy from the storm too. Correct?"

Dr. Maxwell answered, "Yes! You're right, Savage. The storm's electrical activity does hide the energy surge created by it along with your bioelectrical signals. The apparatus was created to draw energy from its environment when needed.

Well, I guess now I have to believe in 'The Shinning One's' tales from Irish folklore. Apparently, Ciara was right to think that you are Brigid."

"Why would you think that Dr. Maxwell?"

"Brigid is Airmed's friend and one of the Tuatha Dé Danann who is associated with wisdom."

Colton snickered. Eden elbowed him for Savage since she was sitting across the room. "Are you ready Charles?"

"Yes, the STG has adjusted to my hand, Dr. Maxwell, and it has more than enough power to create a portal to and from."

"Good. Let's proceed then with our little demonstration."

Charles then pressed two controls on the back on his left hand, turned his hand over and with his middle and ring fingers pressed a control that had appeared in the center of his palm.

There was a barely audible buzz when the portal was created. As soon as it appeared, he walked into it and disappeared.

Although Eden, Savage, and Colton had seen Ciara vanish, they still gasped along with Aiden and Wade at Charles's disappearance.

This time though they thought they had seen a faintly swirling light appearing in front of Charles before he took a step and disappeared. Instantly, Eden thought the light looked familiar but could not recall why.

Once Charles was gone, Colton asked, "Was that a light Charles stepped into? I don't remember seeing a light when Ciara disappeared. Did either of you notice anything glowing? Eden? Savage?"

"No, I don't. But it was really sunny at the time."

"I wouldn't know, Colton. I wasn't in any shape to see anything but stars at that point. My butt is still recovering from it."

Right as she finished talking, Charles reappeared. When he disappeared, it was in front of the chair he was sitting in, when he reappeared it was near the front door of the cottage. It was not all that far, but what was astounding was that he was holding a bag of fresh, pink grapefruits still warm from the Florida sun.

"Here, Eden," Charles said, walking over and handing the bag to her, "I thought you could have these to share at breakfast tomorrow."

"You got to be kidding me!" Wade said after seeing the farmer's label on the bag. Taking them from Eden, he opened the bag and pulled one out. Amazed, he said, "They're still warm from the sun!"

TWENTY-NINE

"WOW! I THOUGHT SEEING SOMEONE DISAPPEARING was cool, but I have to say, the way you reappeared like that was a hundred times more impressive, Charles. The timing was spot on and then the grapefruits just put it over the top, man! Charles, when you returned, I was asking about that light you walked into. That was new. We hadn't seen that when Ciara disappeared" exclaimed Savage.

"Oh, that faint spinning light you saw is caused by the gravity wave created by the STG. If you didn't see anything when Ciara disappeared it probably was because it was during a sunny day. Wait 'til you see one at night. You might want to be wearing sunglasses."

As she was listening to them talking, Eden remembered where she had seen that type of light. She knew Savage would remember too. She wanted Savage's attention but did not want to interrupt. So, she sat there slyly motioning at Savage hoping she would notice.

Savage began feeling like someone was watching her. Looking around the room, she noticed Eden motioning to her, so she frowned back. Eden then made a small spiral motion with her index finger that Savage immediately understood, recalling their conversation about the spiral cave paintings.

Right then, Eden interrupted, saying, "Excuse me, but I have a question about that light and those paintings we saw in the cave with the strange spirals. Are those spirals representing actual gravity waves?"

"Yes, for the most part. That's how the Native Americans saw them."

Savage remembered two of the paintings, and asked, "Okay then. There's a painting in the cave showing us stepping out of one spiral and another showing us leading a child into one. So, these paintings really are about us using a STG to create a gravity wave? This actually happened?"

"Yes, Savage. This was right at the point when Eden accidently sent us all to Ireland," Dr. Maxwell replied.

Aiden still processing what he had seen with Charles's demonstration, asked, "Excuse me, Dr. Maxwell. Is there any chance that being near the gravity wave the STG creates would cause harm to a human?"

"Good question, Aiden, but no. There are no side effects because the force field device attached to the STG automatically shields anyone from direct contact. For the person or persons in the gravity wave, it's just like being in regular gravity. They are safe as long as they stay inside the force field when the gravity wave is functioning. And, if they are using a larger device and inside a container or a vessel, the force field will sense that and will automatically extend around it as well, thus protecting everyone.

You see, a gravity wave forms in front of the person or vessel first, as it forms it distorts spacetime. This allows anyone inside the protective force field to move through time. Whenever you change the flow of the gravity wave it allows one to move backwards and forwards in time, depending on what the need is at the moment."

"So, there's advantages to moving both ways?" asked Wade.

"Yes, but the most important thing about moving backwards and forwards in time is carefully picking the correct time coordinates."

Eden's cheeks grew red.

"Anyway, you'll soon all learn how to do all this when you meet the Sentinels. Along with any other training they will give you to complete your mission."

"And, how soon will that be, Dr. Maxwell? A week or two?" Wade asked.

"Well, I can't give you an exact hour or minute. That's a call that's made higher up the ladder from Charles and me, plus a lot of the timing depends on the five of you. But I can tell you a general estimation is between midnight tonight and midnight tomorrow," he replied.

Hearing what Dr. Maxwell said, the five of them began talking at once.

Colton's voice drowned out the others. "Wait! You're telling us we'll be leaving sometime in the next twenty-four hours? Well, that's impossible! It's not enough time to prepare, to get organized! We'll have to get supplies, pack, tell our parents, and work!"

Dr. Maxwell, seeing the concern on their faces and hearing it in their voices, thought to himself, "If they only knew." He did not need the memories contained in the Memory Keeper since he personally remembered all the time loops. He knew what they had faced previously, and what could possibly go wrong.

After managing to get them to calm down, he said, "Listen, you will be Time Traveling. It's not necessary to let your parents or work know you'll be gone, because you will be back before they even realize you aren't here. You can make your return time a second or even less after you leave.

This will all make more sense once you have had your training with the Sentinels. They will explain in depth how time should flow, and how loops get created since its relative to you when you travel, and they will teach you to understand how to operate all the devices you will need."

The five of them calmed down. They were apprehensive about the whole thing, and especially not saying anything to their parents. As if Dr. Maxwell had been reading their minds, he explained, "I understand your unease but consider this. The reason you shouldn't tell your parents or any people you care about for that matter, is because of Ciara. It's for their safety. If they get on her radar, she'd harm them to get to you.

Charles and I have put protection measures in place, here on the farm and at the dig site. Both areas are showing, at appropriate intervals, random decoy human bioelectrical signals we have set up. Since Ciara's familiar with all yours, she would see these other signals as unimportant people not worth her time, and she would move on.

Now as far as we are aware, Ciara has no idea about any other people but us, and that's a good thing. Charles and I would like to keep it that way. Remember she sees all of us as members of 'The Shinning Ones'. If she would see you interacting with someone else in a close familiar way, she would most likely assume they were also part of the Tuatha Dé and go after them hoping to get to you."

"Geeze! That's one paranoid woman!" Wade said.

"You have no idea!" said Colton.

"Okay, we get it! So, we agreed. No speaking to anyone about any of this. Right guys?" Aiden asked.

"Good! Now that we have that settled. Do any of you have any other questions for Charles and me?"

Savage said, "Dr. Maxwell, we're completely overwhelmed with everything you've told us tonight. I can't speak for the others, but at the moment my mind is numb, and can't think of any questions. Although I'm sure I'll have plenty of them for you later."

"Well, you've had a lot thrown at you all at once, and for that, I am sorry. Ciara's attack was unexpected, and we had to move faster than planned. We've been stuck in this Time Loop far too long. It needs to be resolved. So, think about everything and talk it over when you all get back to the farmhouse. See if there is something that you need answered or cleared up."

Outside a nearby flash of lightening, and the crack of thunder interrupted their thoughts. Then, the rain began to fall harder.

Dr. Maxwell paused a second, listening to the rain fall, then continued, "Charles and I will check with you all tomorrow about what we've discussed tonight and see how you are all feeling about everything. If I were you, after talking among yourselves, I would try getting some sleep."

Without saying anything more, Charles began collecting their mugs and bowls. Eden, wanting to help, went to the buffet. She picked up the large popcorn bowl and pitcher that had held the hot chocolate and followed Charles into the kitchen.

Looking for a place to set them down, Charles said, "Here, just set them on the counter next to the sink. I'll take care of things later."

Noticing she was pale and quiet, he asked, "Are you all right? Dr. Maxwell unloaded a lot on you and your friends tonight, but especially on you, Eden. I really wished we could have eased you all into this, but Ciara forced our hand by attacking you. So, we had to drastically move up our timeline for telling you."

"I'm okay, I guess. Thanks for asking. I think I'm feeling a little numb from trying to digest everything we were told. At first, I wasn't sure whether to trust you and Dr. Maxwell, even after you vanished. It wasn't until after you came back with the grapefruits, I was sure," Eden answered, reaching for the *key*.

"I hope you like them. I wanted to bring back something this time to prove that I had really gone somewhere and that it wasn't just a sham. During the last Loop, Wade was convinced it was some sort of magician's trick. But if you're still not convinced, check the date and farm's name on the label. Then, do a search on them. That should prove it," smiled Charles.

Eden smiled back. She was even more sure now he was telling her the truth. Plus, the pulsing of the *Key* never changed.

"How long have you known Dr. Maxwell, Charles? From the way you two interact with one another, it seems like you've known each other for a while."

"Well, yes, we have known each other for many years. Both of us began our training in the Sentinels at the same time. I'm from Earth too, actually Morocco. When any of the time disturbances originate from Earth, we're assigned to the same team. With everything we have been through, he has become a good friend. I trust him with my life. You can trust him too, Eden."

Eden smiled, letting go of the *key*.

"Why don't you head back into the living room, while I get your raincoats," Charles suggested.

"Thanks, Charles, for everything,"

When Eden walked back into the living room with the others, Dr Maxwell said, "Well now, I think we're done talking tonight. Charles is getting your raincoats. And unfortunately, since I can still hear rain hitting on the roof, I think you are still going to need them."

They all stood when Charles came around the corner holding their dried raincoats. Taking them from him, they put them on, then went to the door.

Right before leaving, they thanked Dr. Maxwell and Charles for their hospitality and the food. Then gave their goodbyes before running out the door and into the rain.

Standing by the open door, Dr. Maxwell and Charles watched as they ran back to the farmhouse. Once they saw them make it inside, Dr. Maxwell told Charles, "Leave the dishes for later. We need to get some sleep. Everything has to be ready for them by daybreak."

THIRTY

THE SUN HAD NOT YET RISEN WHEN EDEN woke up. She could hear the birds singing in anticipation and knew that they were heralding the coming sunrise, but she was not ready for it. At least she was no longer hearing last night's thunderstorm.

Rolling over onto her back and extending her arms above her head, she lay there for a few minutes hoping to fall back to sleep. As hard as she tried keeping her eyes shut, they kept fluttering open.

Giving up, she raised to her elbow and looked over at the clock sitting on her desk. It read 4:54 AM. She collapsed back onto the sofa bed and groaned. For a moment, she regretted giving up her comfortable mattress to Savage, but just as quickly, she concluded that it would not have helped her sleep any better under the circumstances.

Swinging her legs out from under the covers, Eden sat on the edge of the sofa bed trying to figure out what she should do first, take a shower or make breakfast. Her stomach growled, so breakfast won out.

Sneaking into the bathroom, she slowly shut the door so not to wake Savage. Going to her walk-in closet, she quietly slipped out of her PJ's. Reaching inside of one of the storage cubbies, she pulled out some shorts and a t-shirt, then soundlessly went about her regular morning routine. Once she had finished, she pulled her hair into her normal messy bun and grabbed her shoes.

After leaving Savage some clean towels, Eden was silently stepping through the bathroom door when she and Savage, who was on the last step of the loft ladder, almost collided. After the girls had startled one another, they began giggling.

When they had calmed down, Eden told Savage, "I couldn't sleep, so I was going to start breakfast, then run back up here while it's baking to get a quick shower."

"I couldn't sleep either. We'll probably both be dead tired by lunch. Give me a minute to get dressed and I'll come help you," Savage yawned.

Eden smiled, saying, "Why don't you just hop into the shower instead. It might help wake you up. I can handle getting breakfast. I'll just scramble up some eggs and mix them with some tater tots, cheese, and bacon, and put it in the oven. We also have Charles's grapefruits and the yummy cinnamon rolls Mom and Dad bought yesterday at that awesome bakery in Beaver. After I put on the coffee, I'll come back and grab a quick shower.

I know Mom and Dad will be up as soon as they smell the coffee brewing. The guys might get up once they smell the bacon cooking. I know that always works for Aiden."

Savage smiled, leaned back against the loft's ladder, and said, "Yeah, my parents are like that when it comes to coffee too. But Colton and Wade are like Aiden, food driven.

By the way, it was really nice of your parents allowing us to stay over last night and for calling ours to set it up. Colton's a good driver, but I was scared about us driving home during that storm. I heard it coming down hard most of the night, but I haven't heard anything since 3:00 o'clock this morning."

"Yeah, it was bad. Dad mentioned to me that when he talked to your dad, he was expecting to be out on calls all evening because of flood damage and lightning hitting trees. He was all for you all staying here. He also told Dad that there were some slides on some of the back roads and some minor washouts around the creeks, so it was best you didn't try to go home.

Besides, it turned out to be a good opportunity for us to discuss what Dr. Maxwell and Charles told us after Mom and Dad went to bed."

"True but staying up too late talking is why we're so tired this morning. There're still so many unknowns without answers. Although, I must admit, when Aiden was talking about the technical aspects of everything, I could've listened to him all night long."

"Yup! Usually, his rambling on about tech specs is enough cause for anyone to fall asleep. Anyone, but you, Savage!"

"No, that's not what I meant! You see, I know guys. I can usually tell within a few minutes if someone is genuine or not. Your brother is. His voice calms me. And especially since what's been thrown at us, I needed some calming.

Besides, I love his red hair and that cute scattering of freckles across his nose. I hope you don't mind that I'm kind of into him."

"I don't mind it at all! You, I like. We get along, unlike other girls in the past who pretended to like me just to get to Aiden.

Still, he's so inexperienced when it comes to girls. His last girlfriend was in the eighth grade. Although he's never had a shortage of them interested in him, he's been oblivious until now. Even Jenny, from eighth grade, ended up just being a friend.

And even though we're twins, and I think he's a goof, he's still my brother, and I want him to be happy. Since he's met you, he's been smiling a lot."

Savage blushed. Then she said, "Well, there is something that I've noticed that I've been wanting to talk to you about. But I'm not quite sure how you're going to feel about it."

"What?"

Savage let out a breath, and asked, "Haven't you noticed that my brother can't keep his eyes off of you?"

"No! I haven't!"

"Oh, he can be stealthy! When you're not looking, he's been watching you. He won't admit it or may not know it, but knowing him like I do, I'd say he has a huge crush on you."

Immediately, Eden's thoughts went back to Colton's kiss a few days ago, remembering how soft his lips had felt on hers, and the warm spot it had created deep in her stomach. Now, it was Eden's turn to blush.

Savage confided, "Don't tell him I said this, but since he's gotten out of high school, he's matured. He's always been smart, but he's gained some common sense.

I noticed how fascinated he was at the dig site and the operation there. I think he could easily get into archeology. I've also noticed how he falls all over himself when he's around you. I'd have to say he's finally found two things that have really caught his interest. And I think that you find him interesting too."

"Yeah, well you could say that." Eden rolled her eyes and went to get Savage some clean clothes from her closet.

"That's good cause we do get along! So, while you get breakfast started, I'll hop in the shower. Give me fifteen to twenty minutes," Savage said, taking the clothes from Eden.

Eden walked out the door saying, "Okay! That will be about what I need to get breakfast in the oven."

On her way to the kitchen, Eden passed by Aiden's room to check on the guys. She stood outside his door listening for movement but heard no sounds coming from inside. Satisfied that they were not stirring, she went downstairs to the kitchen.

Once there, she went to work on the breakfast casserole. In no time it was in the oven baking. Everything else was set up ready to go because of the prep work they did last night. It didn't take her but a few seconds to put coffee in the coffee maker. While she was setting the timer for it, she noticed the sky was getting brighter.

Running back upstairs, Eden took the steps two at a time. Slowing down, she took the time to walk by Aiden's room to listen again, but still did not hear any noises coming from the room, so she headed back to hers.

Opening her bedroom door, she was surprised to find Savage already showered, dressed, and brushing out her hair. "Wow, you were fast! I thought you'd just be getting out."

"You don't have a Sheriff for a father!"

"Right! I take it that he doesn't tolerate slackers. I won't take too long."

Eden quickly got into the shower and in less than ten minutes was done. She skipped washing her thick hair, so that saved time. When she had finished dressing, she walked out into the lounge area to find that Savage had put away the sofa bed and pulled the linens off it and off Eden's bed in the loft.

"Where should I put these sheets?"

"Here, let me have them." Eden took the sheets and put them in the walk-in closet hamper.

As Eden exited the bathroom, a reflection dancing off the far wall of her room caught her eye. Stopping, she whispered to Savage, "Do you see that light?"

"Yeah, I see it." Savage, unsure why Eden was whispering.

"Ha! I'm not going crazy, Aiden! So there!" Quickly, Eden asked, "How long have you noticed it?"

"When you took the sheets from me, not long."

"Great! I know this is going to sound strange, but I've been seeing this light off and on since we moved here. It sort of follows me. Aiden thinks I'm crazy." You're positive you're seeing it?"

"Yeah."

"Great! Let's go and get the guys. They have to see this, especially that doubter, Aiden." As she said this, she reached for the *key* hanging from her neck. Savage noticed right away.

"I don't know why, but this is important. They need to see it."

"Okay, then let's get them."

Eden rushed out of her bedroom with Savage following close behind. Upon reaching Aiden's bedroom door, instead of knocking, Eden grabbed the handle and burst into the room. Savage standing next to Eden inside the door, surveyed the room.

Aiden, who was sound asleep in the recliner was startled. Immediately he sat up upon hearing the door flying open. Grabbing at the blanket that had fallen to his waist while sleeping, he shouted, "Hey! Hey! Hey! Half-naked guys in here!"

Ignoring him, Eden said, "Come on! You all have to see this now! Hurry up!" Hitting the loft's ladder, Eden shouted, "You too, Wade!" Colton, who was out cold on the sofa bed woke up. Eden and Savage could hear Wade, in the loft, moving around.

"Good grief, Sis! Let us put some clothes on first."

"No, there's no time! It will disappear! Just wrap a blanket around you and move it!

Besides, there's nothing here that I haven't seen before."

"Me either," added Savage, as she winked at Aiden. Aiden, turned red.

By this time, Wade had managed to come down the loft's ladder wearing an old pair of Aiden's sweats and a t-shirt, and Colton had managed to sit up.

"What's up?" Wade yawned.

Standing by the door, Eden grabbed the key again, and pleaded, "Please, hurry guys! This is really important!" Noticing Eden was holding the *key*, Colton perked up and wiped the sleep from his eyes.

"Okay, Eden. Where to?" he asked, throwing back the blanket and standing. He too, like Wade, was wearing a pair of sweats Aiden had given him minus the t-shirt.

"To my room, hurry! You all have to see this, now!"

Eden flew back to her room the minute she knew they were coming. She worried that the light would not be there, until she saw it still flickering on the wall.

After Colton and Wade walked into the room behind her, she pointed to the wall. They were confused at first until they noticed the flickering light. Savage and Aiden followed and when Aiden saw the dancing light, he smacked his head with his palm, and moaned, "Not again!"

"What, Aiden?" asked Savage.

"She thinks it's zombies."

"What?" exclaimed Wade.

"No, I don't, Aiden Pritchard Walker!"

"Then what?" asked Aiden.

"It's this!" exclaimed Eden, taking the *key* from her neck, and handing it to Colton.

Colton took the *key* from Eden, held it in his hand for a second or two. Suddenly he looked shocked. "It's vibrating!"

THIRTY-ONE

"WHAT'D YOU MEAN IT'S VIBRATING? Doesn't it do that all the time?" asked Wade.

"No! Only when there is need for it to. Like when there's danger or when I need confirmation about something."

"Here! Let me feel," Aiden demanded, taking the *key* from Colton. "No way! You're right, it's pulsating!" Aiden handed the *key* back to Eden.

Savage asked, "What does the *key* vibrating have to do with that dancing light on the wall?"

"I don't know. I only know it's important because the *key* started acting up when the light appeared. It's never pulsated the other times I've seen the light."

Wade scratched his head, then walked over to the wall to get a closer look at the beam. After checking it out, he went to the window. The sun had finally risen so he could see outside clearly. As he peered out, he thought he saw something strange, and asked, "Hey, do you guys know if there is anything metallic over in that group of trees in the middle of that wheat field? Cause it looks like the sun is reflecting off something metal or glass maybe."

Instantly Eden ran to the window and stood next to Wade, followed by the others. She pulled up the sash, bent down and looked out, excitedly asking, "Where? Where did you see it Wade?"

"I saw it near that larger oak tree in the middle, just to the left of it, where that maple forks. Right there. See it, Eden?" he asked, pointing.

Before Eden even had a chance to answer him, it moved slightly, hitting Wade in the eyes. The sudden shift in movement caught him off guard. "How rude! Great! Now I'm seeing spots."

As Wade staggered away from the window rubbing his eyes, both Aiden and Colton rushed to take Wade's place to see. In their haste, Aiden unintentionally bumped Eden out of the way. Eden was so upset she stood behind them with her hands placed on her hips.

Not noticing what had happened to Eden, Colton pointed out the window, and shouted, "There! I see it! Right where Wade said!"

"Yeah! Yeah! I see it too!"

Suddenly, Aiden felt a hard slap across the back of his head. "Ow!" he hollered reaching back to rub it. Quickly turning around, he saw Eden standing there scowling at him.

"You knocked me out of the way, but what was worse was that you didn't believe me before when I told you about the lights, and instead, teased me about it being zombies. Now since Wade and Colton have seen the lights, it's all okay!

So, here's what we're going to do. You three are immediately going to go back to Aiden's room, get dressed and we're all going to head out to those trees and put this mystery to rest once and for all!"

Aiden felt sorry about how he had acted. Taking a step towards Eden, he tried to apologize but Eden was not having any of it. First pointing her finger at him, then Colton and Wade, she then pointed at the door, ordering them, "Now move it! We want to get there before it disappears."

The three of them hustled out of Eden's room quickly followed by her and Savage. When they had reached Aiden's room, Eden threatened, "Two minutes. I'm giving you all two minutes to get dressed or Savage and I are coming in after you and dragging you out dressed or not."

As Aiden shut the door behind him, he nervously glanced at Savage. She winked at him again, causing him to immediately turn a brilliant red. Smiling, Savage told Eden, "I just love that it's so easy to make him blush."

Eden smiled. She liked how Savage could unsettle her brother with just a look.

After a bit, Eden looked at her watch and noticed that the guys had half a minute left. Not wanting to wake her parents by pounding on Aiden's door, she moved closer to it and said, "Thirty seconds and counting!" Suddenly, the door opened surprising her.

Colton came out first, barely missing walking into her. He was dressed in the cargo pants he had on yesterday and one of Aiden's white t-shirts that was a little snug on him through the chest, instead of the one he'd spilled salsa on the night before. Wade was following right behind him wearing his wrinkled clothes from the night before, while Aiden remained in his room desperately trying to put on his tennis shoes. When he saw his sister frowning, he slid his feet into the shoes, exited the room staying out of her reach. Under his breath he mumbled, "I really hope I'm wrong about those zombies!"

Quietly they went down the steps and into the kitchen. As they were on their way out the French doors, Eden remembered the casserole in the oven and hurried over to turn it off. As she was doing that, Aiden spied the cinnamon rolls on a plate. As he walked by, he reached out to take one until he saw Eden at the oven giving him a hard look. Quickly he pulled his hand back and hurried to catch up with Colton and Wade.

From there they went out the French doors, around the pool to the far side of the garage, then into the driveway between the garage and the barn. The very same way Dr. Maxwell had arrived and departed the first morning Eden had met him.

Once they had reached the driveway, they followed it until it turned into one of the many tractor paths that followed along the edges of the fields. This track was leading away from the farmhouse towards the grove of trees, so they continued following it. In spite of the path being at a lower angle than Eden's bedroom window, and the four-foot-high winter wheat, they were still able to see the reflection through the trees over the wheat.

Colton and Wade were walking in front of their group, talking between themselves. Eden was right behind them. However, she was not listening to any of their conversation since she had something else she had seen on her mind.

Because she had kept her eyes on the reflection in the trees as she walked along the path, she had spotted something odd. It appeared to her that the reflection was moving. Instead of being in the lower branches of the trees, now it appeared that it had moved to the dense brush under them. She could see it clearly before, but now she could hardly see it above the wheat. Quickly she looked back at her bedroom window at the farmhouse, to gauge if what she was seeing was real.

Colton glancing back at Eden, saw she was confused. Concerned, he asked, "Something wrong, Eden?"

"Maybe, maybe not. I'm not sure yet."

Wade became aware of Colton's concern and asked, "What's up?"

Colton nodded to Wade to wait, then told Eden, "I've seen you looking back at the farmhouse and then at the trees several times. Is it about the reflection?"

"Yeah. I think it might be moving."

"Wade and I both noticed, too. We think it's being manually manipulated. Is that *key* of yours warning you of anything?"

Eden reached for it and felt no change in the pulsing from earlier. Besides that, there was no weight change in it like when they had encountered Ciara. "I don't feel any change, so there's no danger." Eden had come to realize that no weight change in the *key* or frantic pulsating meant the light was not a threat, but given the circumstances, that was perplexing.

"If you're friendly, why are you baiting us by moving around in this group of trees?" she thought. Despite how the *key* was acting, she decided to keep her guard up just in case she was reading it wrong, even though she knew she was not.

Colton and Wade did not say anything to Eden, but they too were on alert expecting an attack at any moment. Even though Dr. Maxwell had told them there would be no way for Ciara to find their bio-electrical signals because of the shield, it did not keep them from being on edge.

It was not long before they realized they had reached a place where the tractor path edging the field was starting to turn away from the trees. Here they all stopped, because they needed to figure out a way to get to the trees without damaging the wheat.

As they were talking about what to do next, Savage began to notice that every so many feet there was a small gap in the wheat that traveled towards the trees. Excited, she said, "Do you guys notice those gaps in the wheat?"

"Yeah, they're called tramlines. They're used for watering and stuff. They're part of a Penn State agricultural experiment that some of the farmers around here are involved in," Wade informed them.

"That's great!" Savage said.

"Don't you see? It's exactly what we need! They're running parallel from this path, directly towards those trees. It looks to me like they're maybe a foot and a half to two feet wide, so we shouldn't damage any of the wheat following one, but the dew will get us a little wet. All we have to do is find the one that's the closest and follow it."

"Yeah, that sounds like it'll work! Plus, we won't be damaging any crops. Dad would ground us for the rest of the summer if we did."

"Ha! So would our Dad, Aiden, along with throwing in some hard labor," Savage said.

They split up and began walking back and forth along the tractor path, searching for the closest tramline to the trees. After going around fifty feet or so back towards the farmhouse, Aiden and Savage thought they had found one that would work and alerted the others.

After agreeing on following it, they began working their way down the line. They also decided to go sideways so to keep from getting the least amount of dew on them, even though proceeding this way would slow them down. They figured they had around two hundred and fifty feet to get to the trees. And because they did not know what they might find along the way, they decided in what order everyone would proceed down the tramline. Colton went first, followed by Eden, Aiden, Savage, and Wade.

As they moved down the line, they were on high alert since they had no idea what they might be facing. Because Colton was in the lead, he kept his eyes on the reflection, and constantly checked with Eden on the *key's* status. Everyone else followed his cue.

As they neared the end of the tramline, they were amazed at how large the grove of trees was, and how dense the underbrush was around it. It was so thick they could not see into the grove, but from what they could tell, the area looked to be at least two acres. It was also circled by another tractor path.

Keeping the moving reflection in sight, they walked around the tract looking for a way into the dense undergrowth. As they followed the light around the trees, it appeared almost as if it was guiding them. By now, everyone was aware the light was moving. However, no one gave an explanation as to why it was leading them.

When they finally reached the back side of the grove, Wade spotted a small path though the brush, and said, "Hey guys, here's a game path we can use, but be careful cause there's some berry bushes and crabapple trees in here. And don't forget about the poison ivy!"

Carefully picking their way through the dense, jagger-ridden underbrush, they were relieved when they had gotten through. As the brush became much sparser, it revealed a shallow spring fed pool lined with various sized rocks.

Also, they could not help but notice how deathly quiet it was. There were no animal, bird or insect sounds to be heard. All they could hear was the water bubbling down a pile of rocks at the far end of the pool. The eerie stillness felt like they were intruding. The whole atmosphere of the place gave them the feeling like time had stopped.

"Wow! This is beautiful!" Eden whispered.

"Yes, yes it is," Savage murmured.

"I wonder why Dr. Maxwell or Charles never mentioned this?"

"Good question, Aiden," Colton said.

Just then, Wade pointed to the light that was now flickering on the large rocks where the water was flowing into the far end of the pool.

Eden gasped, but as soon as she had, the light disappeared. "Where did it go?" asked Savage.

Then, just as suddenly as it had disappeared, the light reappeared but at a different angle than before.

"We're being toyed with, Colton," Aiden said.

"Agreed!"

"I can't tell where that light is coming from."

"Yeah, neither can I, Eden. But I definitely know it's from more than one source, and I'm sure it's directed at the pile of rocks at the end of the pond. What I can't tell is if it's innocently playing with us or if it's dangerous," Wade said.

"I think you're right, Wade," agreed Colton.

"Is the *key* still acting the same, Eden?" inquired Colton.

"Yeah, no change at all."

Then Eden said, "If I can make a suggestion, since there's no difference in the *key's* vibrations or weight, we should go examine those rocks that those lights keep shining on."

"That's a good idea, but when we do, we move slowly, stay together, and keep an eye out for anything suspicious," warned Colton.

Carefully they began making their way to the other side of the pool where the water was bubbling down over a pile of rocks pointed out by the flickering light. As they moved towards it, everyone was keeping an eye out for anything out of the ordinary, including stopping to check out several large rock piles and a fallen tree trunk for anything suspicious.

They had almost gotten to the other side of the pool when a twig snapped startling them. "What was that?" exclaimed Savage. Aiden pulled her close to him.

When they heard the noise, they instantly began looking around to see if they could locate it. As they were searching for the source of the broken branch, a rabbit suddenly darted from some underbrush a few yards away, surprising them.

"I guess there goes our answer to the snapped twig," Savage said nervously, as they watched the rabbit run off into more underbrush beyond them. But something was not sitting right with Colton. He felt the noise was off, not something a rabbit that size would make. As they continued, he remained on guard.

Once they had finally reached the pile of the rocks, the lights guiding them disappeared. But since the lights had been focusing on the rocks before disappearing, they all agreed it was something they needed to check out. So, they moved in for a closer look.

Observing how the water was bubbling up from under the rocks, Aiden said, "Hey! This looks like it's a small artesian spring. I bet this pool is part of an aquifer. That's pretty darn cool!"

Eden could hear Aiden but was not paying attention to what he was saying. She was focused on the fountain. She reached for the *key* for conformation to see if they were moving in the right direction. But again, there was no change in its weight or vibration. Oddly, in that moment, Eden realized she was thinking of the *key* like a guard dog and the vibration as its bark.

As she examined the rocks rimming the bubbling water, they gave the appearance of being normal, but she thought they may have been purposely arranged to look as if they were natural. As she was studying them, she also observed something odd about a large, black slab facing the pool, and rubbed her hand across its surface. It was engraved!

But there was a problem with its placement. It was positioned in such a way that it faced out into the pool, and at an angle to keep them from seeing any of the engravings from where they stood. It looked as if one would have to look at it straight on. So, when Eden slipped off her sneakers and got into the pool, the rest of them wondered if she had lost her mind.

"Eden, wait!" called Colton as her feet hit the water. He did not think it was a good idea. Anything could happen.

"Oh, my!" she squealed, once her feet were in, "The water's so cold!" Encouraged by Eden, the rest of them took off their shoes and climbed into the pool, complaining too when their feet hit the cold water.

As the others got in the water, Eden bent over to take a closer look at the rock. "Look! This hole in the rock looks like a keyhole, and it looks like there's some words encircling it too," she said, rubbing her finger across them.

"Great! Can you make out what they say?" asked Aiden.

Eden, using a trick she had learned from her parents, rubbed the rock with some of the water causing the words to darken. Being able to see them clearer, she told him, "Hmm… yeah, I think so. The first line says, 'Time is always flowing'. The line under the first says, 'The Past, The Present, and The Future'. Those two lines are set over the top of the keyhole in two arches. Underneath the keyhole is another line that says, 'Which will you choose?'"

"Sounds like a riddle to me."

"No kidding, Colton!" Savage said.

"That kind'a makes sense though. Time isn't linear. It's flows like a river," Aiden said.

Eden, still upset with Aiden, was looking at the keyhole again when an idea popped into her head. She took the *key* out from under her shirt and was comparing the hole in the stone with the shape of the *key's* post, when it dawned on her that they matched exactly.

"Hey guys, you're not going to believe it, but take a look at this!"

They gathered around Eden so they could see what she was trying to show them. Pointing to the *key* and the hole, she explained how the shape of the hole in the stone and the *key's* post matched. After checking out both, they agreed with her.

"This is strange. Who would have thought that they would match? Besides, with that *key* supposedly being precolonial, that means the carving and *key* were most likely made at the same time," Wade suggested.

"There has to be a reason each of them match the other," Eden said.

"So, if you're thinking what I think you are, you want to try placing the *key* in the keyhole in that rock. Cause if you are, I'm curious as to which way you would turn it, Eden. If you think about what Dr. Maxwell said about these Sentinels being from the future, the only logical choice is the future. Since they need us to find an orphan from the past, and he mentioned that we needed training first. Who else would be able to train us but the Sentinels?" Wade asked.

"That makes sense," Eden said. "So, do you all think I should try it?"

"I'm all for it," said Savage.

"Yeah, me too. What would it hurt?" agreed Aiden, believing it was only decorative and that nothing would happen when Eden turned the *key*.

"Yeah, same here. To me it looks as if all the clues are leading to it," answered Wade.

"I'm not too sure about this, but if you all think we should, and if there's been no change in the *key's* vibrations, I won't stop you, Eden," Colton said.

Once everyone had weighed in with their opinion, Eden said, "Okay. Let's give it a try."

Taking the *key* from her neck, she wrapped the chain around her hand to keep the *key* secure, and inserted it into the keyhole, saying, "Here goes guys. Future, it is," and turned it to the right.

Nothing happened.

"Yes! Just as I thought!" Aiden said, relieved.

"Well, that was a letdown," Savage said.

"But the clues, the clues were all there! I don't understand what went wrong," Wade mumbled.

Eden sighed, then said, "That's great!" as she tried to remove the *key*.

"No, wait!" Colton shouted, as Eden turned the *key* back to the left under, The Present, to pull it out.

By the time she heard him shouting to wait, it was too late. The second she had turned the *key* back, something clicked. Next the water in the pool began to quiver, growing in intensity. As soon as they saw how it was acting, they tried to get out of the pool, but their feet were immobilized. When they realized they were stuck to the bottom of the pool, they began seeing one another fading. They barely had a chance to scream before they completely disappeared, leaving the water in the pond splashing back and forth, and their shoes sitting alongside the pool.

The moment they had vanished, and before the water in the pool had settled, there was a slight movement in the underbrush where the rabbit had darted out.

A disembodied voice coming from that location, asked, "Dr. Maxwell? Are you all right?"

Charles, removing the face shield and hood of the invisibility suit he was wearing, opened his jacket, and placed a laser pointer into its pocket, then he walked around the pond to the fountain.

As Charles neared the shoes, Dr. Maxwell removed his face shield and hood, and told Charles, "Yes, yes, I'm fine, thanks. Sorry about stepping on that twig. I almost blew it. Colton was warried enough without that happening. By the way, spooking that rabbit was genius!"

Charles laughed, "It was more serendipitous than genius. I looked down and there it was.

Poor thing didn't know I was there until I touched it."

"Either way, it worked! Although, for a minute or two I did think we were going to have the same problems with Colton and

Eden again as the last five Time Loops, but it appears she is following the Memory Keeper's lead this time."

"Well, since this Time Loop has officially begun, we can only hope she continues to."

Dr. Maxwell smiled and held onto Charles's arm, slipping off his invisibility pants, and handing them to him. Charles removed his as well, folded both suits, and placed them into the backpack he had been wearing while under his invisibility jacket.

"We better get back and finish up those loose ends before we leave. I don't want them being upset over disappearing the way they did."

"Don't worry, Dr. Maxwell, I'm way ahead of you. I had everything ready to go before we arrived here this morning to set up. All we just have to do when we get back to the cottage is to wash off this mud and transport."

Dr. Maxwell patted Charles's shoulder fondly as they walked side by side out of the grove of trees. They remained silent as they walked back the tramline through the wheat until they reached the tractor path.

Once there, Dr. Maxwell turned to Charles, and said, "I think that was rather fun this Loop. Now, back to work!"

THIRTY-TWO

CIARA WAS BEYOND DESPERATE. Since Wednesday, she had tried everything she could possibly think of, and still had not been able to locate Airmed's or any of The Shining One's bioelectrical signals. She even returned to Little Beaver Creek, kayaking from where she had initially watched The Shining One's putting into the creek, to where it emptied into the Ohio River, and still came up empty.

Little did she realize that while she was kayaking Little Beaver Creek, she had actually paddled right by the dig where Dr. Maxwell, Charles, the Walkers, and the dig team were working. The stealth cloak that had been put in place as a security measure was automatically triggered by Ciara's bioelectrical signal whenever she was near so, as she paddled by them, only the original woods would be seen and not any of the people or workings of the site.

After all her many attempts at finding them, she had come to the conclusion that they had to be in another time period. But which one? Her instruments were strangely silent, so she had nothing to go on to guide her.

There was one thing though that Ciara was certain of, that this was the doing of Dian Cecht and his grandson, Lugh. Those two had always managed to foil her plans in the past with or without help from the others. Except for that one time, her one victory, when she was able to lose Dian Cecht in the past. That was until Lugh found him, old and weak, many years later.

Even though she now knew that they were human like her, and not the immortal gods called The Shining Ones that she once thought they were, they did have knowledge that she lacked. But all that would end once she had Airmed and her *key*.

Ciara was desperate to get possession of the *Key to Immortality* and all the secrets it held. It was the cornerstone to her plan. She could not return to her time period and begin her conquest of Ireland unless she possessed it.

But how, how could she get her hands on it with Airmed protecting it, and while the others protected her? Somehow she needed to find a way to draw Airmed and them out of hiding and into her grasp. Ciara knew she needed to level the playing field one way or another, but how and by what means?

Suddenly, it dawned on her! Why in the world had she not thought of it before? She already had the bait she needed right in front of her, the beautiful, young woman that she saw Aengus kissing when The Shining One's had first arrived at the creek, the one who had driven off with their truck. Now, what was the name Aengus had called her? Mia, Mia Cooper!

Finally, she had her plan. Kidnapping Mia would be her snare, and their downfall!

THIRTY-THREE

A Step Outside Time

SOMEONE WAS MOANING, BUT IT SOUNDED as if it was coming from far away.

"Who is that?" Eden wondered, but when she tried to look and see who it was, everything was black. Besides the moaning, she thought she could hear a voice, but she was groggy, had a headache, and only wanted to go back to sleep.

"Unitsi Eden, open your eyes," the voice pleaded, as someone gently patted her cheek. Eden tried pushing that annoying hand away, but she could not find it in the dark. As she began to regain consciousness, her eyes fluttered open letting in the light. It was only then she realized the moaning was coming from her.

Squinting her eyes against the brightness, Eden rose up on both her elbows, and looked around the open room, only to find Dr. Maxwell sitting on what looked like a stool next to the elevated, cushioned cot she was lying on.

"There you are!" he said. "Transporting the first time always gives one a migraine. Here, drink this," he told her, as he handed her a small, exquisitely made China bowl, filled with a warm, brownish looking liquid.

Eden, supporting herself on her right elbow, took the bowl from him, and sniffed it, before wrinkling her nose, and asking, "What is it?"

"Well, it's a type of tea that will help with that headache and a few of the other side effects one might get on their maiden time-travel voyage. I know you like tea, and I think you will rather enjoy this particular blend."

Eden took a sip, then smiled as the warm liquid slid down her throat. Dr. Maxwell was right. She did like it. It had a distinctive floral body, ending on a fruity note.

When she went to speak, Dr. Maxwell said, "No, finish it first." After she had drank the last of it, he took the bowl from her and set it on a small utility stand next to the cot she was lying on. "Good. Don't you think?" he asked. Eden nodded.

"This being yours and your team's first occasion to time travel, guarantees you all will get a headache like one on Earth caused by travel fatigue due to time zone changes. One can also get other side effects like a rash, sore throat, or dry mouth, for instance, but they all vary from one person to another."

Eden yawned, and said, "Excuse me." Then while she looked around the sparsely decorated room and it's arched ceiling, she asked, "Where is everyone?"

"They're all here in this room with you."

Reaching for the left sleeve of the strange uniform he was wearing he touched an emblem that was one of twelve. The emblem lit up, revealing the others behind what had been solid privacy walls all in the same room as she. She noticed they were all lying on the same type of cot, being tended to by people she did not recognize, except for Savage who was being taken care of by Charles.

Noticing Eden was awake, Charles smiled and nodded at her.

After being terrified over what had happened to them as they were standing in the pool, she was relieved to now see that they were all fine and had someone looking after them.

Although, she thought as she frowned, she had to admit that she had a sharp tinge of jealousy when she noticed the attendant caring for Colton was an extremely attractive young Hispanic woman around their age.

Dr. Maxwell watched as emotions played across Eden's face. Seeing that she had become aware of the young woman tending to Colton, he patted her hand, and said, "I wouldn't worry, Unitsi Eden. Essie is a shapeshifter. She only took on human form so you all would feel comfortable around her. Besides, Colton's interests are elsewhere."

Eden blushed, and thought, "Great! It must be written all over my face for Dr. Maxwell to say something like that." Then, a thought popped into her head, "Wait! If she's a shapeshifter, why'd she choose to make herself look so beautiful just for us?" But instead of asking Dr. Maxwell, she only nodded her head.

Yawning yet again, Eden began noticing that her eyesight was turning a bit blurry, and that it was becoming harder to keep her thoughts focused. She laid her head back on the pillowed part of the cot, fighting the sleep that was trying to pull her under.

Dr. Maxwell patted her arm, telling her, "Don't fight it, Unitsi Eden. You need to sleep for now. The tea will help. When you wake up, Charles and I will be here."

Eden tried blinking her eyes, fighting to stay awake. But as she did, her eyelids became heavier and heavier until she couldn't hold them open any longer. Finally, she succumbed to the draught that Dr. Maxwell had laced with sleeping potion and drifted off.

回回回

Hearing someone snoring, Eden suddenly sat up and looked around. When she realized the snoring was not coming from her, but instead from one of the guys, she breathed a sigh of relief.

Essie, realizing that Eden was awake, approached Charles. Putting a hand on his arm, she whispered, "Charles, the young woman, Eden, is awake."

"Thank you, Essie, I'll take it from here," Charles said, handing her the bottle he had finished filling.

Walking over to Eden, he said happily, "Good, I see you are awake. How is your head feeling now? Any headache left?" he asked.

"No. In fact, it's feeling pretty good. Thanks."

"Great! Looks like the tea, and potion Dr. Maxwell gave you worked fine on that headache."

"Oh, so that's what was in that tea I drank. I remember thinking something was off."

Swinging her legs over the edge of the cot, Eden was about to stand when Charles stopped her, saying, "Whoa! I wouldn't try standing yet."

"Why not?"

"Well, you've been asleep for over two days. Your legs are probably weak. We don't want you falling and hurting yourself," he said. He then began checking her arms and skin for any rash. "Are you itchy anywhere?"

"No...."

"Good. Sore throat, dry mouth, seeing spots?" he asked. When she answered no to all his questions, he turned and motioned for the large, muscular, bald man talking to Essie to come over.

When something that Charles said before all his questions finally sunk in, Eden exclaimed, "Wait! Did I just hear you right? I've been sleeping for two days?"

"Yes. Think of it as a bad case of jet lag, Eden."

As they were speaking, the man he had motioned to said, "Well, I see our Sleeping Beauty is finally awake, Charles."

Eden laughed. She had been expecting a no-nonsense tough guy instead of the jovial, giant this guy appeared to be. So, she said, "I see you know Earth fairy tales. But in Sleeping Beauty, Princess Aurora has blonde hair like Savage. As you can see, I have red. That's a big problem!"

"Well, we can change that to Merida then," he laughed. Eden's mouth dropped in surprise.

Extending his hand to Eden, he said, "Let me introduce myself, I'm Royce, Keeper of Pop Culture."

"Nice to meet you, Royce."

As they shook, Charles grabbed Royce's shoulder, and told Eden, "Don't believe a word he says about being Keeper of Pop Culture. Like Dr. Maxwell and me, he's just another lowly member of the Sentinels from Earth. He just likes to collect Disney Princess movies."

"I hope you don't mind me asking, but isn't that a strange hobby for a grown man?"

"Believe me, my hobby, as you called it, was an acquired one. You see, before I came here, I had a little sister that loved the earlier classic Disney Princess movies. So, I would save my chore money until I had enough for two tickets for the Saturday matinee. When a new movie came to the local movie theater, we would be first in line to watch it. We never missed a movie... until the fire."

"I'm sorry. I bet she adored her older brother."

"No more than I adored her."

"Now, how about we try standing for a bit?"

"Here, take ahold of mine and Charles's arms and try sliding off the cot. Then just stand there for a minute to see how it feels."

Eden swung her legs off the cot and wiggled herself over until she was sitting on the edge of it. Grabbing onto both of their arms, she stood.

Right away she realized Charles was right. Her legs were weak, and her knees buckled. It reminded her of the time she had the flu and was wiped out for three days. Once she was over it, it took her another day to start feeling like herself again.

After standing there for a few minutes, Charles said, "Okay, let's walk together over to that chair and we'll let you sit there for a half an hour before putting you back on your cot."

Taking the six or seven steps to the chair made Eden feel like she was walking on stumps instead of legs, as her legs began to feel tingly.

Once Charles and Royce had gotten her into the chair, Charles turned to Royce and said, "We'll wake up the others tomorrow. You can tell Essie and Andrei to continue monitoring them for side effects, continue their meds and check on Aiden's rash. I think he'll be needing another application of ointment for it as well. Oh, and give him some more meds for the itch too.

In the meantime, I have to attend a meeting with Dr. Maxwell and Sumi that's going to last a while.

Don't let Eden sit here too long for the first time. Give her something to eat then have her lie back down."

Pausing, Charles laughingly told Royce, "I don't know why I'm telling you this. You have the drill memorized after eleven Loops."

"We should be back sometime after lunch, Eden, and listen to them!" Eden saluted him.

After Charles left, Eden asked Royce, "Charles mentioned that Aiden has a rash?"

"Yeah, it happens sometimes on the first transport. We have been treating it with an herbal ointment and have infused him with an anti-itch medicine. He should be good to go by tomorrow. Although, the itching may last a few days longer. Right now he's a pretty sight.

You should have seen me the first time I traveled! I looked like a strawberry for over a week, but I had a bad case of it. Even though your brother's fair and a red head, his rash is mild. Although, he might not think it is after he wakes up.

I'm sure you couldn't have helped but noticed that I'm an albino, and bald on top of it. They think my condition is what contributed to my exceptionally bad case of the rash. Thank goodness after five hundred Time Loops I've never had it again.

After you eat, Essie will help you get cleaned up and put into some clean clothes. Later, once you are walking on your own, you'll get the standard trainee uniform."

"Okay, that sounds good."

"Royce, can I ask you something before you go?"

"Sure, Eden."

"Well, Dr. Maxwell mentioned that we would be trained before we had to retrieve that young boy. Do you know how long training will take before we leave on our assignment?"

"Ah, it lasts about two weeks after the brain augmentations are done." In a surge of panic, Eden grabbed the *key*, but it was quiet.

Seeing her panic, Royce explained, "Hey, Eden, don't get yourself all upset about it! It's safe, and it doesn't hurt. The augmentation only expands your understanding and physical capabilities. They'll insert some programmed nanites into your blood stream while you sleep to make the changes. You'll wake up needing no time to recover. They have this down to a 'T'. It's very safe. If it wasn't, Dr. Maxwell would never allow it to happen to you all, especially to you and Savage."

Smiling, he bent down at eye level with her, and asked, "Now, are you okay?"

"Yeah, I guess so. My *key* is quiet. But I do have one more question for you. Where exactly are we?"

Royce explained, "Well, to put it simply, Eden, it is a micro-universe outside of the universe that we call home.

The first Sentinels 'tore', for the lack of a better word, a hole in the fabric of spacetime, creating this universe consisting of a single solar system for their base from several rogue planets, and a solitary sun, placing them all inside the tear.

The worlds in this solar system were terraformed to accommodate the different species of Sentinels. This area here is sort of like a crossroads that can interconnect with each of those worlds. It gives us a gathering place to plan and stage our campaigns as they present themselves.

We have a planet much like Earth, complete with a moon. A Demon Class planet where only silicon-based life forms live, that Essie calls home when she is in her true form. A world that is 95% water. And a Gas Giant, where the Sentinels comprised of pure energy call home.

We also have a large solar system sized asteroid belt, which includes a few dwarf planets, that are home to a few lifeforms. And there are a few habitable moons around some of the planets, some of which have asteroid rings.

Time also flows differently here. Even though we keep to twenty-four-hour time periods, beings age very slowly, if at all. I guess you could say that here you have all the time in the world.

I know this is a lot to digest in one sitting. But once you have had the standard brain augmentation and begin your training, everything will come together, and you will understand everything better than I can explain it."

"Now are you sure you're okay."

"Yeah, I'm fine. But you're right. It is a lot to digest."

Just then, Essie approached them with a hovering tray of food. Eden was amazed as the tray hovered for a second then landed gently on an extended surface attached to the utility table next to the chair she was sitting in.

Essie took a beautifully decorated plate from the tray that was holding a warm berry muffin and handed it to Eden. Cheerily, she said to her, "Here you go. I thought you might like one of Andrei's delicious, homemade muffins made from our homegrown berries."

THIRTY-FOUR

AFTER A DELICIOUS BREAKFAST, AN ASSISTED WALK, and a short nap followed by a hardy lunch, Eden was returned to her cot with the back section, and legs raised for support, even though she was feeling better, and her legs felt almost normal. She was told by Royce that they would be taking her for a short walk after supper, and depending on how well she did then, she might be released on her own to wander the facility at will.

Laying on her cot, Eden had nothing to occupy her mind. The inactivity was beginning to cause her to feel abandoned, doubting if Dr. Maxwell and Charles were ever going to return from their meeting with this unknown Sumi person. She knew if the others were awake she would not be feeling this way and she would have had someone she knew to talk to. Although Essie, Royce and Andrei did try to make her feel comfortable and keep her engaged, they had to work.

Aware that Eden needed something to occupy her mind, Royce gave her a device similar to a tablet and showed her how to operate it. It contained data on all the different worlds in the Sentinel solar system and the life forms that called them home. She found that whenever she touched the screen it would give her in-depth information, projecting additional data into the air. From there, it displayed side bars branching off, supplying even more data.

One thing she found utterly amazing was how real all the information appeared. It was as if she was actually there, able to engage all five of her senses. In fact, it was so real her fingers still felt sticky after picking a juicy looking holographic fruit from a bush.

Once Eden had excitedly skimmed through the top layer of the solar system material she then went to the section about the founding of the Sentinels. There she discovered that they were an extremely ancient group of beings bound by the common goal of a pure timeline free of any unnatural deviations. The consortium was formed millions of years ago. Its technology was beyond what she could understand or had seen in any science textbook or heard about in any Sci- Fi movie.

"Aiden and Savage are gonn'a love this," she thought.

She also learned that each galaxy with sentient life had a team that consisted of the beings inhabiting it. Those teams then elected twelve representatives to form the Galactic Council who oversaw the planning and execution of the various missions in their galaxy.

The Sentinels, as a whole, had divided the universe into twelve regions, a dodecagon, for easier administration. From each of these regions, twelve representatives from all the combined Galactic Councils in that area were chosen to form a Regional Assembly totaling one hundred and forty-four delegates.

Then from the twelve Regional Assemblies one representative each was chosen to sit on the Sovereign Senate for one eon which was a little over one hundred Earth years. It was this council of Sentinels that were charged with upholding the principles set down by their founders and for keeping Time and Space deviant free.

After reading about the Universal structure of the Sentinels, it made her feel microscopic.

Eden had just moved to a more in-depth section concerning the development of the Sentinel's core values and their beliefs, when unbeknownst to Eden, Dr. Maxwell and Charles finally walked in. What she was reading had her full attention, and Charles' laughter about something said to the others, startled her.

Looking up from her device, she smiled once she saw it was Dr. Maxwell and Charles.

She knew they would be over to talk to her once they had finished talking with the three aides, so she went back to reading. However, she had not gotten far into the section on the Sentinel's core values and beliefs when they came to her cot.

"Well, I see Royce has given you an IR," Dr. Maxwell said sitting in a chair next to her.

"An IR? Is that what this thing's called?" asked Eden, as she held it up looking at it. "What's the IR stand for?"

"It means, 'Informational Relay'. It's a device that is like a tablet on Earth but has an artificial intelligence instead of a hard drive."

"Oh wow! I thought there was more to this device than Royce explained. I can't wait to show this to Aiden, and Savage!"

Eden had a thought and asked, "Since it's an AI, does it have feelings too?"

"In a manner of speaking because they respond to your feelings. If you are excited, it is excited. If you are sad, it is sad, but within limited parameters. It would not be logical, or even safe, for it to own a full range of emotions. An IR is not a fully formed, sentient AI."

"Are there any fully functioning sentient AIs in the Sentinels?"

"Yes, there are. Originally, they come from a solar system on the other side of the universe, called Sol 12.4. Here they mainly live on the moon that circles the planet that is similar to Earth, called Haven. Mostly, they like to garden, so they supply us with an abundance of various crops. There are some, like Andrei, who like the medical field, and make up much of our medical community."

"Andrei's an AI? Why I'd never would have known that if you hadn't told me! I didn't realize there could be such beings. I must have missed that part when I was reading about the planets in this solar system. There's just so much to remember!"

"That is one of the things I want to talk to you about now, Unitsi Eden. The amount of information you and your team will need to consume in a short time, along with the physical training you all will need, cannot be done without some sort of help."

"You're talking about the brain augmentation, aren't you?"

"How do you know about that? Did you find it in the IR?" asked Dr. Maxwell.

"No, Royce. He explained some of it and tried to reassure me that it would not damage us or change our personalities. He said that the Sentinels have it down to a 'T', and not to worry about it."

R.L. Roush

"He's right about that. Both Dr. Maxwell and I have had the augmentation done. So has everyone here, except for you five, of course."

"I felt a bit better about it after talking to Royce, but I still get apprehensive thinking about it at times."

"Well, let's hope that after you all talk about it between yourselves and talk to Medical, those feelings of apprehension will diminish. Still if you have any questions about it at any time you can ask anyone of us."

"Thanks Dr. Maxwell."

"There's also another issue I need to talk to you about, but it's not anything to be concerned or worried about. It has to do with your *key*."

"My *key*?"

"Yes. Do you remember everything I told you about listening to it, that it remembers all the Time Loops and that it will give you information as needed and will alert you to danger? And that it will become more attune to you, learning you as you learned it?"

Eden nodded.

"Well, at the time I couldn't tell you everything about it because you wouldn't have understood. Now that you've been told a little about AI and will be able to read some about it, I feel I need to tell you that your *key* is also an AI unit. Not a fully sentient AI like Andrei, but much, much more than your IR."

Eden's eyes grew large hearing Dr. Maxwell's information about her *key*. Still, even though he had just informed her of the *key's* full ability, it did not surprise her. She had been feeling for the past few days like the *key* had its own personality. She was beginning to think of it as a guide with a personality.

"You know, Dr. Maxwell, that doesn't shock me. The past few days I've been thinking of it as kind of a dog, a guide/guard dog. Going forward, I think I will refer to it as 'Key', with a capital K. Key's a good name for a dog."

"Well, that's good! I think! And now that we have all of that out of the way, let's see what they are planning for supper. I do

170

hope there's ice cream for dessert!" Dr. Maxwell said, after which he headed towards Essie, and Andrei, with Charles in tow.

After supper had been decided on, Dr. Maxwell and Charles came back and talked with Eden about other things she had read or had questions about. Essie and Andrei also stopped by occasionally to chat as they continued working on the others until supper was ready.

After the meal, they took Eden on a short walk around the campus, showing her the classrooms, the training grounds, and the barracks where they would be staying during training. After the short tour, Eden knew she would have no problem walking, going forward. It felt good being up and about.

Once back in the Communal Recovery Room, they talked a bit more before everyone left for bed except for Andrei. It was his turn to handle the night shift alone.

Eden read for a while. As she was ready to turn in, Andrei came over to speak to her. He then asked, "Eden, would you mind keeping an eye on things here while I run to AI Medical?

I've needed a minor part adjusted since my last mission and I've kept putting it off. Now the pain is making it almost impossible to work tonight. I will only be gone for half an hour.

Don't worry, I'll set everything to run automatically. But, if in the unlikely event something unforeseeable should occur and you need help, just say aloud, "I need help."

Eden was caught off guard. Although she was worried about being responsible for the others by herself, she could not help but wonder what part was giving Andrei trouble. She managed to say, "Sure, no problem."

"Thanks!" Andrei told her, rushing out of the room.

Eden set the IR on the utility table then swung her legs over the edge of her cot. Suddenly she realized she needed to use the facilities. Her land legs were still not a hundred percent for walking fast, but she succeeded in hurrying. She was pleased with herself when she walked back to the Communal Recovery Room a few minutes later, until she thought she heard Colton moaning.

Immediately she went to check on him. As she approached his cot, she could see he was restless and mumbling occasionally. Sitting on the edge of his cot, she took his hand in hers, and said, "Colton, it's alright. It's me, Eden."

His hand felt warm as if he had a slight fever, so she ran the back of her hand across his forehead, and down the side of his face like her mother always did to her and Aiden when she thought they had fevers. But she was surprised to find Colton's temperature was normal to the touch.

As she sat there in the dimmed light, she studied his face. The first time she had seen Colton, she had though his face showed character. He had a strong jaw that merged into a slightly cleft chin, and his nose had a slight kink from a sports injury she recalled Savage telling her about. But she mostly liked his eyes. He had kind eyes. They crinkled when he smiled, causing his cheeks to be accented by dimples.

Then she thought about Colton's lips, and she blushed because it reminded her of his kiss. She was glad the lights were dim, and no one was around to see her face. Aiden was not the only one in the group who turned bright red when they blushed.

Contented with sitting there watching him, she noticed since she had been holding his hand, his restlessness had diminished along with his moaning. Nothing else looked wrong with him physically, except that his hair hung in his eyes. He needed a haircut.

As she sat there, her mind began thinking about possibilities. Lowering her voice, she said, "Who knows, Colton, given time I might…"

Then right at that moment, Colton turned his head causing his hair to fall over his closed eyes making him frown. So, Eden reached up to move it away. As her fingers lightly touched his brow, Colton sighed, "Eden…."

THIRTY-FIVE

AFTER COLTON SIGHED EDEN'S NAME, SHE gasped. Now she was unsure if Colton was really in a medical comma or just asleep. She wondered if he could possibly hear her.

"Colton? Colton are you awake?" she whispered. Leaning in close, she gently placed her hand against his cheek again.

"I don't think he is, Eden. We have him in a medically induced sleep. It is extremely unusual for someone to wake up."

Eden nearly jumped out of her skin when Andrei spoke. She had not heard him come in and was unaware that he was standing right behind her left shoulder. "Oh! Crap! How long was he standing there? Oh, I hope he didn't hear!" she thought in a panic.

Andrei saw her jump, and said, "Oh, I'm sorry, Eden! I didn't mean to startle you. I often forget to make noise when humans are around as they can easily be startled."

Andrei picked up the medical scanner and initiated a routine check on Colton's vitals. After reviewing them, he was relieved to see they were in the normal range.

"Oh, that's alright, Andrei. I, I didn't expect you to be back so soon," Eden managed to answer. "By the way, just how long have you been back?" Eden asked, nervously.

"Not long, just in time to hear him say your name," he said. Eden winced.

"Oh, by the way, in case they forgot to tell you, we'll be waking Savage up in the morning right after breakfast. Colton will be next, before lunch. The other two young men will follow him. If everything goes well, they should all be awake by supper."

"Why not wake them all at once?"

"Good question. You see, they all had different side effects. So, in each case the timing depends on how long the medicines need to work. Savage wasn't as bad as the young men, so we can bring her out of it next. Your brother Aiden was the worst, so he'll be the last.

Remember the tea Dr. Maxwell gave you to drink?" Andrei asked. Eden nodded.

He continued, "That was your second dose of medicine because you had a headache.

They are all now sleeping through their second doses. Some had headaches like you, others had different side effects or combinations, which in turn required additional medicines in their teas. Your brother also needed an ointment for his rash."

"I don't remember waking a first time and being given any medicine, just the second, and the tea."

Andrei laughed, "That's because you didn't. You were all passed out from the time travel. We inoculated all of you after you were examined. Don't worry, it's the same for all first timers, even us AI's."

Andrei picked up the medical device to scan Colton one last time before he went to check on the others, and said, "Hmm, my scans aren't showing anything out of the ordinary, but it was strange that Colton spoke at all."

"I wouldn't exactly have called it talking. It was more like a sigh," Eden told him. Then as soon as the words were out of her mouth, she wished she could have bitten her tongue.

"Ah… now I see! You know, Eden, when someone sighs another's name when they are under like Colton, they must have a strong bond with that person."

Eden's jaw dropped. Apparently, AI's were not only silent but had great hearing.

"So, I'm guessing that you'll be pleased when Colton wakes and you both can speak to each other again."

Seeing the expression on Eden's face, Andrei winked, and said, "Ah, yes! It was that way for Minka and me, too. Don't worry! Yours and Colton's secret is safe with me."

"Now that I am back, and Colton seems to be doing well, why don't you go and get some sleep? He will be awake tomorrow afternoon and glad to see you, no doubt."

"And by the way, thank you, for watching things here for me," Andrei added, bowing his head to her.

"You're welcome."

Setting Colton's hand on his chest, she slid off his cot and went back to hers. Lying there she thought, "Oh, great! I must be an open book. It must be too obvious we have a connection!"

Reaching for the blanket at the bottom of her cot, Eden pulled it up and over her head as she turned on her side, hoping it would hide her glowing face, and that she would be able to fall asleep.

◻◻◻

Eden woke as soon as the sunbeams began shining through the window by her cot. She was surprised she fell asleep so quickly and stayed asleep after what had happened last night. She had totally expected to toss and turn hearing Colton sighing her name all night long. But she trusted Andrei would keep his promise and not say anything, and she hoped Colton would not remember anything if he really was awake.

As Eden thought about the upcoming day, she was excited about them bringing Savage out of her medical sleep after breakfast. She decided to get washed up and dressed so she could be back in the Communal Recovery Room before Savage woke. She did not want to miss a single thing.

As she was leaving, Essie stopped her, handing her what looked like a uniform, boots, and some undergarments. She explained to her that it was the standard daywear for new recruits and for the classes that they would be taking. She also told Eden that when it was time, she would receive a different uniform for physical training.

Eden took the uniform from Essie and was excited to see that it was the same blue as NASA's flight suits, trimmed in yellow. The material felt durable but silky, and she wondered how it would feel once it was on. The boots were sturdy and felt like top end leather to the touch. However, she knew that the boots were not leather, since Essie had informed her yesterday that all food and the clothing everyone used in their solar system was plant based or created from insect/animal by-products. Only the beings of pure energy, who fed off natural occurring radiation, did not have a need for clothing.

Thanking Essie, she quickly made her way to the individual cleaning rooms to get ready. Once there, she found everything else she needed. She did not know how, but they even had her favorite type of hairbrush.

As she was getting ready, she could not help but notice a few of the doors exiting her area were sealed shut. She figured behind them were areas for nonhuman Sentinel use. While bathing, she passed the time envisioning what the facilities for those Sentinel's would look like.

After she had showered, she put on the uniform and found that it fit her perfectly, as well as the boots. The clothes felt as if they were perfectly tailored for her body, giving her room to move without her feeling constricted. This was not what she had expected a uniform would feel like, as she checked it out in the mirror. Even the boots fit like a second skin.

After braiding her hair into a single plat, she then headed back to the Communal Recovery Room hoping she had not missed anything important. But before leaving the area, she tucked her *key* under her uniform.

Walking into the room, she noticed Royce had set up her breakfast, along with a few other place settings, at a table this time instead of at her utility table. It appeared she was going to have company.

No sooner had she sat down, than Dr. Maxwell and Charles came into the room. After giving their good mornings to Royce, Essie, and Andrei, they joined her at the table.

"Good morning, Unitsi Eden!" Dr. Maxwell happily told her as he took his place. "You look like you had a good night's sleep. Am I right?"

"Thank you. Yes, I did." she said, glancing at Andrei, who winked at her. Eden smiled, rolling her eyes at him. "I hope you had a good night too."

"Yes, for an old man."

"And how are you doing this morning, Charles?"

"Wonderful! We'll soon have Savage awake, and the others before the end of the day.

We'll be like one happy family again."

Royce brought over three plates containing scrambled eggs, bacon, home-fried potatoes, and toast, setting one in front of each of them. Before he left, he told Eden, "There is some delicious tea in that blue flowered pot that I thought you would like."

"Thank you, Royce."

Lifting the pot, she poured herself a cup. Motioning the pot to Dr. Maxwell and Charles, they both declined as they had already had coffee.

Time passed in silence as they ate their breakfast. Eden marveled how the bacon tasted like bacon even though it was made from plant protein. The same with the eggs and the butter on the toast. When they had finished, Essie gave them cups of fresh cut fruit. Eden recognized the sticky, sweet berries she had read about on the IR that Royce had given her. They were just as good as she had remembered and made sure to wipe off any juice she had gotten on herself when she was done eating them.

Once they were finished with breakfast, Dr. Maxwell pushed himself away from the table saying, "Everyone, that was excellent. Thank you!

Now let's see about waking up our 'Sleeping Beauty'."

Royce laughed at Dr. Maxwell's Disney reference. Then he said to Eden, "Okay Merida, now it's time for Savage to awaken from her dreams."

R.L. Roush

While Royce was explaining the procedure to Eden, Essie and Andrei had covered Savage's head with a clear dome like mask and proceeded to feed a smokey looking gas into it. Royce picked up the medical scanner lying on the utility table next to Savage's cot and began monitoring her. Eden recognized the device as being identical to the one Andrei used last night when he checked Colton's vitals.

"That smoke you see, Unitsi Eden, is a mixture of oxygen, and a few other needed medicines that will help Savage as she regains consciousness. We like doing it this way because it is less invasive than infusing the medicine from a dispenser into the body through the skin. Plus, it doesn't take as long as the latter either."

"We didn't need to do this routine with you. Besides having a headache, Savage also had issues with a dry mouth and sore throat. The medicated gas will help with both. Do you remember when you woke up and felt like you had just had a great night's sleep?"

"Yeah. I felt wonderful, Dr. Maxwell."

"Savage will as well."

Essie and Andrei left the dome on Savage's head for fifteen minutes before removing it.

"Now, all we have to do is sit back and wait 'til Unitsi Savage finally wakes." In the meantime, he sat there patiently patting Savage's hand, encouraging her to wake.

Eden thought it strange that Dr. Maxwell kept addressing Savage and her with the term Unitsi. What did it mean? But the more she thought about it, she felt as if she had heard the word somewhere before. But for the life of her, she could not remember when. But she decided against asking him in case she missed Savage's waking.

It seemed like it had taken forever before Savage finally yawned and stretched. But when she opened her eyes, she found three strangers staring at her!

THIRTY-SIX

AS SAVAGE OPENED HER EYES, SHE FOUND three strangers hovering over her. Immediately she felt she was in danger. Out of fear she scrambled into a sitting position. Then as her mind began to clear, she became aware there were more than three people watching her. At that point she became combative throwing her hands out in front of her, shouting, "No, No! What... what do you want? Who, who... are you? Leave me alone!"

Eden immediately intervened, and said, "Hey, Savage! Savage, look at me! That's it, focus on my face. Focus! Now take a deep breath."

Noticing confusion in Savage's eyes, Eden told her, "It's Eden, Savage. Listen, you're okay. Ciara's not here. I got you. Dr. Maxwell and Charles have you, too. Understand? See Savage? They're right here."

As Savage began to realize that it was Eden who was talking to her, she started calming down. Seeing Dr. Maxwell sitting next to her, and Charles behind him, helped as well. That was until she realized that the three strangers were standing behind Charles.

"Who... who are they?" she asked pointing out Royce, Essie, and Andrei.

"Savage, they're friends. They're some of the Sentinels Dr. Maxwell told us about. Here let me introduce them to you. This is Essie, Andrei, and the tall one is Royce."

Royce laughed, "Glad to see our Sleeping Beauty is finally awake!" Teasing Savage, he said, "For a while there, I thought we were going to get Prince Charming to kiss you to wake you up."

When Royce talked about finding Prince Charming, Savage realized Aiden was not there and began to panic again. Immediately her eyes began darting around the room until they fell on Aiden lying on a cot not far from her. The second she saw him she sighed in relief.

Considering Savage's reaction to his comment, Royce looked at Eden sporting a huge grin. Ever since he was young, he was a push over when it came to love stories, and happily ever after's. And he sensed one here.

After Savage had found Aiden, she noticed something strange about his appearance, but the lights in Aiden's area were dimmed so she was not sure if what she was seeing was right. She tried squinting her eyes to get a better look, and thought he had a sunburn or a rash.

The first words out of her mouth were concern for Aiden, "What happened to Aiden? Is he okay? He looks bright red!"

Next, she tried swinging her legs off her cot to go to check on him, but before she could, Eden put her hand against Savage's shoulder to stop her.

"Don't try to stand, Savage. You'll fall. Your legs are too weak because you've been asleep for almost three days."

"Wait! What… I've been asleep for three days? But Aiden he needs help!"

"Believe me, he's okay, Savage. Royce told me it's just one of the side effects that can happen when you time travel for the first time. These guys have it all under control."

"Yes, when he wakes, he'll be itchy, and have to apply an ointment, but he'll be as good as new in a day or two. You should have seen me the first time I time traveled. Being albino, I looked like a huge ripe strawberry," Royce said.

Savage looked warily at the massive man, but no way could she ever imagine him looking like a strawberry. After the few minutes of meeting him, he appeared to her to be a bundle of contradictions, powerful but kind, serious but teasing, but definitely not a strawberry. And where did those Disney references come from? She could not even begin to imagine.

Although, she had to admit his humor and kindness was calming.

Dr. Maxwell said, "Now, Unitsi Savage, we are going to get you up and set you in a chair for a bit so you can get some food into you. We are going to put you through the same routine we put Eden through yesterday. Then in about an hour we'll wake Colton. After lunch, we'll wake Wade, then an hour after him, Aiden."

Eden nodded her head, "Yeah, Savage, they'll help you get to the chair. You'll feel better once you eat. Better enjoy being pampered now. In no time the guys will be up pestering us again."

Dr. Maxwell said, "So then, Charles and Andrei, let's move Unitsi Savage."

Eden was excited that the guys would be waking up today. But the minute Dr. Maxwell used 'Unitsi' with Savage's name, she thought, "When I get a chance to get him alone, I've got to ask him what it means and why he's calling Savage that, and me, too."

Andrei and Charles assisted Savage to her chair. As she sat down, she said, "Ooh, you all were all right about my legs being weak. They feel rubbery."

"It's normal, Savage, since you haven't stood on them for three days. They should feel better by the end of the day.

You know, maybe you and I can take a tour. You have got to see this place. It's amazing! I have so much to tell you," Eden said, as she pulled her chair over to Savage's. Dr. Maxwell and Charles did the same with theirs.

Essie went to help Royce who was doing a routine check on the guys vitals, while Andrei was busy preparing a tray of food and drink for Savage. When he was finished, Andrei sent it gravitating to the extended utility table beside Savage. Once the tray had settled on the extension, he took a plate from it holding a huge berry muffin and handed it to Savage.

Seeing Eden's sad expression, Andrei told her, "Don't worry, Eden. Essie told me how much you loved my muffins. I didn't forget and brought one for you too."

R.L. Roush

Handing Eden the other plate, he said, "Here you go! There's some of that tea you like in that pot, and that red container is milk for Savage."

Eden took the plate and said, "Thanks! You read my mind."

"No, I'm just good at reading human expressions, but you are more than welcome, Eden."

"Now, can I get you and Charles anything, Dr. Maxwell?"

"No, no, thank you, Andrei. Breakfast was more than filling," Dr. Maxwell said, patting his stomach.

"Anyway, Charles and I need to be going. We have a few things we must see to first before we wake Colton. However, you can tell Royce I'd appreciate some of that delicious honey butter he makes to put on some of those marvelous biscuits you bake."

Andrei said, "Of course! I'll be sure to tell Royce. And I'll whip up a special batch of those biscuits for you, too."

"Thank you, Andrei! That would make me incredibly happy." Laughter followed them out the door and down the hall.

Andrei said to the girls, "As you can see, Dr. Maxwell sure loves his sweets!" Both of them could not help but smile.

Before Eden could tell Savage what had happened to them the past three days, Andrei came back with an IR. Handing it to Savage, he said, "Here is your personal IR. Eden will show you how to operate it. I'd stay and talk, but I need to get back to Colton to track his readings for Dr. Maxwell since we will be waking him soon." Giving an obvious wink to Eden, he left to go to tend Colton.

"What was that wink about?"

"Well, he found out how I feel about Colton. See, last night he asked me to keep an eye on everyone. He said he needed to run to Medical to get a part replaced that was causing him some discomfort that he hadn't gotten taken care of from his last mission. Well, a bit after Andrei had left, Colton was moaning, so I went to check on him. While I was sitting there, he called out my name. I guess I said some personal stuff to him while he was out.

Apparently Andrei had come back and overheard everything," Eden told her.

"Wait! You just said Andrei needed a part replaced? What did you mean by a *part*?"

"Oh! I haven't had a chance to tell you, but Andrei is an AI."

"You mean he's a cyborg?"

"No! A fully sentient AI, and he's married."

"Wow, and wow! I'd never have guessed. He looks so, so human! And married?"

Eden took Savage's IR and showed her how to navigate it while looking for the section on beings like Andrei.

"Yes, here it is. Info on the AI's. Go ahead and read it. It explains all about them. Oh, and by the way just so you know, Andrei is extremely stealthy and has really, and I mean really, good hearing," Eden whispered.

"I heard that!" Andrei shouted from the other end of the room. At that, both girls burst out laughing.

THIRTY-SEVEN

EDEN GOT THE IR THAT ROYCE HAD GIVEN her. Returning to Savage, they huddled together to research the Sentinel solar system, especially the many life forms that inhabited it. They were not long into their investigation when they realized just how old and extensive the organization was. Overwhelming did not even begin to describe how they felt as they scanned through the layers of information on their IRs.

"Look here", and "You've got to be kidding me," were said many times by both of them as they wandered through the data, sharing it with one another. Often, when one of them had found something they thought was extremely share worthy, they would pull that section off to be displayed into the air for both of them to investigate further.

Savage was playing catch up since she had been in a medical induced coma for a day longer than Eden, but with Eden's help, it did not take her long to catch up. As she explored, she was excited to find that all the displays were interactive. Eden explained how the information they were viewing allowed them to engage all five of their senses. That aspect totally amazed Savage, as much as it had Eden when she first discovered it. Savage was also able to open a few other viewing ports that Eden had not considered.

Not everything they found was always serious or profound. Savage outright snorted in laughter when an odd-looking, furry animal with an elephantlike trunk, unexpectedly tried to spray her and Eden with what they assumed was water, while they were viewing a section on the flora and fauna of one of the Sentinel worlds.

Watching Savage's honest reactions to the holographical information was hilarious. Eden could not help herself and laughed along with her.

It was at the moment they were viewing that odd-looking animal that Dr. Maxwell and Charles returned from their meeting with Sumi and found the girls in fits of laughter.

Not interrupting them, they approached Royce, Essie, and Andrei to review the day's schedule with them. Once things were finalized, they then went to Eden and Savage to update them. It was time to wake Colton.

"Well, I can see you two are making good use of your time," Dr. Maxwell greeted them.

"Oh! Hi Dr. Maxwell, Charles. Sorry, we didn't see you come in."

"That's because we've been engrossed in studying this star system."

"Yes, I could tell when Charles and I walked in. It looks like you both came across the info on the pituitia nasi vellus, or commonly known as a Snot-fluffer."

"A what?"

"A Snot-fluffer. One of the cuter animals in this solar system, if I do say so myself. They're similar to a fox in temperament. Many humanoids here keep them as pets after having their snot glands removed. Just be glad the Holographic View was on, and the True View mode turned off. You both would have ended up smelling like a skunk and needing a deodorizing!"

"Wait! We didn't smell anything!"

"Here, Savage. Let me see both your IRs."

Dr. Maxwell handed one of the IRs to Charles. They began checking the settings, making a few adjustments to them. After comparing what he and Charles had changed, he then handed them back to Eden and Savage, saying. "I think that should do it."

"Ah, I see! Looks like Royce and Andrei had their interface settings set to Monitor Low. Sometimes they are too overprotective. Just be prudent going forward when you view data in the Five Senses mode. For now, Charles and I set the mode to Holographic View for you to view in it for the time being. But keep True View turned off for now."

"Oh! We will!"

"Great! And thanks for the warning."

"Okay! Now that that's out of the way, let's get down to what we need to tell you both.

We want to update you two about our meeting with Sumi, and our plans going forward. The meeting went very well. She is happy with our progress and wants us to proceed with waking all the rest of you by the end of today so we can get started with your training in two days.

The guys will have about a day to adjust to this location and be given an overview on their IRs. It will also give them a chance to meet Essie, Royce, and Andrei, who are members of our support team.

Tomorrow evening before bedtime, everyone will have their augmentations done. That way you all will be able to recover while you sleep. Then, when you wake in the morning, you will have the knowledge and physical strength needed to complete your training."

Eden and Savage were stunned, only two days before their brain augmentations. When he saw their faces, Dr. Maxwell stopped talking. Taking their hands, he said, "Don't worry Unitsi Eden and Unitsi Savage, I would never ask you do anything that would knowingly bring harm to either of you."

For some reason, Eden believed him. He had always been kind to her and Savage, even going out of his way to make sure they were comfortable. But there it was again, his use of the term 'Unitsi'.

Eden asked, "Dr. Maxwell, can I ask you a question?"

"Why yes! Of course! Anything, Eden!"

"I've noticed that you've been calling Savage and me, *Unitsi*. What does that mean?"

Charles anxiously glanced at Dr. Maxwell waiting to hear how the elderly man would handle this question. Charles' reaction to her request made Eden feel uneasy. In fact, it seemed to her that

Royce, Essie, and Andrei had suddenly gotten quiet, pausing their activities as if they were waiting to hear his answer as well.

Unbothered by her question, Dr. Maxwell did not hesitate in answering. He said, "Oh, that! Well, *Unitsi*, you see, is a term of endearment in the tribe I was raised in. I use it because you and Savage are dear to me."

Pausing a second or two, he then reassuringly squeezed both of their hands. He then clasped his hands, and said, "It has another meaning too, but it can wait until you both get back from your mission."

After hearing his answer, Eden was aware that Charles, along with the others, collectively seemed to be relieved when Dr. Maxwell answered her. It made her wonder why he only gave them a partial answer. What was he hiding?

Having his incomplete answer to one question seemed to have presented her more. Plus, they would have to wait until they got back to have the rest of the answer. This was frustrating. But for now, she would have to drop it. Dr. Maxwell had moved on.

Standing, Dr. Maxwell said, "Time to wake up Colton!"

R.L. Roush

THIRTY-EIGHT

WHILE ESSIE REMOVED COLTON'S MASK, Eden and Savage were standing on either side of him anxiously holding onto his hands. Everyone there patiently waited, excited for Colton to open his eyes. After a few seconds they began to move, although for Eden, it was not fast enough.

Colton did not have the fearful reaction his sister had when she woke, because he saw Eden standing there. He smiled. It took another minute for him to realize his sister was standing there as well. He smiled at her, too.

Andrei, who was positioned at Colton's feet monitoring his vitals, was watching everything. He began to hum happily. The sound caused Eden to glance up, and by chance, catch him winking at her. His action caused her to blush. No one except Savage seemed to notice.

Dr. Maxwell asked Andrei, "How's everything looking?"

"Good for now, Dr. Maxwell. However, there was a brief rise in his heartbeat a few moments after he regained consciousness, but not to worry. It's in the normal range now." This time Eden did not look at Andrei but kept her head down. But she could still feel his eyes on her, as well as the warmth of the blood rising up her neck as she blushed. It was moments like this she cursed being a redhead.

Colton was quickly cleared by Andrei. Everyone, except Eden and Savage, went back to their assignments or setting up for Wade's awakening. For now, he was still scheduled to be awakened after lunch.

Savage in the meantime stood there watching her brother smiling stupidly at Eden, and not saying a word. With the way he was acting, normally she would have chalked it up to the medications he had been on. But she knew better. Knowing that

188

she had been dreaming right before waking, allowed her to come to the conclusion that her brother must have been dreaming about Eden before he woke up.

Looking at how happy he seemed made her smile. So, in true sister form, she flicked his earlobe.

"What was that for?"

"Quit griping! That was just a love tap. I couldn't tell from that goofy smile on your face, if you were really awake or under some medication or possibly a magical spell. Don't get yourself all worked up, Colton. I'll leave you alone so you can talk to Eden."

Right before leaving, she added, "That smile was almost as bad as when you were holding Eden's *Key* before you kissed her."

"Wait! Eden, he's not holding that *Key*, is he?"

"No, it's safe around my neck, as always." Eden showed Savage the chain.

"Well, that explains it then."

"Explains what?" asked Eden.

"He's under your spell!" Savage laughed as she walked away.

THIRTY-NINE

AFTER A DELICIOUS LUNCH, WHICH included Andrei's biscuits with the honey butter Royce was known for, they woke Wade.

They used the same routine to wake him as the others, except in his case, the audience was bigger. Eden and Savage stood alongside his cot holding onto his hands, while Colton sat nearby closely watching. As this was his first time observing a person going through the procedure, he did not want to miss a thing. Right on schedule, Essie removed the mask as she had done previously for the others, but this time Royce was monitoring.

In no time at all Wade was blinking his eyes and looking around. His side effects of a sore throat, and being hot, still persisted, but after ten minutes or so they subsided. He also did not freak out when he was introduced to the others, and had no bad dreams, like Savage.

Once they were sure all of Wade's readings were normal, they got him up and sat him in a chair next to Colton. Royce gave him some milk and a couple of berry muffins, which Wade immediately devoured. And being the kindhearted person Royce was he, gave Wade another.

While Wade was eating, Essie joined Andrei at Aiden's cot and began assisting him in readying Aiden to wake. After Aiden's vitals reached a certain range, Essie placed the mask over his face, feeding him the enriched air and potions to aid in his awakening.

"Watch this," Colton said, as he nudged Wade.

As soon as Eden and Savage saw Essie placing the mask over Aiden's face, they joined her and Andrei. Savage slid her hand into Aiden's and sat down alongside him on his cot while Eden, holding his other hand, remained standing. Within a few minutes Aiden's eyelids were blinking and he was waking.

The first person he saw was Savage. As a huge smile spread across his face, and he said, "I thought I lost you."

Savage smiled, and said, "Not a chance, *Pillow Boy!*"

Feeling an itch coming on, Aiden tried to scratch it, but only then realized Eden was holding his other hand. Looking at her he said, "Hey, Sis. You got any food? I'm hungry!"

Eden laughed and released his hand. Turning towards Colton and Wade, she rolled her eyes, and said, "He's fine!" Colton and Wade teased him in good fun.

Aiden realized, as he was scratching, that Dr. Maxwell and Charles were there along with three other people he did not know, one of them being a beautiful young Latina. Dr. Maxwell did the introductions.

Essie noticed Aiden was scratching and retrieved a container of medical cream.

Savage spotted Essie coming towards them with the container. She was curious about what Essie was going to do with it, and asked her, "What's that for?"

Essie held up the container and said, 'It's for itching. I need to apply it where he is scratching."

Savage thought, "Oh, no you won't! Not if I have anything to say about it!"

Instead, Savage told Essie, as she took the container from her, "Here, let me do that for you. This will be one little thing out of all the many others you do for us that you won't need to do going forward. I'll do it."

Essie tried to object, expressing that experience was needed to apply it. But Savage brushed her off by saying, "Don't worry, I know how to do it. If I had a nickel for every time I've doctored my brother and cousin, I'd be rich!" Essie shrugged her shoulders, turned, and walked away.

When Essie rejoined Andrei, he whispered, "I don't understand why you keep trying to get Aiden to fall for you each and every time loop. You know they're a bonded pair like Minka and me."

Essie patted Andrei's cheek, and said, "You know how I like to practice. What if I get sent on a mission to Earth? I need to know how to handle handsome young men like Aiden."

"Maybe his red hair is making you homesick for the fire pits on your planet?"

Essie just scoffed at his suggestion while shaking her head. Knowing his observation was too close to the truth.

"Yes, but I think you like this particular handsome young man a little too much."

"Well, what if I do? One can only try!"

Andrei only shook his head and laughed as he and Essie went to help the others with supper.

Once Essie had left, Savage cheerfully took the lid off the container and dipped her fingers into the cream. Looking at Aiden, she happily asked, "Okay, where does it itch?"

Aiden told Savage that the itch was between his shoulder blades where he could not reach. Without hesitation, she raised his t-shirt and began applying the cream.

Noting Aiden's expression of relief, Eden told Savage, "Maybe you should put some on his face. It might not only help get rid of that cheesy smile, but the red rash, too."

"What's wrong with my face guys?" asked Aiden. Concerned something was wrong, Colton and Wade were no help as they were not holding back their kidding.

"Nothing! Nothing! It's just a side effect. It goes along with the itching. It just looks a little red," Savage told him, hoping he would stay calm. But it didn't help, because when she got to the red part, Colton and Wade burst out laughing.

"What!" groaned Aiden, noticing as he put his hands on his face, that they were red as well.

"It's okay. It'll be gone in a day or two. Royce had the same thing happen to him. He said to use the cream," Savage said reassuringly. Standing behind Aiden, she looked angrily at Colton and Wade while pulling her finger across her neck.

Eden stood there with her hand over her mouth trying to keep a straight face.

At that point, Dr. Maxwell came over to say, "No need to worry, Aiden. Savage is right. Another day or two at the most, and you'll be back to normal. Oh, and supper will be ready soon."

As he left, he added, "I would give him a good coating before we eat, Unitsi Savage. Royce will give him another coating before bed."

While he was talking, Charles and Andrei came over to help Colton to the table. Next, they moved Wade, who still had a case of rubber legs. In the meantime, Savage had been applying the cream to Aiden as fast as she could. So, by the time they came back for Aiden, he was a shade of pink.

Supper was wonderful. The conversation was great, and the food was amazing. It was good being back together again. Time passed quickly.

After supper was finished, Dr. Maxwell gave the guys a brief rundown of the next day's events including the brain augmentation. He answered all of their questions with help from Charles and the others, then shooed them off to bed.

When Eden and Savage got back from getting ready for bed, Aiden was already snoring, and Wade was out cold.

As Eden and Savage passed them, Savage said, "Poor Aiden, he's exhausted. He'll feel better with a good night's sleep." Eden nodded her head in agreement.

"Yeah, maybe by tomorrow his skin will be cleared up. Good night!"

"Good night!"

Savage went to her cot while Eden headed to hers. On the way there, she passed Colton, and noticed he was up. "I see your still awake. You okay?" she asked.

"Yeah, I'm good. It's just been a lot to digest, if you know what I mean. Time travel, side effects, and brain augmentation aren't your everyday events."

"Wait 'til you get your IR tomorrow and start learning about this solar system and the Sentinels. You'll have even more questions than you did at supper."

"I bet! But Eden... there's one question I have left that no one would be able to answer but you."

"Okay... Colton. What is it?"

"While you were sitting on my cot last night holding my hand, you said something but didn't get to finish it before that Andrei guy came in."

"What... what did I say?"

She was right! Colton could hear her. "Darn, he'd heard every word I told him!" she thought.

"You said, 'Given time, I could...' but then stopped. What I'd like to know is what were you going to tell me?"

Looking down at him lying there, she bent over, kissed his cheek, and said, "You'll find out soon enough, Colton."

FORTY

EDEN WOKE THE NEXT MORNING TO LIGHT rain, and apprehension. Tonight was the night they were to have their brain augmentations. Even though she had been reassured it would only enhance her natural abilities, she still felt uneasy about it. Tomorrow morning when she woke, she may never again be herself.

Glancing around the room, Eden noticed that she was the first one to wake, but then again that was not surprising as she always was an early riser. Having become a little familiar with Savage's habits, she knew it would not be long before she would be awake as well. She also took notice of Royce, who was on the other side of the room, methodically going about his morning routine.

None of the guys being awake was a surprise to her. It had been her experience that most guys would manage to get up early for fishing, hunting or sports, but other times they were bears to wake, especially if they were like her brother, Aiden. Then again, they had a pretty rough day yesterday so she thought she would cut them some slack for another hour or so.

Swinging her legs over the side of her cot, she stretched first before quietly sliding off.

Underneath the cot, on a shelf, was a container with recessed handles that held her personal items and the clothing Essie gave her.

After selecting a clean set of clothing, she was about to leave when she heard yawning coming from Savage. "Great! She's awake. Now we can get ready together, then come back and harass the guys," Eden thought happily.

When Savage woke, she yawned and rolled to her side. Rising to her elbow, she looked around and noticed Eden standing near the exit, trying to get her attention. As she watched, Eden put her finger up to her lips and then showed her the clothes, waving for her to come.

Savage slid off her cot and reached into her container, getting her clothes. Soundlessly she made her way across the floor to the exit and Eden. As soon as she caught up to Eden, they waved goodbye to Royce and left the room.

Once in the corridor, they hurriedly made their way to the section housing the individual cleaning rooms. On the way there, Eden told Savage about her plan to pester the guys if they were not awake once they got back. Savage, being Savage, was all in.

Upon entering the room designated for female humans, they proceeded to prepare for the day. And while they were getting ready, they talked about the day before. As Eden stepped out of the shower area she happened to look over to her left. The door connecting one of the rooms used by nonhuman Sentinels caught her attention. As she cautiously approached it, she realized it was oddly covered in condensation.

She thought it strange since she did not remember it being that way the day before. She tried opening it to see what was causing it, but it would not budge.

Taking the towel she had wrapped her hair in, she began wiping off the upper panel in the door. She had managed to wipe off half of it when she thought she saw movement deep within the room. Dropping the towel, she cupped her hands closely around her eyes, keeping out any light and pressed them against the door to get a better look. Unfortunately, the reflecting light from both rooms and the condensation made it difficult to see anything.

As her eyes were beginning to adjust to the light in the other room, she thought she saw the flick of a tail along with beautiful wispy fins. Shocked by what she thought she saw, she looked again.

It was just at that moment, Savage tapped Eden on her shoulder, asking, "What the heck do you think you're doing?"

"Geez! You just scared the crap out of me, Savage!"

"Oops! Sorry! I just wanted to know where they keep the floss. Although, I do have to admit, that expression on your face was funny."

"Listen, I think I saw something in the other room, and you're not going to believe what it was!"

"Okay, what do you think you saw?"

"A mermaid!" Eden whispered.

Seeing disbelief on Savage's face, she said, "You have to believe me! Look, for yourself!"

Eden pulled Savage in front of the door so she could have a look, but the door was fogging over again. Picking up the towel, she began clearing it off. Halfway down the door, Savage nudged her.

Wondering what Savage wanted, Eden stopped and glanced up at her. Savage was staring weirdly at the door while pointing at it. When she looked to where Savage was pointing, she dropped her towel. For there, floating in the water on the opposite side of the door, was the most beautiful creature Eden had ever seen, a mermaid!

Eden noticed the mermaid's features were very fine and delicate. She appeared to Eden to be around her and Savage's age, or maybe a few years younger until she studied her eyes.

Those green, almond shaped eyes were the eyes of an old soul.

The mermaid's long black hair floated away from her face, spiraling around her body causing her flawless skin to blush like a pearl. Although her skin was smooth, Eden could see patches of almost translucent, silver and gold scales reflecting light here and there along her arms and torso. They became thicker and more distinct over her breasts and around her hips going down to her large wispy fins. Here they appeared tipped in a deep forest green, the same shade as her eyes.

The mermaid waved her hand as if in a greeting. Eden was observing her long fingers and long dagger-like nails, also tipped in the same green, when she heard a voice.

"What did you say, Savage?"

"Ah... I didn't say anything."

"Well if you didn't say anything, who was it?"

"It was me!" laughed the mermaid, as she flipped backwards displaying her beautiful fins.

"I said thank you for thinking I am the most beautiful creature you have ever seen. That was very kind of you. It is also nice to finally meet you and Savage." Eden and Savage were astounded that the mermaid was communicating telepathically with them!

"Yes, you both are hearing me, and I am hearing your thoughts as well.

Let me introduce myself. I am Sumi. I wanted to meet you both before your brain augmentations tonight. I thought seeing me might help put your mind at ease, since I have gone through it myself. And maybe, once you are reassured, then you can help the young men.

I come from a water planet on the far side of our Galaxy, called Nibi. I have been with the Sentinels after I became an orphan at the age of nine, which was many millennia ago. So, your observation about my eyes was correct, Eden.

When I had my augmentation, I was concerned as well, but afterwards I was happy I had gone through with it. I found it enhanced the abilities given by the Maker by adding greater understanding and physical attributes. I did not lose anything but fear, and in return, I gained so much more."

"Thank you, Sumi."

Sumi touched her temple, saying, "No need to speak. I can hear your thoughts."

"Will we be able to do this after the procedure?" asked Savage.

"No, this ability only occurs after much practice and many, many years of growth. But you will be able to read each other's body language without saying anything a short time after the augmentation."

"Good! I wouldn't want anyone to know what I was thinking all the time, especially my brother, and cousin."

"I understand! But I will tell you, it is rude and considered bad manners to read someone's mind without a verbal invitation from, or a willful opening of that person's mind.

Now, I must let you both finish so you can get back and speak to the others. There are many meetings for me to attend today. Tomorrow I will come and see all of you before you begin your training.

It was nice seeing you both again. But I do hope this will be the last Time Loop where we must meet again for the first time. Twelve Time Loops have been more than enough.

Oh, and Eden... now what was that Earth saying? Yes! I have it! Remember, 'Beauty is in the eyes of the beholder.' Not everything beautiful is good, or everything that is ugly is evil. Trust your Memory Keeper."

Sumi bowed gracefully to both Eden and Savage before taking her leave. Quickly smiling, and with a flick of her fins, she was gone.

FORTY-ONE

THEY HAD BOTH JUST SEEN AND SPOKEN to a real, live mermaid!

"Amazing! I wonder if all the beings on the Water Planet in this solar system are as beautiful as Sumi?" asked Eden.

"I was wondering that, too. Of course, they could have lifeforms that look like an octopus or a crab, or something totally different. Just imagine it! When we get back to the Recovery Room, we'll have to check out the Water Planet on our IRs."

"Great idea! I have so many questions, my head is spinning. Let's ask Royce or one of the others to start us in the right direction."

Once they were in their changing areas, Savage said, "Eden, I don't mind asking Royce or Andrei, but I really don't want to ask Essie for help."

"Why, what's wrong with Essie?"

"I don't like the way she looks at Aiden. Haven't you seen how she acts around him, all sweet and helpful? If I'm not right there assisting him, she drops what she is doing and rushes right over to help him. Didn't you see what happened last night when he needed more ointment?" asked Savage.

"I just thought she was trying to be helpful."

"Yeah, but you and Aiden didn't see the smirk she gave me, cause her back was towards you both. After that, I wasn't about to let her touch him, let alone rub ointment on him."

"Really, she smirked at you, I wonder what her game is?" asked Eden, pausing before exiting her stall.

"I don't know, and I don't care, except that it's not gonn'a be Aiden, if I have anything to do with it," Savage said, as she shut the door behind her.

Eden was trying to remember something she had been told on the first two days after she woke. "You know, Savage, I remember Royce mentioning to me that Essie stays on the Demon Class planet in this solar system, which means she was originally from one. That makes sense, because Dr. Maxwell also told me she is a shapeshifter and only changed her form to make us more comfortable with interacting with her."

"So, you're saying she's not really human?"

"Yup!"

"Wow, I'd never have guessed that! I mean, she looks like some gorgeous Hispanic fashion model."

"Yeah, which makes me wonder why she chose the form she did. She could have picked any human form she wanted if having us being comfortable around her was all it was. So, why did she pick that one?"

"I have no idea."

"I don't get it either, but I have my suspicions. There must be another motive behind picking out that form other than for our benefit alone. I mean, she, Royce and Andrei are supposed to be part of our extended team, so I don't think it's malicious.

Besides looking at our IRs when we get back, I think I'll also question Royce and Andrei and see what I come up with."

"That sounds like a plan," Savage said.

Savage began brushing her blonde hair vigorously. Eden could tell she was still agitated and said, "Woah! Take it easy or you'll be completely bald by the time you're done."

"Yeah, you're right. I really need to keep Essie from getting under my skin."

"Yup! Just remember she isn't human and may have motives we might not understand."

"Just as long as those motives don't include Aiden, I'll be fine."

Eden set her brush back on the counter in her area. Opening a cabinet, she reached into it and pulled out a container of floss. Tossing it to Savage, she said, "Here's that floss you wanted."

"Thanks! I almost forgot after meeting Sumi."

"Now that we're finished, let's head back. Maybe the guys will be up by now."

"Don't count on it."

Eden laughed.

Walking into the Recovery Room, they immediately spotted Wade sitting tentatively on the edge of his cot, while noticing that Colton and Aiden were still asleep. They did not see any signs that Andrei and Essie had shown up. Savage was relieved.

Joining Wade, Savage asked, "How are you feeling this morning?"

"I woke up feeling pretty good. But the longer I sit here, the more I want a cup of coffee."

"I feel that way about my morning tea. Give me a second. I'll get you a cup from Royce," Eden said.

Savage sat down beside Wade on his cot. "Glad you woke up feeling good, Cuz. Hey! You will not believe what Eden and I have to tell the three of you!"

But after seeing his face, she added, "Maybe we should wait until you have that coffee first. You're looking a little green."

Savage, moved off Wade's cot when she spotted Eden coming back with a mug and a pot of coffee, and with Royce right behind her. She knew Royce would help Wade to his chair, and Wade needed that coffee ASAP.

"Good morning, Wade! How about I move you to a chair? I think it'll be more comfortable to drink your coffee there. Don't you think?"

Assisting Wade down off his cot, Royce gave him a minute to stand on his legs before moving him. Once Wade was ready, Royce walked along with him giving him minimal support.

As he sat down, Royce said, "You did quite well! Your strength is coming back nicely. By tonight, you'll be back to normal."

"Well, that's good to hear!" said Savage.

"Here's your coffee. Black, right? I'll just put the pot here in case you need another.

While you're enjoying your coffee, Wade, I think Savage and I have some sleepyheads we need to wake." Eden nudged Savage.

"Please, whatever you two have planned for those two, be gentle. Yesterday was rough," Wade begged sarcastically.

"Oh, don't worry! They're in good hands," Savage laughed.

"I don't doubt it!" laughed Wade. He saluted her with the mug before taking another sip of coffee.

Then he sighed, "I wish Mia was here. Seems like ages since I've seen her." Savage ruffled his curls, then kissed him on the top of his head.

"Yeah, so do I, Wade. But just remember, with the advantage of time travel you'll be seeing Mia at the same time you would have anyway despite all this happening. She'll not have the chance to miss you."

"Somehow, that doesn't help me missing her now."

"As they say, absence makes the heart grow fonder."

Standing at the end of Wade's cot waiting, Eden asked Savage, "Which one do you want?"

Savage laughed, "Are you kidding? You know it's gonn'a be, *Pillow Boy!*"

Eden smiled. She was hoping Savage would pick Aiden. Her brother had been subjected to her pranks since they were in the womb. To her, Colton would be far more fun and much more interesting to prank than him, besides it meant she would get to be close to him for a few minutes without several pairs of eyes on them.

As she reached Colton's cot, she saw Royce handing Savage a container and saw him mouthing the word 'cold'. Eden guessed if that container held more medicine for Aiden's rash, it appeared Aiden might be getting a rude awakening anyway.

Eden sat on the edge of Colton's cot, but he looked so peaceful lying there that she found it hard to disturb him. She brushed the hair from his eyes and ran her hand gently down his jaw line. Her touch did not wake him, but he did make a few facial expressions.

Leaning slightly forward, Eden took some of her long red hair and used it to tickle his face. The first few times he only turned his head away. The third time he swatted at her hair, but still did not open his eyes.

She tickled him again, moving her hair slowly across his eyes and lips again. This time his eyes cracked open, ever so slightly, to find her smiling at him.

"Good morning, sleepy head!"

"Morning…" he said looking around, "you know, Eden, if we were alone, I'd be tempted to kiss you right now."

"Remember… I said next time you wanted a kiss, you had to ask."

But he was interrupted by a sudden commotion coming from a few cots away. It appeared Savage was happily applying the cold medical cream to Aiden's bare back as he loudly protested.

After she had satisfactorily covered it, she moved onto his chest, arms, and legs; wasting no time in applying the medicine to any other spot on his body that was still the slightest red.

Only until she had deemed all the remaining rash covered, she stopped. "Foiled by my sister again!"

After having a good laugh over her brother's slight discomfort, Eden turned her attention back to Colton, as Wade raised his second cup of coffee to Savage.

"Here, let me help you sit up. Then I'll get you some coffee."

Colton allowed Eden to assist him sitting up, not that he really needed it. His strength was back, and he could walk without assistance, but he did not mind Eden pampering him. It was nice to have her fussing over him, besides giving him a chance to be close to her.

Colton was aware Eden had noticed he was not wearing his tank top when she helped him sit up. He did not think anything of it as it was normal for him to sleep without any type of shirt. But for some reason, this time, it made him feel a little awkward. So, when Eden went to get his coffee, he slipped it back on.

As soon as he had, he was angry with himself. Why was he feeling uncomfortable about it? Last night everyone was dressed in a tank top and shorts to sleep in. In fact, besides him, Aiden and Wade were still dressed that way.

He was confused. He knew girls were always noticing his physique, but it had never bothered him before. He could care less about it, but with Eden it was different. At that moment, Colton suddenly realized that he was developing feelings for Eden. Strong feelings.

He wanted to blame it on that darn *Key* she wore around her neck, the *Memory Keeper*, and the kiss he had given her after Ciara's attack, but he knew better. His heart had started pounding the first time he had laid eyes on her. That mass of glorious red hair, and those hazel eyes that seemed to pierce the depths of his soul, matched with her quick wit and strength had won his heart from day one.

When they were in the cave, and Dr. Maxwell told him that he and Eden had been betrothed in another time loop he thought Dr. Maxwell was crazy. Even after he had heard the music, felt the softness of familiarity on their lips, and recognized the carved stone box and gold broach, he still had doubts, until now.

As he sat there brooding about it, he was curious to know if this was how Wade felt about Mia. When he got a chance, he was going to have a talk with his cousin to feel him out about it. But right now, he would try not to think about it as Eden and Royce were coming his way.

R.L. Roush

Colton slid off his cot and walked by himself to his chair, sitting down near Wade. Royce hovered nearby in case he needed assistance. Once he was settled, Eden poured him a cup of coffee, then handed him the cream to add to his liking. Wade, nursing his second cup, clinked his mug to Colton's.

Just as Colton was taking his first sip of coffee, Aiden showed up, helped to his chair by Royce with Savage assisting.

"Looks like you're not near as red as you were last night, Aiden. You only have a few blotches left that I can see. Seems like that medicine is working."

"You can quit your grinning, Sis. I saw you. But, yeah, most of the redness is gone, and I'm not near as itchy either."

"Well, if you do get itchy again, I have the cream Royce gave me. I'll be more than glad to hit those spots anytime you need." Everyone laughed.

"Are you hoping I'll need it just so you get to use that cold cream on me again?"

"What makes you think that?" Savage, grinned.

At that moment, Royce walked over and handed an IR to each of the guys. "Here you go. I thought Eden and Savage could get you started on learning about this place. You have some catching up to do. They already have a head start on learning about this system, and the Sentinels."

"What are these things," Aiden asked, as he examined the device in his hands.

"They're called IRs, Informational Relays. They're a lot like a tablet, but way more. Let Eden and me get ours and our chairs and we'll show you."

"If they're like a tablet, I think I'll be able to manage."

Aiden began playing around with his IR when an adorable animal suddenly appeared in front of him. "I don't think the sound is on. I can't hear a thing."

"Maybe you should just wait until they can show us," Wade suggested.

206

"Yeah, good idea, Aiden. That creature looks like it's getting ticked off," added Colton.

"No, I got it. It must be this configuration right here."

At the moment Aiden moved to touch his screen, the girls were on their way back from retrieving their chairs and IRs. They saw that the creature Aiden had accidentally pulled up was a Snot-fluffer. It was angry. And it was ready to spray. But before they could shout a warning, Aiden touched his screen releasing the safety, allowing the Snot-fluffer's spray to make full on contact with the three guys.

Eden and Savage stood there with their mouths hanging open. In the background of all the stink, and the guys hollering, they were vaguely aware Royce had shut down Aiden's IR from the Master IR.

Looking at Eden, Savage said, "Well, they did need a shower."

FORTY-TWO

ROYCE COULD NOT STOP LAUGHING. The scene in front of him was just too hilarious!

The Snot-fluffer thoroughly sprayed Aiden before Royce could reach the Master IR to adjust the safety protocols controlling Aiden's IR, and now all of the guys would need to be deodorized.

Aiden, who was still holding onto his IR, had received the brunt of it. Colton, who moved quickly, only had a small section of his back sprayed. While poor Wade, who was still a little wobblily on his legs, was sprayed completely down his left side. But it did not matter how much they were sprayed, all of them were dealing with the effects of the smell, trying not to vomit.

In the chaos that ensued, Eden and Savage had been spared. They were left trying to gain control of their gagging reflex by breathing through their mouths as the odor permeated the room.

The smell was the first thing Royce worked on removing by upping the air flow and exhaust, then releasing an anti-smell agent into the room. Next, he quickly wiped down any surfaces, and items the spray may have had splattered onto with the same agent. He was in the process of maneuvering a hover gurney for Aiden, and Wade, when Andrei, and Essie arrived.

"Whew! Smells like someone in here got sprayed by a Snot-fluffer," laughed Andrei.

Essie holding her nose, complained, "You big tin can! You go ahead and laugh! At least you can turn off your olfactory glands or whatever you call them, while the rest of us can't."

"Don't worry, Essie! It won't last long. I already adjusted the air flow and wiped down any surfaces that were hit. Once we leave to get these young men deodorized and showered, everything should clear out of here in a minute or two. I think your pretty nose can handle it for that long."

"What I don't understand is why you're complaining. You went through the same training as us on noxious smells, plus you live on a Demon Class planet to boot!"

"Well, it's different now, Andrei. I'm in human form." Essie said, glancing over her shoulder at Aiden.

"Okay, stay here with the girls, and finish getting breakfast ready while Andrei and I take the guys to get cleaned up. That way you won't have to put up with the smell any longer than a few minutes."

"But I can ...," Essie objected, before being interrupted by Royce.

"No, that's okay we got it, Essie. Colton can walk on his own, and we can put Wade and Aiden on the hover gurney."

They moved quickly to get Aiden, and Wade onto the gurney and left the room with Colton following behind them. The girls could hear Aiden apologizing to everyone as they proceeded down the hallway, with Royce lightheartedly reassuring him that he was not the first and would not be the last.

As soon as they had left the room, the smell did dissipate quickly, just as Royce had said it would. And they were finally now able to breathe through their noses.

Eden, shook her head, saying to Savage, and Essie, "Knowing Aiden, things could have been worse."

After that, Essie immediately went to the kitchen and began working on Royce's preparations for breakfast, pretending not to be upset about being excluded from assisting with the guys.

"Do you need some help, Essie?" Savage asked, politely.

"No, I'm good. But I wouldn't mind if you both checked the IRs for any damage and around where the guys were sitting, just to be on the safe side. I believe Royce got everything cleaned up because we would still be smelling some odor if he hadn't. I just don't want to find a surprise once they're back."

"Sure thing." Eden answered. As she passed by Savage, she touched her on the shoulder and nodded her head towards the chairs. Savage joined her. Together they looked but found no

R.L. Roush

other places the Snot-fluffer spray had hit. It appeared that Snot-fluffers were very accurate when they sprayed.

Next, they examined the three IRs that Royce had given the guys. After a thorough check, they found they were all in good shape and looking forward to teaching. Once they checked the safety settings to make sure they matched the safety settings on theirs, they set them back on the guy's chairs.

As Eden placed Aiden's IR on his chair, his IR said in a childlike voice, "Thank you! I don't like Snot-fluffer stink!"

"You're welcome! Neither do we!"

Since the guys were not yet back, and they had finished what Essie had asked them to do, they approached her again to ask if there was something else she needed help with.

"Well, I guess you could go ahead and set the table for eight since Dr. Maxwell and Charles won't be having breakfast with us this morning. He just let me know they'll be tied up in meetings with Sumi and the Council all morning but assures me they'll be back in time for lunch."

"Poor Dr. Maxwell! He'll be missing out on having his biscuits and honey butter," Eden said.

"Not to worry! I'll save him some."

It didn't take them long to set the table for breakfast. All they needed was for the guys to make their appearance.

Essie, receiving a message from Royce on their progress, passed it on to Eden and Savage as they finished with the table. "Looks like it's going to be about an hour before the guys get back. So, if you two don't mind, I'm going to check on your training area, and the dorm rooms to see if the secondary team has everything in place for the morning. No sense in running around checking everything right before we need to move you in."

"Sure, no problem! Do what you must. We'll be all right on our own. We'll just do some studying."

"Well, now that we're alone, Eden, let's get our IRs and check on that Demon Class planet, and what Essie looks like in her true form," Savage said.

210

"Good idea! Let's hurry though, before everyone gets back."

It wasn't long before Eden found the information they wanted on their IRs. "Look. It says here the planet is toxic for most humanoid life, and that the lifeforms that do inhabit it are not carbon based."

"Hmm," answered Savage.

Once they were on the same page, they continued to view the planet's biosphere together.

"Here it says that the lifeforms on the planet are mostly silicone based, which allows them to survive and thrive in the volatile environment. This adaptability to overcome extreme conditions enabled their species to develop the ability to shape shift using it as a defense against the environment, and predators."

Quickly looking around to see if they were still alone, and seeing that they were, Eden then projected the true form holographic image of Essie's species, the Ayurea.

"What! This colorful crystal looking statue-like creature is what Essie really looks like?

That's unbelievable!" Savage exclaimed.

"Shh! Not so loud. We don't know when they'll be back," Eden stressed.

"Oops! Sorry! But it's so hard to believe that she really looks like this, isn't it? Is this a female? Or do they even have males and females?"

Eden was surprised at the appearance of Essie's true form as much as Savage, but the more she looked at it, the strangeness of it began to wear off. "Yeah, they have both female and males. The males have different colors. This image is one of a female. Beautiful isn't she?"

"What do you mean? She looks like a colorful, crystalline statue, with extremely dangerous looking sharp edges. It's like something you'd see in a modern art exhibit. Definitely not giving off a Huggy-Feely type vibe."

"Yeah, but if you think about it, having the ability to shapeshift must be amazing!"

R.L. Roush

"I guess so," said Savage, trying not to judge all Ayureans by Essie's actions.

Eden turned the movement and sound modes on so they could watch the way the image moved and hear its true voice. They were both surprised when the female began dancing gracefully and singing. The voice reminded Eden of wind blowing about leaves in the Fall on Earth. Savage agreed.

After they turned off the image, they continued to study the Demon Class planet and how its inhabitants lived. The more they learned the more comfortable they became with the differences between the Ayureans and Humans. When it came down to it, their goals and aspirations were not much different.

Before long, they began to hear the voices of the guys, Royce, and Andrei in the hall. The hour had passed quickly for them.

Walking in, Royce announced, "Well, we're back, clean, and hungry! These three anyway, because I'm always hungry."

Andrei was maneuvering the gurney with Aiden and Wade seated on it, while Colton followed. When they reached the table, Royce helped them off the gurney and onto their chairs. Once they were settled, Savage went to the table and sat between Aiden and Wade to help.

Eden sat between Colton and Aiden at the table. Once she was seated, she took a deep breath, and said, "Oh yeah, you guys do smell better, much better than normal. No more stinky brothers, and cousin."

While Andrei was returning the gurney to a medical storage area, Essie arrived. "I see I almost timed that perfect," she said as she walked in.

"Breakfast is ready when we are. Charles notified me that they have meetings this morning but will be back for lunch." In no time the food was placed on the table, and they began enjoying the hearty breakfast Royce, Andrei and Essie had prepared for them.

After breakfast was done, everyone, except Aiden, pitched in and helped clean up. When they were finished, Royce chased them back to their chairs with Savage assisting Aiden, much to Essie's annoyance.

212

Once they were settled, Eden began instructing them on IR usage. She explained that IRs were also AIs but not fully sentient like Andrei. She told them that they respond to the emotions of the user within parameters and could learn to anticipate the user's needs over time. She also explained that Royce had reset all the overrides to safe mode so they would not have another disaster like this morning's. Of course, the guys grumbled at this.

When all the technical lessons were finished, Eden and Savage informed them that they had met Sumi that morning and explained everything that had occurred. At first, the guys thought they were playing a joke on them when the girls revealed that Sumi was a mermaid.

Savage had to do her childhood pinky swear with Colton. Immediately, they wanted to check out the Water World, but Eden stopped them. She explained that they needed to start at the beginning like Royce had shown her.

After their momentary disappointment, they were soon using their IRs, without difficulty, learning about the Sentinels, their core beliefs, and the solar system they had created. Time studying seemed to pass quickly, even though it was intermittently interrupted with Aiden occasionally saying, "No way!" or "Unbelievable!" When they finally took a break, it was almost lunch, so they each hurried off to clean up, except Aiden, who still needed assistance.

Colton and Savage assisted Aiden much to Essie's displeasure. Wade was now able to walk completely by himself, although Eden stayed close until they reached the female section of the individual cleaning rooms. Here Eden and Savage left them to continue the short distance to the male section.

Before long, they were back together in the Recovery Room, where they found Dr.Maxwell and Charles awaiting them.

As they sat to eat, Dr. Maxwell told them that Sumi had sent her best for their speedy recoveries. He also told them of her desire to meet with them before their augmentation tonight unless there was an unforeseen situation. If there was, he told them that she would instead visit with them tomorrow morning, like she had told Eden and Savage, before starting their training.

213

Although Eden and Savage wondered how her visiting would be possible either time.

Dr. Maxwell enquired how each of them were feeling and expressed how happy he was with their progress. He also mentioned that their recovery was speeding along much faster in this Time Loop than in the previous loops. Secretly, he was hoping that this was a good sign that this Loop would be the last.

As they continued their conversation, Eden and Savage mentioned to him and Charles that they taught the guys how to use their IRs and were now in the process of learning about the different worlds in the Sentinel Solar System. Eden was in the process of explaining how she found the Water Planet, where Sumi was from, to be so beautiful. After which, Savage mentioned the odd silicon-based lifeforms from the Demon Class planet.

Eden immediately noticed Essie's eyes narrowing, and her muscles tensing when Savage had mentioned her planet. Grabbing onto her *Key*, Eden quickly added, "Yes, we could never imagine how different the lifeforms there are from us, but also how beautiful they are in spite of coming from such a hostile environment compared to ours, or the Water Planet's."

Eden's statement seemed to appease Essie, for now. She took note and decided to ask Dr. Maxwell about Essie when it was just him and her.

Lunch proceeded without much drama after that. As soon as it was finished and cleaned up, Dr. Maxwell and Charles left to go meet with the team in charge of setting up the next phase of their training, while the five of them went back to studying.

Eden, feeling anxious, reached for her *Key*. But it was not thinking about the training that was bothering her. It was the augmentation.

As she sat there contemplating what was coming that evening, and the following two weeks of training, the *Key* began to pulse gently. Fortunately, it was reassuring like a purr and not the dangerous pulse. Just like a purring cat, it gave her some comfort.

Unaware, she was slowly being drawn into another memory. Swirls of color began pooling around her, and shapes, and figures began taking form. Suddenly, she was in another time, and place.

Standing at the center of a village, she was watching a group of native children playing lacrosse, when a young boy around nine or ten scored. Suddenly she heard herself cheering and felt herself raising her spear into the air in celebration.

When the boy turned to her and smiled, her heart was bursting with love and pride.

Then just as the children were readying to begin again, from the woods behind her came a loud commotion of whooping and hollering. Spinning around to see if it was friend or foe, she readied her spear while at the same time beckoning the boy to join her.

As the child was putting his arm around her waist, through the woods burst, Aiden, Savage, Colton, and Wade, along with a few other people from the village, carrying two large buck deer tied to poles towards the entrance of the village.

She remembered how six months ago they had walked out of the cave on Little Beaver Creek, and right into the middle of the villagers Spring Planting celebration. The village Medicine Woman had deemed that they were the Messengers that she had foretold of only a week earlier, so they were immediately made members of the tribe. Since then, they had been living there, learning their way of life. Hunting was part of it.

As soon as Eden saw who was doing all the shouting, she relaxed her stance. From what she could see, it appeared that they had great success hunting today and that there would be full bellies in all the lodges that night. Looking down at the boy who was holding onto her, she bent down and kissed his head, saying, "It's okay. Go play."

When she looked back at the hunters, they were now inside the palisade being greeted by other villagers. She also noticed Colton had left them and was now headed her way. As he walked across the open plaza, she could tell he was excited about their hunting success.

Colton, wearing the same garb as the men he had been hunting with and of those in the village, was also carrying a spear along with a sheathed knife at his waist, and he had pulled his now longer, dark hair back at the nape of his neck. As she watched him approach her, she thought he was the most handsome man in the world.

As soon as Colton had reached Eden, he pulled her close with one arm, and beamed down at her, saying, "Did you see what we got in today's hunt?"

Eden, caressing his chin with her freehand, ran her thumb gently across his lips, and said, "Yes, I saw." As she guided his lips to hers.

"Eden! Eden!" A voice in the distance was calling her. It sounded vaguely familiar, like her brother.

Relishing Colton's kiss, she did not want to open her eyes to see what Aiden wanted, but the voice was persistent, bordering on annoying.

Finally she sighed, slowly opening her eyes, only to find Colton looking at her with a mixture of surprise, and another emotion she was not exactly sure of, splashed across his face. She also suddenly realized she was still holding onto his chin, so she quickly dropped her hand.

She was in shock. She was in the Communal Recovery Room now, not the village. She was left wondering if she just did what she thought she had just done. She immediately put her hand on the *Key*, but it was silent.

Momentarily confused, all she could hear was the murmuring of voices in the background, and all she could see was the concern in Colton's gray eyes.

"Eden? Eden? Are you okay?" he asked.

"Yes. But... I could have sworn I was somewhere else a few seconds ago."

"Well, I don't know where you were, but I definitely liked how you came back."

FORTY-THREE

"WHAT IN THE WORLD WAS THAT ALL ABOUT, Sis?" demanded Aiden. He was upset. Being her twin, he could feel something was off with her.

"It was that *Key* again, wasn't it?" asked Savage.

Wade had no idea as to what was going on since he had never actually seen the *Key* in action before this even though he had held it and had heard its fiddle music. The others were going in and out of the Communal Recovery Room and had not witnessed what had happened.

"I think Savage might be right. Eden, can you remember what the *Key* was showing you?" Colton asked calmly, even though his blood was still pounding in his ears from Eden's kiss.

Eden sat there for a few seconds, before she spoke, "I was in a Native American village. It had to be around the late 1000s AD to possibly the early or middle 1100s AD."

"How could you know it was that time period?" asked Wade.

"It was the pottery I saw. Early Monongahela Period."

"Don't forget Wade, our parents are archeologists whose specialty is early Native Americans. We learned a lot growing up because they dragged us everywhere with them. Eden's especially good with pottery," stated Aiden.

"Yeah, that's right! I remember her dad showing her some at the dig site and she knew what it was. Sorry!"

"That's all right. It's not a usual hobby for a seventeen-year-old girl."

"Go ahead, Eden. Finish telling us the rest. We promise not to interrupt again," urged Savage.

"I was watching the village children, especially one small boy around nine or ten. They were playing a type of lacrosse, and he scored. I was cheering, holding my spear into the air. I was so proud! I felt in my whole being that I loved this little boy like he was my own.

They were readying to play the next round, when I heard shouting coming from outside the village. I thought we were being attacked. I called the boy over to me. When he reached me, I looked up and saw all of you, along with some of the villagers, coming out of the woods carrying two large buck deer."

All at once the guys interrupted Eden wanting her to go into detail about the two deer, but Savage stopped them.

"Once I saw it was all of you, I told the boy to go back to playing. I watched as you all carried the deer into the village. Once you all were through the palisade, Colton left the group. I could tell he was happy about the hunt as he walked across the plaza towards me. When he got to me, he put his arm around me, and asked if I saw the deer. After I told him I had, that's when I kissed him. When I opened my eyes, I was here."

"Wow! I was with the hunting party?" Savage gushed in surprise.

"Yeah, you were carrying a bow, and hollering just as loud if not louder than the rest of them."

"Well, what do you know!" Savage said pleased.

Then Colton asked, "Think Eden. Is there anything else you can remember that you can tell us?"

Eden sat there and thought for a minute before saying, "Yes, come to think of it there was something. Something I was remembering while you were walking towards me, Colton."

"This isn't about another kiss, is it, Eden? I rather not know when you're kissing Colton in past Time Loops or even in the present one," groaned Aiden.

Eden was sitting next to her brother and could have jabbed him with her elbow after that comment, but Savage was quicker. "Ouch! That hurt!"

Eden continued, "It has to do with our timing, when we showed up there. The day we arrived in that time period, we unexpectedly came out of the cave and strode right into the middle of their Spring Planting Celebration.

On top of it, their Medicine Woman had just told the people the week before we 'magically' walked out of the cave and into their celebration that five Messengers were coming. Because of her prediction, we were adopted as members of their tribe without question.

The day you all were hunting, we had been with the village for about six months."

"Wait, you mean the cave at the dig site? That cave?"

"Yeah, that cave, Colton. Weird isn't it? That cave must mean something to us, to this mission."

"And we were there six months? That's a long time. We could have slipped up anytime. Do you think that the *Key* could have been showing you where we are going? Or was it showing you one of the wrong moves we made in the past eleven Time Loops?"

"I'm not sure, Colton. But the young boy in the memory; that boy felt right. I think he is the one we are meant to find."

"Shouldn't we ask Dr. Maxwell about all this?"

"Great idea, Wade! Let's ask him when he and Charles get back for supper," Aiden suggested.

However, asking Dr. Maxwell now did not feel like it was the right thing to do Eden thought. He had told her to trust the *Key* and herself. To ask him now seemed to her like a failure. That she needed to have him holding her hand, and that she could not decide without him. She knew he wanted her to be making her own decisions. If this was a test, she was determined not to fail it this Time Loop.

"Guys, wait! For some reason, it doesn't feel right to ask him. Not for now at least. Let's wait until we are done with our training, and he gives us our mission parameters."

"Huh? Why not," asked Aiden.

R.L. Roush

"Yeah, why do you feel like we shouldn't ask him now, Eden?" asked Colton.

"Because of my *Key*, the *Memory Keeper*. Remember the night at Dr. Maxwell's cottage, and he told me to trust the *Key* and to trust myself or we would be doomed to yet another Time Loop? Well, this morning Sumi told me almost the exact same thing.

I don't know if this memory is before the mistake I made or after, but I do know the cave, and especially that boy, are very important. He has to be the one we were sent to retrieve."

"What makes you so sure he's the child, Eden?"

"Because Colton... I loved him like he was my own," she whispered.

Everyone was quiet for a moment. Eden's words rang with the sound of truth, and they all felt it.

"Here's what I think. We shouldn't mention this to Dr. Maxwell until he informs us where we are being sent. That way, we'll know for sure that what the *Memory Keeper* was showing me truly was before the mistake I made, since we were still in the village with the child at that point."

"That makes sense," Savage said.

"Okay, now all that's been discussed, maybe we need to get back to studying."

"Yeah, I think you're right, Sis. Before we realize it, it will be time for supper. Hey, come to think about it, I think I'm a bit hungry right now."

Eden rolled her eyes, and said, "That's nothing new. You're always hungry." The others laughed.

As the laughter faded, they thought they heard a disturbance in the hall. Right then, Royce, Andrei, and Essie walked in. Essie looked like she was sulking. Royce and Andrei headed towards their group, and more specifically towards Aiden.

"Okay, Aiden. It's time for some walking," Royce said.

Aiden got up from the chair and took a few steps on his own with Royce standing beside him while Andrei stood behind. Essie, in the meantime, had disappeared into the largest storage room and was making a lot of noise while in there. The girls assumed she was not happy because she was not assisting Aiden.

"You're doing great Aiden! Now, let's head out into the hall."

As they left, Royce shouted, "We'll be gone around an hour, Essie!"

Suddenly there was the sound of something shattering inside the storage room. Eden looked over at Savage, and shouted, "Do you need any help, Essie?"

"No, I'm fine! Thanks!"

Everyone cautiously looked around at each other. Eden shouted back, "Okay, let us know if you change your mind."

"Ah, maybe we should get back to studying," Colton suggested.

"Good idea!" agreed Wade, briefly glancing towards the storage room.

Retrieving their IRs, they began where they left off earlier before being interrupted.

About an hour later, Royce and Andrei returned with Aiden. As they walked into the Communal Recovery Room, Aiden was walking without assistance although he still seemed a little shaky.

"Well, that was a long walk. Your legs must feel like jelly," Savage said, as she patted Aiden's chair for him to sit. Aiden smiled.

Andrei said, "Aiden had the most severe side effects out of all of you. But I'd say they're pretty good now. While he was walking off and on for half an hour, we alternated with some light lifting."

"Yes, then the other half an hour he had a hot shower followed by full body massage," added Royce.

"Yeah, these guys are good! I'm so relaxed now I need a nap," Aiden said, as he closed his eyes, and laid his head on Savage's shoulder.

Just at that moment, there was a loud crash near the food processing unit. Everyone immediately looked that way. It appeared Essie had spilled a large can of vegetable sauce all over the counter.

"Essie, wait! We'll help you clean it up," Royce said, as he and Andrei rushed over to help her.

Eden and Savage looked at one another. They could tell Essie was upset about something, and both had a pretty good idea what it was about. While Aiden was watching the cleanup, Savage pointed at him. Eden nodded in agreement. After how Essie had reacted when Aiden needed deodorizing, they believed she was upset again for not being included in his rehab.

It was beginning to look like Essie was preoccupied with Aiden. Savage was not happy.

FORTY-FOUR

THEY HAD AN UNEXPECTED GUEST AT DINNER that evening.

Sumi, along with Dr. Maxwell, and Charles, arrived at the Communal Recovery Room after a long day of conferences. They all looked tired. Instead of being his normal jovial self, Dr. Maxwell was quiet and appeared to have something on his mind.

Eden and Savage were surprised to see Sumi with them. They had not been informed that she would be coming for supper, as it was a surprise to everyone. Dr. Maxwell had mentioned to them at breakfast that Sumi wanted to be there to give them some encouragement before their augmentation that evening but had told him she was not sure if she would be able to make it.

Eden and Savage were excited to see her again. They were surprised to see her in an air environment and walking on two legs. Where had her beautiful scales and fins gone? And how was she breathing out of the water? They had questions, so many questions.

Even without her fins, Eden and Savage thought Sumi was stunning. The long, flowing, white gown she was wearing draped at the neckline allowed it to sit on the edges of her shoulders. Its long, wide, translucent, slit sleeves allowed the creamy skin of her arms to peek through. Besides a pair of ornate seashell hair sticks that secured half of her hair in a bun, allowing the rest of her long raven hair hang down her back. Sumi wore no other jewelry, or shoes, for that matter. Her persona did not need anything more.

Eden and Savage joined her. Sumi took their hands in hers, and said, "It is good to see you both again. I really wanted to come before your augmentation instead of afterwards, but I was not sure if I would make it if our meeting with the Sovereign Senate ran later than planned. So, when it surprisingly finished early, we decided to take a much-needed break, and eat first before we report the Senate's concerns to the Regional Assembly."

223

Nodding her head towards Dr. Maxwell, Sumi lowered her voice and whispered, "Besides, Dr. Maxwell needs to refuel and rest before then. Even though he and Charles are the same age, he often forgets to adjust for his mishap." Glancing at the tired, eighty-year-old man, Eden and Savage agreed. But Sumi's mentioning of Dr. Maxwell's accident, and his and Charles's age being the same, caught their attention.

Sumi waved Aiden, Colton, and Wade hovering in the background, over. She asked Eden, "Would you mind introducing the young men to me before we eat, please?"

It was then Eden realized that the table was set, and that the food was being placed.

Apologizing, she quickly did the introductions. As she finished, Royce set the last casserole on the table and announced that supper was ready. Happily, they made their way to the table.

Eden chose the chair between Colton and Dr. Maxwell. As she sat there, she could not help but notice the old man seemed to be lost in thought. Before they began eating, Eden placed her hand over his and squeezed it. Dr. Maxwell looked at her and smiled. She felt relieved.

"Thank you, Unitsi Eden," said Dr. Maxwell.

He thought, "Unitsi Eden always knows how I am feeling. Her kindness is a joy to me. And Unitsi Savage, who is always ready for a quest, makes my adventurous side happy."

He sighed. If only they knew what was coming. Still, he could not risk telling them as he had in previous Time Loops, fearful that his fears would doom them to need to repeat yet another one. This time he decided to keep quiet, leaving them to discover these events for themselves, and hoping that Eden was learning to trust in herself, and her *Memory Keeper*.

The friendly banter while passing the food around the table, along with the biscuits and honey butter seemed to pick up Dr. Maxwell's spirits. Even though the conversation was light, he could feel their unanswered questions assailing him, so he decided to broach the second question that was on their minds by bringing it up, hoping it would lead to the answer to the first question that was bouncing around in their minds.

While buttering his third biscuit with a large amount of the honey butter, Dr. Maxwell looked up at Sumi, and asked, "Sumi, would you be so kind to explain to our guests why you now have legs instead of fins, and can breathe our air?"

After slowly swallowing her last bite of food, Sumi replied, "Hmm, I was wondering who would be the first to ask me that. But you surprise me, Dr. Maxwell that it was you, and not one of our young friends."

"Yes, I'm sorry, Sumi. Even though they have questions, I'm afraid our guests are feeling a bit shy tonight, especially the young men." Aiden, Colton, and Wade eyes widened in embarrassment.

Sumi laughed, "There's nothing to be ashamed of. I know this is all new for you. We do not expect you to understand or even begin to envision the technology that you will be learning over the next two weeks.

First, let me explain. I am not unlike you. I had a family I cared about, and lived on a peaceful, beautiful, blue planet with an abundance of water, and a scattering of a islands at its poles. We were a water dwelling race but over eons, and with the aid of our scientists, we developed the ability to create legs and breathe air to inhabit the islands. So, I am not a true shape shifter like Essie.

Now, situated near one of those islands in an underwater village I lived a peaceful life with my siblings, being taken care of by the adults in our pod. At the age of nine, my family was taken from me in an unprovoked war. Soon after, the Sentinels found and brought me here.

They took care of me, taught me, and became my family. When I reached the age of sixteen Earth years, I had the choice to either join the Sentinels, go live on the Water Planet here or go back to my planet. There was nothing left for me on my home world, and even though there were many occupations on the Water Planet I could learn, I chose to become a member of a Sentinel team. I wanted to give back to them in return for all they gave me.

I remember when I was ready for my augmentation. I will tell you the truth, I was scared. The other members of my team were supportive, but my team leader was the one who put my mind at ease. Tau talked through all my fears. So, by the time I was given the sleeping tea, I was so relaxed it worked immediately.

You can imagine my surprise when I awoke and found it was the next morning. It was like I had only blinked my eyes! I never felt more refreshed and wonderful.

As time went by, I found all my natural abilities were enhanced. Cognitively, where learning math had been difficult before, now I can do it with little effort. It was the same for anything physical. Now I have coordination!" Sumi chuckled.

"Once I had completed the two-week team training course, I was sent on missions. Some were just for the purpose of checking on civilizations with developing technologies, and others were for correcting unnatural time distortions.

When I reached twenty-one Earth years, I decided to have upgrades made to my original augmentation. These tweaks were to enhance my extra sensory perceptions, to make communication with my team flow easier while on dangerous missions.

This is what you and Savage experienced earlier today, Eden, when I spoke into your minds when we were in the cleansing rooms.

I know this is a very brief and simplified version of how I have gotten to where I am presently. However, if you have any more questions, I will stay to answer them all up until the time you are given the sleeping tea before your procedure. We can make our report afterwards."

The five of them were amazed. Initially, they were stunned into silence, but it only took a few seconds before they started firing off their questions. One of their questions would lead to another, and sometimes several.

Royce, Andrei, and Essie quietly went about cleaning up allowing them to talk with Sumi, Dr. Maxwell, and Charles. The three of them understood how important it was since they were also in the same position many years ago. But as soon as they were done, they sat down at the table and rejoined the conversation.

After the discussion, they were all feeling more at ease with the procedure they were facing that evening. In fact, their questions were dwindling down the closer it got to the time scheduled for the augmentation. The occasional lighthearted teasing they engaged in also helped to diffuse most of the fear they had been feeling.

When it was time, Royce got up from the table to make the sleeping tea that they would need to drink before the procedure, while Andrei and Essie left and went into one of the attached storage areas. A short time later, they came back with a levitating cart full of sterilized clothing.

Charles leaned back from the table, and began to explain, "The clothing sitting on the cart is what you will be wearing while you undergo the procedure. You'll need to change out of all the clothing you are wearing now and put on these suits. They are one piece. They'll cover you completely, except for your face. Later, after you are asleep, a protective mask will be added to assist with your breathing, and to allow certain medicines to be added as needed.

After you are dressed, you will all go through the bio-scanner. It will take your readings, while sterilizing you for your procedure. The material in the suits will keep you germ free. From there, we will have you each lie down on a hover gurney and take you over to the Augmentation Center.

When you wake up tomorrow, you will be in the Team Training Center where you will live while learning and training for the next two weeks."

"Thank you, Charles," said Dr. Maxwell. "Now, if any of you have any other questions you may have thought of you have a little time left to ask them before you must get dressed. But before we begin, you must first have some tea.

Royce, would you please oblige our young people here? And were there any biscuits and honey butter leftover from supper?"

FORTY-FIVE

Two Steps Back, One Step Forward

EDEN TOOK THE TOWEL DRAPED AROUND HER neck and wiped the sweat from her forehead, as she and Savage walked to the human female cleansing room. That morning's workout was brutal! Essie had worked them all to the bone and Eden was feeling it.

She could understand why Essie was being so ruthless, since this was their last physical training class before they were to receive their mission objectives before lunch. Essie was just making sure they were ready, getting in a little more last-minute fine-tuning. Although it did seem to her that Essie, during all the physical training classes she instructed, appeared to enjoy giving Savage a harder time than the rest of them. But today, she was unforgiving with her. Yet, through the whole two weeks of training, she never once complained.

Dr. Maxwell was the one who had given Essie the job of instructing them in hand-to-hand, as well as in battle tactics. At first, Eden was surprised. She initially thought that Royce or Andrei would be their instructor, not Essie. But, as puzzling to her as Dr. Maxwell's decision to assign Essie to the combat related classes, his decision to assign Royce with teaching time travel theory and STG usage, and Andrei, with first contact and cultural adherence were even more perplexing.

Eden was really looking forward to a hot shower before lunch, but that thought flew out of her head the minute she and Savage rounded the corner on the way to their cleansing room. There they came across a totally unexpected sight; Aiden standing by the door leading to Essie's area with his arm protectively around her shoulders, and Essie looking at him adoringly!

Suddenly Savage angrily threw her towel to the floor, whispering to Eden, "Just what does she think she's doing?"

As soon as Savage moved forward, Eden grabbed onto Savage's wrist, and whispered, "Let me handle this, Savage. He's my brother. I get to kill him first. If there's anything left after I'm done, it's all yours." Savage backed off. Eden was not aware of it, but she was intimating when she got riled up.

As soon as Aiden saw them, he said, "Boy, I'm really happy to see you two! Essie slipped and twisted her ankle! I'm glad I was close enough to catch her before she hit the floor. I was trying to help her into the room so she could sit down before I went to get help."

Eden stopped where she was and looked briefly at Aiden's face. She could tell he was telling the truth. Still, something was not right. Just as she looked at Essie, she caught her deviously smiling at Savage.

Eden quickly whispered to Savage, "Follow my lead."

"Good thing you were here, Aiden," Eden said. "How about I take Essie in, and you and Savage go get help."

"Good idea! Let's go get Royce and Andrei, Aiden." Savage added.

Eden moved fast, not giving them any time to answer before she was replacing Aiden's arm with hers. When she was supporting Essie, she ordered them, "Okay. Now go get help."

Approaching the room's door, it slid open, and she took Essie inside. Once they were in, she carefully sat Essie on a stone bench inside an alcove. Getting down on her knees, she began examining Essie's ankle. It was then she noticed Essie was not acting like the ankle was tender to her touch.

"Does it hurt here?" Eden asked. Essie shook her head no.

"How about here?" she asked. Again, Essie shook her head no, but followed it with a smirk.

Standing, Eden said, "You know, Essie, I don't think your ankle is twisted at all. In fact, I think you pretended to twist your ankle just so you could end up in Aiden's arms. Right?"

"What if I did? What are you going to do about it?"

"Me? Nothing. On the other hand, once I tell Savage, I don't know what she'll do. But I can imagine, especially after how hard you've been riding her these last two weeks during training.

However, I do have one question. Why my brother, and not Colton or Wade?"

Laughing, Essie looked down at her ankle while moving it around. "It's nothing personal.

I picked Aiden because of his gorgeous red hair. It reminded me of the fire pits on my home world, and because I find him to be very intelligent, and kind.

I manipulated his kindness to see his reactions. And I flirted because I needed practice with male humans for when I get sent to Earth for recon on your technology."

Looking up at Eden, she said with fierceness in her voice, "And I pushed Savage because she is, in Ciara's eyes, Bridget, the warrior-poet goddess. She is your protection, not the young men. And, because Ciara is a woman, they may slack off when it comes to fighting her. Savage won't.

Besides, I'm sick of all the Time Loops. Here in this solar system because we are outside Time, we remember every Time Loop. It has become redundant and needs to move forward." Essie, finished answering Eden's questions, was now bored.

"Even though I can't remember any of them, I agree. It needs to end. I can understand your reasons for acting like you did around my brother, although you need to change your methods in order to learn."

"Truce?" asked Eden, extending her hand.

"Truce," said Essie, taking Eden's hand, shaking it.

Just then, Royce, and Andrei came through the door along with Savage, and Aiden. "She's all yours guys."

Grabbing Savage's, and Aiden's arms, she pulled them from the room and into the hall. Once they were there, she then walked them a good distance away from the door and told them what Essie had told her.

"Aiden, you're my brother, and I love you dearly, but you really need to learn when a girl is flirting with you."

Pointing at both of them, she suggested, "And you two need to have a long overdue talk."

"Savage, I'll meet you in our cleansing room when you're done," Eden said, as she left them behind in the hallway, picking up Savage's towel on the way.

"You know, instead of a shower, maybe I'll take a long soak in the tub."

After she had left, Aiden walked Savage down the hall to stand outside the doorway Eden had disappeared into. There they stood for a long time talking about what had just happened.

"I find it hard to believe that you really didn't notice how different Essie was treating you from Colton, and Wade. She was buzzing around you like an Ohio River mosquito, ready to take a bite, since we got here."

Taking Savage's hands in his, he explained, "Savage, I knew, not immediately. It's not like I've had a lot of experience with girls. But with Colton's and Wade's snickering, I eventually caught on. I didn't encourage it. I was just trying to be polite and was afraid I might cause an interworld incident. You know, new worlds, new species?

Besides, Savage, couldn't you tell it's been all about you after the first time I saw you?"

"You mean, the day when you were wearing the pillow?" She teased.

"Yes, then." Pulling her close, he tenderly kissed her.

Several minutes, and several kisses later, Savage said, "Aiden, we need to stop. We have to get our showers, or we'll both be late for lunch, and that will cause us late for finding out our mission objectives, which is after all, the whole point of us being here."

"Yeah, I guess that's a valid point. Besides, we're both stinky from training anyway and could use a good showering. And I'm feeling a bit hungry."

He gave her one more lingering kiss, then said, "See you back at the Training Center." Holding on to her hand, he reluctantly walked away, until he finally had to let it go.

As their hands let go, Savage answered, "You bet, *Pillow Boy.*"

Walking into the room, Savage was beaming. Immediately, she raised her arms, spinning in excitement, followed with a walkover.

He kissed her! Aiden finally kissed her! What she had been hoping for had finally happened at last. Ever since she had first laid eyes on him hiding behind that overstuffed pillow, she knew that they were meant for each other. She was beyond happy!

Although, she had begun to wonder if he was picking up on any of her signals. At home she had no shortage of admirers willing to jump at the chance to be seen with her. She usually paid no attention to them, but Aiden was different. She loved his quiet, assured, easy-going personality, and for a while, she had wondered if she was going to have to do something drastic like initiating the first kiss. Now she need not worry.

Deep in thought, Savage wandered over to the cabinet holding the towels and removed what she needed. Right at that moment, Eden came out of the tub room. Quietly she stood there for a few seconds watching Savage, before saying, "I was wondering when you'd show up."

Savage blushed. Stuttering, she said, "Well… well a… umm… we were talking… a… about a lot of things."

"I'm sure you were talking. Along with all those other things."

"Well, there were a lot of *other* things, you know."

"Ugh! You don't have to go into details. If you're happy with my brother drooling on you, that's all that counts. Though, I'd rather not hear about it!

But you better hurry with that shower. We only have half an hour to get back to the Training Center. All I have left to do is dry my hair and get dressed."

"Oh, yeah!" Savage said, as reality set in.

Hurrying to the shower room, she juggled her towels, while pulling her training tank over her head at the same time. As she reached the door to the showers, and tubs, Eden said, "Hey Savage! Glad my brother is finally talking, you know, about things."

Savage smiled as she disappeared through the doorway.

While Savage was showering, Eden dried her hair and dressed. Allowing her mind to wander, something she had not had a lot of time to do lately, she thought about what Sumi had told them. She was right. When they had woke the next morning, they all felt great, better than they ever had. Still, Eden believed as the day progressed that they would have had some sort of side effect from the placement of nanites, the gene splicing, and the minor structural realignment, but to her amazement no one had any. There were no physical changes to their looks, or personality.

She was pleased with how they had all pulled together to become a well-functioning team. Physically, by the end of the first week, they were able to do world class gymnastics, fight hand-to-hand, and master several martial arts skills. Their interactions with each other had become intuitive. Plus, it took them no time to grasp the concept and application of time travel. Even the cultural historical knowledge they learned had them understanding the past with new eyes.

However, there was a small learning curve using the STGs. They definitely needed the full two weeks to be taught to operate it correctly.

On a personal note, she had been worried about Aiden's interactions with girls. Even though she could feel how he felt about Savage, he seemed to be extremely slow about showing her. Now that he had finally gathered the courage to kiss her, Eden felt relieved. At least that was one issue that had remedied itself. If only unnatural time displacements would.

Eden was almost dressed when Savage came running out of the shower room, "I'm going to have to fly if I don't want to be late."

Pulling on her boots, Eden offered, "Here, let me help. You get dressed, while I dry your hair."

"Yeah, okay! Great," Savage said, as she tossed her wet towels into the bin.

Pulling the drying apparatus over, and above Savage's head, Eden began drying, while Savage dressed. While she dried Savage's hair, they talked more about what Essie had said. They both agreed Essie's explanation did sort of make sense.

When Savage was done dressing, Eden had managed to dry enough of her hair that it was only slightly damp to the touch. It was then that Savage decided not to finish drying it to save time and just pull it up into a ponytail.

Giving herself one last look in the mirror, Savage said, "I guess this will have to do."

"Not bad, Savage, we still have ten minutes to spare!"

Savage was behind Eden when the door slid open to reveal Aiden, Colton, and Wade standing in the hall.

"My! Don't you all look handsome, and clean for once! Okay, how long have you three been standing there waiting, Colton?"

"Not long, Savage. About five minutes. We would have been here sooner, but one of us was running late."

Aiden bent down and pretended to inspect his boot so no one could see that he was red-faced. Savage, put her head down as well, and began moving everyone down the hall towards the Training Center, saying, "We better get moving. We don't want to be late."

Being privy to what had happened earlier, Eden smiled and laughed to herself. Colton caught her, and asked, "What's the smile for?"

Eden whispered, "I'll tell you later."

Aiden and Savage ended up walking behind the others as they moved through the hallways. Coming along aside her, he took her hand in his. While the others were debating where they would be sent as they walked to the Training Center, they remained quiet. By the time it came into view, it seemed to them their walk back ended all too quickly.

Heading to their quarters, they found Dr. Maxwell, Charles, and the others waiting for them in the Team Meeting Room. Essie was there, behaving, and sitting quietly between Royce and Andrei.

They also saw that there were five sets of clothing, their STGs, and five clear bottles containing an unknown liquid sitting on their meeting table. Further glancing around they detected along the outside wall, near the windows, weapons, very ancient-looking weapons. It was all getting real.

"Please, have a seat." Charles smiled.

Once they were settled, Andrei passed a bottle to each of them, as Dr. Maxwell said, "Well, the day you all have worked so hard for has come. It is time for us to send you on your way, but before we do, you need to drink the mixture that is contained in those bottles. It is replacing your lunch today."

Seeing the disappointment in Aiden's face as he handed the bottle to him, Andrei told him, "Sorry about lunch Aiden, but this is how we always start a mission. The recipe is adjusted for the team's particular biological species and individuals, as well as for us AIs. The formula has to be taken on a nearly empty stomach. Once it starts to be absorbed, it will allow you to go without any food or water for at least a week.

Usually a team never knows a hundred percent what kind of circumstances they will be looping into, so this will help provide some nourishment and keep your stamina up. Now, drink it," ordered Andrei. They all drank, finding the liquid to be rather tasty.

Andrei took their bottles when they had finished, setting them aside.

Dr. Maxwell told them, "Although, in your case, we have somewhat of an idea what you will be facing after eleven Time Loops, thanks to the *Memory Keeper*. But we still don't have the exact place you will step through the Time Vortex. Only you will know that, Eden."

"Ah, about that, Dr. Maxwell, I think I might have that answer already, but in order for me to be absolutely sure, I need to know where you are sending us first and how long you want us to be there before I say anything."

Eden had removed the *Key* from under her uniform and was holding it in her hand. There was no pulsing.

"Hmm... this is an interesting development," Dr. Maxwell thought, noticing what she had done. "Well, we are sending you back to Little Beaver Creek area, during Spring, in the year of 1138 A.D. You will be there until first snow, a few months or so after you find the child."

"Okay, that makes sense. Actually, I can narrow the place for you. We will be sent to the cave you showed us with the pictographs. It will be in early Spring, possibly late April, or early May, during the Native Monongahela Planting Ceremony. I also know we will live with them for almost six months, until sometime in late October, or early November. At least, that is what the *Memory Keeper* showed me."

"Are you positive?"

"Oh, yeah!" confirmed Colton. Eden blushed when she remembered the kiss.

"Was there anything else that the *Key* showed you that you think might be important?"

"Yes, the child is a boy around nine or ten. He's our mission, isn't he?"

"Yes."

Dr. Maxwell was handed a piece of leather by Charles with what looked like a map drawn on it. "Now, keep this safe," he said. Spreading the skin on the table, he had them all look at it while he explained what the markings were. It looked familiar to Savage, Colton, and Wade. It was home territory after all.

As they examined the map, most of the markings were self-explainable, but the map had two settlements marked that Savage, Colton, and Wade knew nothing about. One was on Little Beaver Creek hidden from the Ohio River around the third bend of the creek. The second one was up the Ohio River near where the future bridge for Route 376 would be, right where its first northern pylon would be set, just west of Vanport.

"This is where the village you will be staying in is located. According to past memories the *Memory Keeper* holds, the villagers will welcome you. According to Eden's last memory from the *Memory Keeper* in the last loop, it showed her you will be living with them for about six months. However, it did not reveal the reason, but I'm sure the *Memory Keeper* will show Eden when it needs to reveal it."

"Now, about the boy. From past Time Loops, you will find him in the other village, here," Dr. Maxwell said, pointing to the X on the map.

"I can't tell you much more than... let's just say that it will be a dire situation, so be attentive. You don't know what you might be facing.

The child will be an orphan. He will not have been treated well and will be very frightened. He is the one you need to bring to us."

"You will have one side stop on your way back to us. The *Memory Keeper* will give you the coordinates when needed. Trust them, Eden! Once you have them you will understand everything and will be able to tell the others."

"Wade, during this side stop you are responsible for procuring the *object* we talked about earlier today. No matter what, don't let that object slip through your fingers. Many lives are at stake." He then folded and handed the map to Wade.

"Now, let's get all of you into your period clothing, give you your supplies and the STGs before any more questions. We have half an hour before Embarkation. So, no dragging your feet!" Dr. Maxwell ordered.

Each of them took the pile of clothing Royce handed to them and went into their sleeping areas to dress. Andrei followed the guys to help with the proper placing of their clothes per period, while Essie followed to assist Eden and Savage. After a little adjustment from Royce and Essie, they were ready.

Essie helped Eden and Savage braid their hair into two braids and attached the braid wraps. Their headbands were adorned with beads, shells, and a Mother of Pearl disc, and two eagle feathers each. The guys also wore less ornate headbands, but still had the disc and two eagle feathers tied onto them. The feathers represented acts of bravery.

Each of the outfits they wore were more ornate than the everyday wear used by the natives. They all had necklaces of shells, animal teeth, and purple wampum. Along with the clothing, they all carried an ornate bag holding their everyday wear, the personal items they would need, and gifts to present to the village elders and Medicine Woman.

Before Eden and Savage left their sleeping rooms, Essie surprisingly hugged both of them, and said, "You both will do well. I know this because you have been trained by the best. Me!" She laughed. So did the girls.

As soon as they were all together again, Royce handed them their STGs, while Andrei fitted them with their weapons.

Once they were ready, Charles said, "Now, hold onto your STGs. I would suggest not taking them off for any reason, instead, just activate its invisibility mode. Okay, any last-minute questions?" No one spoke up. They were prepared, and although they were feeling apprehensive, they were ready and wanted to get on with it.

"All right then, time to go."

Together they walked out of the Training Center and took the rail over to the Embarkation Facility. Once they arrived, they were led into the building by Dr. Maxwell, who was unusually quiet, and deep in thought.

The building was not new to them. They had toured it their first week there, along with the Embarkation Platform that it held, during one of Royce's classes. He had explained the whole concept and procedure to them, so they knew what to expect. Still, this would be their first time using their STGs to leave this star system without any safety protocols, and by themselves. That made them feel anxious.

Before Eden and Savage stepped up onto the platform, Dr. Maxwell said, "Remember what I told you Unitsi Eden, trust the *Key*, and trust yourself." Turning to Savage he said, "Keep everyone safe, Unitsi Savage." Then he kissed both girls on their cheeks and held their hands helping them as they stepped up onto the platform.

In her place, Eden was directly facing Dr. Maxwell, while the others formed a tight, outward facing arc behind her. Colton was to her right, Savage on her left, with Aiden to Savage's left, and Wade on Colton's right.

Eden checked her coordinates. They were spot on. After pressing the control to send them into the past, they all clasped hands. For the nano second it took before they began to slip though time, she thought she saw Dr. Maxwell smiling and waving goodbye.

FORTY-SIX

AS SUDDENLY AS THE SWIRLING MAGENTA, blue, and gray lights had appeared in front them, they disappeared. Now they found themselves inside a void of darkness.

Colton deployed the lighting device on his STG, which lit up the emptiness surrounding them. Everyone followed suit. Once they could see, they were all surprised, except for Eden, to find that they were inside a cave, and not just any cave. They recognized it right away as the cave Dr. Maxwell, and Charles, had shown them at the dig site, minus the pictographs.

"Okay, I guess we all know where we're at. The *Memory Keeper* was right so far. Now we leave, and see if we run into the Medicine Woman, and the villagers outside."

Colton walked over to the fissure, but before getting down on his hands and knees to crawl out, he first checked the small rock shelf above it. Not finding anything, he then got down and proceeded to crawl out.

Eden knew what Colton was looking for, the promise of marriage, the golden broach in the carved, stone box. Holding on to the *Key*, she knew the broach was not there. It had to have been placed on that shelf at the same time the paintings were done. Curiously, she wondered if the *Key* would show her who had created the paintings and hidden the box on that shelf, but it did not. Following the others out, she wondered if she would ever know.

After they had all reached the corridor, they made their way to the opening of the cave.

Just as the *Memory Keeper* had shown her, they walked out into the middle of the Native Monongahela Spring Planting celebration!

So far, the *key* was two for two.

Two months had passed since they had been living in this time period, and still no sign of the boy.

They had lived with the villagers since they had walked out of the cave and into their ceremony. Believing they were the Messengers their Medicine Woman had prophesied about, the villagers openly accepted them into their small village with no objections.

Throughout this time, they were living in one of two empty lodges. It was given to them by one of the elders. It had belonged to his youngest son, who was killed by a bear while on a hunting trip the year before. Since it had sat empty for less than a year, it only needed minor repairs. The son's widow, having no children, had decided to return to her village hoping to find another husband. As all the single men in this village were too old or too young, and she had no desire to be a second or third wife.

The lodge looked like any of the other thirty lodges in the village, round, covered with mats made from rushes or cattails instead of the bark they used for winter. Being thirty feet in diameter, it was large enough for the five of them, with room to spare. It even had a smaller attached room used for storage, and minor cooking or food preservation. It's hearth, located in the center, was used for most of the cooking and for heat, while the sleeping berths where along the outside walls. It was a typical layout for a Native Monongahela home.

When they had arrived, the villagers had willingly shared their possessions and food with them, helping to outfit their lodge with the necessities they needed. In turn, they joined the villagers in whatever they were doing for food sourcing, such as foraging, planting, hunting, fishing, and preserving. And they lent a hand with any palisade or lodge repairs, canoe building, weapons making, or security patrols. Whatever else the tribe needed, they pitched in and helped. The five of them had become so trusted, they even sat in the plaza with the rest of the villagers to discuss tribal matters.

Over the past two months, they had made friends within the village. The Medicine Woman, who was called Dekanawida, was a woman in her forties. A widow, with grown children and grandchildren, she was small in stature but big on knowledge. She was held in high esteem by the villagers. Even though decisions were made by everyone of age in the village, her ideas and teachings carried weight with them.

As a teacher, she was instructing Eden and Colton in various local plants, herbs for healing and other uses, along with making a good cup of tea, which pleased Eden.

Dekanawida also spent time with Aiden and Savage. She showed them the signs to look for in nature, and the stars, for when to plant, and when to harvest. For every activity in the village, there was a season for it to be done.

She and Wade spent time tracking and studying the animals. He enjoyed learning from her about animals that migrated, the ones that hibernated, and ones that were around year long.

There was also a young family of four in the lodge beside them. The father, Oneida, and the mother, Tala, were in their early twenties. They had two young boys, Sahale, who was five, and Hinto, who was two. They were expecting their third soon.

Eden enjoyed watching how their little family interacted with each other. They treated each other as equals. There was no line drawn between men's work and women's work, although, when it came time to go hunting, the women with small children under twelve, and some of the elderly stayed behind to take care of the crops and the village. It was amazing watching how everyone pitched in and helped even if they did not always agree.

Tala also made pottery which Eden found fascinating. The type of pottery she made varied from the utilitarian to the ceremonial. Eden tried to learn, but it would take her years to get to the skill level Tala was at. So, she resigned herself to assisting her, which meant finding dry grasses to break into small pieces; limestone and grinding it into a powder; or crushing the shells they had gathered from the Ohio River all to use as a temper to strengthen the clay.

Eden could make the coils or slabs to form the pots, but when it came to paddling the pottery to bind it together, she had a mess. Tala would laugh at her, take her attempt at a pot, and somehow make something beautiful out of it. However, there was one thing Eden was good at; decorating the pots before they were fired.

While Eden and Tala were busy making pots, Oneida was teaching Wade how to play a flute. First, Oneida had taught him how to make them; one was larger and from softer cedar wood, the second was smaller and from harder walnut. The larger flute made from cedar produced deeper, more mournful sounds. The sounds coming from the smaller walnut flute produced higher tones.

After practicing with Oneida, Wade actually became very good at it. Many evenings, after the business of the day was discussed with the villagers, he would be asked to play. His tunes were mostly soothing, but sometimes they were light and happy, depending on his mood.

However, Eden noticed when Wade was off to himself, his playing became sad, and hauntingly beautiful. She assumed that was when he was missing Mia the most. After all, it was explained to them that flute playing was a major way a brave showed his interest in, and love for a maiden.

Suddenly, her thoughts were interrupted by the sounding of drums. Listening for a few seconds, she realized they were not an alarm but calling everyone to the plaza.

"I wonder what's up," Eden thought. As she put down the rabbit pelts she was smoking, she picked up her spear and went and joined the villagers. When she reached the plaza, she could see that everyone who wasn't out on scouting duty, was there.

Colton came up behind her. Putting his arm across her shoulders, he asked, "What's going on?"

"Don't know yet. I think Dekanawida wants to speak."

Motioning everyone to sit, Dekanawida waited until they were all settled before saying, "The *Great Spirit* spoke to me during a dream last night." Right away there was an excitement tinged with curiosity rippling through the crowd.

Many of the villagers whispered amongst themselves, while others were bold enough to ask, "What did *He* tell you?

"*He* has told me our crops are planted, the lodges have been repaired, our village is secure, so it is now time to visit our brothers and sisters in our sister village north of us, to trade and strengthen our bond of family."

"This is good, Dekanawida. None of us have seen them since the first snowfall of last winter," agreed Oneida.

"Yes, it will be good to see them again. Now we must decide who will go, and who will stay to watch over the village and crops."

"When should we set out, and how long will we stay?" asked one of the women whose husband was gone on the current scouting party.

"The *Great Spirit* told me we need to leave in two days' time, and we will be gone for a week."

Eden was relieved. Aiden and Savage were out with the scouting party and were due back tomorrow. She knew they would be disappointed if they missed the chance to go.

Hearing a sad sigh to the left of her, she looked and saw Tala sitting there holding her belly. Eden saw the disheartened look on her face, and asked, "Tala, what's wrong? Is it the baby?"

"No, the baby is fine, Eden. It's just that it would not be good for me to walk to and from the village so close to my time and with two little ones in tow. And, Oneida is a good father, and for us to go would keep him from trading the points he has worked on all winter. Because of us, his mind would be divided, and he would not make trades worth their value.

And I am really disappointed I cannot trade my beautiful pots. I was hoping to have good trades for them. One of the women in that village makes the softest deer hide. It would be perfect for the new baby when it comes."

"I can take them, if I am chosen!" Eden volunteered. "I'll wrap them in my rabbit pelts to keep them from breaking. I can trade them for the hide you want."

"Yes! We can put them in my basket so they will be easy for you to carry."

As they were planning, Colton interrupted them, "Eden, I believe Dekanawida wants to speak to you."

"Oh, she does?"

"I'll catch up with you later, Eden. Go speak with her."

"Okay, see you soon, Tala. Colton, come with me."

After overhearing the two young women talking, Dekanawida thought as Eden and Colton came to see her, "The *Great Spirit* has truly sent us Messengers that are pure of heart."

Putting her hand on Eden's shoulder, Dekanawida said, "You and the other Messengers are to go. Many of the villagers feel this will help elevate our status in the eyes of our sister villagers. But the *Great Spirit* revealed to me that you must go because *He* has someone you must find that will be in our sister village.

The *Great Spirit* also told me that when the leaves begin to turn, *He* will give you a message for me. I will wait patiently, for everything has its time."

Eden was confused. She understood that they were to be going with the others to the village to trade, but how did Dekanawida know they had to find someone, and that who they had to find would be in that village?

And the message that she must give to Dekanawida from the *Great Spirit*, where did that come from? They were not given any message to deliver by the Sentinels, so she had no idea what she meant. Eden just nodded her head instead of asking questions.

"Thank you, Dekanawida, for the honor of representing the village."

"Now, go, make your plans with Tala."

Eden and Colton walked back to their lodge, and found Wade, and Oneida standing outside of his, and Tala's lodge talking about the upcoming trip. They overheard them talking about making flutes and flaking more stone points for hunting.

When Oneida saw Eden, he said, "Tala is feeding the children now, she said to tell you she will talk to you about the pottery afterwards."

"That will be fine, Oneida. I know she is busy. Tell her I will be here when she is ready."

"Oneida, and I, are going to check an old walnut tree not far from the village, but I'll be back in time to help cook supper." Colton nodded at Wade, before he and Oneida walked away.

Once inside, Eden took the basket from the wall that held her pelts and sat on one of the sleeping berths. Colton sat next to her while she began to take out the sixteen pelts it held. She needed to check which ones would be the best to take. The eight pelts she was now smoking would not be ready. Besides, she was hoping to give those to Tala for the baby, and the boys.

"Are these the pelts you want to take?" He took one from the basket, feeling the softness of the fur, and the suppleness of the leather.

"Yes. I'm trying to decide which ones would be the best to trade."

"You really did a great job on them, Eden. I think you should take them all."

"You think so? I know they can be used for making winter capes, and for warm clothing for the little ones. The first few pelts have holes from the points I shot, but they aren't that badly damaged that they can't be used."

As Colton placed the pelt back in the basket, Eden was watching him with interest. After taking the basket from her, he reached behind them with one arm to place it back on the wooden peg. While he was hooking the basket, Eden smiled at him almost causing him to drop it.

He thought, "When she looks at me and smiles like that I..." Then without thinking further, he put his arm around her and kissed her.

FORTY-SEVEN

THE MORNING THEY WERE TO LEAVE, THERE WAS excitement in the entire village. Many had been up before dawn, in anticipation of the approaching trip.

Eden, Savage, and Colton were ready to go, while Aiden and Wade were still fast asleep. In all fairness, they were packed and had almost everything ready before bed the evening before. All they needed to do was wash up, eat, and grab their things.

Savage had started a fire in the hearth and got some nice coals going, ready for Eden to start cooking breakfast. She and Aiden had arrived back from their scouting trip yesterday with a clutch of eggs they had found. Wade thought they were turkey eggs because their size, plus the color pattern and thickness matched what Dekanawida had shown him.

Eden planned on cooking those eggs for breakfast before they left that morning. Taking a large, flat, thin stone, as long as the hearth was wide, she placed it above the coals, bracing the ends on opposite hearth stones creating a crude griddle. While she waited for the stone to heat, she cut up some wild onions and carrots to add to the eggs.

Helping, Savage went to a small root cellar located in the add-on and took out a lidded pot setting it on one of the hearth stones. Inside was rendered bear lard. Usually, any lard kept up to six months without being cool, but they liked putting it in the root cellar because it helped to make it a bit firmer in texture, plus the stone-lined root cellar helped to keep the critters out of it.

She also got several strips of deer jerky from a gourd hanging in the add on and began cutting them into small pieces.

As Eden cracked each egg, she inspected it, looking for any fertilization, before adding them to a pot Tala had made her. She found all fourteen eggs were good to scramble. Next, she added

Savage's cut jerky and her vegetables to them, whisking them together with a stick that she had slit several times on one end.

She handed the pot holding the eggs to Colton and reached for the lard. Taking a large spoonful of it, she dropped it on the now hot stone. It soon melted and began sizzling. Taking the pot back from Colton, she poured out the egg mixture onto the stone. Then she said, "Watch this!"

As the eggs began cooking, the aroma started building in the lodge. Stirring the eggs as they cooked, she glanced over at the two sleepyheads to see if the smell of the cooking eggs was working its magic.

"You two better wake up, if you want any eggs. They're almost done, and they are going to go fast!" teased Eden.

Colton, who had already gotten his wooden plate, laughingly taunted them, "Losers weepers! Maybe you should give me my seconds now, plus theirs, Eden."

Immediately Aiden and Wade grumpily got out of their sleeping berths, quickly pulling on their leggings, then tying them to their breechcloths and moccasins. They hurried because they knew Colton was not teasing and would leave them nothing.

Eden was serving eggs to Savage, and Colton when Aiden, rubbing his eyes, picked up his plate, and jokingly said, "Make sure you only give Colton one serving, Eden."

Wade, coming up behind Aiden, said, "Yeah, Colton doesn't need much cause he's just a little guy." Grinning, he playfully shoved his cousin's shoulder.

"You make me spill my eggs, I get yours," warned Colton, laughingly.

Both the girls rolled their eyes, after which Savage scolded, "Hey! Horse play's for outside guys. We eat, clean up and head to the plaza. We don't want to be late!

I know we all washed in the creek last night, but you two need to wash the sleep out of your eyes. And Wade, you have eggs on your chin." Grinning, Wade wiped them off with his arm. Savage held her tongue, and snook her head.

They ate in silence after that. The guys shoved the eggs and leftover flat bread into their mouths as fast as they could.

Cleaning up did not take long with them all pitching in. Besides, they kept a tidy lodge.

While Aiden and Wade washed up the breakfast items, Eden, and Colton got some deer jerky from the root cellar, and fruit and carrots from the baskets hanging on the poles in the add on. Eden and Colton divided some of it among the five of them to put in their bags so they would have something to eat on the trek to the village. They poured water on the fire and made sure it was out. Once that was done, it was time to go to the plaza.

Before they left, Colton helped Eden put the basket of pottery on her back. He had wanted to carry it the whole trip, but Eden would not let him, so they had decided to take turns. She had the first leg. Instead, he took her personal bag containing her ceremonial clothes, slung it over the opposite shoulder from his bag and picked up her spear along with his.

While Colton was helping Eden, Savage eased a second leather bag over Aiden's shoulder containing the necklaces they had made from animal tusks, shells, and wampum. During which time, Wade finished tying the ends of a waterproof hide containing his flutes with cord and slung it over his head and shoulder. They picked up their weapons and headed out the entry. Once they were all out of the lodge, Eden neatly replaced the hide over the flap and tied it down.

At the plaza, they met up with the others who were going. Oneida and Tala joined them. Tala had sneaked out of their lodge while Shale and Hinto were still sleeping so she could send her husband and the others on their way, and to wish Eden good trades with the pottery.

In total, there was a group of fifty or so from out of the two hundred and eleven villagers, not counting the ten who left on patrol yesterday afternoon. All were there to wish them well.

Their group was made up of ten women and fifteen men. Five of the men, and three of the women were older and well respected in the village for their knowledge. Also, one of the older men and his wife had a daughter and several grandchildren in the village

R.L. Roush

they were heading to. Out of the remaining people, were three teenage boys. All in all, they had a good group of capable people.

The man whose daughter was at the other village was leading them as he and his wife had traveled the trail many times. He planned for them to take the twelve-mile trail along the Ohio River. It was the easiest and the fastest way, even though it would leave them exposed on the right as they walked along the river.

As they were leaving the village at dawn, the villagers wished them a safe journey and good trading. Dekanawida was also there to bless the trip.

When Eden was about to go through the palisade, Dekanawida took her hand, and whispered to her, "Good hunting!"

As the sun rose higher in the sky, it burned the fog from the valley and river. They could tell the weather was going to be good; sunny with some clouds, and a light breeze to keep the temperature perfect for walking.

The plan was to reach the village around the evening meal after stopping a mile out so everyone could slip into their ceremonial clothes. They wanted the people in the larger village to know that even though their village was smaller, they were to be reckoned with when it came to trading.

Eden was aware that the people from their village also wanted their sister village to know that they had the five Messengers sent by the *Great Spirit*. Besides feeling that they were honored by the *Great Spirit* with their presence, the villagers believed it would give them an edge in trading. She hoped their strategy worked.

Not much occurred in the first few hours as they made their way north, other than sighting a few deer, and the occasional discovery of bear, and bobcat prints in the mud of the Ohio River looking for a drink. Along the way, they stopped for two quick breaks, but when it was closer to noon, one of the teenagers saw something unusual across the river.

When the sun was at its highest, they decided to leave the trail to rest a bit and eat in the cool shade of a huge oak tree their guide was familiar with. The tree itself, sat back from the bank of the Ohio where the brush along the riverbank ended. It provided them with cover from the sun, soft grasses to sit on, and protection from danger.

Just as they had gotten through the brush by using a game trail to get to the tree, one of the teens showing off to his friend, dropped a beautifully colored point belonging to his father meant as a gift to the Medicine Man of the other village. Fearing he may have lost it, he panicked and got down on his hands and knees to search for it. His friend laughed at his carelessness and left him to find it on his own.

Fortunately, it was not long before he found it. Relieved, he carefully put it back into his bag with the other points, thanking the *Great Spirit* he would be spared his father's wrath.

At that moment, he heard an unusual call. Stealthily, he peeked through the brush, hoping to see what animal had made the sound. Instead of an animal, he saw an unknown man dressed in strange clothing come out of the brush on the opposite shore.

As he watched, the man bent down on one knee, cupped his hand, and took a drink. He had no sooner finished when another man came out of the woods and shoved him, pointing for him to go back. He could see the men having words with one another before both stepped back into the woods.

While the boy was observing them, Eden felt the *Key* begin to pulse. Colton caught her look of concern, and asked, "Eden, what is it?"

"I'm not sure," she told him before the *Memory Keeper* began showing her a memory.

While Eden was reliving the memory, the boy scrambled out of the brush on his hands and knees to get to the others. Wade had just taken out his flute, and was about to play, when the boy came running towards them with fear in his eyes.

Eden came out of the memory as the boy tripped and fell at her feet. "You saw two strange men on the shore across the river, didn't you?"

Once the boy had caught his breath, he told them what he had seen. It exactly matched what the *Memory Keeper* had shown Eden.

"What should we do, Eden? Continue to the village or go back?"

"They didn't see us, Colton, but we need to go to our sister village and let them know what we've seen. Then they can send out a scouting party to determine if they are friend or foe.

We should also cut our visit short to three days instead of seven. I don't feel comfortable leaving our village without them knowing about this. In the meantime, one of us should go back to make sure our village is secure."

All of the villagers agreed with her. Once they were finished talking, one of the younger men volunteered to return.

After a half-hour rest, and some food and water, they decided to leave the river trail and take the closest inland route not far from that location. It would add a few more hours to their walk, putting them at the village two hours later than planned, but it was necessary for their safety.

Before leaving, a few of them went back to the river's edge, to make sure any footprints were removed, leaving behind a false trail in case someone came looking. The rest of them gathered their belongings, being sure to leave nothing behind, then headed inland towards the trail.

When they reached the trail, the man who had volunteered, handed over his trade goods to his friend, who would trade them for him. He then bid them a safe journey and ran off down the trail heading back to their village.

When the others caught up to them, no one said a word of greeting, as they were only acknowledged with a nod or two of the head. Everyone was as quiet as they could be going forward.

Surprisingly, the trail was not hard, and they made up time which helped to ease their nerves. When they were about a mile out, they briefly stopped to put on their ceremonial clothes just as they had planned. In twenty minutes or so, they would be safe in their sister village, or so they hoped.

FORTY-EIGHT

AS THEY TREKKED DOWN THE HILLSIDE above the village, the trail opened. They were able to see the village spread out before them alongside the Ohio River. As they approached, some of them noticed a few of the village's watchers standing back in the tree line. When the elder guiding them and those watchmen happily greeted each other, they finally felt safe.

When they had entered through the palisade, they were met by a large group in the plaza excited to see them. They first gave the proper greetings, but before any of the gifts to the Medicine Man and elders were presented, they informed them of the strangers they had seen along the Ohio river.

Within a few minutes, two small scouting parties were assembled. They were instructed to remain unseen, to only observe, and not to engage unless attacked. After a few days, send one brave to report, sooner if they found the strangers to be unfriendly.

One of the scouting parties was dispatched east of the village where they were to find and join the weekly scouting party sent out four days ago. They then formed into two groups, with half going north then east, and the other south and east crossing what was known to Colton, Savage, and Wade as the Beaver River. The second party was to wait until dark, traverse the Ohio River, proceeding southwest scouting the trails.

Once it was dark, and after the last of the scouting parties had left, only then did they feel it was the proper time to present their gifts to the Medicine Man and the elders of their sister village. The unique point the young man had brought the Medicine Man as a gift from his father, was well received, along with the ceremonial pot Tala had sent with Eden. Once all the customs were completed, they were welcomed to join their sister villagers in the plaza for a special evening meal.

R.L. Roush

It was dark when they put their items down in a grassy area of the plaza where they would be spending the night and most likely trading their goods tomorrow. Eden assisted Colton in removing Tala's basket and the two bags he had insisted on carrying since they had left the oak tree, then they joined everyone.

Excitement over the arrival of the five Messengers, and their smaller sister villagers was running high despite the fear that strangers were spotted earlier that day. Many of the villagers were eager to see what they had brought to trade tomorrow, and for the chance to show off their goods.

The children of the village, picking up on the excitement of the adults over the arrival of their special guests, were vying to get close enough to see and possibly touch them without incurring their parents' anger, especially the two young women and the young man with the strange colored hair. Grandchildren of the couple who had led them were among them.

Eden enjoyed interacting with the children running in the plaza catching fireflies, and occasionally attempting to tug hers and Savage's braids. As the children played around them, she was secretly looking for the boy she had witnessed in the memory the *Key* had shown her. However, she did not see him among these children.

She was becoming concerned. The *Key* had shown her that he would be here, and Dr. Maxwell had told her he would be here. Dekanawida had even told her he would be here. The only thing she could think of was that he could possibly be with the other children tasked with protecting the village crops that night. She may not find him until tomorrow morning when those children returned after the villagers went out to their fields in the morning.

That evening, everyone from their village volunteered to help their sister villagers, either with the cooking or with the setting up of the deer skin lean-tos they would need for sleeping.

Savage and Eden were glad for the lean-tos. It meant that it would help keep the dew or rain off them while they slept. The three teenage boys from their group were eager to sleep under the stars around the campfire, along with some of the teenage boys they had met from their sister villager.

254

As soon as the meal was ready, everyone gathered in the plaza and ate. There was a variety of grouse, duck, pheasant, and turkey, along with deer, fish, and clams from the Ohio River. They also served wild rice with squash and beans. And, for those with a sweet tooth, there was blueberries, cherries, boysenberries, and wild honey.

After the meal, many joined in dancing around the campfire, while the Medicine Man and elders passed the tobacco pipe. After several lively dances by the young people and a few elders, the celebration was brought to an end. Parents began to gather their children to return to their lodges.

Out of breath, Colton dropped down alongside Eden, who had sat this dance out. He leaned back on his elbows and watched her while the campfire light reflected off her face, catching the golden highlights in her hair. He was captivated by how beautiful and serene she looked.

Sitting up, he leaned in close, and whispered, "Any luck in finding the boy?"

Eden whispered, "Wherever he is, he's not in the village now, even though the *Key* showed me he would be here. Maybe after the older children come in from guarding the crops tomorrow."

She looked worried. In response, Colton picked up her hand and kissed her palm. Before letting go, he squeezed it, whispering, "Don't worry. I'm sure you will find him before we leave."

Eden reached over to brush away the hair hanging in his eyes. He laughed, "At the rate it's growing you'll be able to braid it soon. Or better yet, I could cut the sides and sport a Mohawk." Eden smiled. Colton had a way of making her feel better.

The young woman, who was sitting near Eden holding her sleeping toddler, asked, "I saw how you enjoyed being with our little ones. Do you two have any children of your own?"

Her question caught Eden completely unaware and left her speechless. In desperation she looked to Colton for help.

Colton told the woman, "Not yet! We are only just betrothed."

The woman nodded, then stood effortlessly while still holding her child. As she looked down on them, she said, "I see, but do not wait too long. It's best to have children when you're young and can keep up with them. It is late, and I must get my children home. I hope the *Great Spirit* blesses you both with many children after you are joined. I will see you both tomorrow during the trading." Eden and Colton gave her their thanks and goodbyes as she left.

As soon as she was gone, Eden asked, "Betrothed?"

"You're forgetting about the golden broach! You do realize we've been betrothed for over a thousand years."

Before Eden could answer Colton, Aiden and Savage plopped down next to Eden. "Hey Sis, what's going on?"

"Well, apparently Colton and I are betrothed again."

"What? Wait! I'm confused."

"Don't worry, Aiden, it's the same old, same old. Remember the golden broach and the *Memory Key* showing us stuck in Ireland?"

"Oh, I get it, Colton! But technically, it hasn't happened yet, unless you're counting the Loops."

"I think we deserve to count them, Aiden, since this is the twelfth."

"Well, if you look at it that way, Eden. Then I have to agree, you two are betrothed."

At that moment, the dancing finished. Many of the villagers had already left, and those still there were settling down around the bonfire or reluctantly making their way back to their lodges. Those of their village without family here, were making their way to either the lean-tos or to reed mats placed near the campfire.

Wade, who was asked to play, pulled out the larger of his flutes and began to play a song he had composed for Mia. As he played, beautiful music could be heard throughout the village, allowing over-excited children to fall asleep and weary parents to remember the days when they were courting. Soon nothing else was heard except the flute.

After changing out of their ceremonial clothes, their group quietly made their way to their lean-to to get some sleep. Eden could only hope that tomorrow would prove to be successful.

FORTY-NINE

EDEN LAY UNDER THE LEAN-TO LISTENING to the birds in the trees begin their morning chirping. The sun was not up yet, but she could hear some of their sister villagers getting ready to go tend their fields. That meant the children who were guarding the crops last night would soon be returning. She hoped to find among them the child the *Memory Keeper* had shown her.

Savage, started to stir. Rolling over, she found Eden awake. Rising to her elbow, she motioned to Eden to exit the lean-to.

Understanding what Savage wanted, Eden wiggled out from between Aiden and Savage. Once she was out, Savage followed. Both stood there for a bit, trying to stretch out some of the stiffness their overprotective siblings caused after making them sleep between them last night, all in the pretense of protecting them.

Eden and Savage quietly reached for their bags, then their weapons; Savage grabbed her trusty bow and Eden her spear. They each had their obsidian blades as well. Once they were ready, they set out to the river to bathe.

Yesterday, when they arrived, they had both noticed a small stream east of the village.

They thought it would be a good place for bathing, so they headed there. When reaching the mouth of the stream, they noticed that it had created a small strip of land arcing out into the Ohio River creating a shallower area on the south side of it and deeper on the north. There was also a small island a little further out in the river that would add some privacy.

"This is perfect!" Eden said. Savage agreed.

They removed their moccasins and set them, their weapons, and bags on a large rock on shore, then they removed their braids. Eden then took a small gourd from her bag before walking

R.L. Roush

straight into the water fully clothed. Savage followed right behind her. Once they were in the pool, they submerged.

When they broke the surface, Savage moaned, "Oh, how I miss hot water!"

"Same here, but at least the river is warmer than it was two weeks ago, besides the augmentation is supposed to help us put up with colder water." Still, knowing that did not help. Savage was right. The water was cold.

Grabbing the floating gourd, Eden removed the twig that was sealing the open end and poured out a mixture of dried yarrow and a few other local plants. Before she began rubbing the mixture into her hair and onto her skin, she replaced the twig, and tossed the gourd to Savage. Savage did the same.

Slipping out of their clothing while still in the water, they both used the same mixture in the gourd on their tunics and leggings, washing and rinsing them thoroughly. When they were done, they spread their clothing on some of the large rocks nearby to dry. Then they swam around for a bit longer, watching as the sun's beams streaked across the morning sky.

After leaving the water, they took out their wooden combs and redid their braids. As they were finishing, they thought they heard voices coming down the path to the river.

"Do you hear that?"

"Yeah, Savage, some of the villagers must be coming for a morning bath."

"Or laundry."

"Or both," smiled Eden. "Whatever the reason, we better get dressed." Eden knew the augmentation helped them to hear further than the normal person, so she was aware they had more time than normal. Still, they did not want to take any chances.

Quickly they put on their ceremonial tunics, then pulled on their leggings, tying them to the tunic and their moccasins. They were strapping their blades to their belts when the first villagers appeared.

After greeting them and engaging in some casual conversation, they gathered their wet clothes and weapons, then headed back to the village. They had to prepare for a full day of trading.

When they reached the plaza, they noticed that the guys were gone from the lean-to, including Wade, along with the boys he had slept with around the campfire. They both hoped that the guys had decided to go to the river to bathe, since they were beginning to get a little ripe from the long walk and the dancing.

In their abstinence, Eden and Savage quickly went about spreading their wet clothing over the top of the lean-to so it would dry in the sun during the day. Wearing wet clothes on their trek home tomorrow would be miserable.

Once their clothes were set out to dry, Eden and Savage removed one of the reed mats from their lean-to, so they could sit in the sun and eat some of the food they had brought along. They knew the guys would be along eventually.

As they ate, Eden was relentlessly watching, constantly keeping one eye out for the boy.

She knew her chances to find him would be better closer to noon, after the children who were guarding crops last night had a chance to sleep and have something to eat.

Watching the villagers bringing their goods to the plaza, Eden said, "We have to find the boy today, Savage. He has to be here somewhere. If we don't find him, we fail. I don't want to have to go back and tell Dr. Maxwell we need to do another Loop."

"Remember when Dr. Maxwell told you to trust the *Key*? Didn't your mind link with it and learn it's pulsing? And hasn't the *Key* shown you memories that are correct along with ones that went wrong? It showed you the boy would be here before we left on this mission, and it showed you we should leave here on the third day when we were under the oak. All these things tell me we are on the right path. Don't start doubting yourself now. He'll show up when it's time."

"Yeah, you're right, Savage. I just don't want to go back and start all over, and I don't want to get us stuck in Ireland again all because I panicked again."

"That's not going to happen this time. I believe in you."

"Thanks! That means a lot," Eden said, as she tugged on Savage's braid. At that moment they saw the guys coming across the plaza towards them dressed in their ceremonial clothes.

"Well, at least they changed into the right clothes. Let's just hope they bathed first."

After they reached the girls, they threw their wet clothes out to dry, then they sat in the grass. Eden and Savage handed them their packets of food and teased them about how clean they looked.

"Yeah, I hope you guys remembered to wash your ears, Colton and Wade."

Colton threw a kernel of corn at Savage, and said, "Don't worry, we dunked our heads under the water a few times or so, that should be good enough." Savage moaned, knowing that could possibly be the truth.

When they were done eating, they set up to do their trading.

They replaced the mat under the lean-to and took out their goods, arranging them in front of them much like their fellow villagers in the additional lean-to's. Oneida, who had been visiting with his wife's sister, who was the daughter of the elder who had guided them there, joined them. He set about displaying his axes, awls, and points next to them.

"Oneida, who is the woman who makes the soft deerskin Tala wants?"

He pointed his finger at a woman directly across the plaza from where they were. She was busy spreading out hides in front of her mat. He said, "That is Tekeni Ehnita. Be warned, Eden. She is very cunning when it comes to trading."

"Well, we'll see just how good she is, Oneida. I promised Tala I would get her the softest deer hides that she makes for your new baby. I'm not going to let Tala down."

Oneida grunted in acknowledgement. He had learned that Eden was fierce when it came to the people she cared about. He and his wife, Tala, happened to be some of them.

Without being obvious, Eden could see from her vantage that there were two hides, one lighter and the other a bit darker, that seemed to fit what Tala had told her to look for. As she watched covertly, Tekeni Ehnita pulled them closer to her. Her actions cued in Eden that she prized these hides more than the others. Aware of it, Eden knew she had her work cut out for her.

Eden began looking over Tala's pots and her rabbit pelts trying to come up with a strategy. As soon as she had decided on one, a woman sat down to trade for one of Tala's larger, utilitarian cooking pots. After some bartering, the woman gave Eden thirty-four elk teeth, and a strand of wampum in exchange for the pot. After the bargain was struck, the woman took the pot and walked across the plaza smiling.

Eden noticed the woman sat down beside Tekeni Ehnita, and assumed they were either good friends or possibly sisters, since there was a resemblance. The woman handed her pot to Tekeni Ehnita. She immediately began to examine it. Satisfied, she handed it back to the woman with a look of satisfaction on her face.

Eden had another woman with a toddler, soon after the first, that stopped to look at her rabbit pelts. She looked at the hides that had cuts from the points and chose four of them. She wanted to use them to make winter boots for her child, so she did not need perfect pelts. She traded Eden a large stone around two inches in diameter, that looked like a rose. Eden thought it might be barite.

After the woman had left, Eden stood up to stretch and look around. She noticed their villagers were doing well trading their goods. Savage, who was sitting next to her, had already traded two of the five necklaces they had made. One trade was with a young warrior, who traded for a necklace made of purple wampum, and for Wade's lower pitched flute. Eden thought, "I wonder who the lucky maiden is?"

When Eden sat back down, she noticed the woman who had the hides was coming across the plaza towards her. Instead of watching her approach, Eden pulled two of the best pots closer, smiled at them, setting them in front of her. This would cause the woman to believe that Eden prized these pots like the woman had her deer skins.

Sitting down in front of Eden, the woman began checking out the pots. She found one much like her friend's or her sister's and set it next to her, but her eyes kept returning to the two pots Eden had set in front of her. Eventually she picked up one and examined it. Eden noticed how the woman's eyebrow slightly rose in interest.

Yes! She was interested in it. Eden had her where she wanted her! Now she just had to nail the bartering.

After some friendly going back and forth, Eden gained the two hides, which she later found out from Oneida were buckskins, along with another good quality deer hide for her. The cost was three of Tala's pots for the buckskins, and eight of her better rabbit skins for the other. She thought it was more than a fair trade.

The day progressed with more trading taking place. Everyone was doing business. Wade traded his smaller, high-pitched flute for two large points, which he immediately used when he later went off to hunt with Colton, Aiden, the teenage boys from their village, and two men from their sister village. Savage traded two more of their necklaces leaving only a smaller, feminine child sized one made of pink shells. Even Oneida had traded most of his axes, awls, and points, and a new bow. He had managed to barter for a baby rattle woven from reeds that he knew Tala would love for the baby, and two small drums for the boys.

Eden stood to stretch her legs. The thrill from all the good trades she had made was dampened by the fact she had not seen any sign of the boy. Worry was starting to creep back in. She wanted to take a walk around the lodges to see if he could possibly be there doing chores keeping him from coming to the plaza, but she still had three of Tala's pots left to trade, and Savage did not know enough about them to get a good trade.

Eden grabbed the *Key* hanging around her neck. When she did, Savage noticed and said, "Don't worry, Eden, you'll find him. I just wish there was a way the *Key* could have printed out wanted posters so we would also know what he looks like, and then we could have passed them out in the village."

"Yeah, that might have helped but it probably would have scared the villagers out of their wits. But what would have been better is if it could have given the memory to each of you so you all would have known what he looks like, too."

"You know, it's crossed my mind that this could be a test of trust between you and the *Key*. Everything that Dr. Maxwell talked about, learning to trust in the *Key* and in yourself is bound up in this situation."

"I thought about that too. I just need to quit being a 'worry wart', like Pap Walker likes to calls me."

Since she was standing, Eden began flipping their clothes, so the sun would thoroughly dry them. Savage stood to help her.

As the girls finished, the guys were back from hunting. They waved to them from across the plaza.

"Looks like hunting went well, Eden." As the guys set their catch down near the campfire, they could see they had acquired several types of game.

After Aiden rushed to Savage, he said, "We did okay. But not as good as we would have if you had been with us." His admission made Savage smile.

When Colton and Wade arrived, they propped their weapons along the lean-to. Then Colton said, "We are going to go help dress the animals so they can be cooked for the gathering tonight. We've decided to give our hides to the two sister villagers who came along.

Seeing their friend still trading, Colton shouted at him, "Oneida, how about joining us when you're done?"

"Yes, I'll come as soon as I can."

"Savage, why don't you give me your last necklace so you can go help them. That way my brother will stop looking like a lost little puppy."

"Aw, no I'm not, Eden!"

"Yeah, she's right. You do!" smirked Wade.

"Oneida, why don't you give me your awls, too. I can trade them for you, then you can go with them. Besides, if you all help, it will create good relations between our villages."

Oneida handed her the few awls he had left and went with them. While they all headed to the campfire, Colton stayed behind with Eden, "You going to be alright by yourself?"

"Sure. Besides, this rise that the lean-to sits on is a perfect vantage point for me to watch for the boy."

"Yeah, I can see that. But this has to be so frustrating for you Eden! I wish we knew what he looked like so we could help. Do you think if I held the *Key* that it would show me?"

"I don't know, Colton, but you can try." Eden took the *Key* from around her neck and handed it to him. Colton wrapped his hand around it, but there was no pulsing, no memories, nothing.

"Well, that didn't work this time," he said, handing her the *Key*. "I wonder why."

Eden then explained to Colton what Savage had said earlier about it possibly being a test of trust, and he agreed.

Right then, a few women from the village came to trade, so Colton took his leave to go help with the animals. Eden watched as he left, then turned her undivided attention to the women.

One of the women was wife to one of the men who had gone hunting with the guys. Since her husband was given half of the hides, she traded Eden for the two awls, and Eden's remaining rabbit furs. She explained to Eden she was making a rabbit cape for her youngest daughter for winter and needed another thirty skins to finish before winter.

Eden accepted a leather knife sheath for the awls, and a small child-sized, leather bag for her remaining rabbit skins.

The second of the women traded a large willow basket for the two smaller of the three remaining pots. And the last woman traded a beautiful buckskin bag decorated with dyed porcupine quills for the last and largest of the pots. Everyone left happy.

That left only the child-sized necklace. Eden had an idea about what to do with it but needed to talk to Aiden and Savage first.

After putting it into the bag she had traded for her rabbit skins, she noticed some of the people were packing up their remaining goods, while others were busy making the fire for cooking in the plaza.

The sun was starting to dip in the west. More and more people began to arrive bringing more food. It soon would be time for supper. As she watched, she noticed several children she had not seen before and began studying them. However, they were either too old, too young or girls.

Sighing, Eden finished packing up all her trades, readying for the early trek back to their village tomorrow morning. As she was putting her last item away, she began to hear a loud whooping coming from outside the village palisade. Standing up to look, from her vantage point she noticed people were heading to the palisade's entrance. Curious, she decided to join them to see what was happening.

As she approached, she looked for the others but did not see them. So, she continued to move forward until she caught a glimpse of the Medicine Man's feathers.

Making her way towards him, she came to the edge of the crowd and stopped. There in the middle of an opening created by the villagers was the Medicine Man and two braves she did not recognize. They seemed to be weary and sweaty, as if they had been running for quite a while.

As she watched, they took a small person from the back of one of the braves and laid them down gently in front of the Medicine Man. Kneeling, he proceeded to examine the person laying at his feet. After a few minutes, he stood and looked over the crowd, until he found Eden's face.

At first, Eden was puzzled, until the Medicine Man stepped away and revealed who was laying at his feet. As her eyes fell to the lifeless figure lying on the ground, see saw that they were lying with their back to her.

As she watched, the figure moaned, rolling onto their back. Suddenly, her whole being filled with recognition. It was the boy!

FIFTY

HE WAS UNCONSCIOUS. QUICKLY SHE KNELT and immediately began to examine him. She found a small gash on the right side of his head near his mohawk that had been bandaged with cattail fluff, a poultice of its roots, and wrapped with rawhide. Other than the cut, she could not find any other obvious injuries. So, as she had been taught, she secretly used the medical mode on her STG that was kept in stealth mode.

To the villagers watching, it looked as if she was examining him just as they would have.

When she was done, she looked up at the Medicine Man. He asked, "Is this boy who the *Great Spirit* sent you to find?"

Surprised that he knew about their quest, she was momentarily caught off guard by his question and hesitated a second before answering him. "Yes, he is. What's happened to him?"

"These men are part of our weekly scouting party. They were patrolling north of the village. The other party we sent out yesterday after you arrived. That group told the first party about strangers being seen and the plan for them to divide into two scouting parties.

They became part of the scouting group that went north then east. They told me, before the sun was up today, they came across the bodies of nine travelers that were attacked by a raiding party, near the mouth of Shenango Creek.

After quickly examining the site and reading the signs, they determined that the group was caught unaware with no time to prepare. They believe those of the group not killed were taken captive by the raiding party. They also found the group's belongings had been looted.

These two told me they almost missed the boy because a female had fallen on top of him, hiding him under her. They were wedged between two large rocks. If the boy hadn't moaned when they walked by, they would have missed him to go on with the others to find the attackers.

From the signs, they could tell that he was running with his bow drawn towards the attackers, when he was hit by an arrow and rendered unconscious. They could also tell that the woman was shot in the back. These two felt she then crawled on top of the boy to conceal him before she died. He was found with this placed in his hand." The Medicine Man then handed Eden a man's necklace made of mountain lion and bobcat fangs, separated by purple cowrie shells.

Emotions began rising inside Eden as she looked at the boy and then at the necklace she held. He was a little child! He was someone's son or brother, or even possibly a grandson. He was viciously attacked without cause, shot, and left for dead. Who would do this to a child, and why?

The necklace that the dead woman put in his hand, proved he was loved, and that he mattered to them. It was unbelievable to Eden that his people were either brutally murdered for the few meager possessions they carried or for the price of a slave.

Eden knew this little boy's life would never be the same. It was then, she vowed that she would love him as her own always.

Blinking back the tears that were threatening to fall, she gave herself a moment to compose her feelings by feigning to examine him again. When she was ready, she stood, looking over those in the crowd. As she did, her and Colton's eyes locked.

Colton nodded his head at her as he stepped through the villagers to go stand at her side.

Soon he was followed by Aiden, Savage, and Wade, silently waiting for her lead. "Thank you for telling us what happened."

Then speaking to the two men, who had willingly carried the child to the village on their backs, Eden said, "Thank you for bringing him here. I want you to know he will be well cared for. I and my companions will see to it."

FIFTY-ONE

AS EDEN WAS LEAVING THE LODGE that morning, she could smell the change in the Fall air.

She paused for a few seconds, allowing her eyes to scan the trees around the village. All they needed was a night or two of frost, and the trees would quickly change into glorious color.

They had already been to the crops that morning before dawn. The corn would soon be ready to harvest next week, and the last of the squash and pumpkins were ready to be picked later this week. Now that they had the day's gardening chores done, she and Colton were getting ready to take Will to hunt for nuts.

Oh, how she loved this time of the year!

Today it would just be the three of them. The others had gone hunting with Oneida and several of the other villagers, trying to stock up as much meat as possible before winter set in.

They had left long before first light. Some of them preferred hunting to caring for crops, especially Aiden. Getting out of pulling weeds and watering, made him very happy.

Savage went along to be with Aiden. But she liked hunting and was actually very good at it, proving herself on many trips. And, since Will was not old enough to go with them, Eden was content to stay here with him. And, wherever she was, Colton was there, too.

The sudden wailing of a baby coming from Oneida's and Tala's lodge caught Eden's attention. However, the crying was soon hushed with a soothing lullaby.

The thought of the baby brought a smile to Eden's face. She was born without incident a month after they had returned from their sister village. Her little brothers, Shale and Hinto, and Eden's Will, constantly begged Tala to let them hold her. And now that she was nearly four months old, the boys' antics caused her to burst into full belly laughs.

Eden recalled giving the pink necklace Aiden and Savage had made after she had included the barite she had traded for, to Oneida and Tala as a birth gift from them all. Tala told them that the baby would wear it for her naming ceremony.

While Eden was reflecting on the past six months, Will burst out of their lodge with all the enthusiasm a ten-year-old could muster in anticipation of their trek into the woods to gather nuts. Immediately he flung both arms around her waist and hugged her. Eden smiled down at him as he held on. Bending over, she kissed the scar on his head.

Seeing that scar reminded her how he had come to them, the day the two braves carried him into their sister village. The day his family was slaughtered.

She remembered how she, and Savage nursed the boy throughout the night with the help of the Medicine Man and the healers. She was so concerned the child would not make it to see daylight, when the Medicine Man eased her worry by telling her that the boy would survive. He knew all along about their quest through a dream the *Great Spirit* had shown him.

As he and she were talking about the child, the *Key* began pulsing. Holding it in her hand, it showed her the strangers. They were heading back north towards the Great Lakes but would return by Fall's end with a much larger raiding party. They and their sister village were in danger.

The *Key* revealed that the people of their sister village needed to leave before Fall's end if they were to survive. The sooner the better. If they did not, what it showed her made her so physically sick she nearly collapsed.

The Medicine Man had seen the effect the *Key* had on Eden, and believed what she told him it had shown her. Without hesitation, he called all the people of the village together to plan. By morning all but a stubborn handful had decided to leave within a few weeks. They intended to go up the Ohio to the Monongahela River then follow it south to several larger, better protected villages in the mountains.

Some of them decided to pack up immediately and go with the Messengers to their smaller village on Little Beaver Creek because they had family there. Others of that group, were to follow in canoes several days later, bringing those not able to take the trails and supplies.

Eden recalled being very cautious when they left early the next morning, due to the strangers, but her fear about the boy's survival was gone. Carrying him on a stretcher, made of bear hide and birch poles, they managed to make it back to their village well into the night.

After a few days of tending to the boy's wound, he regained consciousness. Then began the healing of his heart. At first, he was afraid of his shadow, withdrawn, and at other times almost defiant. As time passed, with all the love and help he was receiving, it changed. Now at least, the night terrors he had a couple times a night, were only happening a few times a week.

Looking into his eyes, she could still see a bit of shadow there, but there was much more trust and love than fear. She could not help but smile and hug him back.

"Unitsi Eden, may I carry one of the baskets with the nuts?"

"Yes, you can. But, still, I think that might be impossible if we leave them behind," Eden laughed.

"Oh, the baskets! I forgot to get them!" he yelled, running back into the lodge.

Colton almost ran into him as he was coming out. "Someone's excited." Approaching Eden from behind, he wrapped his arms around her, giving her a quick squeeze first before kissing her neck.

Eden laid her head back against his chest and sighed. Tilting her head up and to the side, she reached up to bring his head lower and kissed him.

Colton turned her around, for the next kiss. Without thinking, he wrapped his arms around her again, this time lifting her up, so their heads were level.

Suddenly, they heard giggling beside them.

Looking down, they saw Will standing there holding the baskets and smiling. "Kiss her again!" he begged.

Eden and Colton had been caught in the act. Still, that didn't keep Colton from giving her another quick peck before setting her down, causing Will to burst into laughter.

Smiling, Eden took all the baskets from Will, before giving each of them one. Taking Will's hand, the three of them set out for the forest to find nuts.

They walked deep into the woods to where she and Colton had spotted a huge oak tree earlier that summer. Nearby were chestnut and hickory trees that they planned to pick as well.

While they walked, they explained to Will about the different types of trees they were passing, about how they could be used without cutting them down, and how their nuts could be used. When they arrived at the oak tree, they quickly went about filling their baskets. In no time, they were done.

"Maybe we should have brought more baskets, Colton."

'No, I think this is good enough for now, Eden. We'll let the villagers know so they can come and pick some when they have time."

"But... what do I do with these?" Will asked, as he turned around, his arms full of nuts.

Chuckling, they helped him unload them into his basket.

When they had finished, they picked up the baskets and began the trek back to the village, stopping to have lunch alongside a babbling stream. Eden and Colton were enjoying their time together with Will, when the *Key* started to vibrate. Out of habit, Eden grabbed it as it began pulling her into another memory.

Aware of what was happening to Eden, Colton distracted Will by saying, "Hey, Will, let's take a look and see if we can find crawdads hiding out under the rocks in this stream." They took off their leggings and moccasins and began looking.

As Eden began withdrawing from the trance, Will had not noticed. He was having a ball, finding it a lot more fun throwing rocks into the stream to splash Colton than looking under them to find crawdads.

Once Eden had cleared her mind, she said, "I think you two are more wet than the stream."

As if on cue, Colton grabbed Will from the water and began putting on their leggings and moccasins. Then he picked up the baskets and handed Eden and Will theirs before saying, "We stayed here a bit too long. It's getting close to supper, and we better get there before Aiden and Wade. If you know what I mean."

"Don't worry, Colton. Unitsi Savage will be there to stop them from eating everything in sight."

"You got that right, Will."

As they walked away from the stream, Colton glanced at Eden to see how she was reacting from the memory. But whatever that memory was, she was not giving him any clues. He knew that was due to Will being with them. Eden would not want him to be scared.

It took them well over the normal half an hour to get back to the village. Carrying the baskets was not the problem, having an overactive ten-year-old along was. With what was weighing on her mind, it was a relief to Eden to finally see the village when they came out of the woods.

Eden needed to see Dekanawida as soon as they entered the village, but she did not want Will to hear what she wanted to talk to her about. However, she did not need to worry about it, for when they reached the palisade entrance, Dekanawida was waiting for her.

"Just the person I wanted to see."

"And I you."

"Here let me take your basket. Will and I will head back to the lodge to check on Aiden and Wade, and get supper started," Colton said as he winked at Eden. "You stay and talk to Dekanawida," Colton suggested, even though he was dying to know what memory the *Key* showed Eden.

Eden watched them walking off, making sure Will was well out of earshot before saying anything to Dekanawida. What she had to say was not something a child needed to hear.

"Let's walk outside the palisade," Dekanawida directed, seeming to know this would be an unpleasant conversation.

As they began their trek around the outside of the village, Eden said, "I think you already have an idea what this is about. You told me that when the leaves would begin to turn, I would receive a message for you."

"And have you received that message, Eden?"

"Yes, I believe I have," Eden replied as her voice broke.

Dekanawida put her hand on her shoulder. Stopping Eden, she said, "Do not burden yourself with worry over the message. You are only the messenger."

"True, but it doesn't make it any easier to tell you what I saw, especially as the people in this village have become our family."

"Yes, but family will always be family no matter how many miles or how much time separates you. You and the others will always be daughters and sons to us."

With tears in her eyes, she told Dekanawida, "I saw an army of blood coming, the strangers. After it attacks and destroys our sister village, it will find and sweep away our village. And those who remain behind will be taken as either slaves or will be left to feed the vultures and wild animals. I was shown this will happen before the last of the leaves fall.

You must leave the village before two weeks is up. Take the canoes. Follow the Ohio River south until you come to the second largest village on this side of the river. These people will not be of your culture, but they will accept you with open arms. Your children, and children's children will be safe with them. But, after that time has passed, they must move west and follow the Great River north. Settle around the big waters. If they do not go, they will not withstand the storm that is coming."

"The message is much of what I thought it would be. I believe you were given this message so some of us would be saved. I will call a gathering tomorrow after the sun rises. We must prepare. Thank the *Great Spirit* winter is many weeks away."

"There is one more thing, Dekanawida."

"What is it, Eden?"

"I… we cannot go with you. I was shown we must remain behind. We cannot leave until the attack."

Dekanawida's sorrow showed in her eyes. "Yes, I thought it might be as such. It is time for you, and the other Messengers, to take the child and return to the future."

FIFTY-TWO

A WEEK HAD PASSED SINCE THE villagers had left.

Today, was Eden's turn to run patrol between the cave, Aiden, Savage, and Wade. As she was starting her rounds, she recalled the morning that the six of them stood on the banks of Little Beaver Creek waving goodbye to the people who had become their family. They stayed there long after the last of the thirty-five thirty-foot, birch canoes, loaded with families and supplies rounded the bend, disappearing into the morning fog.

For her, it was especially hard saying goodbye to Oneida, Tala, their children, and to her mentor, Dekanawida. She would deeply miss the young woman who had taught her so many things and had become like a sister to her.

Shale and Hinto, along with Will, were too young to understand the situation. They were busy playing on the shore, entertaining their little sister, while the adults were placing their personal items and supplies into the canoes.

It took Will three days to understand that they were not coming back. It was the same amount of time it would take the villagers to arrive at their new home.

Everyone, especially the girls, tried to reassure him that their friends were safe and had not met their death like his family. Even then, he seemed to be anxious when Eden or Savage were out of his sight for long. Even though Will was with Colton at the cave site, checking on the others was one of those times.

She then thought about the information cited in their mission parameters as she ran to check on Aiden. Part of it told them that if a war party approached, it would be from two directions; the northeast trail they had used after spotting the strangers, or from south of the village, up Little Beaver Creek. The information also concluded that any attack would not happen soon after their sister village was destroyed, but closer to a week, since the war party's scouts would need time to explore the area around their sister village and make the discovery that there was another village nearby. The data did not have an exact time, only a time span.

Once the villagers had left, they set their STGs to visible mode. They turned on their proximity alarms to continuous scanning, knowing they would only have fifteen minutes notice if the perimeter was breached.

For defense, they had moved to the cave and set up camp there, making multiple trips back and forth from the village. Taking some of the items left behind and placing them outside the cave, gave the appearance that the tribe had moved to it for safety. The dropping of a few of those items along the way, in addition to their many different sized footprints, created a false trail. They had also decided to wear their ceremonial clothes hoping if seen, the raiding party would think they were performing a ceremony.

One of the items that was dropped intentionally not too far from the cave entrance was Eden's first attempt at pot making. Although the pot was lopsided, she had out done herself on the beautiful design work keeping to the early Monongahela period style. She did not consider it a waste when she destroyed it.

At the thought of that, she laughed out loud, and said, "I wonder what Dad would say about that pot he was examining at the dig site now if he knew that I had made it."

A minute later, she came to the location where Aiden was hidden and handed him some deer jerky and one of the apples she had in her bag. Noticing her smiling, Aiden asked, "What has you in a good mood?"

"Remember that wonky pot I made and broke outside the cave?"

"Yeah. What about it?"

"Well, remember when all of us were at the dig site the day we went kayaking and Dad had me examine a broken pot?"

Thinking about it, his eyes few wide, "No way! You're kidding me! That was the same pot?"

"Yeah, funny, huh! Who would have thought I would be examining a pot I made in the early 1100s."

"That's unbelievable! Too bad we can't share that with Dad when we get back."

"Yeah, that would blow his mind, wouldn't it?"

"Okay, got to go check on Savage next, then Wade. Give them their food. Any messages you want me to pass on?"

"If I did, I wouldn't be telling you, Sis. Just tell Savage I said hi."

"That's all you want to say, just hi. Okay, I'll tell her. Aiden, just be careful. Remember, you only have fifteen minutes, if that, to get back to the cave when the alarms go off."

"How could I forget. Our lives depend on it."

"See you later tonight."

"Yeah, see you, Sis!"

Quickly she ran to Savage's location, gave her the food and Aiden's message. They talked about how Aiden was a man of few words. Then she continued to Wade's position to deliver his food and pass some cheer. When all her check-ins were completed, she headed back to the cave.

As soon as she was in sight of it, Will came running to her, practically leaping into her arms. "Hey there, Will! Have you been helping Colton?"

"Yup, Unitsi Eden! We got all five of the torches cut, wrapped, soaked in oil and ready to go."

"Sounds like you two have been busy." She said, hugging him first before setting him down.

"See, I told you, Colton, she would be happy we got them done."

"Yeah, you were right, buddy."

"Hey, Will, would you please take those torches over to the cave entrance? I need to talk to Eden by myself for a minute." Will nodded and went to move them.

As soon as Will's back was to them, he pulled her close and kissed her. "I missed you," he said.

"I missed you too." Behind them she heard giggling and knew Will had seen them kiss.

Ignoring it, she hugged Colton and whispered, "I've had a weird feeling since this morning. Almost like my stomach's...." But before she could finish, the *Key* began to pulse like it did when they first came across Ciara, and at the exact moment it did, their proximity alarms went off.

"I knew it! Call them back to the cave now, Colton!"

Colton did not have to. They were calling him and Eden, letting them know that they were on their way.

Eden called Will to her right as he was setting the torches by the cave entrance, near the fire. She wanted him close to her.

It was not long before they saw Savage running towards them as fast as she could. When she reached them, she ran into her brother's arms. Out of breath, she managed to say, "Huge war party... coming... arrows barely missed me!"

As she was catching her breath, Wade came running into camp from another direction. "Aiden's right behind me! It's a huge war party. The woods are full of warriors."

After two minutes, that seemed more like two hours, Aiden came sprinting towards them.

Because he was the fastest runner in their group, his position was the furthest distance away. Immediately, he ran to Savage and Eden, hugging them both.

"I made sure they saw me as planned. They are headed this way in a frenzy," he panted.

Eden took Will's hand, and said, "Let's go light our torches, then stand near the cave opening, and wait for the others. Don't worry, Will. It is going to be okay."

As they were lighting the torches, they started hearing yelling coming from the ridge across from the cave. The hill there was steep, almost cliff like, and Little Beaver Creek's channel ran deep against it. It would not be an easy crossing for the war party. As for their part, they only had to let the warriors see them moving into the cave while trying not to be hit by their arrows.

Colton and Wade were near the creek when an arrow whizzed by them. Another landed in front of Aiden, who was standing not far behind them.

"They are getting way too close! We need to go now!" Pointing his lit torch towards the cave.

Quickly they moved to the cave's entrance and began entering one by one. Taking the same route they had when Dr. Maxwell had first led them into it centuries in the future.

After moving far enough away from the entrance, so the glow from their torches could not be seen, they put them out, using the light from their STGs. They knew they only had a few minutes to spare until the warriors made their own torches to follow them.

Fueled by adrenalin, they quickly moved down the passageway, eventually coming to the entrance of the small chamber. Taking turns, they got on their hands and knees to crawl through the passage into it. Eden led the way, but before disappearing into it, she told Will, "Stay right behind me. Savage will be behind you, then Wade, Aiden, and Colton. He's going to shut the entrance behind us so it will be hidden. They won't find us." She then disappeared into the dark.

Soon, all of them but Colton, were standing inside the small chamber. It did not take him long to block the passageway, and as soon as they heard falling rock, he popped his head out of the opening. Once he was standing, he shyly turned and checked the ledge above it but did not find anything. He looked at Eden, shrugging his shoulders. She laughed, while Savage moaned, shaking her head. Will, confused by their actions, looked from one to the other.

Wade informed them, "Hey guys, time for me to take that side trip Dr. Maxwell asked me to take. I'll catch up with you in a bit and tell you all about it then." Without hesitation, he pressed the center control in the palm of his hand on his STG creating a vortex. Walking into it, he disappeared.

None of them had time to question him before he was gone. They would have to trust Dr. Maxwell knew what he was doing.

Will's hand tightened around Eden's. Kneeling down, she said, "Don't be afraid, Will. This is what we've been telling you about this past week. You are going to go through a spacetime displacement like Wade, with us. Savage will hold one of your hands, and I will hold the other.

Now, did Wade look like he was scared or hurt?" Will shook his head no. "Trust us, we won't let anything happen to you."

While she was hugging him, there were noises coming from the main passageway. Had the warriors found them? There was no way they could have, but the voices were getting louder.

Taking several deep breaths, Eden calmed the fear that was rising in the pit of her stomach. She was determined not to panic in this Time Loop. She took her time setting the coordinates on her STG, careful to make sure they were correctly set. Then taking ahold of Will's hand, she thought she heard the sound of digging.

Raising her left hand, she said, "Okay guys. Here we go!" and pressed the control.

Eden was proud of Will as they stepped into the swirling light. He put up no resistance.

As they were walking into it, Savage held Will's other hand.

Aiden thought Eden had messed up the coordinates again when they walked out of the time displacement and into Ireland at the break of dawn.

Everyone stopped short.

Not only were they not back on the Embarkation Platform, but there lying on her stomach in front of them unconscious, was a dark-haired, teenage girl dressed in ceremonial clothes, around Eden's and Savage's age with Wade sitting next to her.

"Hey guys! About time you all showed up."

"Was this your assignment from Dr. Maxwell?"

"Yeah, Eden. Take a look. Does she look familiar?"

Eden got down to examine the girl, studying her profile since she was laying on her stomach. She looked familiar, but she wasn't sure. Squinting, she said, "I don't know...."

Then abruptly, Eden stood and stepped back, exclaiming, "No way! It can't be her!"

Savage pushed Will behind Colton and walked around the girl to get a better look. Then she saw it. Grabbing an arrow from her quiver, she positioned it in her bow within a few seconds, then pointed it at the unconscious girl, confirming, "No, you're right. It's her."

"Whoa! Put the bow and arrow away Savage! She's out cold until I release her. Besides, this Ciara is only a budding teen psycho, unlike the full blooming adult version."

"You all know how good I am at quietly tracking animals. Because of that, Dr. Maxwell had me show up half a minute before you guys, so I could sneak up on her while she was hiding and give her an infusion of nanites. They knocked her out just as she saw you coming through the time displacement. They are now busy healing her mind of its psychosis. When they're done doing their job, she won't remember poisoning Elise the Elder, and she'll finally lose her power lust and have the empathy she needs to lead her people under her guidance."

"What do we do about her seeing us coming through the vortex?" asked Aiden.

"Nothing. Dr. Maxwell wanted her to see you exit and then to see us leave. He says it will help her create a false memory that will aid her in her resolve to help her people over her desire for power."

"Okay…, I just hope it's gonn'a be an awful strong memory," Savage said.

Aiden glanced to his right, and noticing a well, said, "Hey guys, look! A well! Anyone want a drink? I'll draw…"

"Stop! Aiden, stay away from that well! In fact, no one go near it. Dr. Maxwell's orders.

He said to say, you can have all the water you want when you see him in a minute, Aiden," Wade shouted, stopping Aiden dead in his tracks.

Ciara was stirring. Wade said, "Colton, help me set her against these ruins. And Savage and Aiden, you two go down the path until you find a veil covering a bowl of water sitting on a large rock. Bring it here. You carry it Savage, and whatever you do don't spill it! Aiden, you protect Savage."

As Wade and Colton placed Ciara in front of the ruins near the well, Aiden and Savage quickly retrieved the veil and water.

"What are these for?" Savage asked, handing them to Wade.

Taking the veil from Savage, he placed it over Ciara's head just as she would have been wearing it earlier. Then he took the water and placed it on her lap, covering it with the veil. He said, "The veil represents purity, and the water is for healing. It came from the well that Dian Cecht built and has been blessed by the first rays of the morning sun, according to the myths of the Tuatha Dé Danann."

"Now, Eden, set the coordinates for the Sentinels solar system, and everyone get ready to leave. I just have one more thing to do." Taking a gold coin from his bag, he placed it in the water.

"There that's done."

"Why the coin?"

"It's coated in an antidote for the poison she has been giving Elise the Elder and some other medicines to heal the villagers. It will also reinforce her memory of seeing us."

He sent a signal to the nanites to begin waking Ciara, and told Eden, "Let's go back, Airmed."

Then squatting down in front of Ciara, he commanded, "Protect the water." She tried to nod her head.

As the time displacement formed, Wade picked up his spear and joined the rest. As they entered, he whispered to no one, "See you soon Mia!"

FIFTY-THREE

CHARLES, ROYCE, ESSIE, AND ANDREI STEPPED up onto the Embarkation Platform and took their places as Dr. Maxwell stood by watching. "I wish I was going with you, but at my age, I would only be a hindrance. So, good hunting!"

Royce then pressed the control on his STG creating a time displacement. Once the swirling light was formed, they stepped into it instantly disappearing.

Dr. Maxwell thought as they faded, "And now we shall see if this will be the end of the Time Loops."

He had no sooner spoken when a new vortex began forming exactly where the others had been standing. Once it was fully developed, out walked Eden and Savage with Will between them, followed by the guys.

As soon as they saw Dr. Maxwell, everyone excitedly greeted him. After a few hugs and handshakes, he said, "I see you had a successful mission."

Eden brought Will forward to introduce him. "Dr. Maxwell, this is Will. And Will, this is Dr. Maxwell." Will shook Dr. Maxwell's hand just as Eden had taught him.

"Pleased to meet you, Dr. Maxwell."

"And I'm very pleased to meet you too, Will!"

"Now what? Back to the Training Center?"

"No not quite yet, Eden," answered Dr. Maxwell, while getting them to move near the entrance.

"Oh, are we waiting for Charles, and the others?"

"In a manner of speaking, Aiden."

Then, just as Aiden finished speaking, another time displacement began forming on the platform.

When they turned to see what was happening, they could hear voices coming from the vortex that sounded like Royce's and Andre's, but they could not be sure due to a woman screaming loudly and cursing.

As the people in the vortex stepped out of the displacement and onto the platform, the *Key* began pulsing and getting heavier. It reacted exactly like it had when Eden first laid eyes on Ciara. As soon as she saw who the woman was with Royce, and Andrei, she tightly grabbed onto her spear, and Will's hand, placing herself behind the others, and next to Dr. Maxwell.

She could not believe what she was seeing, for there between a disheveled Royce and Andre was the adult Ciara! The very same woman who tried to kill them.

The second Ciara saw Eden, she lunged forward screaming, "So, this is where you, and your family have been hiding, Airmed! No matter! I will kill you first, then your father Dian Cecht, along with all the rest! Then no one will be left to stop me from ripping the *Key to Immortality* from your neck!

Ciara lunged forward again with renewed fervor, but Charles, who was standing behind her, quickly gave her an injection. Realizing what he had done, she became more combative, trying to break away from Royce and Andre, but to no avail due to their augmented strength.

Plus, the more she struggled, the faster the compounds in the injection spread throughout her body. In no time she was unconscious.

"Well, that took long enough!" Essie complained. Grasping her bleeding finger, she complained, "That woman is mad! She had the audacity to bite me!"

Stepping over the prone figure of Ciara, she told Dr. Maxwell, "I'm going to Medical to get this checked. Hopefully she's not contagious!"

"Good idea, Essie! We wouldn't want you to get an infection," Dr. Maxwell said, as she left the Embarkation Area.

Royce and Andre retrieved a hover gurney and placed the unconscious Ciara on it. For precaution, Charles stood ready with another injection. Once they had her secure, Royce took the injector from Charles, and said, "We got it from here. We'll take her over to Medical so they can start evaluating her and we can come up with a plan for this Ciara's brain repair and reintegration.

Now that we have her, I think this calls for a Disney Princess movie tonight. Don't you all agree?"

"That sounds good, Royce! I'll make the popcorn for the movie."

"That'll be great, Dr. Maxwell!" Royce said, as he and Andre maneuvered the gurney out of the room.

"By the way, when we caught Ciara, she was in the process of grabbing Mia Cooper. We tried to make it clean, but we believed Mia may have seen something. This might need to be addressed in the future," Charles reported.

"What do you mean Ciara was after Mia, Charles?"

"Don't worry, Wade, she's safe. If she did see Ciara, it wouldn't make sense to her, and she would doubt what she'd seen. She'll be attending that family reunion and soon forget about what she saw.

Now, Royce and Andre are going to need me to help with the evaluation. If you have questions, Wade, I'll be more than glad to answer them later." Charles said before leaving.

Dr. Maxwell then said, "Now, let's get this young man over to Pediatrics and get him cleaned up and checked out." Reaching for Will's hand, Will pulled back from Dr. Maxwell and grabbed Savage's hand. He had never let go of Eden's.

Eden tried explaining to Will that Dr. Maxwell was a friend, but Dr. Maxwell told her, "Don't worry about it, Eden. He's scared. Even though you tried to prepare him, everything is strange and intimidating. He'll get used to me soon enough. You and Savage keep holding onto his hands."

"Now, let's get out of here!"

When they left the Embarkation Facility, they caught the rail to the Pediatrics Center. Will was awestruck! He loved everything about the rail, and especially the scenery flying by them. He had a million questions which Dr. Maxwell patiently answered for him.

Since Will was bouncing from seat to seat whenever something caught his eye, Eden was thankful the cars were enclosed and sealed. If they had been open in any way, she was positive she would have had to use her belt to strap him in his seat.

It took ten minutes to reach the Pediatrics Center, and Will was disappointed when the trip came to an end. However, his demeanor changed as soon as they entered the building. There he noticed other children like him, and others very different from him. Eden smiled, when the questions began again.

Once they were inside, Dr. Maxwell suggested that the guys go back to the Training Center, get cleaned up, and rest. He would stay, and answer Will's questions.

As they began to leave, Aiden told Savage, "See you soon."

Then he said, "Hey, Will, you better keep an eye on Eden. Make sure she behaves. I expect a report when I see you later!" Will laughed.

After Wade ruffled Will's mohawk, he went and stood by the door with Aiden to wait for Colton.

After kissing Eden on her cheek, Colton asked, "Do you want me to stay?"

"No, go get cleaned up, relax a bit. Will and I will see you later," she answered. As soon as she had told him to go, Will gave Colton a hug.

"See you in a bit buddy," Colton said as he hugged him back.

Joining Aiden, and Wade, the guys left the facility, and took the rail back to the Training Center.

After they had left, an AIMA (AI Medical Aid) came and guided them to a private testing area where Will was to be cleaned up and checked out. Eden could see that this AI, though not designed to look humanoid like Andre, still showed the same gentleness, along with an excellent bedside manner.

When the AIMA asked Will to hold out his hand, Will was unafraid and listened. After placing an adhesive patch on the back of Will's hand, it explained that it was to take his biological readings and to tell them what was happening inside of him. The AIMA even took the time to show him a hologram of his heart.

After several more questions, Eden and Savage could tell Will was having a hard time keeping his eyes open. Although he did manage to ask a few more before falling soundly asleep.

The Medical Aid examined him and said, "He's finally under. It doesn't take most children as long as it did him. He was certainly fighting it."

Dr. Maxwell laughed, "Yes, he did. Now you can get him scrubbed up, and into clean clothing without all the questions and finish the exam. The girls will come get him before our Disney movie later. But don't wake him up until then. After what he's been through, he needs some rest as well."

Turning his attention to Eden, and Savage, he said, "Now, why don't you, Unitsi Eden, and Unitsi Savage go and get cleaned up and rest a bit, too."

They tried arguing with him about staying, but he insisted that they go. Finally, they gave in as he could be quite stubborn at times.

Walking out of the Pediatrics Center, they waited for the rail to take them back to the Training Center. Even though fatigue had not yet set in due to the augmentation, they both knew they would welcome a long soak in a hot tub.

As soon as the rail arrived, they boarded. When Eden realized that no one else was going to join them in their car, she told Savage, "There's something I have been holding back from telling you and the guys. Something the *Key* showed me when it showed me the memory of our village leaving. I didn't really understand it at the time, and I didn't want to draw attention to it in case it might interfere with the evacuation."

Savage thought it was something to do with Ciara, and asked, "What's that crazy woman gone and done now?"

"No! No! It doesn't have anything to do with her, thank goodness."

"That's a relief! What then?

"It's about Will."

"He's okay, isn't he? They're not going to find anything wrong, are they?"

"No, he's okay, Savage. It's nothing to do with his physical or mental health."

"Oh, good! You had me worried for a second."

"No, Will's fine. It's just that... well, have you ever wondered why he puts Unitsi before our names? What it means?"

"No, I just assumed it was a greeting," Savage said.

"I did. When I asked Tala about it she didn't know. She'd never heard the word until Will used it. But she did think it could be some sort of form of endearment used in his tribe.

Have you noticed that when we arrived here that Dr. Maxwell uses it when he addresses us."

"You're right! He does! Do you think there's a possibility he could be from the same tribe as Will?" asked Savage.

"Yes, I do. But I think there's a lot more to it than just that."

"Like what?"

"Well, I'm not sure what to make of it, since the *Key* told me the term means *Mother*.

"What? Mother! Are you sure it told you that? I can understand Will using it, but Dr. Maxwell? Well, that's just... strange."

"I thought so too. I mean, I've come to love the man like a grandfather, and I could understand if he called us his granddaughters. But Mother?"

"Are you sure you got the memory right? Or could be he's having some sort of memory problem. He is pretty old after all."

"Yeah, I'm sure I got the memory right, Savage. At first, I thought that it might be something weird with the translators, so I asked Dekanawida. She didn't recognize the word per se. She thought it was a term of endearment or sorts, like sweetie, honey, or possibly a title, or like a nickname. And memory problem? No, Dr. Maxwell is still as sharp as a tack," Eden laughed.

Noticing the Training Center approaching, Eden added, "Then again, it could be the other thing that I thought of. But I'm up in the air about mentioning it to him."

"What about it?"

"Besides being from the same tribe, I think they may be related."

"Related?"

"Yeah, related," Eden answered. At that moment, the doors opened.

FIFTY-FOUR

A DAY HAD COME AND GONE SINCE they had returned from their mission. For the duration, they were staying in their dorm at the Training Center, while waiting for a transfer to the Team Residential Community. For now, Will remained with them.

That morning, Royce had arrived with news, informing them to expect Sumi sometime after lunch for a debriefing. They were not given an exact time due to her having other meetings, so they had to hang out close to the Training Center and wait.

Eden was still trying to process her mission field reports while answering Will's hundreds of questions on what he was finding on the IR Royce had given him. She had made a mental note to herself to thank Royce for it next time she saw him. And she wanted to strongly suggest to him that when another child is rescued that maybe he first tries giving them some building blocks or one of the drawing tablets instead.

As soon as Savage had finished her report, she diverted Will to a game involving colors and numbers, thus sparing Eden more questions. Since, as team leader, Eden had more information to input than the others.

As soon as the guys were finished with their reports, they decided to take Will outside to the Common Area to teach him some Earth sports. On their way out, a friendly argument broke out between them on whether to start with baseball, basketball, or soccer.

With Will gone, Eden was finally able to finish processing her reports quickly. Setting her IR down, she sat back in her chair and told Savage, "I need to apologize to my mom when we get home."

Savage, busy with putting Will's game in a wall cubby, looked over at Eden surprised, and asked, "What for?"

"For all the millions of times I interrupted her with questions when she was in the middle of something important."

They laughed. Savage agreed, "Yeah, I guess my mom needs an apology as well!"

"Have you noticed, Savage, how fast he has caught on to life here in only a day? And how quickly he's learned to use the IR? On top of everything that has happened to him, how loving he's remained?"

"Yeah, he's all that, isn't he? I've been wondering what they have planned for him. Will he stay with us, or what?"

"Believe me, Savage, that's crossed my mind more than once. Also, what's next for us? I'm assuming we stopped Ciara from accidentally creating that corrupted time displacement, so is time moving forward now? Do they still need us? Will we stay here or get sent home?"

"Yeah, I've wondered about all that, too. I guess we'll find out when we see Sumi. Have you decided to talk to Dr. Maxwell about Will and him being related?"

"Yeah, I just need to catch him at the right time. The few moments he's popped in didn't give me much of an opportunity. I also have a nagging feeling there's something here I'm missing. I just need a little more time to figure it out."

"I'm sure it's alright, and you'll get your answers. In the meantime, what do you want to do? We have some time before lunch, now that your report is done." Savage teased.

"You finished first because you had less reports than I did, on top of Will asking me hundreds of questions!

Still, you know, it would be good to get out of here, Savage, help reset my mind. How about we go for a walk?"

Eden and Savage left the Training Center, heading to the edge of the complex where they had heard there was a new garden. When they arrived, they were amazed at the variety of plants, flowers and trees growing in such a limited area. It had the appearance that it had been growing there together for years, instead of a few short months!

It was hard to believe that the garden was near a large bustling complex. It was so peaceful. They had decided to sit on the grass under one of the trees and soak in its serenity while they talked. They reminisced about the village, various people, and the things they had done and learned. They had a good laugh recalling the time Aiden had his legs unexpectedly swept out from under him by a twelve-year-old girl in their first game of lacrosse.

They also talked about how much they would miss being with the villagers, wondering if they had made it safely to their new home. After that, they grew quiet sitting in silence, soaking up the sun. All too soon they realized that it was time to return.

"What you think will happen to the adult Ciara?" Savage asked, as they walked back.

"I'm not sure. I hope they can heal her mind and help her find some peace."

When they got to their dorm, the guys were there with Will, all freshly showered after their sports, busy fixing lunch. Will was helping Aiden set the table, asking him questions about what they were doing and why. Colton and Wade were cooking. Soon they were eating and talking about what they had done that morning, all the while waiting for Sumi's visit.

After a quick clean up, they settled to wait for Sumi's arrival. Aiden and Savage had curled up beside each other talking softly on the sofa. Eden and Colton were sitting at the table with Will, drawing and coloring with him. Wade, sitting in the window alcove, had pulled out his flute and was playing it. He had just started the second song when Dr. Maxwell, Charles, and Sumi walked in.

After Eden made the introductions for Will's benefit, they all sat at the table to talk. Will was sitting still on Eden's lap as she explained to Will that he had to wait to ask his questions at the end.

"I wanted to personally come and congratulate you on the success of your mission! The tear in the fabric of spacetime that Ciara created has been repaired and the Time Loops have stopped. Time has begun to flow normally again. For this, the Sentinels are most grateful!

And, they have also asked me to personally extend an invitation to you all to consider becoming a permanent response team to work in tandem with Dr. Maxwell and the others. I do not need to know now. I only ask that you consider it. You can give your answers to Dr. Maxwell after you return to your time period when you are ready.

Now, please, engage the language symbol on your STGs." Immediately they complied.

"I did not want to cause Will any distress over what we will be discussing now. So, we will be speaking in a language he does not understand for this part of the debriefing."

Sumi then said, "If you all will allow it, I would like to take Will with me when I leave you at the close of this meeting."

Eden's throat suddenly tightened, and panic began to rise in the pit of her stomach. She knew this moment was coming. She and Savage had been preparing Will for this ever since they moved to the cave. But she had never counted on learning to love Will like she had.

"Where will you take him?" Eden asked, careful not to let Will hear the panic in her voice.

"I will take him to the Earth-like planet, the one we call, Haven. He has a family unit waiting for him there. They will prepare him for his life here and train him to take his place as a Sentinel, if he so chooses when he comes of age. Remember, Eden, Savage, all that I told you about my story? It will be the same for him as it was for me."

"Yes, we do. It's just that it's hard to let him go. I… have come to love him as my own.

We, we all have come to love him."

"Yes, I realize this. And I want you all to know, because of that love, he has the potential to become one of our greatest Sentinels, and to spend a long fulfilling life here."

Eden nodded. She understood. Besides, what kind of parent would she be? She was not even eighteen. She could not provide for a ten-year-old boy in her time. She knew that if she really loved

Will, she needed to let him go to his new family and stay with the Sentinels.

"Will I… we, ever get to see him again?"

"Oh, my yes! If you join the Response Team, anytime you come, you can see him. In time, he will even be able to come visit you."

Eden felt a wave of relief come over her. She saw Savage was relieved as well. "I have to explain everything before you take him."

"Of course. Take him into the bedroom to retrieve his belongings, then you and Savage can talk to him there." suggested Sumi.

The girls reset their STGs and got up from the table. Taking Will's hand, Eden said, "Will, come with us. We need to talk to you about what the adults were saying." Will got up obediently from the table and went with them into the bedroom.

While Eden and Savage were explaining to him that he was leaving with Sumi and why, the guys were sitting solemnly at the table.

Sumi said, "Don't feel bad. You all will see him again, and soon. I have seen this juncture in time before."

"So, you are telling us he will be fine, and that we will all get to be a part of each other's lives going forward?"

"Oh, my! Yes, Colton." Sumi answered. She then proceeded to answer any other questions that they had.

After some time, Eden, Savage, and Will came out of the bedroom. Eden had put him into the clothing she had made him from the deerskin she had traded for her rabbit skins and given him the bag. He was also wearing the necklace of mountain lion, bobcat fangs, and purple cowrie shells that was placed in his hand by his father's second wife when she died.

Charles took Will's weapons from Eden and Savage, while Eden got the picture Will had drawn of them all to place in his bag with his team uniform.

Glancing at the picture, she suddenly noticed the style looked very similar to the cave paintings at the dig site. Nudging Savage, she showed it to her. Then, as Savage looked at it, her eyes grew big. Eden shrugged her shoulders, then took the picture and put it into Will's bag.

When they came out of the room, everyone gathered around him for hugs, and to say their goodbyes. Eden and Savage were the last.

"Be good. Make us proud. And always remember that I love you," Savage told him, sniffing away the tears.

"Yes, Unitsi Savage. I will always love you, too," Will replied, while his upper lip trembled.

"Remember what we taught you, Will. And remember, I will always love you, now and until the end of time," Eden told him.

As she hugged him one last time, Will whispered into her ear, "Unitsi Eden, you will always be my Unitsi."

"Oh, yes! Always, Will!" she said, as the tears she had been holding back streamed down her cheeks.

"It's time to go, Will. Sumi will take good care of you. And we will see you soon. I promise!" Wiping away hers and Will's tears, Eden then placed Will's hand in Sumi's. As they went through the doorway, Will waved goodbye.

Once they were gone, Eden turned to Colton and sobbed into his shoulder. Savage did the same with Aiden. While poor Wade, sniffing back his tears, patted Dr. Maxwell's shoulder.

Dr. Maxwell let them cry for a bit, then said, "Come, come! Dry your tears. All is not lost, and you will be a part of Will's life way into the future. Let's all sit down here now. We have some things to discuss." Reluctantly they made their way back to the table, pulled out their chairs, and sat.

"I know you have questions, and before you go back home, I want to give you answers for them all. Now, Eden, if I'm not mistaken, I believe you and Savage have a big one."

Wondering how he knew, Eden said, "Yes... yes, we do, Dr. Maxwell. Our *big* question, is... are you and Will related?"

"Now, what would make you two think that?"

"It's because you and Will use a term for Savage, and me that the STG's translator could not translate. Dekanawida, and Tala did not know what it meant either, except they said it could be some sort of term of endearment."

"Ah! You've always had a knack for picking up on things others miss, Eden. And the answer to your question about us being related is yes, sort of."

"But how does *sort of* work?"

"First, let me tell you what Unitsi means. Both Dekanawida and Tala were right. It is a term of endearment. It means Mother, like Mom, or Mommy, etc."

"Mother!" both girls shouted.

"Wait!" said Aiden. "So, you're saying you and Will have been calling Eden, and Savage, Mother? So, does that mean you're Will's brother?"

"No, but you are close, Aiden. Very close!"

"Are you his uncle?"

"No, I'm not that either, Wade."

"Then just how are you related?" asked Colton.

Dr. Maxwell grinned, "I am not just related to Will. I am Will!" He then pulled out the necklace that was hanging around his neck from under his shirt. The very same necklace of mountain lion, bobcat fangs, and purple cowrie shells Will was wearing when he left!

FIFTY-FIVE

EVEN THOUGH EDEN HAD SUSPECTED that Dr. Maxwell and Will might be one and the same, to actually hear him say it was unbelievable. Still, when she thought about it, the signs had been there all along, and she was angry at herself for not seeing it sooner.

"But why call us Unitsi, Dr. Maxwell? I can understand Will doing it, but as you got older you knew we weren't your mothers."

"I'll tell you why, Eden. See, you, and Savage took a scared, little orphan, and made him understand he was loved and not alone. I had never felt love like that until you all found and saved me.

You see, my mother died in childbirth. The woman who had fallen on top of me was my father's second wife. She was good to me but did not love me like her own children. To her I was a duty. And my father was distant. He blamed me for his favorite wife's, my mother's, death. So, you can imagine, how I, as a child, would cling to your love."

Eden and Savage each took one of the old man's hands in theirs. He squeezed them and smiled. Afterwards, it was quiet for a few moments before they let go.

Eden broke the silence by asking, "Dr. Maxwell, now that we know this, am I correct in assuming that it was you who planned for us to come to the dig site by inviting our parents to join you; you that placed the mysterious *key* on the keychain to your brother's house, the flashing lights following me, the cave paintings, all of that?"

"Yes, but with a few minor adjustments. I don't have a brother, Sam. I am also an architect, as well as an archeologist. The house is mine, so I made sure the *key* was on the keychain. And

Charles helped me with the cave paintings in a past Time Loop. You see, even though I'm an architect, I'm not a very good artist." Eden, and Savage thought of the picture Eden had just put in Will's bag. They smiled.

"But why reveal this to us now?"

"Well, you see, Eden, you weren't the only one to make a miscalculation that gave Ciara the opportunity to create that disruption of time. You didn't trust in yourself and your *Key* and as a result, we've had twelve Time Loops. My mistake was that I didn't trust my team. I went off after Ciara on my own, and she managed to strand me in time for sixty years. I would have died there if Charles hadn't found me when he did."

Eden was finally beginning to understand the problems the two events had caused. As a shiver went down her spine, she also remembered how vicious Ciara could be.

"When Charles brought me back to the Sentinel's Solar System, they repaired me the best they could, but time is now catching up to me and I have little left."

All of them were distressed when they heard Dr. Maxwell's claim. They were aware he was a little over eighty, but also knew due to his many Time Loops, he was much, much older.

"But I thought the Sentinels could extend life for thousands of years."

"Yes, Eden, but unfortunately the Time Loop I was lost in was damaged due to Ciara's thievery and mishandling of Aiden's STG. When I fell into her trap, she attacked, took, and destroyed mine. Then because I no longer had its protection against that Time Loop's corrupted state, my cells became damaged to the point that they cannot be repaired at a quantum level any longer. So, as a result I am dying.

Now since Ciara's time displacement was prevented, the original timeline will continue. The ten-year-old me, who you call Will, has been taken to the coordinates of the timeline when I originally came to this solar system. In it he will grow into a man and become a Sentinel as I had. At some point, you will meet us again. I will be the same age as Charles and possibly, barring getting caught in any other deviant timelines, live to be as old as Sumi. But this version of me will fade and die normally, just as the adult version of Ciara will also die in time.

I am deeply sorry for the deception, Unitsi Eden and Unitsi Savage. Please forgive an old man. I only wanted to be near my family, those I love and who love me, when I take my final mission to meet the *Great Spirit* and my ancestors."

Since they now had the facts and his confession, none of them knew what to say, for Dr. Maxwell had become like a grandfather to them. Wrapping their minds around the idea that he, and Will were one and the same, was mindboggling. And then knowing he was dying, made it even more surreal.

Eden, who was closest to him, reached across the table for his hand and squeezed it. He smiled, then to keep the silence from becoming awkward, Dr. Maxwell asked if they had any other questions.

At that point, Colton asked about their village and their sister villagers.

Dr. Maxwell informed them, that while most of their sister villagers did escape, the several who refused to leave were killed. Their remains, along with some artifacts from the village, were discovered in the Spring of 1974, when the northern pylons for the bridge over the Ohio River for Route 376 were built.

The people from your village did survive the canoe trip down the Ohio River, where they thrived for several generations in the village they joined. Hundreds of years later, their descendants moved northwest to the larger of the Great Lakes.

Eden was still struggling to understand the purpose for bringing them into all of this. She asked, "I'm confused as to why we were even involved to start with?"

"Hmm... let me try explaining it this way. You all are intelligent, you're not an Einstein, a Mozart, or a Michelangelo, but each of you has unique gifts. These gifts when brought together, complement each other, and when you work together as a team, you are unbeatable! Even though you're not orphans, the Sentinels sought you out for that very reason.

That is why Sumi made the offer for you all to be part of the response team covering the Milky Way Galaxy."

Finally! Everything made sense to Eden.

Dr. Maxwell added as he pushed away from the table, "Now we need to get you all back to your time. Charles and I will follow later. There are meetings we need to attend first.

So, go put on the same clothes that you were wearing when you arrived, because when you arrive home, it will only be a second after you left. Leave whatever you want for now. We'll move your items to the Team Residential Community if you decide to take up Sumi's offer. If not, we'll bring them to you later." Then they went to change.

Savage was sitting on her bed dressing when she said to Eden, "Wow! This is incredible!"

"I know! Right?"

"So, what do you think about Sumi's offer?"

"I think they already know our answer. I know mine," said Eden, touching the *Key*.

"Hey! No fair holding the *Memory Keeper* to try and get your answer!"

Once they were finished, they walked back into the main room to find the guys waiting with Dr. Maxwell and Charles.

Seeing them in their normal clothes again was weird. It drew attention to their six months of hair growth. Savage said, "Looks like you three better get a haircut before we get home!

Colton, Wade, you wouldn't want Dad seeing your hair now!"

Dr. Maxwell said, "Don't worry, Savage. We'll fix that during transportation. Everyone and everything will be exactly like you were or it was before you came here."

"Oh, no, there goes my awesome tan!"

"Don't worry about that, we have a pool. You can work on it there the rest of the summer," suggested Eden. Savage gave Eden a big smile because that meant she would be seeing Aiden almost every day.

"Okay, before we leave, everyone please take your STGs off and place them on the table."

As soon as they had removed them, Dr. Maxwell said, "Looks like everyone's ready, so let's go."

Reflectively, they walked barefoot out of the Training Center and took the rail to the Embarkation Facility. Once they arrived, they went directly to the Embarkation Platform.

Stepping up onto it, everyone took the same position they had when they were in the pond. Dr. Maxwell and Charles took theirs at the control panel.

"Charles, and I will be seeing you all soon. Okay, Charles, let's send them home."

The words had no sooner left Dr. Maxwell's mouth than they saw the vortex forming around them, and Dr. Maxwell and Charles fading away. The next thing they knew, they were standing in the middle of the pond in front of the fountain. They were home!

They all stood there for a few seconds. Colton sighed, and said, "Come on, let's get our shoes on and get back to the house."

They quickly climbed out of the pond and slipped into their shoes. Back tracking through the field on the tram lines, then on the tractor run, they made their way back to the farmhouse in silence.

When they got to the French doors of the kitchen, Aiden pulled them open for everyone to enter. Once inside, they went directly to the table and sat down, almost as if they were in a daze.

After a few seconds, everyone began to talk, when suddenly Eden remembered something and interrupted them, saying, "Wait! Before we say anything more, let me first check that breakfast casserole I put in the oven. Then we can talk."

Getting up, she opened the oven, and said, "The oven's still hot, and the casserole is done."

With her hands on her hips, she said, "Well, we could eat and talk at the same time."

"I'm all for that," Aiden exclaimed, as he quickly got up and grabbed one of the plates, and a set of utensils that Eden had placed on the island when she had started breakfast that morning. Colton and Wade were right behind him grabbing their plates. Surprisingly, so was Savage.

Eden looked at them, and said, "Really? We just had lunch!"

"Aw, come on Sis! That was in another Time Loop! It's breakfast time here," he complained. The others agreed with him, so Eden took the casserole out and set it next to the cinnamon rolls. Then she got her own plate.

While they were sitting at the table eating and talking in low voices, Eden's and Aiden's parents came out of their bedroom dressed in old clothes and waterproof boots.

Frank and Barb were surprised to see the teens up so early, especially on a Saturday. "Well, this is a shock. I didn't expect to see all of you up on our way out. I thought you'd all still be sleeping, especially you, Aiden," Frank said.

"I'm surprised too! Aiden, you're always a bear to get up," said Barb.

"Aww, Mom!"

Eden said, "Well, we all didn't sleep too well because of the storm last night, so I thought I'd get up and make everyone breakfast."

Noticing what her parents had on, she asked, "What are you two dressed like that for?"

"We're going to go check on the dig site. I don't think anything blew or floated away last night, cause everything was locked down good, but I'll feel better when I see it." said her Dad.

"Well, before you leave, make sure you get something to eat, before Aiden eats it all," Eden told them.

"Thanks, Squirt, but I think Mom, and I will just grab a thermos of coffee, and a couple of those delicious looking cinnamon rolls. Don't want to chance any artifacts getting damaged if it can be avoided. Besides, Dr. Maxwell has Charles bringing lunch. We won't starve."

Grabbing the empty thermos on the counter, Frank poured it full of coffee, while Barb bagged two of the rolls to take with them. Then they headed to the French doors to get to their ATV stored in the barn's lean-to, but as they stepped outside, Frank said, "Eden, get my card and order pizza for lunch. It's supposed to turn sunny and get very hot today, so I thought you all might want to hang out and use the pool." A minute after they left, they heard the engine of the ATV revving then trailing off.

They continued with their breakfast and resumed talking about Sumi's offer. By the time they were done, they had made the decision to accept it.

Once their decision was made, and after Aiden devoured the last cinnamon roll, they cleaned up. When they finished, everyone drifted into the living room to relax. While they were talking about what kind of pizza to order for lunch, Wade received a text message.

Pulling out his phone, his face broke into a huge grin when he saw it was from Mia. He immediately began reading it. But as he read, the grin soon faded. "No way!" he yelled standing up.

"What's happened?"

"Just a minute, Colton." Then he texted Mia back.

When he had finished, he told them, "Mia is okay. She's at the family reunion, but she told me something weird happened to her when she went to get her jacket from the car. She said after she had it, as she was shutting the door, this dark-haired woman with bright blue eyes, came charging out of nowhere at her. As the woman was about to put her hands on her, she was suddenly grabbed by two men and a woman. Mia said she blinked, and they were gone.

I told her maybe she hadn't seen it accurately because she was tired from all that driving, and after she gets back, we'll talk about it. Not to worry, and just have fun.

R.L. Roush

Dr. Maxwell asked me to evaluate her reaction, and to deal with it appropriately. He left it up to me to say anything, but said he felt she would make a good addition to our team."

"That's awesome, Wade! I don't mean about the attack, but her possibly joining us," said Aiden.

Everyone was happy about the possibility. Out of the five of them, he had suffered the most from not being able to see or communicate with Mia. Eden could tell that after finding out she was fine a huge weight was lifted from his shoulders.

They passed the time discussing her addition to the group and what the timeline might be for it. And they all wondered if they might have a chance to see Will when it happened.

While they continued talking, Eden looked up at the living room clock and realized it was getting close to lunch and that they needed to order the pizza right away. After deciding, they called and placed their order.

As they were leaving, Eden gave Aiden their dad's card, and said, "Here, get something to drink and some chips from the store. I'll stay here and cut up some fruit for a fruit salad and make some iced tea."

As Savage walked by Aiden on the way out, she swiped the card from his hand without missing a beat. As they headed to the door, she said, "Okay, we're going to stop at the house first to get our swimsuits before getting the food. It'll take them half an hour to make the pizzas, so we should be back fifteen minutes after we pick it up."

Colton asked Eden, "Do you need any help?"

"No, go with them. I'll be fine," she replied. Upon hearing her answer, he nodded and left with the others.

Eden made the tea and put it in the refrigerator to cool. Then she set about cutting up some of the fruit. When she was done, she had a nice sized bowl of it that she covered and placed in the refrigerator next to the tea.

Now that she was finished, she decided to walk out to the pool area to check the water's temperature. As she was reading the thermometer, she was reminded of the cool Ohio River water they had bathed and swum in the past six months, and was glad that it read eighty degrees.

Kneeling to lower the thermometer back into the water, she heard a bird chirping. Standing up to see what species it was, she suddenly had a bright light hit her in the eyes.

"What in the world!" she complained as she covered them.

Shielding her eyes to see where the light was coming from, she noticed it was coming from the very same group of trees that held the pond. When she took a few steps, the light followed, letting her know it was being manipulated.

"I wonder what Dr. Maxwell wants now. Maybe he needs help with something?" Eden thought.

Since she was done with the fruit and tea, she decided to see what was up.

After going behind the garage to reach the road hidden behind the pool's landscaping, Eden retraced her earlier steps to the group of trees where the pond was located. All the while, the flashing light kept hitting her.

She was out of breath when she reached the pool. While she stood there, she did not see anyone, so she went around to the fountain side to see if she could find Dr. Maxwell sitting near any of the larger trees or on one of the rocks.

Once there, she still could not find him. So, she thought, if Dr. Maxwell needed her, maybe she would have to get in the pond like before to transport, since she no longer had her STG.

Slipping off her sandals, she placed one foot at a time into the cold water before moving slowly towards the fountain to find the keyhole. Once she saw it, she removed the Key from around her neck just as she had six months earlier, when a hand suddenly reached out to stop her.

Startled, she turned in surprise, only to find it was Colton. "What are you doing here?

You can't be back that fast?" she said.

"I'm sorry I scared you, but I didn't go with them. It's been weeks since we've been able to be alone without having someone else around. So, I thought if I lured you with the light, I could get you out here where we could spend a few minutes together before the others get back."

Eden smiled when she saw how sorry he was for scaring her and after hearing his explanation. He was right. They had not had any time just for themselves since they had left the village and moved to the cave.

"Your forgiven."

Letting go of Eden's hand, he took the *Key*, and placed it back around her neck. After which, he pulled her close, wrapping his arms around her, saying, "Would you mind if I ask you a question while I'm holding you in my arms."

"What question?"

"Well… do you think that you could possibly fall in love with someone… with someone like me?"

Eden placed her hands on Colton's neck, and before she kissed him, she leaned in and whispered, "Possibly, given time…."

Acknowledgements

WRITING IS FUN, but it is also work. Still, for me it would be even harder and much less fun without the help, guidance, and support of family, friends, and God. So, now I would like to take the opportunity to thank those people.

To the Scribes Writers, thanks for all the Saturdays you have spent listening to my ideas and me reading my latest chapter. Your input, proof reading, and support has helped in ways you'll never know. I can only hope to repay you all by doing the same in return.

To my young adult, and adult beta readers, Aubrey Boyd, Kaelynn Bollman, Leah Carlin and Sandra Carlin. Thank you for your valuable input and ideas. They help keep me connected and current with my audience.

Joyce Faulkner, thank you for being there every time I have had a question or needed direction. Your advice is always generous, and your friendship is a blessing.

It amazes me how many times I can read a sentence, miss something, then go back days later and find it, maybe. Thank you, Frank Tatone, for editing my manuscript and catching the errors that were missed. Also, thank you for your insights. They are always most helpful and appreciated.

And thank you, Gia Tatone, for all our many monthly dinners of homemade spaghetti and meat balls, spiced with valuable information on writing, networking, self-promotion, and publishing. Your support means so much, as well as your friendship.

To my family, thank you for being understanding when at times I did not answer a text message as soon as it was sent, or when I was late to a family event after a book signing. And, for putting up with my grouchiness on the days the writing muse struck after midnight, and I was running on only a few hours of sleep.

And to my biggest Fan, your joy is my strength.

About The Author

R. L. ROUSH IS A RETIRED Computer Automated Drafter who loves all science "what ifs". What if you could create bio-mechanical creatures that could aid and assist humans in dangerous endeavors? Or, what if you could create a time displacement that would allow you to flow backwards and forward through time? Can humans be augmented to enhance their natural abilities without harming them? These are the kinds of questions she loves to answer in her Young Adult/Science-Fiction stories. Ramona is also a published author of a series, *The Eagle's Eyes*, *The Cat's Eyes*, and *The Serpent's Eyes*.

Ramona also likes to paint, collect and classify arrow heads, spend time with her family and two spoiled cats, Mia and Calipso.

www.ingramcontent.com/pod-product-compliance
Lightning Source LLC
Chambersburg PA
CBHW050923030726
47503CB00007BB/2443